Other books by Jen

The Gamble Brothers Series
(Full series complete- Adult Contemporary Romance)
Tempting the Best Man
Tempting the Player
Tempting the Bodyguard

For details about current and upcoming titles from
Jennifer L. Armentrout,
please visit *www.jenniferarmentrout.com*

A Wicked Trilogy

Jennifer L. Armentrout

#1 *New York Times* and International Bestselling Author

Torn
Published by Jennifer L. Armentrout
Copyright © 2016 by Jennifer L. Armentrout
All rights reserved

License Notes

Library of Congress Cataloging-in-Publication Data
Torn/Jennifer L. Armentrout—First edition
ISBN 978-0-9864479-9-0

Cover Design by Sarah Hansen. All rights reserved.
Formatting by Christine Borgford, Perfectly Publishable

For the readers and reviewers.
None of this would be possible without you.

Chapter One

My blood, red as a freshly picked rose, bubbled up from the center of my palm like my hand was some kind of volcano of freaking doom.

I was the halfling.

It had been me—it had *always* been me. And Ren—oh my God—Ren was here to find and kill me, because the prince of the mother freaking Otherworld was free in the mortal realm. The Prince was here to knock up a halfling, to make an apocalypse baby . . . with me.

Me.

I was going to vomit.

Like all over the hardwood floors of my bedroom.

I was having trouble breathing as I lifted my gaze. "Why? Why didn't you tell me?"

Tink's gossamer wings fluttered silently as he drifted closer. The damn brownie. The damn brownie I'd found in Saint Louis Cemetery. The brownie I'd made a Popsicle leg brace for and whose torn wing I had carefully wrapped gauze around. The damn brownie I let live in my apartment for the last two and a half years and hadn't killed yet for spending a fortune of *my* money on Amazon like he belonged on an episode of *Hoarders*. The damn brownie was about to get punt kicked into another dimension.

He clasped his hands together in front of his shirt, which was covered with powdered sugar. Sprinkles of white covered his face like he'd face-planted into a pile of coke.

"I didn't think it would ever come to this," he said.

I lifted my hand, feeling wet warmth cascade down my arm. "Well, it did come to this, like right now."

Tink floated to the left. "I thought we'd closed all the gates, Ivy. We had no idea there was a second gate here. We believed that there was no chance of any of the royal court or the prince or princess coming through. It was a non-issue."

Lowering my hand, I shook my head. "Guess what, Tink. It's not a non-issue. It's a huge, Godzilla-sized issue!"

"I can see that now." He flew over to the bed and landed on my comforter. "I never meant to lie to you."

I frowned as I turned around. "I hate to break it to you, Tink, but if you don't mean to lie to someone, you simply don't *lie* to them."

"I knooow." He drew the word out as he walked to the edge of the bed, his bare feet digging into the purple, chenille bedspread and most likely spreading powdered sugar everywhere. "But you wouldn't have believed me if I had told you, would you? Not like I had a thorn stake lying around."

Okay. He had a point there. "But when I first brought it

up to you, you could've said something."

Tink lowered his chin.

I took a deep breath. "Did you know what I was when you saw me?"

"Yes," he said, and continued in a rush, "but it wasn't on purpose. You finding me was a fluke. A coincidence. Or it was fate. I like to think it was our destiny."

"You can stop there." It hurt, knowing that he hadn't been upfront with me this entire time, and it burned deep in my gut and chest. I didn't know who he was.

I didn't know who *I* was anymore.

"I didn't know until you got near and I sensed the weak fae blood in you. But you're right. I should've told you, Ivy-divy. You're right, but I was afraid . . . I was afraid of what you'd do." Tink suddenly threw himself backward onto the bedspread, little arms and legs spread out. "I didn't want to upset you, because you helped me out, and I didn't want you to do something rash if I did tell you."

"What could I have done?" A ball of emotion knotted in my throat. "What can I do?"

He raised limp noodle arms. "You could've, I don't know, hurt yourself."

My mouth dropped open, causing me to wince as the bruised and swollen skin along the left side of my face pulled taut. Hurt myself? I looked down at the thorn stake lying on the floor. "No," I whispered, bending down and picking up the stake. Using my shirt, I wiped the blood off the tip. "I don't want to die."

"That's good to hear." Tink was sitting up, arms still at his sides.

I placed the stake on the dresser, next to my iron ones and the daggers. "I wouldn't hurt myself, Tink."

"But you would try to leave." Tink was closer, in the air

behind me.

I drew in a deep breath that did nothing to help me. Leave? Was that the next course of action? I stepped away from the dresser, avoiding Tink, which was harder than it should've been for someone that was only the size of a Barbie doll. Weary to the core, I walked to the edge of the bed and sat down. The weariness wasn't just due to the numerous injuries that were slowly healing.

My thoughts were spinning too fast. I closed my eyes and eased onto my back, letting my legs dangle off the bed as panic sliced through my belly. The very idea of leaving had my heart jumping all over the place. Leaving New Orleans meant leaving the Order, and that was huge. One simply couldn't just up and leave the Order. It was tantamount to going AWOL from the military. There'd be APB put out on me. Other Order members would be on the lookout, and there were sects in every state. I'd only be able to hide for so long. If I up and left, David would suspect I was a traitor like . . . like Val, and he'd contact other sect leaders. But it was more than my duty to the Order that made me hesitant to leave—way more.

Hell, my duty to the Order dictated that I turn myself over to them, and it wasn't even that. For the first time in my life, the sudden reluctance to do the right thing had nothing to do with my duty.

It had everything to do with Ren.

Leaving meant walking away from him, and the mere thought of doing that caused my heart to end up somewhere down near my dangling feet. I loved him. God, I loved him more than I loved pralines and beignets, and that was hardcore, because my love of sugary, sweet things rivaled the most epic love stories known to man. Thinking of never seeing him again made me want to curl into a ball, and that would be incredibly stupid, because I'm pretty sure, with my busted ribs, it would hurt like hell.

I should've never gotten close to him.

This whole entire time I'd been petrified that he'd die on me like everyone else had. Never once had it crossed my mind that I'd lose him because I would have to walk away. Or run away, fast.

But what could I do? There was no way I could let the prince carry out his plans. A child created from a union of the prince and a halfling would literally throw open all the doors to the Otherworld. They would stay permanently open, and all the fae would come through. Mankind would turn into an all-you-can-eat fae buffet.

"You're thinking it now," Tink announced.

I was thinking a lot of things right now.

He landed on my bent knee, and the only reason why I didn't throw him off me was because I was sure I'd end up hurting myself more in the process. "You think the only thing you can do is leave, but that won't help you. You're forgetting something very important. Actually, you're forgetting two very important things." He paused. "Come to think of it, you're probably forgetting a lot, because you got your head knocked—"

"Tink," I warned.

He stomped up my leg, which felt like a cat was walking on me. "You have to *consent*."

I pried my eyes open. The left one was still pretty swollen, so Tink was a blurry form where he stood by my hip.

He cupped his hands around his mouth. "Sex. Consent to sex with the prince. That's the only way a child can be conceived. No glamour. No magic or compulsion. No tricks. You know, you have to actually want—"

5

"I know what consent to sex means," I snapped.

"Apparently, you don't." Tink jumped off my hip and landed on the bed next to me. "Because he can't make you do it. Well, he *could* make you, and that's just gross and wrong and not completely out of character for the prince, but a child won't be conceived."

"Oh, great to know. He could force himself on me, but hey, at least there's no apocalypse baby. No harm, no foul."

Tink's little nose scrunched. "You know that's not what I meant." He lifted himself up in the air and flew so he was directly above my head. "But there's a bigger problem, Ivy."

I laughed, and it sounded a little crazed. Not even drunken crazed. More like hitting the asylum crazed. "What could be worse than me being a halfling?" Panic lit up my chest. Just saying that out loud made me want to vomit.

"You said the prince tasted your blood, right?" Tink asked. "After you two fought?"

My nose wrinkled. "Yeah. I mean, I'm pretty sure he did after he . . . smelled me."

"Then there is nowhere you can go that he cannot find you."

I opened my mouth, closed it, and then tried again. "Come again?"

Tink zipped down to the bedspread. "He will be able to sense you anywhere. It doesn't matter if you went to Zimbabwe, and I'm not even sure where Zimbabwe is, but I just like saying Zimbabwe, but he'd find you eventually, because you're now a part of him."

I couldn't even think for a moment, couldn't even form a coherent thought that did not involve what in the actual fuck. "Are you for real?"

Tink nodded and plopped down cross-legged beside my arm. He lowered his voice as if he'd be overheard. "When an ancient, like the prince, takes a part of someone into them, he is forever connected to that person. You're bonded, in a way."

"Oh my God." Unable to deal, I placed my hands over my face. A new horror surfaced. "Then he knows where I am right now?"

"Most definitely."

"And he'll know everywhere I go." Holy crap, I couldn't even process the implications. My mere presence would be putting everyone in danger. But what I didn't understand was, if the prince could sniff me out like some kind of halfling bloodhound, then why hadn't he showed yet? It had been a week since we fought. What was he waiting for?

"It's really creepy, isn't it?" Tink said.

Creepy wasn't even the word for it. I couldn't think of an appropriate word for all of that. "Do you know how to kill him?"

"You kill him like you would kill any ancient. You cut off his head, but that's not going to be easy."

No shit. Taking out normal fae wasn't particularly easy. Stabbing them with an iron stake only sent them back to the Otherworld. Chopping off their heads killed them.

"But that's not the most important thing." Tink grabbed my right hand. My wrist had stopped throbbing, another sure sign that the prince had truly patched up some of the damage he'd inflicted upon me. I eyed the brownie. "You cannot let anyone know what you are."

"Gee. Really? I was thinking about updating my Facebook to halfling status."

He cocked his blondish-white head to the side. "You don't have a Facebook, Ivy."

I sighed.

Tink continued, because of course. "I looked for you. Wanted to add you as my friend so I could poke you, and I know people don't poke anymore, but I think poking is a great way to express how one—"

"I know I can't tell anyone, but what's stopping the fae from outing me?" I asked.

"The fae will know if you're outed, because the Order would kill you." He said this like we were talking about Harry Potter, and not about me, you know, being put down like a rabid dog. "The prince won't want to risk that, even if there are other female halflings out there. He won't want to risk the time it would take to find another one."

"Well, I guess that's one good thing," I said dryly.

He let go of my hand. "You can't even tell Ren. Especially not him."

My gaze shifted to Tink.

"I know what he is. I overheard you two talking the morning you left to guard the gate. He's an Elite, and while I think that is as lame of a name as the Order, I've heard of them."

"How have you heard of them?"

He buzzed down until he was standing next to my head. He bent over, whispering in my ear, "I'm omnipresent."

"What?" I frowned at him. "That doesn't even make sense."

He straightened. "It makes perfect sense."

"I think you mean omniscient."

He glanced up at the ceiling. "Huh."

"You're not omniscient," I told him, and then said, "Are you?"

Tink grinned devilishly. "No."

Annoyance flared. "I need you to be up front with me. No more lies. No more bullshit, Tink. I'm serious. I need to be able to trust you, and I'm not sure I do right now."

His eyes widened slightly and then he dropped down to his knees. "I deserve that."

Yeah, he did, because I took him in and he'd lied to me a lot. It didn't matter that he had good reasons. He'd still lied.

And then it hit me like a smack in the face. I was going to have to do the same thing. Lie for a good reason to Ren and to . . . to everyone, so I was really no better.

"I know about the ancients, because I lived in the Otherworld. We had to learn everything about them to survive," he said. "The prince and the princess, and the king and queen, are the most powerful, but there has always been talk of the Elite. Many fae have fallen to them when they used to come and go into this realm as they pleased, before the gateways were closed."

That sounded believable. I guessed.

Tink screwed up his face. "Though I am surprised to hear that Ren is one. He doesn't seem smart or cool enough for that level of badassery."

"Ren is cool and awesome enough," I corrected Tink. "He's a total badass."

"Whatever." He folded his arms across his chest. "We're going to have to agree to disagree. Moving on. You cannot tell him. It is his duty to end you."

My breath caught.

Like it had been his duty to allow his best friend Noah to walk away, knowing that it would be the last time he'd see him. God, Ren had even said he couldn't go through that again, and I couldn't do that to him. I couldn't put that kind of knowledge on him.

"I won't," I whispered.

Tink nudged my arm with his foot. "You have to pull it together, Ivy. Like right now."

I looked over at him. "I think I'm owed a pity party for the next couple of minutes."

"Save your tears for the pillow."

I rolled my eyes and shook my head. "This isn't an episode of *Dance Moms*."

But Tink was right. Not like I was going to tell him that, especially when I was still considering doing minor bodily harm to him. I needed to pull it together. I had no other choice. Leaving wasn't an option. I controlled the whole baby-making aspect and there was no way I was willingly going to knock boots with that freak. I needed to get it together, because the only choice I had now was to stop the prince.

Stop the prince and make sure no that one, including Ren, found out what I was. I shivered. A question floated through my crowded thoughts, pushing everything out of my mind.

"I don't get it."

"What?" Tink asked.

"How . . . how am I a halfling?" I stared at the ceiling. "I don't remember my parents, but Ren said he checked into them. He said they were in love. How could this have happened?"

Tink didn't answer.

He didn't know. Probably no one would ever know the truth. Anything was possible. My mother might've slept with a fae. Or maybe it was like Noah's father. He'd met a fae woman and had gotten her pregnant before he met the woman he ended up marrying. I just couldn't imagine how anyone who knew what the fae were could knowingly sleep with one.

I exhaled shakily and thought that maybe I would expel all my tears onto my pillow. I sort of just wanted to roll over and let it all out. Actually, I honestly didn't want to think about any of it, but that was impossible.

"You need to let him go," Tink said quietly.

I turned my head to him. "What?"

"Ren. You need to let him go. Push him away. Break up with him. Whatever. You need to get as far away from him as possible."

I stiffened and my response was immediate. "No."

"Ivy—"

"No," I repeated, waving my left hand. "End of discussion."

Tink stared at me mutinously, but he shut up. I knew that letting Ren go and pushing him away would be the smart and right thing to do in case things went south, but I couldn't bring myself to even consider that. That probably said really bad things about me.

Okay. It definitely said really bad things about me.

But I had just found Ren. I'd fallen underwater, completely over my head, for him, with him, and I couldn't do it. I was too selfish. He was . . . he was *mine*, and I'd be damned if I lost that too due to things completely out of my control. It wasn't fair. I . . . I deserved him.

"Fine," Tink muttered finally.

Lying there for a few moments, I gathered what remained of my composure like it was a tattered blanket, wrapped it around me, and sat up, wincing. "I need to shower."

"Thank Queen Mab!" Tink buzzed to the foot of the bed, giving me room. "You were starting to get a bit rank."

I shot him a dark look as I rose.

"And your hair looks like I could cook French fries in it." He twirled in the air and what was left of the powdered sugar hit my face. "It's *that* greasy."

My shoulders slumped as I shuffled to the bathroom. "Thanks," I said, pushing open the door.

Suddenly Tink was right in front of my face, causing me to jerk back. "I know you're mad at me and you probably want to slice and dice me up and wear my skin as a new bracelet."

I glanced around. "Um. That's not exactly what I want to do."

Hope widened his eyes.

"But I kind of want to flush you down a toilet," I amended.

He gasped. "I'd get stuck! And these pipes are old. How would you even do that? I'm not a goldfish."

I rolled my eyes.

Tink swayed and then shot forward, placing his tiny hands on my cheeks. "I'm sorry."

Blinking, I tried to remember if Tink had ever apologized for anything. Not even when he knocked my laptop off the balcony when he'd decided he wanted to watch *Harry Potter* outside. Or when he caught the stove on fire and then tried to put it out with my favorite blanket. Or when he . . . Well, there were a lot of examples of when he should've apologized but hadn't.

"You might not believe this, but I didn't stay with you because of what you are." His pale Otherworld eyes met mine. "I stayed because I like you, Ivy. I stayed because I care about you."

Oh gosh.

My lips parted, and that messy knot of emotion

ballooned in my throat. I wanted to cry again. I was such a mess, a hot and stinky mess.

Tink grinned and his eyes glimmered. "And, okay, I also stayed because you have the magical and wonderful Amazon Prime."

Chapter Two

Exhausted physically, mentally, and most definitely emotionally, all I managed to do was pull on a pair of pajama bottoms and a tank top after my much-needed shower. There was no way I was going to have the energy or even the desire to dry the mass of wet curls on my head, so I twisted them up and shoved a thick bobby pin into my hair.

I roamed back out into the living room around eleven. The entire time I was showering I fought down a hot mess of emotion and locked it away and threw away the key. Well, to be honest, I probably only lost the key to the Pandora's box level of emotional breakdown, but I stayed in that shower until I was confident I could handle everything.

I had to handle this.

I walked into the kitchen, noticing that Tink's bedroom door was cracked open and the room was dark inside, but

I doubted he was actually asleep. Stomach grumbling, I headed for the carryout container Ren had showed up with earlier. Mentally crossing my fingers, I flicked open the lid and sighed.

There was one beignet left.

One.

Shooting Tink's door a glare, I snatched a paper towel off the counter and scooped up the piece of sugary heaven. Then I grabbed a root beer out of the fridge and the can of Pringles out of the cupboard.

Healthy eating at its finest, but I figured I deserved it.

Back in the living room, I eased down on the couch and turned on the TV. Settling on a show about child geniuses, I did the whole hand to mouth thing, getting more sugar and potato-chip crumbs on my chest than in my mouth while I got way too engrossed in the TV. I was equally fascinated by how incredibly smart these kids were, and somewhat shamed because I had no idea what the capital of Tajikistan was when a ten year old did.

I must've dozed off, because the next thing I knew I felt the soft brush of fingertips coasting down the right side of my face. My eyes flickered open, and the first thing I saw was a powerful forearm covered with vines shaded in deep green. I followed that tattoo up to a dark-colored sleeve, knowing it formed the most amazing design under the shirt, and over a sexy throat. I never knew throats could be sexy, but they could be. Oh yes, they could be.

Ren was sitting on the edge of the couch, and my heart did an unsteady flip as a horrible thought invaded my sleep-hazed consciousness. Would he be sitting here if he knew I was a halfling? I squeezed my eyes shut. Of course I knew the answer. He'd be as far away from me as humanly possible. Probably in a different time zone.

"Hey." Ren's deep voice was sex on a stick. Good sex, too. Perfect sex. Mind-blowing sex. It was smooth like chocolate and cultured. I really need to make my brain stop. "You okay?" he asked.

I cleared my throat. "Yeah," I said, telling myself that I'd pulled it together earlier. I opened my eyes and saw that Ren was holding a Pringles can in his lap. "What are you doing with the chips?"

A dimple appeared in his left cheek. The boy had a set of dimples that were absolutely kissable. And lickable. Actually, Ren's entire face was all that and a bag of beignets. His jaw was like marble. His cheekbones were broad and high, and his nose was slightly hooked, as if it had been broken at some point, which was highly possible considering our line of work. His lips were full and expressive, and those eyes of his were absolutely stunning. Thick, dark lashes framed irises so green they looked like emeralds freshly picked from a mine.

Ren was gorgeous, almost so attractive that he could compete against a fae in the looks department, and that was saying something, because the fae were extraordinarily beautiful in their glamoured and true forms—especially the latter. But Ren had them beat. Fae didn't have an ounce of his warmth and humanity.

"Chips?" he said, laughing as he held them up. He shook it. "How about an empty can?"

I frowned. "I was hungry."

"You were cuddling the empty can." A wayward curl fell across his forehead.

My brows lifted. "Was not."

"Was too. You were holding it to your chest like it was a treasured possession. I had to pry it from your fingers."

"Well, I do like Pringles a lot."

"I can tell." He leaned over, placing the can on the coffee table. The other dimple appeared as he eyed my chest, and I got all warm and fuzzy. "You have sugar and crumbs all over you."

Oh.

The warm and fuzzy vanished. "I was hungry *and* tired."

Ren chuckled as he lowered his head, kissing the corner of my lip. Another wretched thought started to break free. Would he kiss me if he—I cut the thought off, and focused on a better one. I couldn't wait until he could really kiss me again. A split lip sucked ass.

He lifted his head. "Did that ass save you any of the beignets?"

One of these days he might actually refer to Tink as something other than a body part. "One."

He cursed under his breath. "And it looks like your chest ate most of it."

"Thanks," I muttered, shifting onto my side so he had more room. He scooted in, resting his arm on the back of the couch as he angled his body toward mine. "What time is it?"

"A little after two in the morning." His lashes lowered as he dragged his finger along the neckline of my tank top. I shivered. "The streets were dead. No sign of the prince or any of the warrior knights that came through the gates. Saw a fae, but he disappeared on me near Royal."

I started to sit up, but his finger did another pass, this time skating down the center, between my breasts. It was hard to concentrate on important things when he was touching me, but I managed. "Something is going on. I don't understand why they'd be lying low like this, especially after busting the prince free."

"They're probably trying to stay alive." More fingers got involved as he coasted them carefully over my bruised side and still achy ribs. "After all, they're probably focused on finding the halfling."

My breath caught.

He moved his hand away as his eyes flew to mine. "Did I hurt you?"

"No." I swallowed hard as I pushed up into a sitting position and leaned against the arm of the couch. I curled the palm I'd sliced open into a fist, hiding the wound. Though I was a mess all over, I doubted he'd notice it. "Did you see David tonight?"

His eyes searched my face. "Only for a bit at headquarters. He was busy getting the new members sorted."

"How many did we get?" We'd lost sixteen the night the fae opened the gate to the Otherworld at the LaLaurie house—the night my best friend, my closest friend, had betrayed us.

"Five for now, I think." He leaned over, resting his weight on his arm and his cheek against his fist. "He said that he's trying to pull more in from Georgia or something. While he was in the middle of yelling at someone on the phone and yelling at the new members, he asked about you."

Surprise hit me. "Really?"

He nodded. "Wants to know if you're still planning to come in tomorrow. I told him I thought you could use a few more days."

Twelve hours ago I would've pitched an absolute bitch fest at the suggestion, but after what I'd recently discovered, I wasn't sure about returning tomorrow. "I don't know if I'll be . . . ready."

"I think you need to take a couple more days." He

reached over with his free hand and picked up a dry curl. "David agrees. You've come a long way in a week, but sweetness, you . . ." He stopped as he stretched out the curl and then let it go. It snapped back into place. "You were hurt bad. I don't want you on the street until you're at a hundred percent."

My gaze drifted to my closed hand. I wasn't sure I'd be a hundred percent anytime soon. Physically? Yes. Everything else? Ha.

"Hey." Two fingers curled under my chin and lifted my head. His eyes were bright and beautiful. "You sure you're okay?"

I forced a smile. "Yeah, I'm just tired." That wasn't exactly a lie.

"Then let's hit the bed."

I didn't protest as Ren rose and picked up my hand, gently hauling my butt off the couch. He led me toward the bedroom door and I glanced over my shoulder, expecting to see Tink peeking around the corner, but he was nowhere to be seen. I was surprised that he was missing a prime opportunity to annoy Ren.

I climbed into the bed and got settled on my side—because now I had my own side, the left side, and Ren had the right side since he'd been staying with me each night for the past week. I watched him strip down. It was a show I didn't want to ever miss, no matter what was going on in my head or with my body.

Ren always started with his shirt, and he took it off in a way that I found fascinating. He reached behind him, grabbing the fabric at the nape of his neck and tugging it off over his head. I don't know what it was about that, but it made all the lady bits stand up and take notice.

So did his abs and pecs.

Because our job required us to go toe to toe with a creature that could punt kick you like a football, we had to stay in shape, but I had a feeling that his flawless six-pack and defined chest had been some kind of gift from God. As were those amazing indents on either side of his lean hips. They were so perfect they were almost indecent.

Ren unhooked the band that circled his stomach, just below the chest, and got down to removing the daggers at his side. He placed them next to mine on the dresser. His and hers weapons were the way of romance in the Order. Then he kicked off his boots and two more stakes joined his stash. Then his socks came off.

His chin was bent as his hands dropped to his tactical pants. A button come undone and down went the zipper. I clutched the bedspread, and he lifted his gaze. "You like what you see, don't you?" he asked as he shucked off his pants.

I nodded and then said, "Yes," in case he doubted it.

A slow smile graced his lips. "I like you watching me."

Ren sometimes went commando, and that was incredibly hot to think of. Today he had on tight black boxer briefs, and I could tell he really did like me watching. I could see the hard, thick ridge of that approval straining the material.

My stomach dipped as he picked up his clothes, folding them neatly and placing them on the chair by the door. Then he disappeared into the bathroom. We obviously hadn't done anything of the fun and naughty nature since last Wednesday, and we only had sex that Tuesday night and Wednesday morning. Before then, we'd messed around, and it had been wonderful, but we hadn't spent a lot of time together. And before Ren, there had only been Shaun and the one time. A burst of sadness lit up my chest at the thought of the boy I'd loved and lost three years ago. The pain was still there, probably would always be there, but it was fading like I guessed . . . I guessed it was supposed to.

But now there was Ren, and I refused to lose him, too.

The bathroom door opened. Our relationship was still so new that a fine tremble coursed through my belly as he approached the bed.

"So, I'm wondering about something," he said, stopping at *his* side.

I focused on his face. "What?"

"Why are you clutching the blanket like it's going to run away from you?"

"Oh." I let go of the blanket and scooted down onto my back. "I don't know."

A half-grin appeared as he slipped under the covers. He turned off the lamp and rolled over onto his side, facing me. "You're really weird tonight."

Oh dear. "No, I'm not."

He carefully placed his arm over my hips and shifted so the front of his body was pressed against mine. I tipped my head back and turned toward him. I couldn't make out his features at all since I kept heavy curtains on my windows. The room was pitch black, but I could feel his gaze.

And I could feel his hard length against my hip.

I couldn't help it. I immediately thought of him in this bed, moving over me and in me. An ache blossomed between my thighs. I shifted, wiggling my hips, and Ren let out a deep, rumbling sound. I moved again.

His fingers splayed across my outer hip as he dipped his head, brushing his lips over my temple. "You moving like that is going to drive me crazy."

My toes curled. "We could, you know, do something

about it."

He made that sound again, and I felt the tips of my breasts tingle. "Ivy, we've got to take things easy for a little bit."

"What?" I whispered, turning onto my side. I placed my hands on his chest. In the darkness, he kissed my forehead. "Do you not . . . want to?"

The second I asked that question I wanted to kick myself in the face. What in the hell was wrong with me? I was a halfling. And admittedly, I was feeling a wee bit unsure about things, like, for example, should I even be coming onto him when I was this . . . *this thing* he was here to literally kill? Was I betraying him in a way, his—

"Babe, I want nothing more than to get between those legs with my hands, my mouth, and most definitely my dick, but I'm not going to risk hurting you." His hand flexed along my hip. "So for right now, it's me and my hand on my dick and thoughts of you naked underneath me, coming and screaming my name."

My body flushed hot at the image of him touching himself. "That's not helping."

"Ditto."

Easing onto my back, I exhaled softly and closed my eyes. His hand stayed on my hip as he settled back in against me. Several moments passed, and in that time, a hundred different things filled my thoughts. I pushed aside the whole halfling business, and almost wished I hadn't, because I started thinking about Val.

I still couldn't believe what she'd done. I mean, I'd accepted that she was a traitorous bitch, but I just couldn't understand why. How long had she been working with the fae? There was no way it could've been since I met her three years ago. Or at least I hoped not. She hadn't been under compulsion, because she'd been wearing the four-leaf clover incased in her bracelet. I'd seen it, and the simple, yet extremely powerful thing prevented a fae from manipulating a human. She was using free will while aiding the fae, and even when she went back to headquarters, removing some weird, random crystal David had kept in storage. She made that choice.

How could she do this to everyone?

Heart pumping, I opened my eyes. "Ren?"

"Yeah?"

"Did . . . David say anything about Valerie?"

He didn't answer immediately. "Order members are looking for her, but no one has seen her."

That was because they didn't know where to look or know her like I did, but I was going to find her. I had to, because I had to make sense of how she could do this.

"She's a big concern. She knows a lot about the Order, and David isn't keen on the fact she's probably shared a shitload of secrets with the fae." He paused. "I still want to kill her."

And I still had a hard time hearing that.

I got his anger though. I was also furious. After the gate had opened and the prince had strolled through, kicking ass and not taking names, I'd followed them back to the Order's headquarters, and she . . . she had left me there with him. There was no doubt in my mind she knew what was going to happen, and she *left* me.

"But it's more than that." His voice was heavier, tired. "He's not questioning the whole halfling shit anymore. He knows we've got to find her."

Understanding rippled through me. "You think Val is the halfling?"

"Yeah, babe. It's what I've been thinking for some

time. It's why I wouldn't tell you who the other person I was looking into was. Didn't want to put that crap in your head if it turned out not to be the case," he explained.

Holy Sunday-sized shit balls.

Ren and David, the sect leader, thought the halfling was Val. To them, it made sense. Then didn't they have to be worried out of their minds that Val was already in the process of getting pregnant with the doomsday baby?

"She must've figured it out somehow. Maybe a fae got to her and found out," Ren added, and then yawned. "I know her parents are denying it. Both are claiming that they're her actual biological parents, but who would fess up to that shit?"

My stomach sunk. "Where are her parents now?"

"Don't know. Don't really care."

Pressure clamped down on my chest. I opened my mouth to tell him . . . to tell him what, exactly? That I knew for a fact her parents were innocent of shacking up with a fae? How could I prove that without incriminating myself? I closed my mouth, and oh God, I was a terrible person, a legit horrible human being.

Well . . .

Nope. Wasn't quite a human being now, was I?

Oh my God, I needed my brain to, like, jump off a freaking cliff. What in the hell was I going to do? I couldn't let her parents go down, because I seriously doubted they had anything to do with what she'd done. And they *would* go down. That was the way the Order operated. Her parents would've been deemed a threat and there was only one way threats were dealt with. Unease blossomed in my chest, along with a hefty dose of fear.

"You sure you're okay?" he asked suddenly.

"Yeah," I breathed, forcing my tense muscles to relax.

I refocused. "Has David said anything about that crystal Val took?"

"He doesn't know what it is." Ren paused. "Or he's not saying. Not sure if he trusts anyone at the moment, but I've put some feelers out to see if anyone in the Elite has an idea."

Couldn't blame David for not trusting anyone. Hopefully someone knew about the crystal. I thought about Merle. She'd randomly mentioned a crystal once before, but I was reluctant to involve her and her daughter. I didn't want to bring trouble to their doorstep. They'd been through enough.

His hand tightened along my hip, and then he found my cheek in the darkness once more, and kissed me there. I let him fall asleep this time, but I stared into nothing as my mind jumped from one screwed up situation to the next. Stupid tears burned the back of my throat, but I fought them back, because if they fell, Ren would wake, and I was feeling too weak, too ripped open to keep this very big, very horrific secret under lock and key.

But as I lay there, the fear inside me grew like one of the vines that had crawled its way up the wall and over the balcony railing. There was no shaking the feeling that no matter what I did, things were going to go bad.

And they were going to go bad fast.

Chapter Three

I'd originally planned to get my butt out of my apartment and make my way to the headquarters on Thursday, but that's not what I ended up doing. Instead, I checked in with Jo Ann, my only non-Order friend. Unsure of how to explain why I had disappeared from class and hadn't been very communicative, I went with the trusty old "I got mugged" excuse, which was sadly believable, but there was a good chance that was the second time I'd used that excuse to explain away random bruises. I really needed to come up with something more creative, because I was sure there was going to be another instance when I was going to have to lie to her.

And that sucked.

Besides the fact that I liked her and enjoyed how genuinely kind she was, being around Jo Ann made me feel . . . normal. Like I was any twenty-one-year-old about to turn twenty-two in two months. That I could have things like a degree and a boyfriend. Like I wasn't shirking my duty by enrolling in classes at Loyola—classes I was most likely going to fail.

That served as a cold reminder that I wasn't normal.

I spent the bulk of Thursday dealing with my rather ineffective attempt at being normal. I'd tracked down the syllabus, but only managed to get a return call from my statistics professor, of all people. After bluntly telling me I'd missed way too much time, he explained I needed to talk to my advisor and then mic-dropped on me by hanging up.

My advisor didn't call me back until Thursday afternoon, and it wasn't a good call, but honestly, out of everything else, it almost felt like not a big deal. Just another reason to eat my feelings through the last box of pralines.

I'd missed too much time, a week here and a few days there, and I had a choice that really wasn't much of a choice at all. Fail classes due to already missing so much time, and it was only the beginning of October, or withdrawal from the semester.

I was going to have to withdraw, and it was hard not to laugh at the tiny, almost pathetic voice that said I could reregister in the spring or once things calmed down. As if things were ever going to calm down.

As I tossed my phone on the couch cushion, I told myself that I was still Ivy Morgan. I was still *her* even if I had to drop out of college, even though I was a halfling. I was still *her*. No matter what.

I had to keep telling myself that.

So I stayed in my apartment, on my couch, Thursday and Friday. Ren and Tink were relieved about that. Their reasoning for me "taking it easy" came from two very different places.

Ren worried about my health—physical and mental. He didn't want me back on the streets until I was ready for both.

Tink didn't want me stepping out of the apartment, because he feared I'd be exposed as a halfling or snatched up by the prince.

But I wasn't going to stay hidden away forever. I couldn't. I just had to be smart about all of this. The bruises were fading, and in probably another day or two I could go out in public without people staring at me. The ache deep in my body was also fading. I could protect myself if necessary, and I was pretty sure by Sunday I'd be fine enough to get back out there.

I hoped so at least, because I was already going stir crazy. I had too much time to think and try to figure things out. There were a lot of things I didn't understand. If I sat down and started listing them, I'd be doing it for the next week, but one of the biggest things was why the prince hadn't come knocking or busting down my door. According to Tink, after the prince got way too familiar with my blood, he could sense me out, so he had to know where I lived.

I asked Tink that question when Friday evening rolled around and Ren was out on the streets. "Why hasn't the prince showed up here?"

"Huh?" he murmured, squinting at the TV.

I sighed.

Tink was sitting on the couch beside me and he'd commandeered my laptop at some point. *The Walking Dead* was on the television—well, it was on the Amazon Fire Stick TV thingy that the little bastard had ordered a few days ago unbeknownst to me. On my laptop, he was watching old episodes of *Supernatural*. I think he was on season three judging by the current length of Sam Winchester's hair.

At least it wasn't *Harry Potter* and *Twilight* this time, because I was getting really tired of hearing him quote Edward Cullen and Ron Weasley at the same time.

"Why are you watching both of them?" I asked, folding my arms loosely across my chest as I leaned back against the cushion.

"I think it's good to be prepared," he said from his cross-legged position.

"Prepared for what?"

He stopped the show on his laptop. "Zombie apocalypse or a demon infestation. You'll thank me when people start eating each other or when a yellow-eyed demon shows up and starts burning people alive on ceilings. I'm going to be like Daryl and Dean and grab a bucket of salt and a bow with unlimited arrows—hold up!" He held up his hand as he zipped into the air above the laptop, focused on the TV.

Everyone was standing in front of a barn and psycho Shane was pacing in front of the locked barn doors. Psycho Shane went full crazy after he shaved his head. At least, that was my opinion.

"'Things ain't the way they used to be!'" Tink shouted at the same time Shane did, thrusting his little brownie fist into the air. He then turned to me, expression serious. "Things ain't the way they used to be, Ivy!"

"Oh my God," I muttered, pinching the bridge of my nose.

"God doesn't have anything to do with it, Ivy Divy."

"Can you just answer my question?"

He tilted his head to the side as he buzzed out over the coffee table. "What question?"

Taking a deep breath, I counted to ten, then reached over and snatched up the remote. Tink shouted like I had taken away his favorite toy and shattered it in front of him. All I did was pause the TV. I held on to the remote. "I was thinking—"

"That's what I smelled!"

I stared at him.

"You know, the smell of wheels burning as they try to turn over . . ." He drifted up toward the ceiling and rolled his eyes. "Never mind. Carry on."

My fingers tightened around the slender remote. "I was *thinking* that if the prince can sense me, why hasn't he showed up here?"

"I don't know." Tink came down to the coffee table and started marching across it. "I'm not the prince, but if I was the prince, I'd be buying time."

"Buying time?" I scooted to the edge of the couch.

"Yeah, because he's got to win you over." Tink swiped up the straw he'd had in his Coke. It was nearly the size of him. "That's basically what he has to do if he wants to impregnate you."

I cringed, like a full body cringe. "Please do not use the word impregnate ever again."

"Why? That's what he wants to do." He started dancing with the straw, the kind of dancing you see in the clubs. Hips gyrating all over the place. "He knows coercing or tricking you isn't going to get the deed done, so he's probably trying to learn how not to be a sexed up dickhead."

"Sexed up dickhead?" I repeated.

"Uh-huh." Tink dipped the straw as one would a dancer. "Remember when I was telling you how I saw the prince getting it on with three females once? He's totes sexed up. And he's a dickhead. In other words, he has no empathy or compassion. No humanity."

"Most fae don't."

Tink twirled the straw. "Yeah, but the ancients are worse. They're as far away from human as you can get. He's going to have to work on wooing you."

I slowly shook my head. "That's . . ." There were no words.

"That's what I'd do." Tink dropped the straw and whipped around toward me. "Or he's plotting something major and any moment he's going to knock down the front door and storm the place."

"Wow." A fine shiver curled down my spine. "That's really a relaxing thought."

He zipped over to the couch and sat on the arm. He tipped his head back and stared up at me. "Don't worry. I'm here to protect you."

I just looked at him, because other than ordering shit off of Amazon, the only strength he had was the unique ability to annoy the crap out of me while somehow still managing to be endearing.

Tink grinned. "Trust me, Ivy. The Prince is *not* going to want to mess with me."

~

My body was the first to wake, and I was slow to open my eyes. At first I didn't understand why I felt so hot. I could feel the blankets pushed down to my hips and my shirt was bunched up. Cool air caressed my belly, but pressed to my side was a hard, warm body, and a rough, calloused palm glided back and forth below my navel. Soft lips brushed my temple. *Ren.*

Air caught in my lungs as every sense I had fully awakened. He was in bed with me, and I wasn't sure when that happened. Normally, he was off on the weekend, but with members down, it was all hands on deck. I'd fallen asleep Saturday night a little after midnight, and he'd still been out. *Home.* It felt so strange and wonderful to think of Ren and home in the same sentence.

"Ivy." He murmured my name in that deep, smooth voice of his. His hand stopped at the loose band on my pajama bottoms, with the tips of his fingers just under them.

A deep flutter kicked around in my belly as I tipped my head back. "Hey."

It was dark in the room, and I had no idea what time it was, but I had a feeling he was smiling, and I bet his dimples were out. "I didn't want to wake you." His hand slid down an inch and the muscles low in my stomach tightened. "But you were making these sounds."

I was super close to making all kinds of sounds. "I was?"

"Yeah." He brushed his lips over the curve of my cheek as I reached over, placing my hand on his hard stomach. The muscles and skin seemed to jump in response. "These soft, little, breathy moans."

My eyes widened. "Really?"

"I would not lie about something that was so fucking sexy." His hand was venturing further south. "I'd just about dozed off when you started. Those moans went straight to my cock."

Heat swept through my blood. "Sorry?"

He chuckled and then the sound faded away in the darkness. "I want to kiss you."

Air lodged in my throat. I wanted that. "You don't need my permission for that. Just assume it's always granted."

"I like the sound of that, but your lip—"

"My lips are fine," I told him as I lowered my hand, loving the way his body stiffened against mine when I reached the band of his briefs. "Actually, they're not okay. They're lonely and they feel abandoned by—"

Ren's mouth silenced me. His kiss was soft, and it felt like it had been so long since I got to enjoy this that I felt the kiss all the way to the tips of my toes. When I didn't scream in pain or anything, he deepened the kiss, nudging my lips apart. His tongue moved against mine. I loved the feel of his mouth on mine, and the way he tasted.

"Goddamn, you're so sweet," he said against my mouth. "I got another request. I want to touch you. I need to."

My breaths were coming in short pants and my hips rocked even though he hadn't even touched me there yet. "That's another thing you can assume you have permission for."

"You just made my night. Hell, my week." He kissed me again, dragging his tongue over the roof of my mouth. "Fuck it. You made my life."

Those words lit me up more than any touch could. His hand slipped down between my legs and his mouth covered mine, silencing the moan that ripped from my lungs. Sensation flooded my body, acute and delicious, but a horrible thought snapped at its heels.

Was this wrong?

Ren thought I was like him, that I was a hundred percent human. He had no idea I had fae blood in me, and all Order members, including Ren, hated the fae. I knew, deep down, that he wouldn't be here right now if he knew the truth. He wouldn't be kissing me like I was something special, to be treasured. Nor would his hand be between my thighs, pressing on the bundle of nerves with just the right amount of pressure.

He would be disgusted.

No.

I am no different.

His hand stilled, because I'd stopped kissing him back. "Hey, sweetness, you okay? Did I—"

"I'm okay. Promise." I moved my hand under his briefs and my fingers brushed the head of his erection. My breath caught when he groaned.

I was okay.

I had to be.

I was still Ivy Morgan. I was still the girl who fell in love with Ren. I had no idea if he felt that strongly about me, but I was the same girl he cared for—the same girl he wanted.

I kissed him, sliding back on track. Shifting slightly, I spread my legs and reached further down, wrapping my hand around him. He made that incredibly sexy sound again, the deep rumble that never failed to make me hot. His finger slipped through the wetness gathering and my entire body jolted.

"I haven't forgotten how much you like that, but damn if it doesn't feel like the first time." He slid that finger almost all the way out and then thrust it back in, causing my back to arch.

We'd done this before. Once. Not in bed, though, but on the couch at his place. The second time we'd actually had sex, so I wasn't counting that. So this was kind of like the first time.

I started moving my hand, remembering the way he seemed to like it, and I guessed I was doing it right, because his back bowed and his finger started moving faster in me. He lifted himself up, somehow managing to push down his briefs while not even taking his hand away, and that took amazing talent. Our breaths mingled as the bedspread tangled around our legs. I wanted him in me, thick and hard and wonderful, but we weren't going to make it that far. Oh no.

He added another finger, and I cried out. My senses twisted with each hot dip of his fingers. "Fuck, Ivy, I. . . ."

I could feel him swelling in my hand, and I all but face planted into his chest when the orgasm hit me. I came, my hips riding his hand as I moaned against his skin. He came in my hand, his cock swelling and then jerking. My name was a heated curse on his lips.

"Christ," he grunted after several moments. "I can't even . . ."

"Me neither," I murmured, easing my hand away. A part of him was left behind, on me, and I didn't even care. Sweet aftershocks still rocked my body.

A sexy chuckle radiated out from him as he slipped his hand away from me. I immediately missed it and wondered how inappropriate it would be to keep it there for, like, forever. "I can't believe I came that fast," he said. He lifted his chin and kissed the corner of my lip. "You got a magic hand."

I laughed at the absurdity of the statement. "I always wanted to excel at something. Who knew it would be hand jobs?"

"I'm a lucky man." He rolled away and stood. "Be right back," he said, and a second later, the light from the bathroom came on. He grabbed a towel and turned the tap water on while I glanced at the clock he'd been blocking. It was a little after three in the morning. The light turned off and Ren returned. He sat on the bed. "Give me your hand," he said.

Doing as he ordered, I smiled as he moved the warm, damp towel over my hand. In those quiet moments, those three little words bubbled up, but I kept quiet.

Ren disappeared again and returned quickly. This time he rolled onto his side and tugged an arm around my waist, pulling me down so I was nestled against him.

"How's your ribs?" he asked once he appeared satisfied with where he had me.

"Fine. They barely ached all day."

"You telling the truth?"

I grinned as I wiggled in closer to him. "Yes."

"Hmm." He fisted the front of my shirt. "I just realized I didn't even make it to your breasts. That's like a huge sex fail. Those beautiful babies most definitely feel abandoned."

Giggling, I folded my hand over his. "It's okay. You can make up for it next time."

"Oh, you better believe I will. I'm going to shower them with so much attention I might have to name them and take them out to dinner."

I laughed outright at that. "How was work?"

"Boring as being forced to sit through *New Moon* repeatedly," he replied.

"You better not let Tink hear you say that," I warned. "Or he'll find new ways to torture you with how he's convinced Jacob and Edward should've gotten together. He's into something called slash fiction now."

"You know," he said slowly, "I'm not even going to touch that with a twenty-foot pole."

"I wouldn't." I paused, closing my eyes. "So, no fae? Nothing?"

"Not a damn thing."

I traced the outlines of his knuckles. "That is so freaking bizarre."

"Yep."

A couple moments passed while I thought about what I wanted to do tomorrow. "So I was thinking . . ."

"That's what I smell."

"Geez." I rolled my eyes. "You and Tink have more in common than you want to admit."

"I might have to kick you out of the bed for that."

I snorted. "Um, yeah, you can't kick me out of my own bed. Sorry."

"Whatever," he replied. "What were you thinking about?"

I drew in a deep breath. "I was going to go out tomorrow—not to work. Just to get back out there."

"Sounds good. I got the evening shift again." His hand flattened against my belly. "You can come out with me."

I opened my eyes and winced. "I kind of wanted to just go out and do my own thing."

"Why?"

My wince turned into a frown. "Does there need to be a why?"

"Yeah, I like to think so."

I stopped tracing his knuckles. "I just want to get back out there. It's not a big deal."

"And you have to do that alone?" he queried softly.

"Well, yeah. I kind of want to do it alone." I flipped onto my back. "It's nothing personal. I just—"

"I know, Ivy," he said with a sigh. "You've got to prove you're still the badass that you are. You don't want a babysitter or a guard."

My brows inched up my forehead. "Why would I need either of those two things even if I weren't a badass? No one has seen a fae in days."

"Has nothing to do with the fae," he replied. "You need a damn babysitter because you want to get out there and find Valerie."

Chapter Four

Oh shit.

"Yeah, you think I don't know you that well, do you?" he stated.

I laughed dryly and muttered, "You don't."

Ren stiffened. "What the hell?" He lifted his hand and I felt the bed shift as he rose up onto his elbow. "What in the hell is that supposed to mean?"

I screwed my eyes shut. Okay. I probably shouldn't have said that for a ton of obvious reasons. "I'm sorry. "

"You really don't sound like you mean that."

I shook my head even though he couldn't see it. Frustration rose, and I knew I was the one who was in the wrong. Not him. He was right about the Val thing, but there was no way I'd find her with him tagging along. For some reason, and maybe it was a dumb reason, I felt like if I could find Val by myself, she wouldn't run from me.

There was also the whole finding Val's parents thing.

Ren wouldn't and shouldn't be along for that ride.

Ren exhaled heavily. "I know you need to find her. She was your closest friend, but she betrayed the Order *and* you. She nearly got you killed. No matter what questions you have for her or how she answers them, it's not going to change what happened."

I pressed my lips together.

"And if you find her, you might actually find fae," he added.

"Well, that would suck, but . . . if I do find fae, I know how to do my job, Ren."

"I'm not saying that you don't know how to do your job." He leaned over, switching on the nightstand lamp. "But I am going to be really honest with you."

My gaze flicked over to him. Dammit, why did he have to be so hot, because it was really hard to be irritated with him when I wanted to kiss him. "Of course you are," I muttered.

He ignored that. "You are strong and brave, but you were seriously injured a week ago—"

"A week and three days ago," I corrected him.

Ren eyed me. "Do those three days really make a difference?"

"Yes," I snapped. "Look, it's late. You just got off in more than one way—"

"So did you," he reminded me.

I shot him a look. "Can you turn off the light so we can go to bed?"

"No."

My eyes narrowed. "Ren . . ."

His green eyes met mine. "You're not ready to be back out there."

"Oh, so you're a doctor now?"

"You almost died, Ivy."

A slice of bitter panic lit up my chest. "Thanks for the reminder."

"Obviously you need one, so could you try to use some common sense and just say yes, Ren, I'll be happy to join you tomorrow night?"

I wanted to say that. I also wanted to say a lot of other things. I chose to say none of it. "I don't need your permission. You do realize that, right?"

Ren shoved his hand through his hair. "I'm not trying to be an ass."

"Well, you should try harder, then."

He stared at me, and I could tell there was a lot he wanted to say, but like me, he kept that pretty mouth of his shut for a moment. "Whatever." He turned and switched off the light.

"Finally," I muttered, flipping onto my side and giving him my back.

He ignored that as he shifted back down onto his side. A moment passed, and then I felt his arm around my waist. He dragged me back against his chest. "Just think about what I said, okay?" When I didn't answer, he said, "Ivy?"

"Okay," I whispered, lying, because I'd already made up my mind even though I felt terrible about it.

~

I was walking out of the bedroom Sunday morning when there was a knock on the door. A shadow moved past the window near the porch, heading down the steps. I immediately had a sinking suspicion of what it was, and glanced down the short hallway toward the kitchen.

Ren easily stepped around me. "I'll get it."

"You know, I can do that."

He kept going. "I'm just being a gentleman."

"More like he's being an overprotective bully," Tink commented from where he suddenly appeared in the hallway. "I was hoping you'd be gone by now. Alas, Queen Mab and your God both hate me."

I shot Tink a look that said shut up. Things had been a little tense between Ren and me this morning, and he was not helping.

"You know, if you weren't actually the size of an overgrown rodent, your opinion might actually matter." Ren opened the door. "What the hell? They deliver on Sundays, too?"

I peered over his shoulder and sighed. "Yep. Tink, it's for you."

"Me? All for me?" Tink buzzed into the living room. As he got closer, I realized he was wearing an Elf on the Shelf sweater, and yeah, I wasn't even going to question that. He bumped into Ren's arm. "Excuse me."

Ren tipped his head up and stared at the ceiling, exhaling slowly. Tink screeched when he saw the packages— there were four of them. One large box and three smaller boxes. Knowing how Amazon packed their stuff, I figured there was either something ironically small in the big box or there were ten things shoved into it.

"You going to stand there or actually be helpful?" Tink demanded. "Pick up the boxes for me?"

"Tink," I snapped.

"If I pick up those boxes," Ren said, "I'm pitching them into the courtyard."

Tink jerked back, smacking his hands against his

cheeks. "You wouldn't dare."

"I'd so dare."

"Oh Jesus," I muttered, stepping around Ren. I picked up the boxes and carried them inside, dumping them on the couch.

"Careful!" shrieked Tink. "There could be priceless, fragile items in there." He spun in the air as Ren was closing the door behind him. "And you! You made a lady carry boxes inside."

I rolled my eyes.

Ren exhaled heavily. "God, you're so annoying."

"So?" Tink hovered in front of the couch, his wings furiously beating the air. "I'm rubber and you're glue!"

Ren turned to face the little guy. "What?"

"Whatever you say bounces off me and sticks to you!"

Ren stared at him and then slowly shook his head as he turned back to me. "It's like living with a two-year-old with the mental capacity of a fifteen-year-old boy."

My lips twitched, and I turned to hide my grin. Ren didn't stay long, and by the time afternoon rolled around, I was sitting in my chair in the bedroom, lacing up my boots. The apartment was oddly quiet. Tink was sulking in his bedroom, because he knew what I was about to do, or he was playing with the stuff that showed up today. Ren was still at his place, doing laundry or listing all the reasons why he wanted to strangle me or poison Tink, and then heading out to work.

Which was why I was slipping a dagger into one boot and carefully hooking the thorn stake into the other. Getting back out there to do my duty wasn't the only reason I wanted to return to work so quickly. Besides feeling like I was going to murder someone (most likely Tink) if I stayed in this apartment a minute longer, I also needed to find Valerie. It was Sunday, and while I doubted she'd stick to a normal routine, I knew what she typically did on Sunday evenings.

There was a good chance that I'd run into Ren, but I'd cross that pissed-off bridge when I came to it.

I stood up and straightened the loose gray shirt I wore. It was long, coming to my thighs, and it successfully hid the stake I had secured to my hip. I made a pit stop in the bathroom and leaned onto the sink, studying my face in the mirror.

The bruises on my left side had faded dramatically, and the concealer had done wonders with covering what remained. A touch of lipstick camouflaged the mark on the center of my lip. Good chance that would be an actual scar.

I left my hair down just in case people looked too closely and realized I was hiding a mess of a face. Maybe I shouldn't care about that, but whatever. I wasn't the best-looking thing out there, and I had no idea how I'd really snagged Ren's attention, but I didn't want to look like a walking accident victim.

Then again, Ren was probably questioning his life choices at the moment. He hadn't exactly been the happiest camper when he'd left this morning.

I started to push away from the mirror but stopped. My eyes. They were blue. A very deep blue, like the color of the sky right before it gives way to dusk. I had no idea what the color of my parents' eyes were or which one of my parents was a . . . fae, but all fae had blue eyes— pale eyes that were the color of glaciers. I was guessing all the creatures from the Otherworld had those kinds of eyes, because Tink also had them. Did my mortal parent's genes deepen the eye color so they . . . looked normal?

God.

I squeezed my eyes shut and took a deep breath. No matter what half of my blood said, I was still Ivy Morgan. For twenty-one years, I had operated like any other human being. Well, a human being warded at birth to see through the glamour of the fae, but whatever. I was still Ivy.

With that thought in mind, I left the bathroom. Grabbing a lightweight purse with a shoulder strap that wouldn't get in the way of things, I strolled out into the living room. I wasn't a big handbag fan, but I'd found the black, fringed piece of awesomeness at a thrift shop off of Canal, and I'd used it before. I grabbed my book bag, digging out the thin wallet, and that went into the purse with my cellphone.

"You're insane," Tink announced.

I didn't look to see where he was as I lifted the strap of my bag over my head, draping it across my body.

"You shouldn't go out," he said, voice closer. I could hear his wings fluttering.

"Am I supposed to stay in here forever, Tink?"

"Yes. I don't see anything wrong with that. Amazon does one-hour delivery now and you can get almost anything out of their pantry." He was hovering by the window when I turned to him. His hands were folded together under his chin. "And you can use Man-Boy to get us beignets, since it's the only thing he's good at."

There were a lot of things Ren was good at, but I wasn't going to spend the next hour arguing with Tink. "I'll be back," I said.

"You hope." He followed me to the door. "Ivy—"

"I'll be careful." I turned the knob and glanced over at the brownie. "I promise, Tink. I'll be home in a little bit."

He opened his mouth, but I stepped outside and closed the door behind me. A second later, something smacked into it, and my brows rose. I doubted it was Tink. Probably something I didn't want him throwing at the door.

Shaking my head, I went down the staircase and out into the courtyard. The purple and blue periwinkles and bright pink hibiscus flowers were multiplying like rabbits along the stone walkway. Leafy green vines covered the fencing and the wrought-iron cornstalk gate. That stuff was going to take the whole place over, but I kind of liked it wild and out of control.

The weather wasn't unbearable, probably in the mid-seventies with the sun behind the clouds, but I fished out my sunglasses anyway and slipped them on. Walking down Coliseum Street felt a little weird. With every step I took, I expected the prince to pop out from a courtyard or from behind the heavy moss. It was ridiculous, this ball of nerves weighing in the center of my stomach, but I put one foot in front of the other as I headed toward Perrier.

First things first. Find out where Val's parents were and somehow, I didn't quite know how yet . . . Wait. Change of plans. I needed to make a pit stop at Cafe Du Monde on Decatur. I needed a beignet—a fresh beignet. It had been forever since I had one that was still all warm and toasty, and hadn't been brought home to cool off.

I caught a cab, because there was no way I was waiting around for one of the damn trolleys, and rode over to Royal. I hopped out, making my way toward Decatur as I kept my eyes peeled for fae.

It felt good to be out, to be walking, which was something I never thought I'd say, but being cooped up in the apartment had me yearning to just be out in the fresh air and get my muscles working.

The streets were busy even for a late Sunday afternoon. Tourists were everywhere, snapping pictures of buildings. Drunken stumbling was at a minimum, but I knew in a couple of hours there'd be someone, most likely multiple someones, who would be sitting down on the narrow sidewalks because they simply couldn't walk any longer.

A wry grin tugged at my lips. Most locals stayed far, far away from Bourbon, staying off the known streets and into the lesser parts of the French Quarter or hanging in the business district. There were times I'd rather take a swim in the muddy Mississippi than walk on Bourbon, but when I was gone for a while, I missed the craziness. Probably because I hadn't lived here my entire life, and in many ways, I was still a newbie to Nola.

Cafe Du Monde was about five minutes from the heart of the Quarter, but the space under the green and white pinstriped awning was always packed, as it was today.

Sighing, I sidestepped a couple who'd apparently decided holding hands while walking at the speed of a three-legged turtle was an appropriate thing to do. The line up ahead was ridiculous, but I'd come this far, so I was getting a damn beignet—

A cold draft stirred my curls. Goosebumps raced across my skin as I stopped under the covered walkway. My right hand floated to my side as I whipped around, ignoring the startled curse from the boy in a waiter's white uniform. My heart jumped into my throat.

The prince stood behind me.

Chapter Five

Holy shit.

I took a step back, bumping into someone. The person said something, but I didn't hear them or care. Part of me couldn't believe I took an actual step away, like I was afraid, but I was beyond caught off-guard.

The prince of the damn fae stood in front of me, and he looked like he belonged in the Otherworld.

Or in an Anne Rice novel.

His raven-colored hair brushed broad shoulders cloaked in a white linen shirt. Like before, he must've forgotten to button it completely. Unlike normal fae, his skin wasn't silvery, but bronze, and stood out in stark relief against the whiteness of his shirt. He'd ditched the breeches, though. He was rocking some leather pants now and . . . *combat boots.*

Actually, the prince looked like he belonged in New Orleans.

Snapping out of my surprised stupor, I became aware of the hum of conversation around us and I felt the warm breeze return. The sugary scent of beignets filled my nostrils, and I saw a middle-aged brunette openly gawking at him, and even though I found his very being to be disturbingly unsettling, I could admit that his perfectly symmetrical, angular face was beautiful. It was the kind of beauty that was almost hard to look upon. Like if he was just a picture on the Internet, you wouldn't believe he was real. But he was, and there wasn't a flicker of warmth or compassion in his features.

I lifted my right hand, reaching for my iron stake out of instinct, even though I knew it would do no good against the prince.

"You shouldn't do that." His voice was deep with what reminded me of an English accent. "I know you want to, but it would be very, very unwise of you, Ivy."

My hand twitched.

Creepy Prince smiled slightly. "Your friend has been very helpful."

That got my hackles up. I slid my sunglasses onto my forehead and forced my tone to stay calm and level. "I'm sure she has. Speaking of Val, happen to know where I can find her?"

His lips curled in a semblance of a smile as he stepped closer. The prince was tall, taller than Ren, who was pushing six foot two. My entire back stiffened as I forced myself to hold my ground, even though every instinct demanded that I run and run super fast, because he had almost killed me once before. Correction. He would have definitely killed me if he hadn't realized what I was and had, I guessed, healed me.

"I've been waiting for you," he said, instead of

answering my question, his pale blue eyes fixed on mine.

My hand curled into a useless fist. "That is extremely creepy to hear."

That cold smile returned. "Why don't we talk? There are seats across the way."

"Yeah, that's not going to happen."

The slow smile increased but never reached his eyes. "Oh, I know it is."

Fine hairs rose on my arms.

"What exactly can you do right now?" he said in the same coldly polite voice. "Refuse me?" Creepy Prince laughed, and it wasn't a bad sound. Again, it was something that was just *cold*, as if he were mimicking what a human would do. "You can't."

"I can." My palm itched to grab the thorn stake secured under my pant leg, but I held still. I might be reckless, but I wasn't stupid.

"Really? I will have to beg to differ on that. You see, humans surround us. So many of them, and I have an extraordinary appetite." His eyes appeared to glimmer as his gaze slithered from the top of my curly head down to my toes. "A rather impressive appetite for many, many things."

"Okay. First off, ew." My lip curled. "Secondly, I don't want to hear about any of your appetites."

One dark eyebrow rose. "Oh, but you should know that I could kill twenty of these humans in less than five seconds and feed on the rest, leaving them to believe that it was this little red-headed girl who murdered these innocent people." His voice dropped even lower as he leaned in and icy air brushed my cheek. "You deny me this, those lives will be on your hands, little bird."

Anger flushed hotly as my eyes met his. There wasn't

a single part of me that doubted anything he said. He had me. God, I hated to admit it, but he had me.

Pivoting on my heel, I marched to the corner of the street and then crossed it, heading towards Jackson Square. I didn't have to look behind me to know the prince was following. I could feel him, his iciness beating upon my back.

The whole entire time, my heart raced so fast I was sure I was going to go into cardiac arrest on the sidewalk. This was insane on so many different levels. I was about to have a conversation, albeit an unwilling one, with the mother freaking prince of the Otherworld on a lazy Sunday afternoon. At any minute, he could kill a dozen people before anyone knew what he was up to. Any Order member could stumble across us, and how would that look, me being chummy with the prince?

Man, I really should've listened to Ren.

Then again, would the prince have stayed away if Ren were with me? Creepy Prince said he'd been waiting for me. He could've come anyway, and Ren would've gone ape shit, and his life would be in danger.

It really was a no-win situation.

All the benches were full, but the prince strode right up to the first one that was under the shade of a leafy tree. An elderly couple took one look at him and then struggled to their feet. Not a single word was exchanged. They ambled off as fast as their tired, old bodies could carry them.

"I bet you're real useful on a crowded bus," I remarked.

He sat down on the bench. "Sit."

"I prefer to stand."

Those eerie eyes locked onto mine. "And I prefer you to sit."

My fingernails dug into my palms. "You wanted to talk,

then talk."

His eyes were no longer glimmering. They were as hard as chips of ice. "Sit, little bird."

"Don't call me that," I snapped.

There wasn't even a flicker of surprise or anything that gave a hint about what he would do next. He simply lifted a hand and crooked one finger. A second later, a horn blew and someone shouted—several people shouted.

I looked over my shoulder. "What the . . . ?" I trailed off, eyes widening as a young man, no older than me, stood in the middle of the busy street. It was the waiter who'd cursed earlier when I'd whipped around. A car door opened as the young man dropped to his knees in the middle of the street.

"Sit, or I will make sure his insides are on his outside."

Oh my God. Heart dropping to my toes, I pressed my palm to my chest. "How did you . . . ?" I'd seen fae manipulate humans, but never like this. Never from this far away and without touching them.

"I am the prince," he replied. "You have met no other like me. Sit."

Holy shit.

I sat.

I sat as far away as I humanly possibly could on the bench. The prince smiled, and the young man shuddered. A look of confusion crossed his face as he looked around hastily. He rose to his feet and stumbled across the street where people surrounded him.

"The mortal realm has changed," the prince said after a moment, and I looked over at him. He was staring at the road, dark brows knitted. "The last time I was here, horses carried people where they needed to go. There was no world wide web or TV."

My brows inched up my forehead.

"It has taken me a few days to . . . adapt to all of the technology and people. They are everywhere. Ready to serve." He smiled again as he stretched out his long legs. "My people will do well here."

Pressing my lips together, I inhaled through my nose and remained silent.

"My world is dying, little bird. It is dark and dead. Nothing new is reborn." The prince extended an arm along the back of the bench. If he touched me, I'd puke in his lap. For real. His chin tipped toward me. "The only way I can save it is to permanently open the gates."

I knew this already. Tink had told me.

"Our food source is nearly depleted. It will not be much longer before everything is gone."

When he spoke of the food source, I knew he didn't mean cheeseburgers and bacon. He was talking about humans. When the fae didn't feed, they had normal human lifespans, but when they fed from humans, they could almost become immortal. It wasn't something any of the Order members liked to think about, because there was nothing we could do about the humans that had been snatched from our world long ago, when the fae came and went through the gateways as they pleased. From what we'd learned, they raised humans in their world like cattle.

It was repulsive.

"You've done this to yourself," I said, voice surprisingly calm. "You've killed your own world. You're not going to do the same to ours."

The prince dipped his chin. "What do you know of my world, little bird? What do you know at all?"

Prickling irritation danced across my skin. "I do know

I want to stab you in the eyeball every time you call me 'little bird.'"

His lips twisted into a cruel smirk. "You do not like me."

"No shit," I muttered.

"Perhaps if we met under better circumstances—"

"One where you didn't beat me within an inch of my life?"

A woman walking past us looked over at us sharply but kept going when the prince nodded. "There is that, but I do recall giving you ample opportunity to leave without injury. You chose not to. You fought me, and yes, I would've killed you if I had not realized what you are."

I choked on a laugh. "Wow."

He didn't appear to find anything he'd said amusing. "But now I know how important you are."

My fingers curled around my knees as a breeze lifted a curl and tossed it across my face. A strange scent surrounded the prince. It wasn't exactly unpleasant, but it reminded of something. Beaches? No. I frowned.

His gaze flickered over my face. "You will open those gates for me."

I laughed again. "Yeah, that's not going to happen."

"I figured you would say that," he replied, casting his gaze back to the street. "Let me impregnate you and you will want for nothing."

My brows snapped together. "Yeah, that's probably the most unappealing offer for sex in the history of mankind."

He stared at me. "You are not afraid of me, are you?" Then he leaned over and inhaled deeply. "No. I smell fear on you, and yet you speak to me as if you have no concern for your well-being."

"Did . . . did you just smell me again?" I asked, my pulse pounding in my throat. The truth was, I was scared. Terrified, honestly, but I couldn't show that.

The side of his lips curled up. "You are confident because of your importance to me, or you are foolish. Either way, you will bear my child."

All I could do was stare at him, because this was by far the most bizarre conversation I'd ever had with anyone or anything, and I'd had a lot of strange convos with Tink.

"You can make this easy and come with me now or—"

"I can make this hard? I know how this works. You can't force me to have sex with you," I said, voice low. "And if you threaten the lives of others to get me to go with you, you're still forcing me." I met his stare, calling up every ounce of bravery I had. "You can make me sit here and talk to you. You can even expose what I am to the entire world—"

"Why would I out what you are? Your kind, your Order, would kill you before you took your next breath. No one who wishes to not incite my wrath will betray you."

Well, that was . . . kind of good to know. At least I could mark that one thing to freak out over off the list. "Anyway, you can make me do a lot of things, but you cannot make me do that. Ever."

His head cocked to the side. "Is it because you're in love with the human male?"

I blinked, jerking back. He said the word love like he was utterly unfamiliar with the term. "What?"

"The man who rushed to your side when you were injured. The one who has been spending every night at your place."

Oh no. I started to stand but my legs were weak.

The smile reappeared. "How much do you value his—?"

"Don't," I warned, voice barely audible. "Don't threaten him."

He chuckled then, and it almost sounded real.

"Loving someone else has nothing to do with it. Even if I were single, I wouldn't have sex with you."

"I would," a man said as he stopped in front of the bench. He grinned at the prince. "Just saying."

The prince winked in return.

I waited until the other man had roamed off before I continued. I made sure my voice was low. "I am not having your child and ensuring that your kind takes over the world. Sorry. That's not going to happen."

"Are you a wagering type, little bird?"

I stared at him a moment. "This is insane. You nearly killed me. You're a fae that wants to take over the human realm. There is literally nothing you can say or do that will—"

The prince moved fast, too fast for me to track. He was suddenly directly in my space and his cool hand was curved around the nape of my neck, smashing my curls. I tried to pull back, but yep, I was getting nowhere without breaking my own neck.

"Let go of me," I ordered, moving my hand to my left side. If I had to stab him, even if the only thing it did was piss him off, I would.

"You can fight this all you want, but I know the game and the rules," he said, and my stomach roiled as his icy breath coasted over my cheek. "I know how this ends, little bird. And trust me, you will be consenting sooner than you realize."

Chapter Six

The prince just got up and walked away. Walked on down Decatur like he was out sightseeing wearing leather pants in seventy-degree weather. I think he might've walked into Jackson Square. Maybe he was going to check out the statue of Andrew Jackson? Or maybe he'd cross the street again and try some beignets or coffee mixed with chicory?

And I just sat there, sort of stunned and kind of wanting to laugh. Not the good kind of laugh. I was back to the slightly crazed kind.

What had just happened?

I was trying to comprehend the entire conversation, but the prince getting up and walking away was perhaps the most unexpected part. He didn't try to force me to go with him. Oh God, was Tink right? Was the prince going to attempt to woo me? Nausea hit me in the stomach, and I might've puked a little in my mouth. Was that why he had only creeped me out but didn't try anything else?

I knew I needed to say something. It was my duty to inform David that the prince was out and about.

Pushing up from the bench, I drew in a deep breath and slid my sunglasses back onto my face. What could I say though? How could I explain to anyone that I'd seen the prince but he hadn't attempted to harm me? It might be believable if I was any other Order member and not the one who'd chased the prince down and spent one-on-one time with him, getting my ass handed to me. I could say that the prince hadn't seen me. That wasn't entirely impossible.

Nervous energy filled me as I waited for the traffic to clear on Decatur. The best thing for me to do was keep my mouth shut, but I couldn't. I had to warn other members that the prince was out and moving around the city. It was a safety concern. But it was more than that. It was my duty—a duty ingrained in me since birth and I couldn't deny it.

The Ivy before the whole halfling business would've done the right thing, and I was still her.

As I crossed the street, I thought about texting Ren, but I didn't. Not yet. There was something I needed to take care of first, the reason why I was out in the first place, and that had nothing to do with getting beignets.

I headed northeast on Decatur then turned left on St. Phillips, making my way toward the headquarters of the New Orleans branch of the Order. The twenty minute walk helped slow down my heart rate, but it did nothing to ease the anxiety building within me.

When Mama Lousy's gift shop came into view, I noticed right off the bat that things had changed. The shop was closed, and since it was Sunday, that was unheard of. The gift shop was really just a front for the Order, selling fake voodoo stuff and yummy pralines. Jerome, a grouchy retired Order member, usually ran the place. I hoped nothing had happened to him. He could be a real dick, but he was kind of a lovable dick.

Dylan was standing outside, leaning against the deep burgundy wall next to the door that led upstairs. To the average passerby, he looked like some strange dude loitering, which meant he blended right in with his dark denim jeans and gray Henley shoved up to his elbows. He was wearing sunglasses and his built arms were crossed over his chest.

My steps slowed as he turned his head in my direction and said, "Oh look, she *is* alive."

I arched an eyebrow as I stopped in front of him. Order members weren't exactly a warm and friendly bunch. Probably had a lot to do with our high turnover rate. Most of us died before you could even get to know someone. Val had been different, though. From the first moment I'd met her, she'd welcomed me while everyone else was standoffish. Another reason why her betrayal cut so deep.

Ren had been different, too.

He was friendly and warm, but he also had wanted to get in my pants from the moment he saw me, and that was straight from the horse's mouth, so . . .

"Why is the gift shop closed?" I asked.

"Jerome came down with a cold and David didn't see the point of bringing anyone down for this," Dylan explained. That made sense. There weren't a lot of retired Order members around these parts who would want to come in and deal with the public.

"Glad to hear he's otherwise okay." I glanced into the dim shop. A few fake skulls sat on a stack of praline boxes.

"You were worried about that old coot?" Dylan

laughed. "He's going to outlive a nuclear war."

My lips twitched. "Probably. So, what are you doing out here?"

"Fae know our location now since that bitch led the prince here." Dylan propped a booted foot against the wall. "The door has to be guarded."

I wanted to point out that one Order member probably wouldn't be able to stop an ancient, but figured that wouldn't win me any friends. "Makes sense," I murmured, reaching for the door.

"Hey." Dylan stopped me halfway in. "Glad you're doing okay."

Surprised, I looked over my shoulder at him. All I saw was my reflection in his sunglasses.

"And sorry about that shit with Val," he continued. "I know you were close to her. That isn't easy to deal with."

My fingers tightened on the handle. "No, it's not," I admitted, angling my body toward him. "Did you suspect something?"

"Not until David had me watching her, but I didn't see shit that would've made me suspect anything."

And David had put Dylan on Val-duty because Ren told him that he suspected she was the halfling.

"Strange thing is, Ivy, I saw her kill fae." He laughed, but there was no humor in it. "Like, how fucked up is that? She was working for them and still killing them?"

"She had to keep up appearances, I guess." Saddened by that fact, I turned back to the stairwell. "I'll see you later."

"Yep," he said.

I pushed my sunglasses up onto my head and started climbing the steps—steps that I had almost bled out on when an ancient had shot me with a gun he'd manifested out of thin air. An ancient that David had refused to believe was around.

The stairwell always smelled like sugar and feet, a gross combination. I hesitated on the second-floor landing. Irrational dread formed like a lead ball in my gut. The last time I'd stepped through this doorway, I'd found Doc Harris dead on the floor, his gaze blank and fixed on the ceiling.

Taking a deep breath, I hit the buzzer and looked up at the small camera. I had no idea who was monitoring the door. If there wasn't anyone, I had a key and could—

The door opened suddenly. Ren stood there. I so was not expecting to see him already. "Uh . . ."

He leaned against the doorframe. "I thought you were going to think about what I said, Ivy?"

My lips pursed.

"I can see that you didn't."

"I did," I insisted.

"And I also thought you weren't coming out to do anything work related, and yet you're here."

Um . . ."Are you going to let me in?"

Ren sighed as he stepped aside. I shot him a look as I walked in. The first place my gaze went to was the floor. The beige carpet had been pulled up. It made sense considering Harris's blood had most likely bled straight through the to the boards below.

"Huh." My throat felt oddly hoarse as I stared at the floor. "Who knew there was hardwood under there? Like, why would they have covered that up with crap carpet?"

Ren curled his hand around the nape of my neck. The touch was so different from how the prince had done it. He turned me toward him, and I opened my mouth to speak, but he lowered his face to mine and kissed me.

It wasn't a soft kiss, but it was sweet and long. My lips parted, and I tasted chocolate on his tongue, which made me start to grin as his arm circled my waist. He drew me against him. Out of instinct, I looped my arms around his neck. When he moved his mouth to the side, he kissed the corner of my lip.

I was a little breathless when he settled me back on my feet.

"You looked like you could use the distraction."

"Oh," I whispered.

He slid his hand up through the mass of my curls. "I'm not in your head, sweetness, but I know what you were seeing when you were staring at the floor."

I closed my eyes as I rested my forehead against his chest.

"It's the same damn thing I saw when I first walked in here and every time since then, but it's not the doc I see on the floor." He lowered his head as I dropped my hands to his waist. I knew he was talking about me. "I keep telling myself it'll get easier."

"Has it?"

"Not really."

"That's motivational," I murmured.

Ren drew back, and I lifted my gaze to his. "What've you been up to?"

"Nothing really. Went to get beignets, but . . ." The truth rose to the tip of my tongue. *Tell him*, ordered Good Ivy. *Keep your mouth shut*, ordered the voice that sounded strangely like Tink.

"What?"

I lowered my gaze. "The place was packed."

Tink would be so happy.

"And that stopped you?" he asked.

A door opened and a heavy, irritated-sounding sigh forced us apart. I turned around. I was kind of relieved to see Miles Daily, the *de facto* second-in-command. The reason I was "kind of" relieved to see him was because I was pretty sure Miles didn't like me and also had thought I was the traitor.

Miles raised his dark eyebrows as he glanced between us. "Am I interrupting?"

"You going to get pissed if I say yes?" Ren said.

I bit down on my lip to hide my grin.

Miles rolled his eyes and turned back to the room he'd just been in, which was probably the most emotion I'd ever seen from him. I could never get a read on the guy. He was worse than David when it came to figuring out how he felt and what he was thinking.

There were daggers and files on the oval desk inside the room. One of them had Denver, Colorado, written on the tab. Huh. That was where Ren was from. Was someone that he knew coming down? That could be interesting.

TV monitors lined one side of the room. Obviously Ren had been in here with Miles. I stared at the files. "What were you guys doing?"

"Looking over prospects." Ren slid his hand down my back before stepping away and heading back into the office. "Well, that's what Miles was doing. I was just being annoying."

"Truer words have never been spoken," Miles muttered. He stopped in front of the monitors. There were more out in the main room. The Order had cameras randomly placed throughout the Quarter and surrounding neighborhoods.

As far as I knew, there were none near Jackson Park, thank God.

"Ready to get back to work?" Miles's expression was inscrutable as he watched the monitors.

Ren faced me.

I ignored his look. "Yeah, I think I am."

Ren squinted.

I also ignored that.

"Sounds good. We need every able-bodied person out there." Miles turned back to the table. "The fae may be lying low right now, but we know it's not going to stay that way. It's only a matter of time. We need to be ready."

This was the perfect time for me to mention the whole prince thing, but the words wouldn't even form on my tongue. I glanced at the wall of monitors and started to look away when one of the images snagged my attention. My eyes narrowing, I turned fully to the monitor on the left, on the last row. It was a house—an old antebellum, which wasn't odd since there were a lot of homes like that, but I recognized this one.

"You're watching Val's parents' house?" I asked.

"Yep." Miles picked up a folder and opened it. "Have been for the last week."

Shit. That meant going to Val's house was off the table. She wasn't dumb, though. She'd be nowhere near that place. I still planned on checking out Twin Cups, a bar a few streets off the Quarter that was actually a hidden bar within a bar. Val like to go there to relax and chill after work. The likelihood that she'd be there was slim, but it was a start.

I looked over at Ren. His gaze was trained on me. A lazy half-smile was on his face, and I was thinking, based on that expression, that he wasn't too mad about me being out on the streets. The problem with that was he was going to be hard to shake while I went looking for Val and her parents.

Knowing that the Order was probably still questioning them, there could only be a few places where they'd be kept. Definitely not here. I glanced at the wall again. Two of the TVs were off. Both would've linked to two different facilities the Order had. One was over in the warehouse district. The other was an old mansion, most likely haunted, out near the bayou. Those damn monitors would tell me where they were without me having to waste my time or get caught sneaking around. What I was going to do once I figured out where they were was still up in the air.

I was kind of winging things right about now.

I placed my hands on the back of a chair. "How are things going with Val's parents?"

"Her parents are no longer a concern," Miles tossed the file onto the desk.

The breath I took got stuck. "What does that mean?"

"You know what it means." Miles walked around the desk, grabbing a dagger. He pushed up his sleeve, showing a forearm holster, and shoved the dagger in place.

My gaze flew over to Ren. His lazy smile was gone. A muscle was flexing along his jaw. Oh no, no. I looked back to Miles. He was heading out the door, into the main room. "Did they confess to anything?"

"No." Miles snorted. "Not like either of them was going to admit to fucking a fae. Doesn't matter. They were compromised, and the sooner we find their daughter, the better. And if we're lucky, that bitch isn't knocked up yet. Doubtful, but we can hope."

Oh God.

I closed my eyes tight.

I was too late.

Chapter Seven

The floor shifted under my feet. Val's parents were dead. Miles didn't need to confirm it. I knew. I was too late. Instead of getting my shit together the moment I'd learned that the Order had her parents squirreled away, I'd moped around my apartment for days, and now I was too late to even attempt to do a damn thing.

"Hey." Ren's voice was soft. "You okay?"

I exhaled slowly as I lifted my gaze to his. "Did you know?"

"Know what?"

"That they'd taken her parents out?"

"What?" He stared at me a moment and then started toward the door. He closed it and faced me, brows knitted. "I'm pretty sure everyone in the Order knew that was going to happen, including you."

He was right, but I thought there was time. Hell, I don't even know what I thought.

Ren approached me. "How can you be so surprised?"

"I . . ." I wet my lips. "Do we have irrefutable proof that Val is a halfling?"

He placed a hand on the chair. "No, but—"

"But we don't. And let me guess, her parents maintained their innocence this whole time," I said, knowing I needed to keep my mouth shut but couldn't. "Right? So what if we're wrong? What if Val is just a traitorous bitch, but not a halfling, and the Order just flat out murdered her parents? They were good people, Ren. Dedicated their entire lives to the Order."

And that was true. They were good people, and now they were *gone*. A bitter sadness blanketed me.

A moment passed and his expression softened. "You knew them."

"Of course I did. Not really well, but that's . . ." I trailed off, closing my eyes. Guilt churned the acids in my stomach. By staying quiet, had I gotten Val's parents killed? They would've been walking a very fine edge even if no one believed her to be the halfling, based on her actions alone, but I couldn't help thinking of the role I'd played in Shaun and my adoptive parents' deaths.

"I'm sorry." Ren circled an arm around my shoulders and tugged me to him. I went, but my arms were still limp at my sides. "I want to forget that you were close to her. That's wrong of me." He paused, letting out a rough breath. "And I get why you want to be out here and why you feel you need to find Val."

I squeezed my eyes shut again.

"There's something I should've said this morning when we were talking about it," he continued. "I don't want you out there looking for her, because if you do find her, it's going to be hard—too hard for you. I don't mean that in a bad way, like you can't handle yourself, but this will be rough on you, Ivy. You're going to find yourself in a really bad position."

"I know."

"Do you?" he asked quietly. "Are you ready to face her? Go toe to toe and take her down? Because that's what you have to do, and I don't want you to have to make that decision. I'd rather it be me, or anyone else. You don't need to live with the kind of shit that's going to be left behind. I can shoulder that for you."

Oh gosh.

My heart imploded into goo. I wanted to be mad at him, because it made . . . well, it made hiding everything from him so much easier, but how could I when he said all the right things?

"You're too good." I whispered the truth.

"I am pretty awesome."

I cracked a grin. "And so modest."

Ren turned and leaned against the table. He brought me along with him, positioning me so I stood between his legs. A finger curled under my chin and lifted my head. "I really am sorry for what she has done."

Me too. But he didn't even know the half of it or why he really was too good for me, and why I didn't deserve this . . . with him. I knew that, and yet I was still standing here.

"You haven't eaten anything?"

I shook my head.

"I was thinking about trying out this place on Canal. They have fried alligator."

My nose wrinkled. "Ew."

"I've never tried it." His eyes danced with amusement. "I'm thinking today is the day. Come with me."

"I don't know. I'm not really hungry." Plus, I had other things to do. Important things.

"Checked out their menu. They have Tater Tots."

"Hmm?"

"Tater Tots with cheese and bacon smothered on them," he added.

My eyes widened. "Sold."

~

After leaving the diner on Canal, I was rocking a decent-sized food baby, the only kind of baby that would be getting into my stomach anytime soon.

Ren had eaten the fried alligator and determined that it sort of tasted like a cross between chicken and pork.

And I sort of thought that sounded gross.

Ren took my hand as we walked down Canal, toward the Quarter, his fingers threaded loosely through mine. I didn't know how to feel about this since I hated having to navigate people holding hands, but I liked my hand in Ren's. I liked the warm weight and how . . . grounding it was.

Ren squeezed my hand. "You going home or . . . ?"

I knew this was coming. Dinner had been nice and normal despite what I had learned about Val's parents, my weird meet and greet with the prince, and all the other messed-up things going on. It was weird how all of us Order members could easily bounce back from the Three D's: danger, death, and destruction. Maybe it was the fact we constantly faced certain death that made us seize each second of the day while continuously pushing forward.

Well, some of us.

Up until recently, I'd really been living in the past.

Hung up on my own missteps and guilt, afraid of letting go and moving on, and now that I finally had done that, everything I knew about myself was a lie.

I swallowed a sigh that would have sounded so pathetic I could have won a Daytime Emmy for it. "I'm going to head home in a bit."

"But not right away?"

I didn't answer.

Ren stopped, pulling me off the sidewalk so we weren't in the way. We were at the corner of Canal and Royal. "Okay," he said after a moment. "Just remember what I said earlier. If you find her, think before you act. Call me. I'll take care of it. Make sure she's brought in alive."

I appreciated what he was saying, more than I think he realized. I stood on my tiptoes, placed my hand against his smooth cheek, and kissed him. Then I smiled at him. "Are you coming to my place when you get off?"

"I was planning on it," he said. "Can you text me when you get back to your place?"

He was giving me permission to go do my thing. He wasn't exactly saying it, but he knew what I had planned, and he was stepping aside. Geez, I sort of wanted to strip right here and have sex with him.

"I will," I promised.

His gaze held mine, and there was so much warmth and strength in those emerald eyes, but there was something else. A deep, unfathomable emotion. "Ivy, I . . ."

I held my breath, for real. Because what was in his eyes mirrored how I felt, and if he was going to say those three words, there was a good chance I would strip down, right here and now—

"I'll miss you," he said finally.

Oh.

Well then.

Ren leaned down and kissed me. It was short but powerful, and better than cheese and bacon-smothered Tater Tots.

He swaggered off down Canal, heading back in the direction we came from, and I was left standing there, staring at him, a little weak in the knees.

Goodness.

Drawing in a deep breath, I looked down and fished out my cellphone. Dusk had fallen, and since it was a little too early for Val to be at Twin Cups, I decided to go ahead and make my way there. It wouldn't hurt to scope out the place and talk to a few of the bartenders.

Twin Cups was located about two miles past the Quarter, in the Bywater neighborhood, and it was hidden inside another bar that looked like any other bar outside the Quarter—slightly less smelly, a little quieter, the floors a little less sticky.

With the night just kicking off, the streets were crowded and it took about forty minutes for me to hoof it to Bywater. The whole time I kept an eye out for fae. I didn't catch sight of any silvery skin, but an ancient could be around. They were harder to pick out since they didn't use glamour like the rest and blended in with humans.

Muscles aching in my butt and legs, I wanted to sit down by the time I reached my destination. Laughter and shouts greeted me as I walked into the bar, squeezing past the high top tables. No one paid attention to me as I headed for the hall in the back of the two-story building. I passed the restrooms and stopped in front of a Coke vending machine.

Reaching into my purse, I snagged two dollars out of my wallet and fed them into the machine. Instead of hitting one of the soda options, I reached around and hit the button along the side.

The machine rumbled to life and I stepped back. No soda dropped, but what looked like a regular wall beside it cracked open.

So fancy and secretive.

Grinning, I opened the door to a narrow staircase that led upstairs. At the top there was another door which opened with a turn of the knob. Nothing extraordinary there. Just a regular door.

The Twin Cups was super low key. TVs were on, and like downstairs, some game was playing, but the volume was turned down. There weren't any high top tables, just couches and low chairs surrounded by coffee and end tables. A wall of books faced the doorway. One time, when Val had been a bit tipsy, she'd ventured over to the shelves and discovered that some of the books contained old, hand-drawn maps of the city. Others had drawings of buildings. Pretty cool.

I almost could see Val standing there, her curly hair falling prettily around her shoulders, wearing something bright, most likely in orange or fuchsia. She'd be in a loose-fitting skirt, and multi-colored bangles would be dangling from her wrist.

But she wasn't dancing in front of the shelves.

Only a few people were in Twin Cups. Two men sitting on a couch, and a group of women surrounding a coffee table with books stacked on it. It looked like a book club or something, and I was immediately envious of their smiles and whispered conversation about book boyfriends. For a moment, I allowed myself to imagine sitting with them, chatting about books. I could picture Jo Ann with me. Maybe even Val.

But that wasn't my life.

It never had been.

My chest heavy, I turned to the left and recognized the bartender. He was an attractive, dark-skinned man in his mid-twenties. His name was Reggie, and he went to Tulane. I was pretty confident he and Val had hooked up in the restroom behind the bar more than once.

He looked up from whatever he was doing and smiled. "Hey there, Curly. Been a long time."

"It has." I made my way to the shiny, polished bar and hopped up on a stool. I snagged my sunglasses off my head and placed them in my purse. "How've you been?" I asked him.

"Good." He moved a tray of shot glasses to the back bar. "Only have two classes this semester that are really giving me trouble. How's Loyola?"

"Um, it's going . . . fine." Stupidly embarrassed, I was unable to admit that I was dropping out.

His brows furrowed as he walked over to where I sat. "You sure you're okay? Looks like you have a black eye."

And I guessed my makeup was fading. "I got mugged about a week ago."

"Fuck. For real?" He leaned his elbows against the table. "This damn city, man."

My eyes widened slightly as I stared down at my hands. "I have a question for you," I said.

"Ask away."

I smiled. "Have you seen Val recently?"

"Val? Hell, I haven't seen her in . . ." His brown eyes rose to the ceiling. "I haven't seen her in a couple of months. Probably not since July."

Dammit.

Reggie worked every Sunday evening and most of the

nights throughout the week. If he hadn't seen her, she probably hadn't come by and wasn't going to. But for her to not have been here in months? Obviously, the whole working for the fae thing wasn't something new that had happened in the last couple of weeks.

"Did you two have a falling out or something?" he asked.

"You could say that."

A wry grin formed. "Sounds like a good story. I got time."

I started to respond, but my phone rang from inside my bag. Holding up my hand, I hopped off the stool and pulled my cell out. It was Brighton, which was weird because that woman was terrible when it came to using the phone, finding the phone, and returning calls. Needless to say, I was surprised.

"Hey," I answered, turning and leaning against the bar. "What's—?"

"My mom is gone," Brighton blurted out.

My spine stiffened. "What?"

"She's gone, Ivy. But that's not all." Her voice was pitched and strained. "Can you come over? I . . . This isn't something I can talk about over the phone. You have to see it."

"I'll be right there."

~

Brighton and her mother Merle lived in the Garden District, not entirely far from my apartment. They lived in a gorgeous antebellum with one of the nicest kept courtyards, the kind that put my overgrown mess to shame.

Normally Merle would be out back, and Brighton would be watching over her. The doors would be open and jazzy music would be drifting out from inside the house.

The front door opened as I stepped through the wrought-iron gate and approached the sprawling porch. Brighton stood in the open doorway, her blonde hair in a loose ponytail at the nape of her neck. She was in her mid-thirties, gorgeous in an all-American, beauty pageant winning way.

"Thank you for coming over right away." She stepped back, letting me into the cool interior of the house. The place was very traditional, with old furniture and walls papered with dainty flowers in muted, pastel colors. It probably had been that way since the house was built, lovingly taken care of through the ages. "I didn't know who else to call. I don't really trust the other members and I know things are really bad right now."

I couldn't blame her for not trusting the Order. Merle had been fed on by the fae and hadn't fully mentally recovered from that. A lot of the Order members were dicks when it came to Merle, but before the incident with the fae, she was pretty high up there.

This wasn't the first time Merle had disappeared. Sometimes she roamed off, but I'd never seen Brighton this stressed out about it before.

"What's going on?" I asked her.

She walked through the sitting room and into the dining hall. There were several journals and handwritten notes laid out on the oval, cream-colored table. "Mom hasn't been acting right since the gate opened." She paused, picking up a short glass of what I assumed contained liquor. "More so than normal. It's like she knew this was going to happen."

I thought back to the last conversation I'd had with Merle. The woman had known a lot—all about halflings, the fact there were two gates—and she'd always had a major problem with Val. I'd always believed Merle was just being a Judgey McJudgers over Val's dating habits like some older people tended to be, but now I was wondering if she was just seeing something we'd all been blind to.

"Tell me what happened."

She took a swig of her drink then stopped. "You want something to—"

"No, I'm fine."

Brighton wet her lips then swallowed hard. Her knuckles on the hand holding her glass were bleached white. "She hasn't been sleeping a lot since the gate was opened. Maybe an hour a night, and I would wake and hear her pacing in her bedroom, murmuring to herself about how it wasn't safe here anymore. At first, I wasn't too concerned. It may not be safe for anyone since the knights and the prince came through the gate, but three days ago it changed. She started talking about these places where the fair folk lived."

My brows rose. Fair folk was another name for fae, one not commonly used outside of people who believed in fairy tales. "Was she talking about the Otherworld?"

"That's what I thought at first, but she started talking about communities, and I realized she was talking about here, in our world."

I frowned, not following the importance of that. The fae that had crossed over into our realms lived among humans. Hell, there could be one living a block from here.

"I know what you're thinking, and I thought the same thing. That she was just talking about the fae." Brighton coughed out a stressed, hoarse laugh. "Then this morning she came downstairs with all these papers and told me that it was no longer safe for her or me to be here. I tried to calm her down, but nothing was working. She was in a fit." Lifting the glass to her mouth, she downed the contents in one impressive gulp. "She was saying that the Order couldn't stop the knights and the prince. That only the fae could, and the Order knew that."

I watched Brighton walk to the other side of the table. "I should've followed her immediately when she went outside, but I didn't. Maybe five minutes passed, and when I went to check, she wasn't in the courtyard. I searched all the nearby streets. It's been decades since she's gotten in a cab. She was just . . . gone. You know she couldn't have gotten that far, but she was gone, Ivy."

Okay. Unless Merle called an Uber, which was unlikely, that was very weird.

"When I came back in, I saw these journals, and once I picked them up and started reading them, I couldn't stop. If you look at them, you'll understand why." She placed her glass down on the table then reached over, picking up a leather-bound journal. "You need to read this."

I reached over the table and took the journal from her. The thing was old, the leather worn and soft, and the paper had a faint yellow tint. I turned it around and started reading as Brighton started walking back and forth.

At first, none of it really made sense. It was like picking up a book and starting it in the middle, but as I turned the pages and kept reading, things started to piece together.

Disbelief flooded me as I really started to make sense of what I was reading. "My God," I whispered, staring at the journal. "This can't be . . ."

Brighton stopped pacing and crossed her arms. "That's what I thought too, but my mom's not *that* crazy. They're not the rantings of a lunatic."

"I know she's not, but this is . . . it would be insane." I reread the lines again, recognizing names of past Sect leaders—names connected with other names I didn't recognize, but attached to dates of when they'd either crossed over into our world or had been born into ours. I sat down in the chair before I fell down. "No, not insane but unheard of."

"But not impossible," Brighton said, dropping into the seat across from me. "You know nothing is really impossible."

She was right about that, but this . . . this was beyond something any of us had ever imagined. If what was in this journal was true, then my world had just been blown to bits all over again.

Because what I was reading stated that there were fae who lived in our world—fae that did not feed on humans.

Fae that had worked alongside the Order in the past.

Chapter Eight

I sat back in the chair. I was currently knee-deep in a stunned daze as I flipped back a couple of pages to where the names of past Sect leaders were listed. It stopped about two decades ago, on Lafayette Burgos. The other names listed beside the Sect leaders I assumed were fae, based on the bizarre nature of some of the names.

"There are good fae," Brighton said, and my gaze shot to her pale face. "I'm almost too frightened to even suggest that. As if an Order member will appear out of nowhere and accuse me of treason against my own kind." She laughed again as she glanced up at the ceiling. "But if you keep reading, that's what you'll see. Fae who came into our world, but decided not to feed off humans. They lived normal lifespans, much like our own. They worked alongside Order members in the past."

My thoughts were wheeling as I started flipping through the journal. Entries were meticulously dated, detailing investigations, searches, and even kills. Many of the entries included the names of Order members and the fae they worked alongside.

Brighton reached across the table and picked up a deep blue journal, a much thinner one than the journal I'd been looking at. "My mother took detailed accounts of everything. I'm not even exaggerating. I had no idea she had all of this hidden away. This book lists all the members of the Order, up until when she . . . when she left." She placed it on the table. "I got curious and checked on some of the names associated with the fae. Some of them are still alive but have moved out of the city. But there is one still around. Jerome."

"Holy . . ." I couldn't even begin to picture Jerome working with a fae. It went against everything I knew about him. "If this is true, why has this been hidden— erased from history?" I asked. "Why wouldn't this be something known?"

"I don't know." She gestured at a dozen or so journals and a stack of loose sheets of paper scattered across the table. "There's a good chance that there's some sort of explanation in there, but as of right now, I have no idea."

I sat forward, resting my elbows on the table as I dragged both hands through my hair, holding the curls back from my face. I opened my mouth but had no idea what to say.

A sympathetic look pinched Brighton's features. "I know you're already dealing with a lot, but I didn't know who else to go to. You've always been so patient and understanding with my mom. She trusts you. I trust you."

I nodded and drew in a deep breath. Neither of them would trust me if they knew the truth, but that was neither here nor there. I scanned the table as I collected my thoughts. Okay. First things first. "Do you have any idea where she could've gone?"

"Before she left, she told me it wasn't safe any longer and that she was going to them. I didn't know what she meant at first," Brighton explained. "But I think she was going to them—to these fae who don't feed on humans."

Other than how absolutely crazy that sounded, I wondered why Merle would leave Brighton behind if she felt things were no longer safe. That didn't sound like Merle at all. No matter what kind of mental state she was in, her daughter was always a priority. There was more to this than we knew.

A hell of a lot more, I thought as I stared at all the journals. "So do we have any idea of where these . . . good fae could be living?"

"Maybe." Brighton reached over, choosing a longer and wider journal. "This one has maps of the city, places marked where hunts have been carried out and locations of kills. I'm hoping there's something in there. It's just going to take a little bit to search through it. Not like I can skip a page."

"Are there anymore like that?"

"Not that I've found." She placed the journal in front of her, then pressed her fingers to her mouth. "There was something else she said before she left."

At this point, I had no idea what to expect. "What?"

Her cornflower-blue eyes met mine. "Before she left, she told me to contact that young man Ivy brought with her. Ren? She said Ren would know what to do."

~

Ren would know what to do.

Back at my apartment, I sat cross-legged on my bed and stared at the journal Brighton had allowed me to take. I'd spent the last couple of hours reading through it, and if any of this was fake, it was an extremely well put together hoax, spanning decades.

"It's not a hoax," I whispered, reaching up and tucking a stray curl behind my ear. I was convinced that this crap was true or that Merle believed it to be true, and she had believed that for *years*, well before she was captured by the fae.

Closing the journal, I glanced at the clock as I rubbed the back of my neck. It was a little before one in the morning. Ren would be here soon. I'd texted him when I got back to my place, but I hadn't mentioned anything about Brighton or Merle. I figured that would be a conversation to have in person.

Ren would know what to do.

Did he know there were fae that were . . . good? How could he not have brought that up at some point? I squeezed my eyes shut as I dropped my hand. He was a part of the Elite, and they probably had access to all kinds of information we normal and not so cool members didn't. And could I get mad at him for not telling me? All things considered, probably not.

Good fae? I laughed under my breath and opened my eyes. How could that theory be so surprising? I lived with a creature of the Otherworld—a brownie. Tink was annoying. He was *expensive*, and he had this horrible habit of not being exactly forthcoming with information, but he wasn't evil. Before I met him, I'd assumed that all creatures from the Otherworld were bad. Obviously I had been wrong. So it could be possible that there were fae who were like . . . like humans.

82

I had so many questions though. Without feeding, how did they use glamour to hide their appearance? From what we knew of the fae, they had to feed to use their magic. Were we fed false information?

I'd asked Tink about good fae when I got home. He'd been busy on *my* computer, creating *If Daryl Dies We Riot* memes. He'd genuinely appeared confused by my line of questioning. According to my pint-sized roommate, all fae were bad. There was no such thing as a good fae.

Something had occurred to me while I'd watched him concentrate, the white glare from my computer lighting up his face. "Do you ever leave this house, Tink? Go anywhere?"

He'd frowned up at me like I'd asked him why I should watch *The Walking Dead*. "Why would I leave? This place has everything I need, and if it doesn't, I can order it from Amazon." He'd paused. "Though, on second thought, we could use a live-in chef, because you can't cook for shit."

I'd left the conversation at that point.

So there was a good chance, if Tink was being honest, that he hadn't been out to possibly figure out that there were good fae. I thought about the day I'd stopped over at Brighton and Merle's looking for them and saw what I'd first believed was another brownie. I'd caught a glimpse of translucent wings. I'd chalked it up to me seeing things, but now I wasn't so sure.

I wasn't sure about anything anymore.

But what changed with the Order? And why was it buried so effectively, that a few decades later, no one even knew about it with the exception of the older members?

All this thinking was giving me a headache.

Flopping onto my back, I flung my arms out to the side

and lay there until I heard a key turning in the front door. I didn't move an inch. My bedroom door was halfway open, so I knew he spotted me the moment he entered. Or spotted half of me.

A few seconds later, my bedroom door creaked open and I heard a low, sexy rumble of a chuckle. "What in the world are you doing?"

I threw my hands up in the universal I-have-no-clue gesture. His footsteps approached the bed and then he came into view. His wavy hair was wet and the shoulders of his shirt were damp. It must have started raining at some point.

"You look weirdly adorable right now." He put his right knee on the bed and planted his left hand beside my head. "Though I have a question."

"About what?"

"Why are you wearing shorts and knee socks?" He leaned over, caging me in. "Why not just wear pants?"

I arched a brow. "First off, I'm not really wearing shorts, *shorts*. I'm wearing sleep shorts."

"And there's a difference how?" he asked as he lowered his head and kissed my cheek.

"There's a difference." I waited as he kissed my other cheek. "Secondly, the socks are comfortable and they're fuzzy, which makes them better than pants."

"Okay." He chuckled again, kissing my forehead.

"And finally, it's the perfect combination. I'm not too hot or too cold," I explained.

"Whatever you say." He kissed the tip of my nose. "All I know is that I'm going to love pulling them off you later. With my teeth."

My eyes widened and my stomach dipped, the muscles there tightening. My body really loved the sound of that.

His mouth was now aiming for mine, and I knew if I let him kiss me, he would be taking *all* my clothes off with his teeth, and unfortunately for my libido, I couldn't let any of that happen. Yet.

I placed my hands on his chest, and when I spoke, my lips brushed his. "There's something we need to talk about first."

"Okay." His tongue flicked out, tracing my bottom lip and causing me to suck in an unsteady breath. "Are we going to talk about how your breasts feel abandoned? Because I've been planning all day to rectify that." He cupped my left breast and his thumb swiped over my nipple. "No bra? Perfect."

Sucking in a sharp breath, I called on every ounce of willpower I had and said, "Merle is missing."

His mouth hovered over mine. "What?"

"And she left all these journals and paperwork behind, some dating back several decades."

"Uh-huh." His thumb made another pass.

My toes curled. "And in those journals she lists names of the previous sect leaders and—" I gasped when he plucked the hard nub through the thin cotton of my shirt. "And she detailed how the Order used to work alongside the fae."

Ren's hand stilled, and I didn't know if I should be happy or sad about that. Slowly he rose up a little so I could see his face. "Come again?" he said.

"And talks about how there are actually . . . good fae—fae that don't feed on humans."

He blinked slowly. "Are you high?"

"I wish," I muttered, hoping his reaction was genuine. "But if you let go of my boob I can show you."

Ren hesitated. "Do I really need to let go of your boob?"

I stared at him.

A dimple appeared in his right cheek and he slowly, finger by finger, removed his hand. "Okay. What exactly are you talking about?"

"It's all in the journal that's about an inch from your knee."

His gaze flickered over my face and then he tilted his head to the side. "You're being serious, aren't you?"

"Uh. Yeah."

Frowning, Ren leaned over and snatched up the journal. He sat beside me, book in hand. "You said Merle is missing?"

I sat up. "Yeah, Brighton called me after we had dinner. She said that her mom hadn't been acting right since the gate was opened, more so than normal, and this morning she must've come downstairs with all these journals and stuff."

"Okay," he said slowly.

"She told Brighton it was no longer safe for her and then left. When Brighton went to look for her about five minutes later, Merle was just gone. She checked several of the surrounding blocks and there was no sign of her."

"Is it possible she hailed—"

"It's possible, but not likely. Anyway, when Brighton came back inside, she started looking at all the stuff— including the journal—and that's when she called me. I skimmed through it then brought it home. I've been reading the stuff for hours, and Ren . . . I think it's real."

One side of his mouth quirked up. "Ivy, there aren't fae who don't feed off humans."

"According to that book, there are."

His brows knitted together. "I'm not trying to be rude or anything, but Merle struggles—"

"Yes, she struggles, but this stuff has been chronicled for decades, Ren, before she was caught by the fae." I scooted onto my knees and reached around him, taking the book from his hands. "Trust me, I didn't believe it at first—couldn't believe it, but look at this." I opened the book to an entry made in the seventies and turned it over. "Read this and pay attention to the date."

His gaze held mine for a few beats and then he looked down at the book. I knew which part he was reading. It was a joint mission between the Order and the fae, where they helped locate several teenage humans who'd been kidnapped by other fae. I remembered the good fae's names—Handoc, Alena, and Phineas. Of course, the last name made me think of *Phineas and Ferb*. Ha.

Ren's mouth opened and snapped shut. He gave a little shake of his head. "I . . ."

Smirking, I reached over and flipped the pages to the list of names. "Take a look at this. List of Order members who apparently co-hunted with fae."

He scanned the page. "I . . ."

"And there's more. Seriously. You could spend all night reading this. There's no way these are all some wild delusions that spanned decades."

I let Ren read for a few minutes. He stopped every so often, as if he was reading things more than once. When he finally looked up at me, his expression was adorably confounded.

"Most of the Order members from that time have re-tired and moved out of the city or didn't make it to retire-ment age," I said. "But there is one who is still kicking and is accessible. Jerome."

Ren's brows flew up.

"But there's something else." I pushed off the bed and

stood. "Before Merle left, she told Brighton to contact you. That you would know what to do."

"What?" His response was immediate.

"That's what she was told." I folded my arms. "To contact you."

He shook his head as he looked down at the book. "I have no idea what to say."

"So you didn't know about this? That there could be fae that were . . . good?"

"I have honestly never heard of this, and as a member of the Elite, we know everything. That's why this is impossible."

"You know nothing is impossible," I said, repeating what Brighton had said earlier. "If it's true, the Order and the Elite hide it well, practically erasing all evidence, and those who are still alive obviously don't speak of it."

He turned back to the journal. "This . . . I honestly don't know what to think or believe, but I'm telling you for real, I have no idea why Merle would tell her daughter to come to me. No idea whatsoever, because I've never heard of this before."

Staring at him, I knew, just knew, that he was telling me the truth. Unlike me, who was lying.

"If this is true . . ." His gaze flicked up to mine again. "Then we need to find one of these good-natured, non-human-eating fae, and we need to do it quickly."

"Yeah." I watched him skim the pages. "You make that sound like it's something easy."

"Hell." He laughed dryly. "I think we've learned nothing is easy."

"So true," I murmured.

I tugged my socks off and stretched out, dipping my feet under the covers while Ren was nose-deep in the journals. I kept quiet, knowing his head had to be spinning much like mine had been when I first read them. Hell, my head was still whirling around.

Surprisingly, I fell asleep while he read, stirring awake sometime after he'd climbed under the covers. Something about his warm, hard body must've reached deep into the recesses of slumber, because I was wide awake. I had no idea how much time had passed, but I was curled against his side and he was on his back. He'd left the nightstand lamp on, and as my gaze traveled over the surface, I saw one of the journals lying on the edge of the bed. He'd fallen asleep reading, and for some reason I found that incredibly adorable.

And sexy.

There was a lot of skin pressed against mine. Ren had undressed, and as I drew my leg up over his bare one, I quickly discovered that he'd stripped down to his briefs. The hair on his legs tickled mine as I slid my calf over his.

Ren shifted, and his hand, once lax against my waist, tensed. He fisted my shirt, and my heart stuttered. I placed my hand on his chest, tracing the chiseled definition of his pecs. His body was amazing.

And as I lay there, pressed against his side, I wasn't thinking about everything that had happened. I wasn't thinking at all, and it was blissfully perfect. It felt like it had been forever since my thoughts weren't occupied and my body wasn't aching.

Well, parts of my body were aching but for a whole different reason.

Biting my lower lip, I slid my hand down his flat stomach, over the taut ab muscles there. He tensed as I went lower. Ren was awake.

"Ivy," he said, voice guttural and deep. "What are you

doing?"

Instead of answering, I pushing the covers down our legs, then I shucked off my bottoms. I reached for the band on his boxer briefs, and when he didn't stop me, I carefully tugged at them. He lifted his hips and I slid them off.

"*Ivy.*" He groaned my name again as his hand trailed down my back. I flushed.

I lifted myself up and straddled him. My heart pounded in my chest as I stared down. One side of his mouth curled up as his hands landed on my bare thighs. I leaned my head down, pressing my lips to his. I followed the path of his mouth and then my tongue, working the seam of his mouth until he parted. His hands moved, sliding up my thighs and under the loose shirt I was wearing, to my hips. I slid my body down, gasping at the friction and the deep, achy pulse between my thighs.

I knew he wanted this as badly as me. His erection pressed against my center, and I could feel it in his heady gaze and the way he clutched my hips. I pushed down with my hips again, reveling when he let out a sexy as hell groan. Moving slowly, I rubbed against him until my breaths were coming out in shallow pants. His hips lifted, and it was like we were dancing.

"Ren," I murmured against his mouth, only able to force out one more word. "Please."

"You don't have to beg, sweetness. His hands slid over my hips, gripping my butt. "Grab my wallet out of my pants. There's a condom in there."

Throat dry, I nodded and then scampered off of him, quickly finding his pants on the floor. I pulled out his wallet and fished out the condom. "So cliché," I murmured.

"I wanted to be prepared. I planned on using it as soon

as I got here, but I ended up distracted." He sat up and took the condom from me. I placed a knee on the bed and watched him roll it onto an impressive erection. When he was done, those green eyes burned. "Get back here," he said.

Hot all over, I did just that, and I was back where I began, my knees on either side of his hips.

"Damn." One hand lifted and curled around my neck. He dragged my head back down. His mouth was on mine again, and this kiss went deeper and longer than the last. Our tongues tangled, and when I pulled away again, he nipped at my lip, causing me to gasp.

I reached down and curled my fingers under the hem of my shirt before I lifted it and tossed it aside. Completely nude, I resisted the urge to shy away as he looked his fill.

His gaze moved over my chest and then his hands followed. He caught my nipples between his fingers, plucking at them until they stung with pleasure, and all the wonderful feelings pooled between my legs. My chest so did not feel abandoned now, especially when he curled up and closed his mouth around my breast, sucking deep and wrenching a cry out of me. My head dropped as he moved to my other breast, every pulse in my body pounding.

"I need you inside me now," I whispered

"Fuck," he groaned. "Keep talking like that and I don't know if I'm going to make it to that point."

Empowered and feeling a little crazy, I laughed. "I have faith in you."

"Yeah?" His voice was husky as he gripped the base of his cock.

I slid my knees down slightly. "Yeah."

A low moan parted my lips as I lowered myself onto him, inch by inch. Both of his hands flew up to my hips.

"Oh God," I whispered.

"Damn," he said, sliding his hands up my sides. He held me in place for a moment. "I could keep you right here." He lifted his hips, wrenching a gasp out of me. "Right like this."

At this moment, with all these wonderful feelings building inside me, I totally agreed. I sat up, rocking my hips as I planted my hands on his chest. It was so much fuller this way, so much more intense. My toes curled as pleasure spiked throughout my body.

"Am I . . . I doing this right?" I asked. "I've never done it this way before."

"Sweetness . . ." He cupped my breast with a hand, his thumb sweeping over the tip. "You couldn't possibly do this wrong. Ever."

My pace picked up and his followed. He went deep, then somehow even deeper. The angle made it feel like he was touching every part of me. He lowered his hand to where we were joined together and that thumb got busy swirling around. "You feel so amazing," I said, grinding down as tension coiled tight. "I think I'm gonna . . . *oh God.*"

Ren said something, but it was lost in the rush of sensations pouring into my body. I threw my head back, welcoming the powerful release surging throughout me. It was like every nerve ending decided to fire at once, and they kept exploding.

I was still coming when he shifted, rolling me onto my back and thrusting fast and hard. His hips pounded into mine, and all I could do was hold on. My legs curled around his waist, and I clutched his arms. His hips plunged once more and then he stilled, his face buried into my neck as he let out a ragged groan.

Still swimming in the aftershocks, I ran my hand through his silky hair. God, this . . . he was amazing. Everything about him.

Ren held me tight as he pulled out and rolled onto his side, pressing me to his body. I could feel his heart racing against mine as I pressed my lips to his throat and kissed him.

I love you.

Those words whispered through me. I wanted to say them, but I couldn't speak them out loud, so I said them over and over again in my head.

I love you.

~

A pounding on the front door woke us both at the same time. Sluggish, I sat up as I pushed the mass of curls out of my face. Ren was already looking at the clock on the nightstand. "It's after three in the morning. Who is at your door?"

I glanced over at him. "I have no idea."

"I seriously doubt that's Amazon delivering." Ren was on his feet, pulling his pants on. He left them unbuttoned, and my mouth watered a bit at the sight.

I jumped out of bed, pulling my shorts and shirt back on. As Ren opened my bedroom door, a horrible thought filled my mind. What if it—

From where we stood, I could see the knob turning on the front door. My gaze flew to the deadbolt. Ren hadn't thrown it. Cursing, I shot forward, snatching an iron dagger off my dresser just as my front door swung open.

A knight stood in the entryway.

Chapter Nine

The fae walking into my apartment was most definitely a knight—an ancient fae who'd come through the gate with the prince. He was tall and broad, with the same deep olive skin tone. His dark hair was buzzed close to the skull. He had no weapons in his hands, but I'd seen an ancient manifest a gun out of thin air before.

He was kind of dressed like a badass biker, wearing a dark shirt and leather pants, and Ren took one look at him and laughed. He actually laughed as he stood there, shirtless, his pants zipped but unbuttoned. "Oh, you just busted into the wrong house," he growled.

The knight's response was a tight-lipped smile, and then he strode forward, chin dipped down. There was no time to question why the knight was at my place. Fae didn't typically seek Order members out. We were the hunters, not the hunted.

Ren was in front of me, becoming a living, breathing

obstacle, and while I appreciated his protective nature, I could hold my own. My fingers tightened on the handle of the dagger as Ren brandished the thorn stake.

The knight took a swing with his meaty fist, but Ren was wicked fast. He dipped under the knight's outstretched arm and sprung up behind him. Planting one leg, he spun halfway, landing a brutal kick in the back of the knight.

Stumbling forward a step, the knight easily caught himself and pivoted around. Taking the advantage, I sprang forward as Ren swiped the business end of the stake at the knight's throat. That was the only way to take down an ancient. The head had to come off, and I was really hoping and praying it wouldn't be messy.

The knight sidestepped Ren's throat-jab, then lifted a hand in my direction. He didn't touch me, didn't come anywhere close to me. All he did was lift his hand, and suddenly my sock-covered feet were slipping backward across the hardwood floors. I hit the wall.

"What the hell?" I yelled, my eyes wide, staring at the knight.

Ren swung out with his other fist, landing a blow on the fae's jaw. The knight turned his cheek and laughed. "That was funny?" muttered Ren. He flipped the stake, then lunged forward, slamming it into the knight's chest. The knight grunted as Ren dragged it in a downward motion that would not end pretty.

"Whatever," the knight replied, and then swung out with one arm, backhanding Ren across the face and knocking him aside. Ren crashed into the end table. The lamp fell to the floor, shattering into several large shards.

Oh hell to the no, he did not just hit Ren.

Seeing red, I pushed off the wall and launched myself

forward as Ren got back up and kicked out, catching the ancient in the knee. The knight went down on one leg just as I reached him. I grabbed him by the top of his head and jerked his head back, my arm arcing—

The knight flung his hand out, and a second later, I was scooting across the room, bumping into a plant stand. The fern went over, spilling dirt all over the floor. This time I ended up over by the balcony doors.

"What the hell!" I shouted again.

Ren sprang forward, swinging out, but the knight dodged the attack. He caught Ren's arm and spun him around, drawing his back to the knight's chest. I pushed away from the doors, racing across the small distance. Shoving the dagger into the knight's back, I yanked the blade out as I was then thrown across the floor once more, back toward the bedroom as the knight let go of Ren.

A cold, harsh reality set in as I caught myself by grabbing the doorframe. The knight was purposely keeping me out of the fight while going toe to toe with Ren.

Ren caught the knight by the shoulder with one hand and lifted his leg, thrusting his knee into the fae's gut. The knight exhaled roughly as he shoved Ren back into my chair. The little footstool Tink used went flying.

Then they were going at each other, fists flying, with a lot of dodging and dipping. I shot forward again, this time determined to not get shoved aside like a piece of clothing. I was a foot away when movement to my right caught my attention.

Tink appeared in the hallway, just beyond the bathroom, his wings moving lazily as he yawned. He was wearing a . . . tiny *nightcap*? What in the holy fuck? He was even wearing miniature pajama bottoms, blue and white striped, and I had no idea where he'd gotten them from. No idea at all.

He was in the process of stretching his little arms out when he looked around the room. "What kind of tomfoolery is this?"

Tomfoolery?

The knight was distracted for a moment, eyeing Tink with surprise. A second later, the brownie's eyes widened as all sleep vanished from his face. Tink shot into the living room as he ripped off his dainty nightcap and tossed it aside, the pale blue cap floating to the floor.

"Thou shall not pass!" Tink shouted, throwing out his hand in the direction of the knight and Ren.

I stopped.

Ren halted mid-swing.

The knight caught Ren's arm, blocking the jab as he turned and cocked his head to the side, staring at the brownie.

Tink blinked slowly. "Well, shit. That worked in *The Lord of the Rings.*"

Oh my God.

Ignoring Tink and hoping he managed to stay out of the way and make it out of this alive, I darted toward the knight.

"This needs to stop right now. You're cutting into my sleep time," Tink announced, lowering his arms to his sides as he hovered near the coffee table. "And you don't want to mess with my sleep time. I give you one more chance, sir. Leave, or else."

"Jesus," muttered Ren, ducking as the knight lunged for him. "What are you going to do, Tink? Annoy him to death? Because that might actually work."

"You have no idea what I am capable of," Tink shot back.

I shot forward, grabbing the knight's arm and trying to flip him, but the knight turned suddenly. Lifting his arm *and* me, he tossed me over the back of the couch and dumped me onto the cushions. I started to scramble away when I saw Tink move toward where Ren and the knight were brawling.

"Stay back, Tink!" I shouted. Dammit, this was getting out of hand.

"I got this." Tink looked at me, then drew in a deep breath. "I'm sorry, Ivy."

I frowned as I rose from the couch. "You're . . ."

A fine shimmer surrounded Tink, like a misty cloud of golden dust. He was completely covered, body and wings. The dust expanded, forming a cyclone that swirled down to the floor and halfway to the ceiling. It moved so fast and was so thick that I couldn't see Tink inside of it.

I took a step forward as fear for Tink rose in my gut, but the shimmering cyclone stilled and then fell to the floor in a rush of sparkling golden dust and . . .

"Holy shit," I whispered.

The knight stopped fighting. So did Ren. The entire world would have stopped, because they were seeing what I was seeing, which was insane. Absolutely freaking insane.

A man stood where Tink had hovered—a fully grown man who was as tall as the knight, and that man, whoever he was, looked like Tink. He had shockingly white hair and blue eyes. Tink's handsome little face was now transformed into a normal-sized handsome face. He was tall and broad, with defined pecs and abs, and—oh my God, he was naked. Like legit naked! And I couldn't un-see any of that, because . . .

Because this fully grown male was Tink.

"Oh my God." I took a step sideways and then my knees gave out. I plopped down onto the couch.

"What in the actual fuck of all fuckdoms?" Ren exclaimed.

That summed up everything.

Striding forward, Tink headed straight for the stunned knight. Ren stepped aside, and I think it was completely out of shock, because there were *things* hanging and dangling—and I was scarred for *life*.

"There are none of your kind in this realm," the knight said. "You're not to be—"

"Nope. Nope. Nope. It's the middle of the night and I ain't got the time nor the care to listen to you," Tink stated.

Then Tink moved so fast that one second he was stalking all naked-like toward the knight, and then the next second the knight's neck was splitting wide open. Bluish-red blood poured down the front of the knight's shirt as the head rolled to the side and off the shoulder.

The sickening *thump* of its head hitting the floor echoed in the silence, and then the body followed, folding like a paper sack.

"Yeah, ancients don't go poof. We're going to have to do something about the body. Probably before morning," Tink explained. "Because they tend to decompose fast, and there's going to be a lot more than just blood seeping through the floorboards."

Um . . .

Tink handed the thorn stake back to Ren. Somehow, I had no idea how, he'd gotten it from Ren. Tink smiled proudly as he brushed his hands together and looked down at the body of the fallen knight. "Good day to you, sir!"

"What in the actual fuck?" Ren demanded again.

My mouth gaped open.

Ren was staring too, his gaze moving from where the knight lay in pieces, to the fully grown Tink—fully grown, *naked* Tink. His jaw was moving, but it was like he couldn't find the words. I couldn't blame him. All I could do was stare at Tink.

"How?" I whispered, and I didn't know if I was asking how he managed to get rid of the ancient or how he was fully grown.

It took Tink a moment to realize I was talking about him. "I'm very powerful, Ivy. I've told you that a hundred thousand times before, but you probably just ignored me. Big things come in small packages."

"That . . . explains nothing," I stated.

He cocked his head to the side. "Well, I am kind of like a house elf."

"Oh my God!" I shrieked, jumping off the couch. "You are not a house elf! This isn't the wizarding world of fucked up! You're fully grown. Like *man-sized* grown."

"I'm going to pretend you did not speak of the wizarding world in such a tone,'" he replied snottily. "Anyway, I'm a brownie. We have a remarkable ability that allows us to shrink ourselves. It's sort of like a defense mechanism. Just like opossums playing dead."

My entire face scrunched up. "That . . . that is not the same as an opossum playing dead."

"But it's the same idea. We can make ourselves smaller so that we are grossly underestimated," Tink explained with a shrug. "It works. Obviously. None of you thought I could—"

I held up a hand, and he must have read the crazy in my face, because he shut up. "So, you're telling me that this entire time you've actually been pretending to be small?"

"Not exactly pretending," he replied thoughtfully. "Being small is the same as being large."

I widened my eyes. "That makes no sense."

"I warned you, Ivy. I even asked you if you knew what you had living in your house." Ren kindly took that exact moment to remind me of this.

I turned devil eyes on him. "Did you know he was actually six-and-a-half-feet tall and anatomically correct?"

Ren's nose wrinkled. "Well, no."

"Then shut the hell up!"

Ren threw his hands up. "Alrighty then."

"Why would you think I wasn't anatomically correct in the first place?" Tink asked, sounding offended.

Turning back to naked, person-sized Tink, I ignored his question and shouted, "And where are your goddamn wings?"

He frowned. "I have them hidden now. In this form, they're pretty big and would be knocking shit over left and right, and considering how unstable you are, I doubt that's—"

"I'm unstable because you're not the size of a fucking Barbie doll."

"I don't see how this is a problem," Tink responded. "I'm actually more useful this way. You don't have to carry my deliveries when I'm—"

"Oh my God!" I screamed once more. I couldn't believe it. Tink wasn't the size of a doll at all. He'd just chosen that size, and the whole time he'd been living here, he was really like Ren-sized, and he'd seen me in my bra and undies, and . . ."Oh my God, I'm going to kill you!"

Tink drew back, his eyes wide. "That's a little drastic."

"I can get behind that thought process," Ren said dryly.

"I saved your life," Tink gasped, whirling toward Ren. "How dare you?"

Ren rolled his eyes. "I had it handled."

"It looked like the only thing you had handled was the art of getting your ass kicked."

I sat back down on the couch, having absolutely no idea of what was happening.

"Keep telling yourself that." Ren came around the side of the couch and picked up the damaged lamp. He placed it on the end table. "Can you put some damn clothes on?"

Tink arched a brow. "You have a problem with male nudity?"

"I have a problem with your dick hanging out."

"You didn't have a problem walking around the apartment with your junk all out and in everyone's face," Tink retorted, referencing the first morning those two met.

"That's because I didn't know you were here."

Tink smirked. "You know what I think the problem is? You're intimidated by my size."

Oh my God.

Ren laughed. "Yeah, I'm not intimated. That's not a problem."

Considering I fortunately knew Ren's size and unfortunately now knew Tink's size, I could confirm that was, indeed, not a problem. Picking up a throw pillow, I tossed it at Tink. He caught it and sighed, holding it so it covered up parts of him I hadn't wanted to ever see.

I pressed my fingers to my temples. "This is a nightmare. I'm going to wake up in a few minutes, the lock on my front door won't be broken, there will have been no knight, and Tink will still be a foot tall playing with troll dolls."

"Oh, I'll still play with them," Tink replied. I squeezed my eyes shut.

"If it makes you feel better, I can return to your Tink-approved size," he offered.

"It's not going to make me feel better." I opened my eyes. "Now that I know you're really full grown."

"Okay." He sat down on the edge of the coffee table, bare ass and balls just *everywhere*. Jesus. He stretched out his long legs. "So . . . this is awkward."

No shit. This entire time I thought I'd been living with this cute little brownie, but really I'd been living with this extraordinarily hot, super tall, fully-grown male creature of the Otherworld. Because I'd thought of him as this tiny thing with wings, I had never really worried about accidentally flashing him with my boobs or worse.

"While this shit show over here is a pretty big deal," Ren said, gesturing at Tink, who, as expected looked offended by his word choice, "I'm going to have to ask one more fucked-up question in a series of fucked-up questions." Ren sat on the arm of the couch. "I know things were crazy—well, are still crazy." He eyed the new life-sized version of Tink. "But that knight was gunning for my ass, and I mean that. He didn't want anything to do with Ivy."

My eyes widened. Oh no. Ren had noticed that. Of course he had. Not like the knight wasn't being particularly obvious about it. I had no idea what to say. And I didn't get a chance to really get creative, because Tink spoke from his naked perch on the edge of my coffee table.

"Probably because the knight went after the one he viewed as more of a threat," he said. "That's what I would do. Take out the one who is stronger first."

My brows slammed down.

Tink studiously ignored me. "Knights are very tactical. They're strategists."

I had no idea if he was telling the truth or just covering for me.

Ren looked over at me. "This is a big deal," he said.

Everything about the last twenty-four hours was a big deal.

"If the knights are coming to Order members' houses in the middle of the night . . ." Ren thrust his hand through his hair then dropped it to his side. "This changes everything."

My gaze met Tink's. Everything had already changed.

Chapter Ten

"I'm sorry, Ivy Divy." Tink followed me into my bedroom.

"Stop with the cute shit." I cut him off as I walked to my closet and yanked the door open. "Calling me 'Ivy Divy' isn't cute anymore, not when you're like two freaking feet taller than me."

"I'm not that much taller than you."

I looked over my shoulder at him, shooting him a glare worthy of shriveling up the man-parts now concealed by a towel wrapped around his waist, because apparently he didn't have any dude-sized clothing on hand.

"Okay." He backed off . . . by a couple inches. "I never said anything, because I—"

"Let me guess. Because you never thought it would be an issue?" I laughed harshly as I pulled a sweater off a hanger. Shoving the door shut, I faced Tink—man-sized Tink. "I've heard that excuse before."

"I know." He glanced out into the living room. Ren

had left with the body to go do God knew what with it, but he could return at any minute. "It's just that when we enter the human realm, we always take this form. It's a protective measure, and you found me in that form, and I thought it was best—"

"Oh my God, Tink, you could've just said something. Like, oh, I don't know. 'Hey, I may look small, but I'm really a giant dickhead.' That would've been helpful." I pulled the sweater on over my head then stomped out into the living room, walking around the shimmery blood that smelled faintly of berries and cream. I just couldn't even deal with that. "You're cleaning that up!" I shouted at Tink.

"I'll clean it up, Ivy, but I don't like it when you're mad at me."

I snort-laughed as I walked into the kitchen, grabbing the broom and dustpan out of the pantry. "Then how about being honest with me, completely honest with me? That would stop me from being pissed at you."

Tink followed me back into the living room, watching as I brushed up the pile of dirt. "If you knew that I could be this size, you wouldn't have been comfortable with me staying here," he said.

I stopped and looked up at him. Damn straight I wouldn't have been comfortable. "Correct."

"See?! You probably would've tried to kill me. You knew me in my smaller form, so I stayed that way until I felt like I had to intervene." Tink sighed. "Look, Ren might've handled the knight, but knights are extremely deadly and powerful. I reacted without thinking."

I returned to the mess on the floor, scooping up more dirt. "I'm glad you took care of the knight, but that doesn't change the fact that you haven't been up front with me this whole time." Bending down, I picked up the dustpan and brought it over to where the lamp had landed, stepping around the puddle of bluish-colored blood. "There's so much you haven't been honest about."

Tink was quiet as he righted the plant stand, then plopped the fern back onto it. By some act of dark magic, the towel secured around his waist stayed there.

I didn't know what to say to him. There was so much going on and my mind was focused in so many different directions that I almost didn't have the brain space for him.

Tink appeared at my side. "Hey, at least I killed the warrior with my sheer strength and skill."

I snorted as I brushed up the pieces of broken lamp. "More like you shocked him with your nakedness."

"Well," he said, grinning. "My girth *is* impressive."

"Ew," I muttered, and then faced him. A couple of moments passed. "I need to seriously know if there is anything else that you haven't told me. I'm being so serious this time. If you lie to me again—" I cut myself off and swallowed a sudden knot in my throat. If there were more lies, that was it. It was too much. "Now is the time to be completely honest."

Tink's pale blue eyes met mine. "There's nothing else, Ivy. You now know everything about me."

"What I asked you earlier about . . . about communities of fae that might not be . . . bad? Were you telling the truth then?" I asked.

"Yes." He nodded for extra emphasis. It was hard holding his stare right now, because Tink was . . . he was hot and that just made me feel kind of gross. I had never thought of him that way before. It never once had crossed my mind. "I've never heard of such a thing. They may be out there, but I honestly don't know. And I really haven't left here," he said, his brows knitted together. "It was overwhelming when I came through the gate. Everything was so loud and . . . and yeah, I haven't gone back out."

Was Tink actually afraid of going out into the world? That could explain his obsession with Amazon. I'd always thought it was because, well, he was tiny and it was kind of hard to blend in when you were only a foot or so tall and had wings. Obviously, he could've switched into this form at any time when I wasn't around and left this apartment to party it up on Bourbon Street.

"You've really haven't gotten back out there?" I asked.

Tink shook his head. "I've thought about it, but I haven't taken this form since I came to this side." He glanced down at himself. "It's weird. Being this size, that is." Drawing in a deep breath, he lifted his gaze to mine and said, "It's easier being smaller here. There's none of my kind. No one. It's just easier for me."

I suddenly felt pretty bad for Tink, and I didn't want to, because he'd lied to me so many times. Harboring anger was easier than forgiveness and understanding. He had valid reasons for his lies, but they still stung. I set the dustpan on the coffee table.

"Are you still mad?" Tink ventured closer to the couch. "I can stop ordering from Amazon. Okay, well, I can cut back on ordering from Amazon. Like maybe down to three orders a—"

"You don't need to stop ordering from Amazon." I clutched the broom as my gaze drifted to the door.

Ren was stopping at the Walmart about ten minutes down the road to pick up a new lock. It was going to be a long night, and even with the lock changed, how safe was it to be here now?

"We never had to worry about the fae searching us out before," I said. "This . . . I don't even know what to think of this."

Tink said nothing, because what could be said?

Ren and I were going to have to talk to David about what had happened. There was no way around that. This was too important, too dangerous.

I thought about the prince and how the knight had behaved. My fingers trembled around the broom, so I propped it against the couch. "I saw the prince earlier."

"What?" Tink's response was sharp and high.

I repeated myself. "I saw him when I left here. I went to get beignets and he walked up behind me."

"And you just now say something?" Tink vaulted over the couch. Like, jumped up and cleared the back and landed, standing on the center cushion.

I gaped at him. "How in the world did your towel stay on for that when I can't even get one to stay wrapped around me when I get out of the shower?"

"Magic," he replied. "Seriously. What the hell, Ivy? What happened?"

"If you get off the couch, I'll tell you."

Tink pouted, but stepped off the couch. He sat down, folding his hands in his lap all proper like. "Waiting."

I sat down on the edge of the coffee table—not the same part his man-parts had been all up on. I told him everything, finishing with the part about the prince just walking off, ambling down the street. "He didn't try to take me or anything. He—"

"He was wooing you. Like I said." Tink reached across the space and tapped the tip of my nose. And that was just weird as all hell now. I drew back, shooting him a look of warning. He ignored it. "Or he could just be trying to understand you so he can figure out what his next step is."

"I think we know what his next step is," I said, folding my arms loosely in my lap. "The prince knows about Ren, and the knight had no intention of fighting me. He kept pushing me out of the way. Didn't even bruise me. He was, like Ren said, completely focused on him. I think he was here . . ." Biting down on my lip, I couldn't finish that thought.

Understanding flared in Tink's gaze. "The knight was sent here to kill Ren. To take out the competition."

Chapter Eleven

As expected, the night was long. Ren was quiet as he set about replacing the lock, and I didn't ask him what he'd done with the knight's body. I was just grateful that his truck was here and he hadn't had to attempt hauling a body around in the back of a Ducati. It was near four in the morning when we retired to the bedroom, locking the door behind us.

And we really didn't talk then either other than me asking if he was okay and vice versa. Then he circled an arm around my waist, tugged me to his chest, and shoved his leg between mine.

It was hard to fall asleep knowing that a knight had found me—found us—but the weariness that had settled into both our bodies allowed sleep to drag us under. We slept with an iron dagger under our pillows, and it wasn't until late Monday morning that Ren and I untangled ourselves from one another and hit the shower. Sadly, the shower thing was separate. We both had gotten texts from David. There was a meeting this afternoon.

When I shuffled out to the bedroom while Ren was doing his thing, I saw that the fae blood had been cleaned from the floors, and then I was dealt a surprise when I entered the kitchen.

Tink had returned to, well, the Tink size I was used to, wings and all. He was sitting on the counter, eating the cereal he'd dumped next to him while watching an episode of *Supernatural* on my laptop.

"You know what I was thinking?" he said as I went to the cabinet and grabbed the coffee. "I never thought I could pick between Sam, Dean, Castiel, or Crowley, but I think I can."

"Uh-huh?" I murmured, dumping about ten scoops of coffee into the maker.

"Yeah. I would have to go with Crowley."

I closed the lid and blinked. That was unexpected. Turning the coffee pot on, I turned around and leaned against the counter. "You picked the king of hell?"

He nodded his little chin, and seeing him this small again wasn't as weird as I thought it would be. "I have my reasons. One of them is that he has a great English accent."

I raised a brow as I turned to grab a mug, loading it with coffee and sugar.

"And I like his boy crush on Dean," Tink continued. "Who wouldn't have a crush on Dean? If you didn't, I couldn't believe that you were real."

"Uh-huh," I repeated, taking a sip. I was not nearly awake enough to process this conversation.

Tink pointed at the screen. "Just look at those baby blue eyes. That grin of his is what heaven looks like."

I left the conversation at that point, switching places with Ren. I hoped he didn't kill Tink while I showered and got ready. I was pleased to see that I had to use less concealer around my eye and jaw today.

When I came out of the bathroom, I found Ren sitting on my bed, suited up for work, my coffee cup dangling from his fingertips—my obviously empty coffee cup.

His grin was sheepish. "Sorry. I went out to the kitchen, lasted about five seconds and then came back in here. Saw your coffee. It was too sweet to pass up."

"Did Tink try to talk to you about someone named Crowley?"

"Yes." He leaned over and placed the cup on the nightstand. "I have no idea what he's talking about, and I don't want to know."

I walked over to him, smiling when he put his hands on my hips and tugged me between his legs. Ren's gaze slid up the tank top I wore. "Glad we had some time together last night before the shit hit the fan."

"Me too." I warmed as I clearly remembered the time we had carved out for ourselves. Our eyes met. "What do you think about Tink?" I asked.

"I'm going to be real honest with you," he said, squeezing my hips. "The fact that the asshole isn't the size of my boot bothers me. I don't care that he's back to that size, eating cereal on your counter like a damn pet rat."

My brows lifted.

"I'm not saying you should kick him out. I'm not asking that, even though I would one hundred percent support that decision," he continued with a wry grin. "Just letting you know that I'm not too fond of the whole thing."

"Duly noted." I bent over and kissed him, loving the way his lips curved into a smile under mine. We had to head to the Order soon, and we only had a couple of minutes, so I kissed him again and spent the short time making out with him.

It turned out that wasn't exactly the brightest idea, because I wanted more minutes than we had, and based on what I felt under me, so did Ren.

He made this deep growly sound that had me wiggling in his lap as his lips coasted up my cheek, toward my ear. "Tonight, when we get done working, it's going to be all you and me, and I don't care what kind of shit we've got to deal with or think about or plan for. As soon as we're done, I'm going to get you naked."

My fingers dug into his shoulders. "I like the sound of that."

"I bet you do, but I'm not done." His tongue flicked over the lobe of my ear a second before his teeth caught the fleshy part, eliciting a sharp gasp from me. "After I get you naked, I'm going to spend some one-on-one time with various parts of your body, and then I'm going to get you under me, then on me again, because that was fucking hot, and then in front of me. I'm going to fuck you. Hard."

"Oh God," I moaned, my hands flexing on his shoulders. I liked that. A lot.

He kissed me on my neck. "Got a really bad pick-up line for you."

"Yeah?"

"Yep. Heard it not too long ago and I've been saving it for just the right moment."

I grinned. "Waiting."

"You're a work of art." He paused. "I'd like to nail you to the wall."

"Oh my God." I laughed loudly. "That is so terrible. Holy crap."

Ren chuckled. "I know. Now get off me so the hard-on of the century goes away."

I laughed again and then rose from his lap, but I didn't go too easy on him. Reaching down, I found that hard-on of the century and squeezed him. His harsh groan echoed in the room.

"You hussy," he muttered.

Grinning, I let go and backed away. "Whatever."

Ren closed his eyes and appeared to count under his breath. "It's not really warm outside. Heads up," he said.

"Thanks for the weather update." I turned to the closet and grabbed a black thermal, pulling it on. Then I grabbed my weapons and secured the thorn stake to my calf, hidden under the leg of my pants.

Ren was walking a little stiffly as we left the bedroom, and when he stopped at the door, his eyes narrowed on my smile.

"Be right back," I told him, then walked into the kitchen. Tink was nowhere to be found, and my laptop was missing. Cereal crumbs remained on the counter. Some things never changed. I rapped my knuckles on his door. "Tink?"

"Yo," he yelled back, and it sounded like normal Tink, not full-sized Tink.

"We're heading to work," I told him, shifting my weight from one foot to the next. "I just wanted—"

The door suddenly opened, and Tink appeared, his wings moving lazily. "You're letting me know? That's different. Typically you just leave without saying anything."

I frowned at him as I noticed he was wearing a pair

of doll gym shorts, and they were tiny, like disco-dancing tiny. And they were satiny and silver. Wow. "I've told you—"

"You're worried about me because of what happened with the knight. Don't worry. I can take care of myself." Floating forward, he flicked the tip of my nose. "Be careful, and tell Ren he is more than welcome to stay at his own place tonight." Then he closed the door in my face.

I was so not telling Ren that.

"Everything okay?" he asked when I joined him.

"Yeah, I was just checking on Tink." I paused as I grabbed my bag and draped the strap over my shoulder. "I'll admit," I said in a low voice, "I'm a little worried about leaving him here. He doesn't have the thorn stake like last time."

Ren opened his mouth, seemed to think carefully about what he was going to say, and then closed it. "I'm sure he'll be okay."

"Uh huh."

He smiled crookedly and opened the door. We headed down the staircase and out across the courtyard. It was chilly outside, cooler than normal, but I wasn't complaining. Not too long ago I was wishing for a polar vortex to make New Orleans its bitch, but it was unseasonable for this time of year.

The drive into the Quarter wasn't too bad as it was a pretty decent time in the afternoon. I swore I saw someone in a T-Rex costume mowing grass, though.

Somehow, by some kind of magical happening, Ren nabbed a parking spot in the garage the Order used, which was closer than usual since there was no parking on Phillips. Typically there weren't spots available, because locals had figured out you could park there without having to give your keys and car over to someone, but Ren was obviously super special.

"You ready to have this talk with David after the meeting?" Ren asked as we started toward headquarters. "We're going to be dumping some crap on him."

That was the understatement of the decade. On the way into the Quarter, we'd decided to hold off on mentioning the unproven community of good fae. We would talk to Jerome first, get a read on him, and see what we could get out of him before going to David.

"He's not going to be happy that we didn't call him last night, but at least we can butter him up with the good news of one of the knights being gone."

"That won't go a long way."

I nodded and scanned the streets. Ren did the same. He was looking for fae, but I was keeping an eye out for the prince. So far, we weren't seeing anything other than a whole lot of tourists underdressed for the cold snap. A block from the headquarters, he reached over and tugged on a curl of mine. I looked at him.

He winked. "I just can't stop myself from playing with them."

I knocked his hand away and shook my head. "Save that for later."

"I don't know about that." He reached over, sliding a hand down my back. "Gonna be playing with other things then."

Oh dear.

The building came into view, and I shook it off while Ren chuckled. One of the newer recruits stood guard outside. Mama Lousy was still closed, which meant we were most likely going to have to visit Jerome at his place. It was probably better that way since the gift shop was wired with video.

I smiled at the new guy, and he nodded in my direction.

"Hey Glenn, what's going on?" Ren asked as he opened the door.

"Nothing much," he replied. Glenn was tall and dark-skinned, his head bald and smooth. Sunglasses shielded his eyes and he gave off a great "don't screw with me" vibe. "Got some new people upstairs."

"Not surprised about that," Ren said as I headed into the stairwell.

"Yeah, but these guys are different."

I exchanged a look with Ren, and he shrugged. As we reached the door, it opened for us. Rachel Adams was on the other side. The tall and slender Order member was in her early thirties. I didn't know her well, and like most members, she kept to herself. Beyond her, I could tell that the room was pretty full.

"Glad to see you're back up and moving around," she said, stepping aside.

"Thanks. Glad to see you're not dead." My eyes widened as I realized how that sounded. "I meant that you didn't die in the battle, not that I'm glad anyone else died, but yeah . . ."

She stared at me and arched a brow.

"Nice," Ren murmured under his breath, and I casually jabbed my elbow out, catching him in the side. He grinned, and the dimple on his left cheek began to appear. I was thinking about hitting him again when David suddenly appeared in front of us.

I hadn't seen David since I left the hospital, and for a man who usually seemed so ageless, he didn't right now. The salt and pepper sprinkled at his temples had expanded up the sides of his head. Deeper wrinkles had formed at the corners of his dark skin, around his eyes. He looked tired.

And pissed.

But he always kind of looked pissed.

David nodded at Ren and then looked down at me. He placed a hand on my shoulder and squeezed gently. "Good to see you finally walking back through that door."

I blinked once, twice, and then murmured, "Ditto."

He stepped back, and I felt like I could've fallen over, because that was actually nice coming from David, from the man I always felt like I was letting down and who never really seemed to be overly happy with anything I did or said.

I almost wanted to do a little jig.

I looked around the room but didn't see Miles. Feeling antsy, I glanced over at Ren. That's when I noticed Ren's grin starting to fade. Two men I'd never seen before had joined David. One was tall, had dark hair, and was probably in his mid to late forties. The other was shorter with pale, pale skin, and had red hair brighter than mine, and that was saying something. Ren stiffened as the dark-haired man approached him.

"Ren," the man said, extending a hand. "It's been a while. Good to see you're doing well."

"Likewise." Ren shook the man's hand, but there wasn't an ounce of warmth in his voice. "What are you doing here, Kyle?"

My eyes widened. Kyle? *That* Kyle? The one who killed Ren's best friend because he turned out to be a halfling? Holy shitballs.

"Here because we're needed." Kyle turned to me. He extended his hand in my direction. "You must be Ivy. David was telling me about you."

"Nice to meet you," I lied—lied straight through my teeth as I shook his hand.

"Same to you." His gaze flickered over my face. "Fought the prince of the Otherworld and lived to tell the story. Amazing."

I forced myself to show no reaction. "Barely lived to tell the story." I smiled tightly as he let go of my hand. He turned sideways, and I felt a weird pressure clamping down on my chest.

David moved to the center of the room. "Okay guys, listen up. We've got two members from Colorado here. Their names are Kyle Clare and Henry Kenner."

A muscle was flexing, doing overtime along Ren's jaw as he folded his arms across his chest. There was not a single doubt in my mind that Ren was very unhappy that they were here.

I wasn't too thrilled myself.

"I'm going to cut through the bullshit. Henry and I are here to find the halfling," Kyle announced. There weren't any gasps of surprise from the other members. Apparently they'd been filled in on all that and the whole secret society of Order members known as the Elite, but unease was brewing in my belly as Kyle's dark gaze flickered around the room. "Here's the thing that all of you are missing. If that girl was truly the halfling and the fae knew that, they wouldn't have her anywhere near that gate," Kyle said. "They would've kept her safe and sound. She isn't the halfling."

~

I hauled ass out of the meeting the moment I could without looking suspicious. I had to, because the longer I stayed in there, the more it felt like the walls were closing in. Panic burned my lungs and the acids were churning in my stomach.

I'd barely heard anything else Kyle and Henry had said, and there was no way I was hanging around to talk to David about what had happened last night. I knew I needed to, and I knew it was important, but I had to get out of there for a moment.

Once outside, I sucked in deep mouthfuls of cool air and headed down the street, not really paying attention to where I was going. I just needed to get far away from Kyle, from the Elite member who had discovered that Ren's childhood best friend was a halfling, and had calmly followed the young man from Ren's home and killed him.

He was here, and he knew that Val wasn't the halfling. The others would soon realize that, and they would—

"Ivy," Ren called out, and I kept walking, stepping around people. "Ivy, just slow down." He caught up to me easily, catching my arm and drawing me to a stop. "Are you okay?"

My heart was pounding so fast I could hear it in my ears. I shook my head, feeling sick.

His brows knitted together, and concern filled his emerald eyes. "What's going on?" When I didn't answer, he pulled me aside, into the narrow alley between two buildings. "Talk to me," he said.

I could barely breathe as I stared up at him. What had Ren told me before? That he couldn't go through that again. Having to make a choice between someone he cared about and duty. And he was smack dab in the middle of that horrible situation again.

"Babe," he said, cupping my face, his thumb sliding

across the curve of my cheek. "What's going on?"

Two choices loomed in front of me. I could continue to keep Ren in the dark about what I was and hope for the best. Pray that Kyle wouldn't figure out it was me, and that somehow we'd be able to deal with the prince and the ancients without me getting outed in the process. But I knew as I stared into his eyes, that was a lot of foolish hoping and praying—a dangerous level of it.

Telling him the truth, which was my only other choice, was so incredibly risky. I loved him. I was *in* love with him, and maybe that made me a little blind, but because I loved him, I couldn't do that to him. I couldn't allow him to find out through Kyle or other members of the Elite. I didn't know what would happen if I did tell him, and I fully recognized that I would virtually be handing him a loaded gun. I had no idea what he'd do, but I knew if I spoke those words, it was over between us.

And I couldn't ask him not to do his duty. He would be required to turn me over to the Order, or worse, to take me out himself. I knew I couldn't let him do the latter. I was too much of a fighter for that. I knew myself. I would fight anyone who came for me even if I understood why I'd be turned in.

"You're really starting to scare me, Ivy." His eyes searched mine. "For real."

The sound of traffic and the hum of conversation faded into the distance as I took a deep breath. I had to tell him. He had to know, because I wouldn't let him be blindsided again. I couldn't lie to him anymore.

My breath lodged in my throat. I had to do the right thing.

Chapter Twelve

My heart felt like it was about to stop in my chest. "I'm the—"

"Hey, what are you two doing down here?" a voice called from the mouth of the alley, halting me. I jerked back, and my heart nearly fell out of my chest when I saw Henry standing several feet away.

Holy crap on a buttered cracker, I'd almost admitted to being the halfling in front of Henry—an Elite member.

"Well, nothing like explaining the obvious," Ren said. "We're talking. You know, something two people, sometimes more, or hell, even when a person is alone, like to do without interruption."

I gave Ren a long side-look.

Henry strode down the alley, the color of his cheeks starting to match his hair. "Kyle warned that you were a smartass. I see he wasn't exaggerating."

Ren smirked. "What's up?"

"Kyle needs to speak with you." Henry glanced in my direction, and apparently decided I was not worthy of being a part of the conversation, because he refocused on Ren. My brows rose.

"Kind of doing something right now." Ren folded his arms. "I'll be up to see Kyle when I—"

"It's an order." Henry cut him off, mirroring Ren's stance by folding his arms. "So whatever you're doing right now is going to have to wait."

For a moment I thought Ren was going to continue being a smartass. The hard set of his jawline told me there was a really good chance of that happening. I also recognized that certain gleam in his eyes. Time to step in. "I can wait," I told him, touching his arm. "Go see what Kyle needs."

"Hell," Ren muttered under his breath, and I knew talking to Kyle was the last thing he wanted to do. "We'll continue this later. Okay?"

I nodded, dropping my arm.

"Times a-ticking, my man," Henry commented.

Ren ignored him as he lifted his arm, curling his hand around the back of my neck. He lowered his head as he drew me toward him, and I went, guessing Ren was not going to hide his relationship with me in front of the newcomers. I couldn't decide if that was a good or bad thing.

He placed his mouth beside my ear and whispered low enough for just me to hear. "You okay?"

I didn't know what I was at the moment. "I'm fine."

Ren hesitated for a moment, then pressed his lips to my cheek. I thought that would be it, but then his mouth was on mine, and he kissed me deeply. It was not a chaste or sweet kiss, and I almost forgot that Henry was standing there.

"I think she just got pregnant," Henry said, clearing his throat.

Ren slowly lifted his head, his eyes locked on mine. "I think you better keep your month shut if you want to use it later for things like breathing and eating."

My eyes widened. Oh dear.

Whatever Henry replied was lost in another quick kiss, and then the three of us were walking out of the alley. "Text me when you're done," I said.

"Will do."

I looked at Henry, who was studiously acting as if I didn't exist. "Bye, Henry," I said.

He grunted.

I rolled my eyes while Ren gave me a half-grin. Wiggling my fingers at him, I pivoted around and started off in the opposite direction from headquarters. I waited until I reached the corner of Royal and then stopped, leaning against the wall.

"Holy shit," I murmured, bending over as the full reality of what I'd almost done sank in. "Holy shitstorm in the making."

My stomach roiled. I'd been a hundred percent prepared to tell Ren that I was the halfling, and those words had been right on the tip of my tongue before Henry showed up. I still needed to tell him, but this was like getting a governor's reprieve seconds before execution.

My face scrunched.

That was a terrible way of looking at it. Okay. That was probably the most realistic way of looking at it, but seriously, it wasn't helping.

I stood there for a couple of moments while I gained my bearings. No one paid attention to me. They probably thought I was going to puke. Luckily that sensation had passed by the time I straightened and looked around. Exhaling roughly, I started walking toward Bourbon.

It was hard to focus on the job at hand, especially when there were still no fae in sight, so my mind was bouncing around like a tennis ball in a tornado. I had no idea what Kyle wanted with Ren. Most likely normal Elite business, but I'd totally zoned out on whatever Kyle was saying after the whole halfling thing. I should've probably paid attention.

I hung around on Bourbon, and it was close to eight in the evening when I decided I was done waiting for Ren. I was going to stop at a diner to grab something quick to eat, and I was considering my options when I saw a flash of fuchsia near the intersection of Conti Street.

A strange sense of familiarity struck me, and instinct took over. A logical part of my brain knew it was unlikely that it was Val, because she would have to be insane to be down here, but then again, Val was obviously a little crazy.

I reached Conti Street and scanned both sides. Someone bumped into me and muttered under their breath as I turned left, onto Bourbon. There! I recognized the fuchsia shirt. My breath caught as I started in that direction and the people thinned out on the sidewalk. I spotted caramel-colored curls as tight as corkscrews.

Holy shit.

It was Val.

Deep in my core, I knew it was her and not just some random girl with curly hair. Tension poured into my muscles as I picked up my step, keeping close to the edge of the sidewalk as I followed her. She was still on Bourbon, now nearing the corner of Bienville when she looked over her shoulder.

My heart stopped. Even though we were nearly a block apart, I could swear our eyes met. She turned back around quickly and started running—like full-on sprinting.

I took off after her, dodging people, which was not easy at this time of night, but there was no way I was going to let her get away from me. Heart pumping and my bag thumping off my hip, I kept going.

There wasn't time to call Ren or any other member of the Order, and to be honest, confronting Val in front of anyone wouldn't be wise. Since she was working with the fae, she had to know what I was.

Darting around a group of college-aged guys who were watching someone bravely stagger across the street, I almost lost sight of her as I hit Iberville. I thought she might've turned down that street, but then I spotted her further up on Bourbon, nearing Canal.

Dammit. She was fast.

I couldn't let her cross Canal. From there, she could hop on one of the trollies and end up in God knew where. So I dug in and really pushed it. My stomach ached, reminding me that I had, in fact, almost died not too long ago, but I ignored the burn and kept going.

I was quickly gaining on her, then she turned left on Canal and raced down the block. Without warning, she darted into one of the hotels. I followed, bypassing a startled-looking bellhop.

Music and laughter filled the lobby of the hotel. I turned wildly, scanning in all directions. A door across from the elevators drifted shut, and I knew, just freaking knew it was her.

Motherfucker, she'd gone up the stairs.

Jesus, I was going to punch her in the face just for *that* alone.

Calling on every ounce of willpower I had left, I threw open the door and charged up the stairs. Reaching the second floor landing, I looked up and saw her two floors above me. "Val!" I shouted. "Stop!"

She didn't.

Of course not.

Not when she knew how much I hated stairs. Running up them was like lying down in front of a slow-ass moving, heavy as hell trolley and letting it run you over.

Halfway up the stairs, I was grasping the railing as I fought to keep going. How many stories was this hotel? A hundred? Just when I thought my legs were going to give out, cool air washed over me and invaded the warm, stale air of the stairwell. Rounding one more fight, I saw the door to the roof was wide open, the pieces of a rusty handle on the dirty cement floor.

I burst out onto the roof and immediately saw Val standing in the center, her back to me. The sun had set, and moonlight flowed across the pavement, giving way to deep shadows near the churning units covering most of the roof.

Winded, I stopped and placed a hand to my side. "Stairs?" I squeaked. "Really?"

"I was hoping you wouldn't follow." She turned slowly, facing me. "You hate stairs."

"No shit," I gasped, wondering if I was going to pass out. "How did you break the handle on the door?"

"Drop kick," she replied. "You know I have strong legs."

Legs of freaking steel right there. Dragging in deep gulps of air, I focused on her—on the girl who used to be my best friend. We stared at each other for several moments, neither of us saying a word. Then Val spoke first.

"You just had to follow me, didn't you?" Val pushed the curls back from her face and then dropped her hands, shaking her head. "You couldn't just not have seen me and went on your merry way?"

I stared at her. "That's a stupid question."

She sneered at me.

"You were down there, where any Order member could've seen you. Are you surprised that one did?" I asked.

"I've been careful," she said, and the sleeve of her bright blouse slipped off her shoulder. "No one has seen me until now."

I kept my hands at my sides, watching her closely. "Why would you be down in the Quarter?"

"Ivy, I'm not going to tell you that."

"Of course not," I muttered as she met my gaze again. The pain of her betrayal blossomed in my chest like a noxious weed. "Why?"

"Why what?" she asked.

"Don't pretend like you don't know what I'm talking about." I stepped forward, and she tensed. "Why did you do this? How could you betray us like you did?"

Her pressed her lips together, not responding.

"People died, Val. People you knew. Who you worked with and who trusted you," I continued, and the bitter betrayal gave way to red-hot anger. "I almost died, Val. Your best friend. The person who trusted—"

"I didn't want you to get hurt," she fired back, her hands closing into fists at her sides. "You followed me, Ivy. You followed me and the prince. Who the fuck does that?"

"Me!" I shouted. "I kept thinking they had you under their control. That they were manipulating you. That was why I followed. I followed you because I care about you and you almost got me killed."

"But you didn't get killed, did you?"

"That's not the point, dumbass."

Her eyes rolled. "Why are we even standing here talking about this? I know you've been given orders to kill me or bring me in, but you want to stand here and talk me to death."

"I want to know why the fuck you did this! I don't even care about the Order," I admitted, my voice cracking with raw emotion. "You did this to me! I want to know why."

Val's shoulders rose, and I could tell she wanted to look away, but knew better than to do that at this point. "You don't understand."

"You're right," I snapped back. "You got your parents killed, Val. Do you know that? They were executed because of you."

She flinched. "That was . . . sad."

"Sad?"

Her nostrils flared. "Jesus, Ivy, sacrifices have to be made. It's not like they didn't live a long and happy life."

My mouth dropped open. "I can't believe you."

"But you should."

"Stop talking in cliffhangers!" I was losing my patience.

"Jesus, Ivy, are you really happy working for the Order? Spending what limited time you have on this Earth, putting your life on the line every day for a bunch of people who literally can't even stop from drinking themselves to death? You're happy getting up every morning knowing that there is about a fifty-percent chance you're going to die that day and get paid shit for it?"

My jaw worked. "We get paid pretty well."

"For going out there and defending those fuckers,

knowing we're going to eventually die doing it?" She flung her arm out toward the ledge of the roof. "No. We don't get paid enough for this shit. And you know we can't just quit. We were born into this, cosmically pulling the short straw on life."

She was right about the not quitting part. It wasn't exactly unheard of, but it wasn't easy.

"And I know you're not happy," she continued. "That's why you take college classes—"

"Yeah, I take college classes, but I don't betray everyone I know," I shot back in a state of disbelief. "If you were this unhappy, you could've just walked away from it."

She snorted. "I could've done that, but I . . . You don't know, Ivy. You see the world one way, but you have no idea what the other side is like."

"Other side?" I repeatedly dumbly.

"You have no idea what the fae are capable of, and I'm not talking about taking over the world. They are . . . well, let's just say once you go fae, you never go back."

"Are you fucking serious?"

"And when they feed?" She licked her lips. "It's better than a shot of heroin."

"You've . . ." There were no words.

"Don't look at me like that—like I'm repulsive. When it happened, it wasn't like it was planned. I got cornered on a hunt, Ivy, months and months ago. He didn't kill me. I'm not even sure why. He wanted to . . . play with his food, I guess. I thought I was going to die, but he took me to Marlon instead."

"Marlon . . . the ancient?" Marlon St. Cryers was an ancient who lived a very public life as a renowned business developer. I'd been *this* close to him when I'd been at Flux.

Val nodded. "We worked out a deal. He wouldn't kill me if I helped them find the Order members who were guarding the gates. And you know, it sounded like a deal I should take, considering I liked living and breathing. So I did. But after a while, it wasn't even like I was being forced, Ivy. I began to see how this was all going to end. They're going to win, Ivy. Especially now that the prince is here. They are going to take over eventually, and you know what? I'd rather be on the winning side. And girl, like I said before, the fae know what they're doing."

I stared at her, horrified. "Do you even hear yourself? You enjoy being fed on? Holy shit, what is wrong with you?"

"Don't knock it, babe, until you get with one who doesn't want to make you hurt. And it doesn't hurt. It's like a full-body orgasm. Trust me." She shrugged. "There's freakier shit out there."

"No. No there's not." Then it struck me. "The new guy you were dating. He's a fae."

"Took you that long to figure that out?" she replied wryly.

"Marlon?" When she didn't answer, I resisted the urge to knock her upside her head. "You've been feeding him information, getting people killed and betraying everyone, just so you can stay alive and basically get fucked and fed on? Wow, Val."

She moved, stopping a handful of feet from me. "I know what you are," she stated, her voice low. "So how dare you stand there and lecture me on what is right and wrong? You're the halfling. You're going to be screwing the prince soon enough."

I shot forward, getting right up in her face. "First off, I'm not going to be screwing the prince, because I actually have taste in men. And secondly, I didn't choose to be this, Val. I didn't wake up one moment and decide to be a fucking coward and betray every person who trusts me, because that's basically what you are. A fucking coward who fucks everyone while fucking them over—"

Val swung on me, and that flipped my oh-hell-no switch. I dipped and then shot back up. Cocking my arm, I threw a punch. I didn't miss. My knuckles connected with her jaw, snapping her head back.

She stumbled a step and then her head whipped in my direction. She worked her jaw. "Bitch."

"Really? You deserve that and more."

Her chest rose. "You know I can't kill you, and I know you won't kill—"

Swinging again, I punched her in the face. Pain spread across my knuckles, but this time she didn't back off. Val launched herself at me like a damn tiger. I went down, landing flat on my back, the air knocked out of me.

"Hitting isn't nice, Ivy." She gripped my shoulders and started to lift me up.

That wasn't going to happen. Rocking my hips, I wrapped my legs around her and flipped her faster than she could blink. Stalling her, I planted a hand on her chest, holding her in place. "You know you can't beat me in a fight, Val."

"I don't know if I want to when you're grabbing my boob like that," she said.

"I'm not grabbing—"

She threw a punch at my jaw. I rolled to the side as I saw stars for a second. Holy crap, she could hit.

Val sprang to her feet. "That was almost too easy."

"Really?" Planting my hands, I shifted my weight and kicked out, sweeping her legs right out from underneath her. "How about that, bitch?"

She shrieked as she went down, and I jumped to my feet. Val was only down for a second. She rose and rushed me like a damn linebacker, shoving me backward. We slammed into an air unit and the ancient thing rattled.

I lifted my leg, going for her very active lady parts, but she anticipated my move, and I caught her in the side, which earned me a nice sucker punch in the stomach. I doubled over with a grunt as I stumbled away from the unit.

Val grabbed me from behind, wrapping one arm around my neck. "This is getting really old. Why don't you chill the fuck out and—"

Twisting in her grasp, I used her weight against her as I grabbed her arm. I flipped her over my shoulder, and she hit the floor with a satisfying yelp. Breathing hard, I stood over her. "I can't believe you, Val. You know I can't just let you walk away from here."

"What are you going to do?" she asked from her prone position. "I know you're not going to kill me. You don't have it in you. So you're going to try to take me in, and yeah, I'm not into that. I just need to delay this."

"For what—?"

Val leaped to her feet like a damn ninja and coldcocked me. Blood leaked out of my nose as the pain exploded. I spun, kicking out with my legs. Val darted and then lurched forward, grabbing huge handfuls of my hair. I shrieked as fire spread across my scalp.

"You're going to pull my hair?" I gritted out, grabbing her arm. "That is low, Val."

"That's the lowest thing you think I've done?"

"Oh, I know there's more." Digging my fingers into her wrist, I put the pressure on her until she yelped and let go. Springing backward, I spun and kicked out again. Val tried to dodge my legs, but they caught her in the hip. She went down on one knee. "You're pretty much wallowing in—"

An icy wind whipped across the roof, stinging the sore spots on my face. Val stiffened and then slowly pushed to her feet. She stepped back, giving me a wide berth. I opened my mouth, but a large, winged bird landed on the ledge of the roof.

It was a raven.

The thing was huge and glossy black, and totally not a normal bird.

My heartbeat stuttered, and all I could think was, *not again* as the air rippled around the raven, and a second later the prince was crouched in its place.

Chapter Thirteen

The prince was still for a moment, and sort of reminded me of the statues perched on rooftops, made of marble and consisting of no warmth or life. Only his midnight-colored hair moved in the breeze, playing across his chiseled features.

Instinct forced me to take a step back, and it was in that moment when I realized I had no weapons in my hands. I'd been fighting Val, and not once had I pulled a weapon. Her earlier taunts rang true. I couldn't kill her.

But right now that wasn't the most pressing issue to focus on.

The prince was back, and something else Val said had surfaced. *I just need to delay this.* She knew he'd come. "Bitch," I hissed.

"I knew he'd come," she confirmed in a low voice.

Anger bubbled up like lava. "I want to punch you again."

"Girls," the prince murmured as he straightened to his full, impressive height. "What do humans say? Why fight when you can make love?"

"That is incredibly cliché," I said, widening my stance.

A smirk formed on the prince's near-perfect lips as he stepped off the ledge. He was dressed much like yesterday. Wind tousled his shirt, pushing it back against his hard stomach and chest. "And your hair is still obnoxiously bright, even at night."

I stared at him, brows raised.

He drifted a few feet closer, and his chin rose, nostrils flaring. "I smell your blood."

"This just keeps getting better and better," I muttered.

The prince cocked his head to the side. "I can think of many ways to make this evening so much better."

Ew.

Val moved closer to the prince, and I stiffened. "Don't get near him," I warned.

She raised a brow. "Babe, I've already been near him. Like, really near him if you get my drift."

I totally got her drift.

And I totally wanted to barf.

I also totally didn't get why I was trying to protect her at this point.

"Why are you bleeding?" the prince asked. When I didn't answer, he looked at Val. "Explain."

"We were fighting," she immediately answered, her tone timid. I'd never heard her like that before. Val was the opposite of a quiet, little mouse. "She attacked me. I had to defend myself."

The prince raised an eyebrow. "You were to bring her to me. Not beat her."

"I wouldn't say she 'beat' me," I muttered.

They both ignored me, and there was no mistaking the nervousness in the way Val fidgeted with her fingers. "I wasn't planning for her to see me tonight. You know what I was doing in the Quarter. It was what you asked."

"What *were* you doing in the Quarter?" I asked, and was ignored, yet again.

The prince angled his body toward Val, which worked to my benefit. I slowly kneeled and reached under my pant leg.

Val shifted her weight from one foot to another. "I told you we needed to give her time, but I promised—"

I unhooked the thorn stake as the prince said, "You promised to bring her over. I do not see how involving fists would accomplish that."

I also didn't understand how Val could promise anything that involved me, but I kept my mouth shut as I stood up.

"I will. I just need time. Ivy is difficult, Drake." Her eyes were wide. "I just need more time."

Drake? That was the prince's name? I stowed away that little piece of knowledge for later, then kicked off, bum-rushing the prince.

He lifted a hand without even looking at me. I hit an invisible wall and was gently shoved back, my booted feet slipping over the pavement as he said, "You do not have permission to address me so directly."

"I'm sorry," Val quickly whispered. "You're right. I overstepped."

I stopped sliding, and I couldn't stay quiet any longer. "Did you just apologize for overstepping? *Overstepping?* Are you on crack? And she isn't going to woo me to the dark side. I'm un-woo-able. So I don't know what she's been promising you, but it's a whole lot of nothing." I started forward, relieved to see I wasn't blocked again. "You can't use her to get to me, *Drake*."

He turned his head in my direction and smiled. My stomach flipped, and not in a good way. "I didn't give you permission either."

I spread my arms wide. "Look at all the fucks I have to give. I give zero. Zero fucks."

"Ivy," whispered Val. "You need to stop."

That cold smile of his increased. "Oh, my little bird doesn't know when to stop. She's lucky that she's necessary, but you . . ." He focused on Val. "You are not so lucky."

It happened so fast that I didn't see the prince move. One second Val was standing next to him, and the next, he was by the ledge and Val was gone, and noise was streaming up from the street below.

Horns blew. Tires squealed. The whipping wind sounded like screams as I stood there, frozen for several seconds in panic. "You . . ."

"She was a problem for you, wasn't she?" Drake queried, his voice without emotion. "I took care of her."

Took care of her? My horrified gaze swung in his direction. "How? She was helping you."

"As you said, I couldn't use her to get to you." One broad shoulder rose. "She was expendable. You are not."

Oh my God.

"She betrayed you. I served retribution for you."

Oh. My. God.

Drake stepped toward me, and I raised the thorn stake. "Don't get near me."

His gaze dropped and he sighed. "Remember what

happened the last time you pulled a weapon on me?"

A shiver coursed down my spine, because oh yeah, I remembered, but I held my ground. "Do you really think that's going to stop me from fighting you?"

"No," he replied. "Apparently, you do not learn from previous experience."

My hand tightened on the stake as I glanced toward the ledge. "Maybe not, but I don't have to worry about you hurting anyone else right now either. We're alone."

"And that should make you much more wise." He lifted his chin, the dark strands of his hair brushing his shoulders. "I could do anything I wanted to you and there would be no one, including you, to stop me." Those words sent chills down my spine. Several seconds passed and then his icy smile returned. "Goodbye. For now."

The air around him seemed to distort, and in a heart-beat the large raven was back. Spreading its long and broad wings, it swooped back over the ledge and disappeared from sight.

I drew in a shaky breath as I slowly lowered the stake.

Rushing to the ledge, I placed a hand on the cool stone and leaned over. The roar of wind caught the loose strands of my hair and blew them back from my face. I don't even know why I tried to look. I already knew what I was going to see.

There. On the roof of a dark SUV was Val, arms and legs splayed in broken, unnatural ways.

Val was dead.

~

Numbing instinct took over. I knew I had to get away from the hotel without being seen, and that wasn't going to be easy considering I'd run into the hotel, chasing Val . . . the woman who was dead outside.

Oh God.

Emotion clogged my throat as I raced down the stairs and then entered one of the hotel hallways, making my way to an elevator. Luckily, I didn't need a card to use it. I pulled my hair up, twisting it into a knot. The lobby was full of people crowding the glass revolving doors. Squeezing past them, I slipped out onto Canal and headed right, ignoring all the sounds—what the people were seeing, the shocked gasps, the sirens. Once I was back on Bourbon, I pulled out my phone. I started to call Ren, but since he hadn't texted me, I knew he was still busy. In a weird, detached daze, I decided not to bother him. I knew I had to report this, so I searched for David's number and hit SEND as I blindly made my way down the street.

David answered on the fourth ring. "What."

He always answered like that. What. Not a question but a demand. For some reason, hearing something so familiar settled the tight knots building in my stomach. "It's Ivy."

"Sort of figured that out when the caller ID showed your name," he replied dryly. "What's going on?"

An older woman noticed me, and her face pinched with concern. I wiped my sleeve under my nose, forgetting it was bloodied. "Val's dead."

There was a sharp expletive that blasted my ears. "I need a little more detail, like about five seconds ago."

"I saw her on Bourbon, and she ran. I chased her up to the roof of one of the hotels on Canal," I explained, keeping my voice low as I made my way toward the street. "She was down here doing something, but she wouldn't tell me what it was. We fought, and she . . ." My breath caught because I couldn't tell the complete truth, and what did that make me? I'd have to unpack all that mess later. "She fell off the roof."

"Shit," muttered David.

I took a breath that seemed to get stuck. "I didn't kill her." David didn't reply, and I don't even know why I continued speaking. "I asked her why she did this, why she betrayed us. She—"

"It doesn't matter, Ivy. The why does not matter. She did what she did. She made that choice," David replied with a heavy sigh. "She still out on Canal?"

My stomach turned. "Yeah."

"I'll send someone out. Call Robby. Let them know she's one of ours." There was a pause. "You're off for the rest of the night."

I stopped in the middle of the sidewalk. Someone knocked into me, and I shot the woman a look that warned her not to say one word. "Why? I'm fine. I can—"

"You were close to her. You just saw her die. I don't care what you say you are, you're off for the rest of the night. Get your ass off the streets or you'll find yourself off tomorrow too," David advised. "I'm being serious. It's an order."

Starting to walk again, I gritted my teeth and immediately regretted it, because my jaw ached. "All right."

"I'm gonna need you to come down tomorrow and fill out a report," he said. "Don't forget."

I was so not looking forward to that. I hung up and walked about four steps before my phone rang again. It was Ren. I answered. "Hey."

"Just heard about Val. Where are you?" he asked.

"Um . . ." I looked around. "On Bourbon. Across from Galatoire's."

"Hang out there, and I'll meet in you in a couple of minutes."

"Ren," I whispered, my heart flipping all over the place. I really wanted to cry. "You're busy doing special Elite stuff, and you don't need to come to me."

"You need me and that's where I need to be," he replied. "I'll be right there. Okay?"

Ren hung up before I could respond, and I had to breathe deeply so I didn't break down. I looked around, and not finding any place to sit, leaned against the mustard-colored wall and waited while this horrible burning sensation churned in my stomach, slowly crawling up my throat.

Val had betrayed the Order. She had nearly gotten me killed, but . . . she'd been my best friend, and now she was gone. Dead on the street because of the choices she'd made, the trusts she'd broken and horribly misplaced in others. I didn't understand how I could feel so much pain for a person who'd done one of the worst things, but I did and the heartbreak wasn't any less because of her actions.

It was more.

~

Ren showed up about twenty minutes later, shaving off about five minutes of that walk, which was rather impressive. He didn't say anything when he spotted me leaning against the wall, and neither did I. Partly because I was just so . . . relieved to see him—that wonderfully messy, wavy hair of his, those bright, warm green eyes, and everything that was alive about him.

He walked up to me, and a second later, I was in his arms, and he was holding me so tight and so close. I didn't care what we must look like to others on the street. I wrapped my arms around him and held on. One of his hands slid up and down my back, and we stood there like that for what felt like eternity.

"You okay?" Ren leaned back and brushed his lips over my forehead. "Looks like your jaw is a little red."

"I'm fine." My voice was hoarse.

He circled his arm back around my shoulders, dragging me in against his chest once more. "I'm sorry, sweetness."

My fingers dug into his shirt. "I didn't kill her, Ren. It—"

"It doesn't matter how it happened," he said, but it did. There was so much I was hiding. "You facing her down was the last thing I wanted for you. That's too heavy," he said. "I know what you're feeling."

My eyes slowly opened. Ren did know. Kind of. His best friend hadn't betrayed him, because he hadn't known he was the halfling, but Ren had been standing on the other side when it came to someone he cared about.

And he was doing it again now, but had no idea.

My mind raced back to earlier in the evening. I'd been seconds away from telling Ren the truth, but I'd stopped. Henry's appearance and what had just happened with Val didn't change anything else. I pulled back, clearing my throat. "So, what did Kyle want?"

Ren's gaze moved over my face as he tucked back a few loose curls. "He wanted to talk about the halfling and plans to try to ferret out some of the fae. See if we could capture one of them and get them to point us in the right direction, but with Val . . ."

My heart was pumping again. I had no idea how many fae knew what I was, but there was a good chance a lot did. There was no escaping any of this. If what just happened with Val had taught me anything, it had taught me that. "She wasn't the halfling, Ren."

His brows knitted. "I know Kyle thinks—"

"I'm the halfling," I whispered.

Chapter Fourteen

Oh my God.

There. I'd said it. I'd told the truth—an earth-shattering truth while standing in front of some building that was most likely a bar.

Ren's brows were raised and his full lips were parted. Several seconds passed while my heart thundered in my chest. "What?" he said finally. "Ivy—"

"It's me." My voice was shaking as were my hands. "I didn't know until about a week after I fought the prince. I didn't—"

"Stop," he said, holding up his hands. "I don't know why you think that. I don't care what Kyle said in there. Val was the halfling. That makes sense."

"No. No, it doesn't." I took a step back, swallowing hard. Tears clogged the back of my throat, but I needed to pull it together. I breathed through the burn. "What Kyle said earlier is the truth. If Val had been the halfling, they wouldn't have risked her that night to open the gate. She wouldn't have been out here tonight. They'd do everything to keep her safe so she'd be available to the . . . to the prince. It's not her."

"Okay. All right." He thrust a hand through his messy hair. "I can see why you'd believe that, and you've been under a ton of stress, but—"

"It's not stress, Ren. You're not hearing me. It's not some whacked-out theory I've come up with. I don't even understand how myself. You said my parents were in love and there was no evidence of one of them being with someone else. Maybe it was like your friend. I don't know, but it's me." I closed my hands into fists. "It's *me*."

He stared at me, his chest rising sharply. "That's impossible."

Exhaling roughly, I grabbed his hand and pulled him past several buildings and into a well-lit alley that fed into a courtyard. The alley smelled faintly of mold and questionable bodily fluids, but it was the closest semi-private place.

I looked toward the mouth of the alley and saw people passing by, oblivious to what was happening a handful of feet from them. "I know I should've told you the moment I found out, but I . . . I was hoping it wouldn't come to this. That I would never have to tell anyone, and I know that's wrong, but I . . ." My gaze shifted back to him. He was staring at me. "I can't lie to you anymore. Not when they're here. I can't do that to you. I don't want you to be caught off-guard by it."

His lips parted as he took another deep breath.

"I'm sorry," I whispered. "You must be so disgusted with me."

Ren slowly shook his head. "Disgusted? I could never

be disgusted with you."

Hope sparked alive. Was he saying that he still accepted me, even knowing what I was? He wouldn't turn me in and we'd—

"I don't know what's going on in your head, but we can figure this out." He stepped closer, lifting a hand. "Try to get to the bottom of why you think this about you."

Disappointment washed away the hope. He didn't believe me. God. "I'll show you," I said.

His brows knitted together as concern slashed over his handsome face. "Sweetness, you don't have to show me anything."

An ache lit up my chest as I reached down and yanked the thorn stake out of my pant leg. I straightened and angled my body so what I was doing was hidden from the people on the sidewalk. Ren's eyes widened and he shot toward me, but he was too late. I sliced my palm, over the same spot I'd sliced before. Air hissed between my teeth as I glanced up, watching Ren, because I already knew what my blood was going to do. It would bubble and fizz, and even in the poor light of the alley, he'd see it, and that shit wasn't normal to say the least.

Ren jerked back. Stumbled. And I imagined he rarely ever lost his step like that. He paled and his mouth moved without sound.

Swallowing the lump in my throat, I closed my hand as I lowered the thorn stake. "I'm the halfling, Ren."

His stark gaze rose to mine. Those beautiful green eyes were full of horror and a raw emotion I couldn't quite place.

"I'm sorry. So sorry. I just couldn't lie. Not with them here. I'm not asking you to lie for me or to do anything or not to do anything," I rambled on. "I hate to do this to you, because I love you—" I sucked in a sharp breath. Oh no. Those three words totally came out of my mouth. Terror filled me. "Ren . . ."

"You what?" he whispered.

Now my heart was lodged in my throat. I couldn't repeat it. I couldn't say those words again.

His expression changed, and he looked stricken as his gaze moved from my face to my hand. "You tell me that you are this—this thing, and then you tell me that you love me?"

Oh my God.

"How is this . . . ? How have I missed this?" he asked. I didn't know what to say as I folded my arms. The thorn stake pressed against my side, a heavy reminder. His gaze drifted over me as he shook his head. "You . . ."

I couldn't breathe right. Only tiny puffs of air were getting through, and that was doing nothing for me. There was this tearing feeling in my chest I'd felt once before. "Ren, that's not—"

"I just can't." He held up his hand, silencing me. "I can't even process this right now."

Tears filled my eyes.

"I . . . I still need to go talk to David," he said, and my heart stopped. I swear to God my heart stopped in my chest. When he spoke, his voice was rough and abrasive. "He needs to know about what happened with the knight."

I blinked slowly as what he said sunk in. "You're not—"

"I just can't." He took a deep breath. "I can't do this right now."

The ripping feeling increased, gouging open a hole I knew would never be filled. I said nothing as he walked away, leaving me in the alley.

~

I didn't go home immediately. I don't know why. I just roamed around for the next several hours, expecting Kyle or other Order members to spring out from the horse-drawn carriages rolling up and down the narrow streets, or from the insides of the dark, tinted vehicles, and snatch me up as I patrolled the Quarter.

It didn't happen.

I just didn't want them to come to my apartment and take me in, not with Tink there. Maybe that was why I didn't go straight home. But finally I wore myself out, and knowing I was supposed to go home hours before, I called it a night.

I'd crossed paths once with Dylan and then with Jackie, another member, but neither of them hissed "Halfling" and then proceeded to try and kill me. Ren hadn't told anyone yet, or if he had, they weren't making their move. I didn't even care if Dylan and Jackie told David that I was still out. That was the least of my problems.

Every time I heard tires squeal, or someone walked up behind me too fast or too close, I tensed. That wasn't good. I was a mess as I alternated between anger and sorrow throughout the evening. There were no fae to take out my aggression on, which was a damn shame, so I wanted to punch random, innocent people on the streets. Like drive-by throat punches. The messy, violent swelling of emotion was almost too much. And then when I realized how terrible it would be to just run around punching people in the throats, I felt horrible, which was worse.

Then I thought about Val and the pain increased.

And then I thought about Ren.

My heart broke all over again. I loved him—I was in love with him, and he . . . God, he had to hate me now. I kept checking my phone as I roamed the streets, and I didn't even know why. Only a tiny part of me believed I would get a text or a missed call from Ren, a very small, dumb part of me. Of course, every time I checked my phone, there was nothing. But that small part destroyed the rest of me.

It took everything for me to keep walking, to keep looking for fae and not break down in the middle of Orleans Avenue, to not sit on the curb and just sob. I'd never been more relieved when my shift was over and yet reluctant at the same time, because I'd grown so accustomed to Ren coming home with me.

But not tonight.

Probably never again.

I was in a daze during the cab ride back to Coliseum, and when I walked into my apartment the lamp by the door had been turned on. Tink had also kicked the ancient furnace on, so the apartment wasn't freezing, but the whole place smelled of burnt hair and dust.

I lifted the strap of my purse over my head and dropped it on the chair by the door. I looked down the hall and saw that Tink's door was closed. There was no light peeking through the cracks. I walked to my bedroom, quietly closing the door behind me. I placed my phone on the nightstand. I didn't really undress. All I did was toe off my boots and strip off my weapons, placing them on the dresser with the exception of one. I took my pants off, leaving them in the middle of the floor. I brought the thorn stake with me and climbed into bed, placing it next to my pillow.

I didn't sleep.

My eyes were open and I stared into the darkness, not really seeing anything. The hurting in my chest was a very real pain that tripled with every heartbeat.

Part of me, as bad as it sounded, regretted telling Ren the truth. If I hadn't, he would be here right now with me, fulfilling all those things he'd whispered in my ear before we left for work. His arms would be around me, making me forget all about Val and her fate. His lips would be on mine, and even though it wouldn't change what I was or what we would have to face, it made it all seem . . . easier somehow. I wouldn't be alone in any of this. We'd be together.

But I would have been lying to him.

I squeezed my hand tight, ignoring the pain in the palm I'd sliced open. Telling him had been the right thing to do, but that didn't mean it wouldn't hurt, wouldn't keep cutting deep. What had Ren said?

This thing.

That was what he'd said I was. A thing. Maybe he hadn't meant it, was just lost in the moment, but he was right. I wasn't really even fully human. I was a thing, and I'd been an idiot.

Why did I even fool myself into thinking we'd had a chance? The moment I found out I was the halfling, I should've known right then. I should've ended things and walked away from him. Actually, I should've never gotten with him in the first place. I'd always known this wouldn't end well. I'd resisted and I'd pushed him away, but in the end I'd caved, and now look at me.

I closed my eyes, trying to breathe through the burn crawling up my throat and crowding my eyes, but it wasn't working. Tears fell, and the moment that happened, I knew I'd lost all control. The tears quickly turned into sobs, the kind that shook my entire body. I smacked my hands over my face, smothering the sounds.

This, oh God, this was a familiar feeling. I'd felt this before after Shaun. It had been different, because there'd been a lot of guilt mixed in with the pain, and Shaun had died. Thank God Ren was still out there, but what I was feeling right now was just as intense.

And it ripped my heart to shreds.

I hadn't known Ren as long as I'd known Shaun, and even though Ren and I had messed around, we only had that one night and morning. There was so much we didn't get to experience together. The same with Shaun. His life had ended because of my stupid mistakes before he got a chance to really live. And Ren?

The truth was, things were over between Ren and me before they really ever got started, and I didn't know who I was crying for more. If it was for me or for what Ren and I never really had a chance to find, or if it was over Val.

Chapter Fifteen

Waking up Tuesday morning hurt skin deep and further down, into the bone and muscle. My eyes ached and my temples pounded from the lack of sleep and the crying. I'd cried so much last night that I was sure there were no tears left in me.

I rolled onto my back, staring at the ceiling, and drew in a deep, even breath. My face felt crusty. That was gross, maybe even a little bit pathetic. Not that crying made you weak or pitiful. Once upon a time, I used to think that, and then I grew up.

But I had gotten the tears out. Even though my chest felt like I'd driven a stake through it and all I wanted to do was plant my face in the pillow, I couldn't.

I was hurt. I was grieving Val. I was heartbroken, but I couldn't wallow in any of it.

There was too much to do, and I didn't know how much time I'd have. At any moment, the prince—Drake—could reappear, and while I was convinced of my badass ninja skills, I knew I wouldn't win a battle against him. Not yet at least, especially with how easily he . . . he had taken care of Val last night. I hadn't even seen him move. If he came to take me, I'd be gone.

And who knew if I would be turned over to the Order or the Elite by Ren? They could come for me at any second, even if . . . even if Ren didn't turn me in. This Kyle guy could figure it out all on his own, because he knew the halfling hadn't been Val. So there wasn't time to waste.

I needed to check in with Brighton to see if she had discovered anything about the supposed communities of good fae. I needed to fill out a stupid report even though going to the headquarters felt like I'd be walking into the lion's den with meat hanging around my neck. Paying a visit to Jerome was also on the list.

I also needed to go withdraw from classes.

Time to get moving.

With a low groan, I rolled over onto my side and swung my legs off the bed. My thoughts started to drift toward Ren as I undressed the rest of the way, but I pulled the brakes on that car crash of a thought process. Then Val's face popped into my head, and I had to hold my breath until I felt dizzy. Nope. Nope. A thousand nopes. I was not going to spend a single second thinking about him, Val, or how I felt when I had work to do. Later, when I had time, I'd let myself have those moments again, but until then, I had to keep my shit together.

After showering, I started to walk out to the kitchen in my old, tattered robe, but stopped at the bedroom door. The thing was practically see-through in certain areas, and Tink wasn't this asexual little brownie anymore.

My cheeks heated as I recalled every time he'd

gotten an eyeful. No need to repeat that. Pivoting around, I changed into a pair of worn jeans and a long-sleeved thermal.

Hair half dried, I twisted it up in a knot and secured it as I walked into the kitchen. Tink was standing by the sink, peering down into it. He didn't look up as I walked to the fridge. "You came home alone last night," he said.

I ignored the question as I opened the fridge door and grabbed a Coke.

"And he's not here now," Tink continued. I turned around and realized he had a little stick-looking thing in his hand with a fine thread dangling off the end of it, disappearing into the sink. "Not that I'm complaining. I needed a break from him."

I popped the tab off the Coke and took a drink. Tink had filled the sink up with water. I had no idea what he—

Tink cocked his arm back and moved the stick—no, it was a pole—forward. My eyes widened.

I shot forward, almost dropping the soda. "What the fuck? Tink! Are you *fishing* in my sink?"

He looked up. "Yeah," he said, drawing the word out.

Sitting the Coke on the counter, I slowly approached the sink. "If there are fish in my sink, I swear to God, I'm flushing you down a toilet."

Tink shot me a bored look. "As if I'd fit down a toilet."

"Tink!"

He sighed. "Relax. They're not real fish." Dropping to his knees, he reached into the water and pulled out a small, red plastic fish. "I tried to order real ones from Amazon, but alas, they do not sell them."

I fell back against the counter, breathing a sigh of relief. Thank God for the small things in life.

"So where is Renny Tin Tin?"

Knowing that Tink wasn't going to drop it until I answered the question, I decided to go with the partial truth since I wasn't exactly feeling ready to discuss what had truly happened. "We had a fight yesterday."

"Really?" He sounded way too happy about this as he dropped his fishing pole into the water.

I nodded as I picked up my Coke and took a huge drink that burned my throat. "I don't think he'll be around for a while."

"That big of a fight?" Tink cocked his head to the side. "You . . . you didn't tell him, did you? About what you are?"

There wasn't a moment where I considered telling him that I had, because there was no point in freaking him out. "I didn't tell him."

He studied me for a moment. "Then why did you fight?"

"It's not something I really want to talk about." I finished off the Coke and dumped the can in the trash. I looked over at where he stood as something occurred to me. "Why are you this size now?"

"Why not?" he said, hopping along the edge of the counter.

"Because I know you're not really this size," I pointed out. "So why are you staying small?"

He shrugged. No answer.

As I watched him hop back along the counter, going in the opposite direction, I thought of something else. "What would you do if I died?"

He stopped, one leg raised. His head turned slowly in my direction. "Why would you even be thinking about that?"

It was my turn to shrug. "I've thought about it before,

but just . . . you know, with everything going on, there's a chance. There's always been a chance, Tink. What would you do?"

Tink opened his mouth and then closed it. His wings drooped. "I don't know what I'd do," he said. "I guess I'd have to go find someone else who has Amazon Prime."

"Nice," I said, shaking my head. "Seriously. You'd have to leave here eventually, you know? Take on your . . . um, bigger form. Granted, you won't necessarily blend in that way, but you wouldn't be the size of a doll with wings."

Tink was surprisingly serious when he answered, "I know what I'd have to do, Ivy. You don't need to worry about me."

A weird sense of relief hit me, and I nodded. I started toward the hall and then stopped again. I turned back to him. "Do you want fish? Like, as a pet? Not to fish for in my sink."

His eyes widened into little saucers. "You'd get me some if I said yes?"

"Yeah," I replied, deciding that I would. "I can start you off small. Like with a beta or a goldfish—"

"Can I have a ferret?" he interrupted.

I blinked. "What? No. No ferret."

Tink pouted as he flew over to the table by the window. "What about a cat? Sometimes I see cats out in the court-yard. I watch videos of them on the YouTube. They seem to be . . . sort of mean, and I kind of like that about them."

"Tink, a cat would probably eat you if you stay that size." I paused. "And it would definitely tear one of your wings."

"Nah." He planted his hands on his hips. "I think a cat would love me, especially if you get me a kitten and I raise it."

"Obviously you've never been around a cat," I said dryly. "It doesn't matter if you've raised it—the cat will try to kill you at some point."

His brows knitted together. "I refuse to believe that."

I sighed. "How about a tortoise?"

He rolled his eyes. "What would I do with a tortoise?"

"I don't know." I threw my hands up. "What would you do with a cat or ferret?"

"Pet it. Hug it. You can't do that with a damn tortoise."

"I think you can pet it," I reasoned.

He rose into the air. "I want something fluffy."

I shook my head and turned around. "You know, forget I said anything about this—"

"Nope. Not ever going to forget." He followed after me as I walked down the hall. "I will never forget this. Ever."

I rolled my eyes as I picked up my purse and then went into the bedroom, dropping my phone into my bag and then weaponing up. "Look, if you had a cat, you'd have to take care of it."

"I know that." Tink flew up to the ceiling fan and grabbed one of the blades, dangling from it. "I'd have to get a litter box—preferably one of those self-cleaning ones, and cat toys and—"

As I exited the bedroom, I hit the switch and turned on the fan, grinning when he shrieked.

"That was screwed up!" he shouted as he was flung across the room. "I'd never do that to a kitten!"

"Goodbye, Tink." I closed the door, shutting him out, and stepped out onto the porch.

Cold air immediately greeted me. Holy crap was it chilly. I was glad I'd grabbed a long-sleeved thermal. What the hell was up with the weather? Normally it was still in the eighties during October.

Making my way through the courtyard, I noticed that some of the vines were withering. I slowed my steps, walking up to the wrought-iron fence. Vines were hardy creations. They lasted all year usually, and I'd only seen them affected once during a severe drought. I scanned the length of the fence. The whole network of vines looked dull and frail. And that was weird, because just a few days ago they were flourishing and taking over everything.

I reached out, curling my fingers around a section. The plant immediately shrunk up and then broke apart, scattering into tiny pieces that slipped through my fingers until only a fine layer of dust remained on my hand.

~

After making a pit stop at Loyola to withdraw from classes, which was full of suckage, I called Brighton before I caught a ride over to the Quarter. She was still poring over the maps, and there were many according to her, but none of them were marked with helpful asterisks that identified the places of good and happy little fae.

She still hadn't heard from her mother, and when I told her I was stopping over at Jerome's, she hadn't been exactly hopeful that I'd get any information from him.

I was praying I could prove her wrong.

What other choice did we have if she couldn't find anything in the maps? Especially since her mom was MIA.

Jerome used to live in St. Bernard Parish, but his home was destroyed during Hurricane Katrina. Ever since, he'd lived over in Tremé, in a Creole cottage. Tremé gets a bad rap. Of course there were some grittier areas, but the neighborhood was ancient and beautiful and proud of its heritage. There was more crime over in the Quarter, and walking in Tremé wasn't like you were in Little Woods—an area absolutely devastated due to the storm, and years later still forgotten—or Center City, which could get a wee bit rough.

Tremé had received minor damages during Katrina, mostly due to the raised porches on the old homes, but there'd been a decent amount of work done on the neighborhood. Or at least, that was what I'd been told.

Since I didn't have homemade cake to bring him, I stopped at a bakery on Phillips and picked up a chocolate pie, which I thought was the next best thing, and then hoofed it over to his house.

Jerome's place was small and white with a bright red door and a raised porch. I passed three kids chasing each other on the sidewalk, one of them carrying a basketball. The wood creaked under my feet as I climbed the steps. Shifting the boxed pie to my other arm, I knocked on the door.

"What?" boomed Jerome's voice from inside, followed by a hacking cough.

My eyes widened as I turned sideways. "It's Ivy."

"So?" came the response, but it sounded closer. Kind of.

I bit back a retort. "I came to see how you were feeling."

"Feelin' like I don't want visitors." The door opened, though, and Jerome was standing there in a forest-green robe. He looked haggard as hell. We eyed each other for a moment. Then his gaze dropped to the box I held. Without saying another word, he shuffled aside.

Stepping through the door, I glanced around the living room. I'd known where Jerome had lived for a while, but I'd never been to his place before. The leather furniture screamed single man. So did the game playing on the flat-screen TV.

"Ya look like crap," he said, squinting at me. "Thought ya should know."

"Well, your house smells like dust and Vick's VapoRub," I replied.

Jerome snorted and then coughed as he made his way over to the recliner and plopped down. "Insultin' me while I might be dyin' is a new low even for ya, the red-headed demon."

I rolled my eyes. "But hey, I brought you chocolate pie."

"That goes some distance for makin' up for your rudeness." He adjusted his robe as he said, "Put it on the kitchen counter, will ya?"

That wasn't so much of a question, but I decided not to point that out as I walked the small distance to his kitchen and placed it on the counter next to a sparkling clean coffee maker.

"Where's that boy of yours?" he asked.

Pain pierced my chest as I walked back into the living room. "He's out doing . . . guy stuff."

Jerome shot me a look that was a cross between "are you stupid?" and "why are you wasting my time?" "Heard about Val," he said.

"Yeah." I cleared my throat, not wanting to go there. I sat down on the edge of the couch and placed my hands on my knees. "So, you're not feeling any better?"

That look on his face increased. "Girl, I know ya ain't here to check on my well-being."

"I'm kind of insulted by your lack of faith in me," I said.

"Shit." He laughed and then coughed. "Why ya here?

Did David send ya to tell me to get my ass back to the shop? Because ya can tell him to go shove that—"

"Yeah, no. David doesn't even know I'm here. No one does, actually."

That silenced him, but that wasn't the only change. His right hand slipped off the arm of the recliner, inching toward the crease in the cushion, and I knew immediately what he was going for.

A dagger.

Or a gun.

"Jesus," I said, throwing up my hands. "I didn't come to kill you. What the hell, Jerome?"

His hand stilled. "Ya can't be too safe these days."

That was sad but true. "Look, I'm here for a reason. I have a question to ask you."

Suspicion still clung to his features. "Uh-huh."

I decided not to beat around the bush. "I want to know about the fae who don't feed on humans."

Disbelief flickered across his face a second before his features settled into their typical grumpy position, but I'd seen it. Mother-freaking bingo. I'd seen it. "I don't know what ya—"

"Yes, you do," I went on, leaning forward. "And it's important."

"Ya crazy." He shook his head, looking away. His dark eyes narrowed. "Ya shouldn't be asking questions like that. Ya don't know—"

"I know that the Order worked with these fae before, up until a couple of decades ago, and I know that the Order buried it so deep that no one knows about it."

He was silent for a moment. "Merle's been talkin'."

Excitement rose. "Actually, not really. She's missing."

His gaze shot to me. "What?"

"She's gone. I think she might've gone to one of these communities."

"No way." He shook his head again. "That ain't possible." His slippered foot started tapping. "And not because of the why ya think. Those communities ain't in existence anymore."

Holy crap, I was a bit breathless. Jerome was actually talking to me. "You—so, you're saying that there are communities of fae that don't feed on humans? That are good?"

"I said 'was,' and that means in the past. They've all been . . . dealt with."

I frowned.

Jerome rubbed a thick hand over his forehead. "David don't know about this. This was before he came on as sect leader and was just some boy workin' the streets. Ain't no one around here besides Merle who knows about this. And that's the way it needs to stay."

"Wait. What?"

"All of that is in the past and it ain't a past anyone is revisiting. Sorry to hear that Merle is missing, but she ain't with no good fae. And there ain't nothin' to tell."

"Jerome, please. You obviously know something about these fae." I fought to keep my patience. "What can it hurt by you telling me about it?"

He laughed. "Girl, ya don't know anything."

"That's why I'm here."

"There's nothin' to tell," he repeated.

I counted to ten before I continued. "Obviously there's a lot to tell. There were fae who didn't harm humans at one time. Why can't you tell me about them, about what happened?"

Jerome was quiet.

"You know the knights and the prince came through those gates and—"

"And that got nothin' do with what used to be some thirty or so years ago. They can't help ya, because they ain't existin' no more," Jerome snapped, his voice thick with the cold. "Sorry I ain't got the kind of news ya lookin' for, but it's time for you to go."

"Jerome." My hands curled into fists.

"I mean it, Ivy. Ya need to go. Now." His gaze cut to mine. "Don't make me ask ya again."

I held his gaze. I didn't get it. He knew something. He'd pretty much confirmed that there had been good fae once upon a time, but refused to go into any detail about it and I couldn't figure out why. Why was it such a big deal for it to be known that there were fae who didn't feed on humans?

"Ya know where the door is," Jerome said.

As much as it ticked me off, I knew when it was time to give it up when it came to Jerome. Pressing my lips together, I rose. "Hope you enjoy your pie," I said.

He didn't say anything until I reached the door, and then he stopped me by saying, "Don't go around askin' other people about that either. Heed my advice on it. There ain't nothin' you need to know about any of that."

I didn't respond as I walked outside, closing the door behind me. As I walked down the steps, my phone rang. I pulled it out and saw that it was David. My heart skipped a beat and I willed my voice to stay level as I answered it. "What's up?"

"Is Ren with you?"

I stopped walking. "No. Why?"

"Shit," grumbled David. "He was supposed to come

back and talk with me last night about some shit that was urgent. He didn't show. I called him last night and this morning. No answer. Like he's done dropped off the face of this planet."

Chapter Sixteen

The conversation with Jerome and the whole situation faded into the background. My heart was thumping fast as I stared at my phone. Ren couldn't be missing. Twenty-four hours hadn't even passed since the last time I'd seen him. Granted, the length of time didn't matter, but I refused to believe he had just disappeared. No way. My brain couldn't even process that.

There was a good chance he was taking some unplanned and unapproved leave time after I'd dropped that bomb on him, but would he really not tell David? Ren was too responsible to do that.

As I walked back toward the Quarter, I ignored the way my pulse was all over the place, and called Ren. The likelihood of him answering my call when he wasn't answering David's was slim, but I had to try.

The phone rang and went to voicemail. For a moment, I didn't know if I should leave a message or not, and then told myself I was being stupid. The words tumbled out. "Ren, this is Ivy. I'm calling you because David is looking for you. He's been trying to reach you and you—well, obviously you know you haven't returned his call." Rolling my eyes, I stopped at the corner of St. Louis and Basin. "Anyway, can you call him back? I don't expect you to call me. But just call him back. Please."

Hanging up, I slipped my phone back in my bag and then brushed the fine wisps of hair back from my face. I glanced over at the cemetery. Nervous laughter could be heard as a tour guide regaled them with stories about Voodoo queen Marie Laveau and her daughter.

Acid churned in my stomach like I had drunk bad milk. What if the prince had gotten hold of Ren? The mere thought of that robbed the air from my lungs. Ren could hate me and want to gouge his eyeballs out at the sight of me, but I wanted him to live.

Okay. There was no need to panic right now. I had to go to the headquarters because David reminded me about the stupid report before he'd hung up, but I'd be passing where Ren had parked his truck yesterday afternoon. I could see if it was still there. If it was there, then that . . . yeah, that could be something to get concerned over.

I picked up my pace, and it took about fifteen minutes to get to where Ren had parked. Entering the small, dimly lit garage, I shivered since it was at least ten degrees cooler here than outside. He'd parked on the second level, the top floor. I headed toward the cement stairs. The garage was small, only fitting about fifty cars, but some days it was packed like a can of sardines. Today was one of them. The entire place smelled of gas fumes and body odor.

I rounded the second-floor landing and hurried toward

the back of the garage, walking around the stained pillars as I scanned the row of vehicles. I knew he'd parked somewhere in the middle, but as I reached the back, I didn't see his truck anywhere.

That was a good sign, I told myself as I looked out the dust and dirt-covered window, down to the street below. His truck being gone meant he came back to it at some point last night. The truck being here would have meant he'd never made it back, and there would be very limited reasons that didn't include something horrific for why that would happen.

Still, as I turned around, I wasn't exactly relieved. I took a step and then stopped as I heard footsteps. My gaze swung to the right as my eyes narrowed. My paranoia blew through the roof, and my hand drifted to the dagger concealed at my hip, under my shirt.

A second later, a tall and slender man stepped out from behind a dark green van. On first glance, he looked super normal. Long-sleeved shirt and denim jeans, but within seconds the façade of normalcy faded away, revealing the truth beneath the glamour I'd been warded at birth to see through.

Holy shit.

He was a fae.

There was an actual fae in the garage, and normally this wouldn't be a big deal, but since no one other than my lucky ass had seen a fae since the gate had opened, this was huge.

The fae walked into the center of the garage, his steps slow and measured. He appeared older than most, and his silvery-white hair was shorn short. I unhooked my dagger.

He stopped, raising his hands at his sides in a universal

don't-kill-me gesture, which I knew better than to trust. I tightened my grasp. The fae opened his mouth as if he were to speak.

Another fae appeared at the top of the stairs. Crap. A female stalked forward purposefully. No fae in days and days, and I end up with two of them?

Oh, but I had a lot of pent-up aggression to work out of my system, so this could be a good thing.

The male turned, his arms dropping. "No—" His words were cut off as the female fae rushed forward, her long, icy-blonde hair streaming out behind her. She held something—a dagger, most definitely an iron dagger.

Before I could say a word or do a thing, the female fae slammed the dagger into the gut of the male fae. His surprised shout was lost as his body folded into itself.

"What the fuck?" I stared at the spot where the one fae stood. "What just happened?"

I didn't expect an answer from the female fae, and I sure as hell didn't expect what happened next.

She ran straight toward me. I widened my stance and lifted my dagger, expecting her to try to grab me or take a swing. Nope. She right straight into me, and into the dagger.

My mouth dropped open as I stepped back. Her pale blue eyes met mine a second before she folded into herself, disappearing. Her dagger clanged off the floor, and I stood there, mouth gaping so wide people could've walked by and thrown things into it.

The female fae had legit impaled herself on my dagger. She ran right up and into the pointy end.

I looked left and then right.

"All righty then," I murmured.

I sheathed my dagger as I mentally added another

WTF to the ever-increasing list I was now going to officially keep track of.

I bent down and picked up the dagger the female fae had used, then I got out of the garage and walked quickly to my destination. It was Miles who opened the door to headquarters. I barely forced a grimace of a smile in his direction. "Where's David?" I asked.

"Office."

Angling sideways to get inside, because he sure as hell didn't actually step out of the way, I handed over the dagger the female fae had used. "Here you go."

He took the dagger, frowning. "What the hell am I supposed to do with this?"

"Well, most Order members use them to actually kill fae," I replied. "You know, when they go out there and work."

Miles muttered something under his breath that sounded an awful lot like "itch." Grinning, I walked across the common area. David's door was open, and as I approached his office, I saw he wasn't alone. Kyle and Henry were with him.

Ugh.

My weak grin faded.

The three men looked up as I entered the room. "I just saw a fae in the parking garage we use," I told them. "Actually, I saw two of them. One killed the other and the other sort of . . . impaled herself on my dagger."

David blinked slowly. "Come again?"

"Yeah, if you heard what you think I said, it's what I said." I walked further into the room, giving the other two dudes a wide berth. I stopped at the corner of David's desk. "I've seen a lot of weird stuff, but that was . . . Yeah, that took the cake."

"I don't even know what to do with that info," David replied, leaning back in his chair. He glanced at the two Elite members. "You guys?"

"Nope." Kyle eyed me. "Did either of the fae say anything?"

"One looked like he was about to, but the other—a female fae—killed him before he could. She had one of our daggers."

"Thanks to Val, I'm sure," David muttered, and my chest clenched.

"The fae have long since adapted the use of iron for their own in a self-policing sort of way," Kyle replied, casually tossing his arm over the back of the chair. "Though, it *is* rare that they use it against one another."

I glanced at him. Real helpful intel right there.

"It's good that you're here," Kyle added. "Got some questions to ask you."

My stomach dipped. Obviously they couldn't care less about the two fae. "What's up?"

"Last night we were chatting with Ren, and then he left here to meet with you. David advised us that you two are seeing each other," he stated.

I glanced at David, who looked rather bored with the conversation. Then again, he looked bored with everything. I lifted my chin. "Well, I'm also sure Henry told you that since he saw us kissing."

Henry arched a reddish-brown eyebrow. "Still surprised you didn't get pregnant from that kiss. Jesus Christ."

I wrinkled my nose at him, but refused to actually answer the question, because I was sure that Ren and I weren't dating anymore. "You guys still haven't heard from him?"

"No," answered David.

"That's why I was in the parking garage," I explained. "Ren parked there yesterday, and his truck is gone. So he must've gone back there. I was thinking—"

"Ren was asking some off the wall questions last night." Kyle kicked his booted feet up on the desk. "He was asking if we knew anything about fae who didn't feed on humans."

Oh. Oh, shit.

"Do you know why he'd ask something like that?" Kyle asked, his head tilting to the side. "Because that's a strange thing to ask."

Double shit. Instinct told me to lie, but then lying meant I was leaving Ren, wherever he was, out there hanging on his own. He'd done that to me when we'd first met, and I remembered how crappy that made me feel. But telling them about what Brighton had found would turn Kyle and Henry's attention to her and Merle, and there was something about those two I didn't trust.

And I probably didn't trust them because I was the halfling, but whatever.

Plus, I remembered what Jerome had said about talking about that.

So I shook my head. "I don't know why he'd ask that, but Ren's always curious about things."

"Huh," replied Kyle. "What a weird thing to be curious about. Maybe you need to find better ways to occupy his mind."

I started to frown.

"His absence and its timing is strange," Henry stated from his corner. "Do you have any idea where he could be?"

My Spidey senses were tingling now. "No. I mean, I

was thinking about checking his place, but this . . . isn't like him." I looked to David and admitted, "I'm a little freaked out about this."

"Yeah, well—" David's phone rang and he picked it up. "Yeah?" he grumbled, rubbing his hand over his head. I hoped it was Ren, but the way he suddenly stiffened and then stood, told me that if it was, it wasn't good. Several seconds passed. "I'll send a team down there now."

My little ears perked up with interest. "What's going on?" I asked.

He hung up the phone. "Jackie just called. She and Dylan said there was a lot of police activity down at Flux. Several cars. Reporters setting up outside."

"I thought you guys checked that place out," I said.

"We did. There were no fae there when we went," David replied, thumbing through his phone contacts. "This may not have anything to do with fae, but it warrants investigating."

"I'll go." I turned and jerked back, finding Miles in the doorway. God. Was he there the whole time, lurking all quiet-like? Creeper.

"Not you," David called out, stopping me. "I want that report about Val filled out. Now."

I pivoted around. "But—"

"Why is it that I always have to tell you an order is an order?" David walked around his desk, a folder in his hand. "Every single time."

He had a point.

I took the folder from him as Kyle stood up. Henry was the first out, glancing down at my folder. "I'd rather be shot in the fucking head than do paperwork."

Um. Wow. Okay. I hated paperwork too, but that was excessive.

Kyle said nothing as he walked past me. I was half-tempted to toss the folder back on David's desk, but I knew better than to do that.

Under Miles's watchful gaze, I walked out to the common room, plopped down at the table, and picked up a pen. I opened the folder and was about to relive something I really didn't feel like doing at the moment, but stopped when I felt eyes on me.

Lifting my gaze, I saw Miles leaning against the wall, staring at me. I waited a second and decided to make use of the fact that he was being a creep. "Can I ask you a question?"

"If I say no, you still going to ask?"

"Probably." I twirled the pen between my fingers. "The crystal that Val came back and took from here. What is the significance of it?"

One shoulder rose, but there was a forced casualness about it that I didn't trust. "Just a piece of shit gem that doesn't mean much."

"Then why would she come back and take it if it's nothing?"

He shrugged. "Probably because she's a dumbass and thinks it holds some value."

Okay. Yeah, I wasn't believing that for one second, but it was obvious he wasn't going to tell me anything else. I got back to filling out my report, and when I peeked up again, he was still being a creep. I sighed. "What?"

Miles smiled, but it didn't reach his eyes. "You and I don't really know each other."

I tilted my head. "To be honest, no one really knows each other in the Order."

"Except you and Val. You two knew each other fairly well, and she betrayed the Order and is now dead." He pushed off the wall, approaching the table. "Fell off a roof. Huh."

There wasn't a single part of me that missed the fact that he *didn't* refer to Val as the halfling.

"*And* you're close with Ren. You two are dating." He sat in the seat across from me, which sucked, because that meant he wasn't planning to leave anytime soon. "And now he's MIA. An Elite member missing. That's odd."

I dropped my pen. "Where are you going with this, Miles?"

"Nowhere, really. Just thinking out loud."

"Can you not do that?"

The chair squeaked as he leaned back. "You know what else I can't not do?"

"I don't know," I replied. "Your double negative is confusing as hell."

"I can't shake this feeling I've had for about three years that there is something very, very off about you."

My breath caught as our gazes locked.

"David trusts you. He even likes you." Miles's stiff smile slipped from his face. "I don't know why, but I don't trust you, Ivy."

I didn't look away as I tensed, but hey, good to hear David actually did like me. "Well, thanks for letting me know your personal, irrelevant opinion of me. I appreciate it."

"You're welcome," he replied, smirking. He leaned forward, placing his elbow on the table. "I'm going to be real cliché as hell, too. I'm keeping my eye on you, Ivy."

Chapter Seventeen

I finished my report, which was just a generic breakdown of events leading up to Val's death, under the watchful eye of Miles. I managed to ignore him and not spin kick him upside the head when I left. I pushed the episode with him to the back of my mind. I had other things to stress over.

Namely Ren.

The prince.

The fact my womb was a walking time bomb.

I caught a ride over to the warehouse district, to Ren's place. As I rode the industrial, cage-style elevator up to his floor, I worked through the multiple scenarios of how this could play out. If Ren wasn't here, I didn't know what to do next other than scouring the streets for him, but I knew I'd have little luck. After living in New Orleans for three years, I knew the streets could swallow people whole. And if Ren was at his place? Oh gosh, I'd probably just cry out in relief, hug him, and then scamper off. If he was at his place, avoiding David and my calls, he didn't want to be found.

My heart was bouncing all over as I walked up to his door. My hand froze as I went to knock on it. Fear held me still. Ridiculous. I could face down a pack of rabid fae, but I was too scared to knock on Ren's door?

I rolled my eyes.

Rapping my knuckles on the steel, I stepped back and waited . . . and waited. I knocked again and waited probably five minutes. Nothing. Either he wasn't in there or he spotted me through the peephole and wasn't answering. Either way, I felt sick to my stomach.

I gave up and went back down the elevator. Outside his apartment, I fought to not give in to the panic building in my stomach. I needed to refocus, and since I was close to Flux, I decided that was better than nothing. And it would totally be worth David's glare when he saw me.

It took me about fifteen minutes to get to the stretch of newish buildings and old warehouses converted into clubs and restaurants. There was no missing the fact that some serious crap had gone down at the club. Blue and red lights lit up the street, casting alternating colors along the shiny windows of the nearby buildings.

My steps slowed as I neared Flux. Yellow police tape spanned the area, roping off the entrance to the club. Reporters were being kept at bay by several police officers. I scanned the crowds but didn't see David or any other Order member. Remembering the back entrance where Ren and I saw the fae talking with the officers, I skirted around the crowd and cars and headed for the alley.

Walking past the stone benches and potted plants, I stopped and peered around the corner. Several dark SUVs blocked the doors. There was a back entrance where food service and staff entered. One that I doubted would be easily—

"Hey."

Swallowing a yelp, I nearly came out of my skin as I whipped around. Glenn stood behind me, dark brown eyes wide and brows raised. "Holy crap, are you part ninja?" I exclaimed. "I didn't even hear you walk up behind me."

"It's called being quiet," he replied, grinning. "I'm pretty good at it."

"I'll say."

He stopped beside me. "Whatcha doing?"

I turned back to the loading area. "I was hoping I could sneak in the back and see what the hell is going on in there."

"It's a freaking horror show."

"You've been in there?"

Glenn nodded. "Got here when David put the call out. Haven't seen anything like it. Seriously." He lifted a hand, rubbing it over his skull. "You don't have to sneak. Only members are inside, and a handful of detectives that David knows."

"Crap," I murmured. If the police were here and most of them were outside while only members and the cops who knew about us and the fae were inside, this was some serious stuff. "Let's go."

Glenn led the way to the doors where the SUVs were parked. "So where are you from?" I asked, realizing I knew very little about him.

He looked over his shoulder at me. "You're the second person to ask me that."

I glanced around. "Oh?"

"Yeah. You and Ren."

"Oh," I said again, much lower this time.

A handsome grin appeared on his face. "I'm from New York City. It's taking me a bit to get used to this place."

"I've never been there. Always wanted to see it though." We walked around one of the SUVs. "I'm originally from Virginia."

"So the summers are as bad here as I've heard?" He opened the door, holding it out for me. "I was expecting it to be warmer by now. Sort of feels like I'm still in the north."

"Yeah. The weather right now is a little weird."

Glenn stepped around me and led the way down a narrow hallway with several closed and opened doors. A break room. A door marked "Manager." A storage room that was open, with liquor bottles everywhere.

"I'm not sure what you've seen before. I'm guessing you've seen some crazy stuff since we all have, but this . . ." He trailed off as he stopped in front of a gray door with a small window. "Yeah, this is something else."

Unsure of what I was preparing myself for, I walked through the door he opened and made it a couple of steps before I came to a complete stop. Horror rose within me, robbing me of the ability to speak or even think.

The house lights were on, glittering like sharp diamonds. I spotted David standing next to Miles and Henry. Dylan and Jackie were standing near what used to be the shadowy corners. And then there were detectives staring up, and I had to wonder if they had ever seen anything like this before.

People hung from the ceiling.

Humans.

Their bodies were swaying like branches in the wind.

People were scattered across the floor.

Their bodies left behind like discarded trash.

Some were nude, and some were fully clothed. They looked like staff. The men were in black slacks, and some were still wearing white uniform shirts. Others were bare-chested. Some women wore slinky black dresses. The closest body to me belonged to a female. She had one high heel on her foot. For some reason I looked down to see if I could find the other shoe, and I don't even know why that was important, but I looked and then I saw her.

It was the waitress I'd seen the night Ren and I had come to Flux. She'd been serving Marlon and the ancient whose blood had opened the gates. I'd suspected she'd known what they were, based on her wariness around them, and how she seemed to know that she was about to be fed on when the ancient had grabbed her. Now she was dead and cold on the floor, staring up at the dazzling lights.

They were all dead—dozens and dozens of humans. Some hanging from the ceiling. Others splayed across the floor and in between tables and chairs.

And all of them had been fed on until there was nothing left but pale skin and tainted, darkened veins.

~

It was late Tuesday night when I got home. Tink was asleep, or at least that's what I guessed he was doing, because his door was closed and no sound was coming from inside. But I was too disturbed to sleep.

I sat on the corner of the couch, wrapped up in the soft chenille blanket. The TV was on, the volume turned down low, and I had no idea what was being said or what was happening.

I couldn't un-see what I'd seen in that club.

As long as I lived, I would never forget the sight. Glenn had been right. I'd seen a lot of crazy and messed up stuff, but nothing ever like this. So much death—senseless death.

Even David had been unsettled, and it wasn't because he couldn't hide that many deaths from the public. The detectives were going to spin it as some kind of cult—mass suicide or something—but people weren't stupid. Some were going to be seriously suspicious, but they'd never believe the truth anyway.

I'd overheard Kyle say he'd seen something like this before once in Dallas, where the fae had turned on the humans that had served them for one reason or another, feeding on all of them until they were gone. That too had been pawned off as a cult offing themselves because a comet hadn't shown up or something.

I didn't understand why this had happened. The fae didn't need humans for anything other than food, but having their assistance in some areas had to be helpful. Why would they kill them, and why now? There were too many questions.

Before I left, I'd closed the waitress' eyes, and on the way back to my place I'd called Ren. There was still no answer, but I didn't leave a message for him this time.

Ren's face blurred with the waitresses' and back again, and instead of seeing her, I saw him, lying on his back, his beautiful green eyes dull and unfocused, all life gone from them. Once that image was fully implanted in my brain, I couldn't get it out.

Hours passed, and I might've dozed off, but it felt like

I blinked and then it was morning and Tink was sitting on the arm of the couch, a few inches from my face. And not tiny Tink. Oh no. This was full grown Tink . . . in pants.

A hell of a way to wake up.

I jerked into a sitting position and drew back, staring up at Tink dumbly. "You're . . . people-sized."

He cocked his head to the side. "There's something about using the word 'people-sized' that just sounds offensive."

My gaze dropped. "And you're wearing jeans."

"You like them?" He looked down at himself and nodded. "Got them off of Amazon. They were something called True Religion."

"You . . . you bought True Religion jeans?"

Tink batted his blue eyes at me. "They were like two hundred dollars, so I figured they were good jeans."

I stared at them and plopped down on the other end of the couch, planting my face into the pillow.

"I thought you'd be happy about the fact my junk isn't hanging out," he said.

I closed my eyes.

"And here I thought I was doing a good thing." Tink paused. "I guess I could go naked—"

"No."

There was a moment of silence. "I think I have a rather attractive form when I am small *and* tall. I also think that most women and a lot of men would be more than happy to see me naked."

I closed my eyes.

"You should be happy," he continued.

I grimaced.

"Because I'm quite attractive," Tink added. "Just in case—"

"I get it, Tink."

"Goody gum drops." Another pause. "Why are you sleeping on the couch?"

I didn't answer.

Tink nudged my leg with his hand, which felt weird because he was people-sized. "Are you and Ren still fighting? If so, there's a chance you might want to see my junk."

I pried one eye open. "I don't want to see your junk *again*, Tink."

"Huh," he said.

Several seconds passed and then I said in a scratchy voice, "A whole bunch of people were killed last night. They were fed on until they died, and some of their bodies were hung from the ceiling."

"Whoa," Tink said. "That's a buzzkill."

"Yeah," I murmured, sucking in a deep breath. "And Ren is missing."

"What?" Tink shrieked, startling me. I sat up and he jumped—all six and a half feet of him—onto the coffee table. He crouched there, on the edge in a feat of anti-gravity. "What do you mean he's missing?"

I broke it down for Tink, skipping the whole "telling Ren what I was" part and ending with, "I don't know what to do."

Tink hopped down and sat on the coffee table. "I don't know what to tell you. I mean, who knows? Maybe he's off licking his man wounds? Or maybe the prince has captured him. Both make sense. Ren's his competition."

My heart flopped over in my chest as I rose, unable to sit or be in the apartment any longer. My muscles ached from sleeping in a cramped position. "That's not helping," I said.

"Sorry?" He stood. "I'm really not good at saying sorry

and sounding like I mean it, but I *do* mean it."

I walked around the couch and stopped by the bedroom door. "I get it."

Tink followed behind me. "Would now be a bad time to talk about getting that kitten you—"

Shutting the door behind me, I walked into the bathroom. I showered and changed in record time, gathering up my wet hair and securing it in a knot. I grabbed my weapons and walked back out.

Tink popped up from the couch. "You're leaving already? It's like nine in the morning."

"I know." I walked to my purse. "I just can't sit in the house. I need to be out there."

"Doing what?"

That was a good question and something I'd thought about while I showered. We had some intel at headquarters on possible locations of fae cells—homes where we had evidence fae lived. Places we kept an eye on, but hadn't raided because we weren't a hundred percent positive fae actually lived there. I was *this* close to knocking on their doors.

"You're going to do something dumb, aren't you?"

"No." I picked up my bag and draped it over my shoulder. "I'm just going to go out."

Tink leaned over the back of the couch. "I can go with you."

I raised an eyebrow as I picked up my keys.

"Not like this. I haven't gotten around to buying a shirt yet, but I can make myself small and you can put me in your purse," he offered.

"I am not putting you in my purse."

Tink folded his extremely well-muscled arms over an extremely well-defined chest. "It could work. I can help you look for Ren."

I walked to the door. "Maybe next time." I stopped, thinking of something I should've done a long time ago. "Order a new phone from Amazon for me, one that comes with an answering machine."

Tink wrinkled his nose. "Why? I don't use the house phone."

I exhaled noisily through my nose. "I know, but I can call it and leave you messages. Like if I'm running late or if there's a problem."

"Oh." His gaze roamed to the ceiling. "Good idea. I bet I can one-hour that shiz. Let me see." He started toward the kitchen, and I couldn't, God help me, couldn't help but notice how low his jeans hung and that he really had a—oh God, no! I blinked tightly as Tink itched at his scalp. "I just realized I've never used the home phone to call you before. I could have kept tabs on you. How have I not thought of that?"

"Guess my luck with that just wore off," I muttered. "Order it, please."

I left before Tink could convince me to bring him with me, which wouldn't be hard, because there was a part of me that kind of wanted to stash him in my purse. With the way things were going down, he was a good ace to have up my sleeve.

I caught an Uber into the Quarter and got dropped off on Decatur. I walked past Cafe Du Monde and crossed the street, entering the park.

It was early enough that it was relatively quiet as I made my way down the pathway. Frost covered the grass, and if it were a couple of degrees cooler, my breath would be leaving little puffy mists.

I really needed a better game plan than busting up on

random doorsteps. I could go back to headquarters and pour over the intel that we did have on best possible places. If I could find a fae that wouldn't kill itself immediately, I could possibly find the prince—find Drake.

I stopped in front of the statue of Jackson and folded my arms around my waist. Maybe that was why I was out here. Maybe, deep down, I came to this park because I'd seen the prince here before. Tink was right. Being out here, hoping to lure the prince out, was stupid, but if Ren was missing, it had something to do with him.

If anything happened to him, I could never forgive myself. I hadn't even really forgiven myself over what had happened to Shaun yet, and that seriously *had* been my fault. I'd made a horrible series of choices that inevitably led to his death, along with my adoptive parents, Holly and Adrian.

I looked up at the statue of Jackson, exhaling roughly. I knew that I hadn't done anything on purpose other than getting close to Ren, but God, I didn't want to go through this again. I didn't want to—

"Ivy."

My heart stopped in my chest. I recognized that voice. I *knew* that voice. Half-afraid it was my imagination, I turned around slowly. My breath caught in my throat, and emotion exploded in me like a Roman candle.

Ren stood behind me.

Chapter Eighteen

"Ren," I whispered, staring up at him, almost not believing he was standing there. Suddenly I was tossed back in time, to the first time I'd seen him.

I'd lay bleeding on the steps of the headquarters from a nifty little gunshot wound, and I'd thought I was seeing things. He'd reminded me of one of the angels painted on the ceilings of old churches. It sounded ridiculous, but the classic hard line of his jaw and those chiseled features had been almost perfectly pieced together. Even the mess of curly waves was like the painted angels I'd always been fascinated with. I'd seen a ton of hot guys before, especially since moving to New Orleans. Sometimes the city was a melting pot of hotness, but Ren could hold his own compared to a fae, and that was saying something.

He reminded me of that now, standing before me like an avenging angel.

My heart pounded so fast that I felt sick, and I spoke

the first thing that came to mind. "Where have you been?"

Ren stepped closer, so that he was standing under the shadow of Jackson with me. "I've been around."

"David has been trying to call you. I've called. I thought . . ." I took a deep breath, willing my heart to slow down, but nervous energy had taken over. Standing in front of him now that he knew I was the halfling was seriously overwhelming. "I thought at first you just disappeared because of what I told you about myself. And then I feared that the prince had taken you—oh God, I haven't even told you about all of that." I winced. "I was going to tell you. I swear, but you left after I told you about me being the halfling, and I didn't get the chance to tell you everything."

"Ivy—"

"I saw the prince twice. He was actually here, just outside the park, the first time I left the apartment, and he showed up when I chased Val." I rushed on, needing to get it all out before he uttered another word. "He was the one who killed Val, Ren. He knocked her right off the rooftop like she was nothing but a discarded . . ." I sucked in a sharp breath. "Like a piece of trash. Then you came to see me, and I'd planned on telling you the truth earlier in the evening before Henry interrupted us. I couldn't go another second without you knowing, so I told you and then you disappeared—"

"Ivy." His hands, cool from the morning air, cupped my cheeks, silencing me. Ren was touching me. He was actually touching me despite what he knew. "It's okay."

I had to be hearing things. "I don't understand."

He smiled crookedly. "What don't you understand?"

Wanting to return the touch but unsure of his reaction even though he was touching me, I made fists at my sides.

"I'm the halfling, Ren." My voice was low. "I'm this . . . this abomination."

His head tilted. "You are not an abomination."

My breath caught. "You can't mean that."

"I do."

Disbelief thundered through me. "That doesn't make sense. You know what being a halfling means. I'm not even completely human. The prince wants to knock me up to have an apocalypse baby—"

"I wish you would stop calling it that." His brows furrowed.

"But it's true." I stepped back, and his arms fell to his sides. "I mean, I'm still Ivy, but I'm also this . . . this *thing*, and you came to New Orleans to find the halfling. How can this be okay? Especially after what happened to your friend when you were growing up? And now that Kyle and Henry are here, members of the Elite who know that Val wasn't the halfling, how can any of this be okay?"

His emerald gaze flickered over my face. "Because I will make it okay."

Ren said it so simply that I almost believed him. I opened my mouth, but there weren't any words, so I just shook my head. I didn't understand how he could make it okay.

Ren reached for me. "Ivy—"

I held up a hand, warding him off for reasons I didn't fully understand. "You called me a '*thing*' after I told you that I loved you, and then you left me standing on the street. And look, I'm not really even judging you for that. Yeah, it was kind of shitty, especially since you disappeared afterwards, but I dropped a massive truth-bomb on you. So I get why you needed time to deal with everything, but I don't get—"

Ren moved fast, curling one hand around the nape of my neck, and before I could take my next breath, his mouth was oh-so close to mine. "I shouldn't have reacted the way I did, but I was shocked," he said. "Now I've had time to think about it and everything will be okay."

It was like my brain had shut down and I'd lost all critical thinking abilities, because I heard what he was saying, but I couldn't believe what I was hearing. There had been a tiny part of me which had hoped Ren would accept what I was when I told him, but I had recognized how foolish and naïve that was. Our duty had been ingrained in us since birth. To Order members, fulfilling our duty was the most important aspect of our lives, and with Ren being an Elite, even more so.

I could hope all I wanted, but reality was . . . well, it was the cold, harsh truth that was inescapable.

"Are you hungry?" he asked.

I blinked. "What?"

"Would you like to get something to eat?" Ren drew back and a half-grin appeared on his face.

All I could do was stare at him.

His grin increased, but I didn't notice any dimples. He reached down and took my hand. "Let's eat."

In such a state of shock, I let him lead me out of the park and across the street to Cafe Du Monde. I stood there when we got in line, painfully aware of his cool hand wrapped around mine. When I looked up at him, I found him staring at me, and I was pretty sure he hadn't stopped doing that since he'd said my name.

"Is this some kind of joke?" I asked.

His brows furrowed. "I do not see how since I'm not sure why this would be funny."

A plug was sealing off my throat as I whispered, "Okay.

Is this some kind of plan then? You pretend everything is okay and then hand me over to the other Elite members?"

Ren shook his head and leaned over. His lips were close to my ear. "This is not a trap, Ivy. And the Elite will never get their hands on you."

I started to respond, but that plug had completely cut off my ability to speak, so I nodded and then stared straight ahead, tears blurring my vision. Was this really happening? Ren was here and he forgave me? Everything was okay, and we were going to order some beignets?

Apparently that was what was going to happen. We ordered beignets for takeout and a bottle of water to share. There was a table open on the pavilion, which was another oddity that I had to chalk up to the mere presence of Ren.

I watched him open the container and pull one of the beignets apart. All of this was incredibly surreal, like I'd wake at any moment and be devastated to discover this was just a dream.

It took several minutes for me to be able to trust that I could speak without breaking down. Even after waiting and finding something sort of normal to talk about, my voice was hoarse. "Have you . . . checked in with David?"

He shook his head. "I will later. He's not really my priority right now."

I widened my eyes. "He's so not going to like the sound of that."

"I cannot say I care." Another quick flash of a grin.

Oh, he was going to care when David laid into him. "What about Kyle? Henry? He—"

"They're not really my concern either." He paused as he held the pastry between his fingers. "Are you going to eat?"

Feeling out of it, I snatched up a beignet and took a bite. Of course, powdery sugar exploded everywhere, but I barely tasted the fluffy piece of heaven.

Ren took a bite of his beignet and his face twisted with disgust. He turned and pitched it into a nearby trashcan.

"Was there something wrong with your beignet?" I asked, brow raised.

He brushed the powdered sugar off his fingertips. "It didn't taste right."

I chewed mine and paid attention to it this time. "Mine's fine."

Ren shrugged. "Didn't like it."

"That . . . that is sacrilegious."

One side of his mouth quirked up. "I can think of a lot more interesting and naughty things that would be considered sacrilegious besides throwing away a beignet."

I warmed at his words but was hesitant. I finished eating my beignets, then took a gulp of water.

Ren took the bottle. "You done?"

I wiped my mouth with a napkin and nodded. Ren downed the rest of the water, and that too went into the trash. We rose and walked out to the sidewalk. Nerves were riding me hard. This seemed all too easy, too perfect. "Are you sure you're okay with what I am and everything . . . everything else?"

His gaze found mine and he took my hand, drawing me close. "I told you, Ivy. I've thought about everything. I've made . . . peace with it." He paused, holding my cheek with his other hand. "You don't believe me?"

"I do." I *wanted* to. "It's just . . . I really thought you'd be disgusted with me." I lowered my gaze to his chest. "I thought you'd be so repulsed."

"I could never be repulsed by you." His hand slid to the

back of my neck and he squeezed. "I wish you would not think that."

I felt like a broken record. "But you work for the Elite. It's your duty—"

"I don't care about my duty. Not when it comes to you."

I started to speak, but he lowered his head, and every concern I had vanished as his lips neared mine. Ren was going to kiss me, and I hadn't thought that would ever happen again. That we would be standing here like this. Our breaths mingled and our mouths hovered for a few precious, heart-pounding seconds, and then he was kissing me. He tasted of sugar and . . . winter mint, and as the kiss deepened, he pulled me even closer. So close that I knew we had to be drawing stares from those around us.

"Let's go somewhere." Ren's lips brushed mine. "So we can be alone."

My heart was beating all over the place, because I figured going somewhere to be alone meant he wanted to expand on the whole naughty thing he'd mentioned earlier. We had time. We weren't due into work until that evening, but Ren really should be checking in with David.

"What do you say?" he asked, kissing me again and scattering my thoughts once more. "I just want to be alone with you right now."

I wanted to be alone with him, too. As crazy as all of this was, it was what I needed—we needed. "Tink's at my place."

"What?"

"Well, of course, he's always there," I said, realizing how stupid that announcement was. "He actually wanted to come out and help look for you. I think he was being kind of genuine, which is a pretty big step," I rambled on, suddenly feeling like Ren and I had just met. And maybe it was really like that, because now he knew what I was. There was nothing hidden between us. "He wanted to hide in my purse, but I figured the last thing I needed was getting caught with a brownie in my bag."

Ren's gaze sharpened. "Let's not go to your apartment."

"Your place then?" When he nodded, I ordered myself to remain cool and not break down in giddy hysterics. "Where'd you park?"

"Didn't park," he answered.

"No truck or motorcycle?"

Ren shook his head.

I stared up at him, brows furrowed. Why in the world would he take a cab or public transportation when he had his own vehicle? "Did you take a cab or something?"

"Didn't feel like driving," he replied, smiling at me. Still no dimples. "Had a lot on my mind."

That was understandable, but also didn't really answer why he hadn't driven in a way that actually made sense. "Let's head further down on Decatur," I said. "It will be easier to catch a cab there."

We did just that, catching a ride over to his place in the warehouse district. I did most of the talking while Ren did most of the . . . staring. His eyes were on me the entire time. That was not an exaggeration. I squirmed in the backseat of the cab, flustered and a little unnerved. His quietness was a little bizarre, but he had to have a ton of things going on in his head.

When we arrived at his place, he paid the cabbie and then we were riding up the elevator, and before I knew it, we were inside his flat.

I hadn't even seen him unlock the door. That was how out of it I was, how caught up in my own head. This all felt like a dream.

Ren tossed his keys onto the coffee table, so obviously he had unlocked the door. "Want anything to drink?" he asked.

I shook my head as I unhooked the daggers at my waist, placing them on the coffee table next to my bag. Then I sat down on his couch. "I'm fine."

"You're nervous," he pointed out, dropping into the seat beside me. "I don't want you to be nervous."

"Is it that obvious?"

"Yeah." He glanced up at my messy knot. "I get that things have been . . . tough recently."

"Tough?" I laughed, sliding my hands along my knees. "I'm just . . . I don't know. I keep thinking this is some kind of dream. That sounds stupid, doesn't it?"

"It's not stupid." Ren twisted toward me, placing his hand over mine. "I left you without giving you a chance to fully explain. I dropped off the map. It was wrong, especially after what happened to your friend."

"Yeah, that was kind of . . . dickish."

Ren's eyes shone like cut gems. "I overreacted. Trust me, I regret it."

"You do?"

"More than you will ever know," he said.

I took a deep breath that felt like it went nowhere. "How are we going to make this work?"

"I don't know," he answered. "But I know we will."

There was a lot to be said. A lot. I felt like my brain was cycling on repeat, but when he leaned in, pressing his forehead against mine, I closed my eyes and let myself just be here, in this moment, with the man I'd fallen deeply in love with.

I gripped Ren's arms, and I don't know how I ended up on my back, but he was over me, and the tips of his fingers were trailing down the side of my face and over the curve of my jaw. I was finding it hard to breathe.

Ren brought his mouth to mine. The kiss didn't start off slow. He nipped at my lower lip, causing me to gasp. As my lips parted, he took full of advantage of that. He still tasted of mint, and as his tongue curled around mine. I reached up and dragged my hand through his messy, silky hair.

A thousand questions were whirling in my head. There was so much we needed to talk about, but I couldn't think beyond the way he felt and tasted, of how his body felt on top of mine.

I jerked when his cool fingers coasted over the skin of my stomach and up my side, to the strap of my bra. His lips left mine, trailing down my neck. Eyes closed, I tipped my head back, giving him more access. His hand closed over the cup of my bra, causing my back to arch. My hips rose out of instinct, moving restlessly against him.

I paused, my eyes fluttering open. I didn't *feel* him, which was odd, because for Ren there was normally no hiding how interested he was, and he was *always* interested. Was he really into this or—Oh gosh, I stopped that mess of thoughts from continuing, but I planted my hands against his chest. "Do you . . . do you want to slow down?"

"Stop?" He shifted then, sliding a strong leg between my thighs, hitting *that* spot with shocking accuracy. "That's the last thing I want to do."

"You don't—"

His mouth silenced my questions, and he was kissing me again like before, leaving little room for thought.

Ren's hands got involved again, and his touch had warmed, so when I jumped this time it was because his fingers had made their way under the cups of my bra.

"Amazing," he murmured, sliding his other hand down to my hip. He urged me to move, and it really didn't take much. I rocked my hips, riding his thigh as I slipped my hands under his shirt.

His mouth lifted. "Do you want—?" A knock on his front door drew his attention. He turned his head, looking over the back of his couch. A moment passed and then his eyes found mine. "Ignore it."

I was down for that.

Ren's fingers shoved my bra aside. The knocks got louder. His thumb coasted over my nipple.

The banging at the door continued, this time followed by a voice. "Ren, if you're in there, I need you to open this damn door right now."

Vaguely recognizing the voice, I groaned under my breath as I pulled my hands out from underneath his shirt. "You should probably get that."

Ren made a low, growly sound in the back of his throat as he lifted himself up off of me. It was a little scary and kind of hot, even though I wasn't entirely sure he was *that* into what was going on.

He swung his legs off the couch and rose swiftly. I sat up and fixed my bra so I didn't have a boob hanging out, then tugged my shirt down. Ren was by the door when I peered over the back of the couch. He opened it, and I saw immediately why I had recognized the voice.

Henry strode right on in, brushing past Ren. His gaze cut to where I was peeping over the cushion, and he sneered in a way that made me feel like he was a second from spitting on the ground. "Well, that fucking explains why you haven't been answering your damn phone."

Ren shoved the door shut then turned, facing Henry.

"Where in the fuck have you been?" Henry demanded.

"Kyle said you were reliable and that we could count on you. So far the only thing we can count on is you spending your time getting fucked."

My brows rose. "Hi, Henry."

He twisted toward me, giving Ren his back. "Thought you haven't heard from him, huh?"

I smiled tightly, deciding I didn't feel like clarifying that I hadn't heard from Ren until an hour or so ago. I was really beginning to not like this guy's attitude.

"This is bullshit," Henry snapped, his gaze drifting over my face like he could actually see what he'd just interrupted and he was disgusted about it. Now I was feeling pretty insulted. "Ren, you cannot be ser—"

Henry's neck twisted abruptly to the right. I straightened, pushing off the back of the couch as I noticed Ren's hands on either side of Henry's head. Then Ren removed his hands, and Henry folded, smacking to the floor with a deafening thud.

Ren had snapped Henry's neck.

Chapter Nineteen

The sound of bone snapping echoed in my head, bouncing off my skull. A moment or two passed and Ren looked up, exhaling heavily. "He is quite annoying."

My mouth dropped open.

"Well, he *was* quite annoying," Ren clarified as he glanced down. "Not so much anymore."

I exploded off the couch like a detonated bomb. "What the hell?"

Confusion flickered over his handsome face before his features smoothed out. "Ivy—"

"You just broke his neck!" Holy crap. *Holy shit.* I shot around the couch, my stomach dropping to the floor when I saw Henry lying there, arms splayed out, eyes glazed over, his head twisted at an unnatural angle. "You just freaking killed him."

"Yeah," he said. "I did."

Blinking, I tore my gaze from Henry and looked at Ren.

"That's all you have to say? Yeah, you did? Ren," I all but shrieked, "you just killed him!" I pointed at Henry just in case he was confused about who I was talking about. "Holy shit, Ren. Why would you do something like that? I mean, yeah, he was annoying, but you can't just kill someone because he has bad timing." I bent over, grabbing my knees as my stomach churned. "Shit, Ren, we're going to be in so much trouble. So much—"

"He knew what you are."

I stiffened like steel had been dropped down my spine. "What?" I whispered.

"He knew that you were the halfling," he repeated. "He had to die."

Maybe it was the shock of everything—Ren unexpectedly returning and being okay with what I was and then snapping Henry's neck like it was a twig—because I suddenly wanted to laugh, but nothing was funny about any of this.

"How?" I croaked out. "How did he know?"

"I don't know," he answered.

My brows furrowed. "Then how do you know he knew? And if he knew, then that means Kyle knows. And if they know, then how am I still standing here? They've had ample opportunity to come after me." I scrubbed my hands down my face. "They don't seem like the type to wait around."

"They will if they believe you will lead them back to the prince," Ren replied, kneeling at the side of Henry's body. He reached into the pocket of the man's tactical pants and pulled out a cell phone. "After all, they wouldn't want to just take out the halfling."

But taking me out would be an end to one of the major problems we faced. At least temporarily, until the prince located another female halfling. But with me out of the picture, they'd have more time to figure out how to kill the prince. Having a special stake was only going to get them so far.

Ren shoved Henry's phone into his pocket and rose. "I'm sorry that this bothered you, but it had to be done."

I inhaled sharply. Did it? If Henry knew what I was, he was a danger to me. So was Kyle. I got that. I also got that Ren was protecting me, but he'd just killed a man and it hadn't even fazed him.

"I need to take care of the body," he said, stepping over said body. Then he was in front of me. I jerked when he curved his hand around the nape of my neck. "I should do this alone."

I was at a loss for words, my heart beating so fast I felt sick.

"It'll be okay. I promise." He lowered his head, kissing me, but I didn't feel it. My entire being was numb. "I'll catch up with you later," he said.

I found myself nodding and then I slipped free. I gathered up my weapons and started to pass Ren, but he caught my arm. My gaze flicked to his. "You know I had to do this, right?" he asked.

I nodded, even though I wasn't sure of why I was nodding. All I knew was that leaving his apartment was a good idea, because I needed to get out of there and think.

"I'll catch up with you later," he repeated. "You meet me back here?"

"Okay," I managed to force out as I lowered my gaze, staring at his throat.

Ren let go and I beat feet across the room. At the door, I stopped and looked back at Henry's body. All I kept thinking was that this man, this human being, was dead by Ren's hands. Literally. Sometimes humans get caught in the crosshairs when it comes to fighting the fae, and they get killed. Other times a human gets fed on too much, they get out of control, and have to be . . . put down. I hated that—hated that part of my job more than anything, but it happened. This though . . . A shudder rolled through me. This was different. No matter how I wanted to spin it. Whether Henry knew I was the halfling or not, this was in cold blood.

And I never, not even once since the moment I met Ren, had thought he could so efficiently, *coldly,* end another human's life. No way. I thought about the day in the Quarter when the guy was killed in the street and Ren had been unable to save his life. That had gutted Ren. I'd seen it in his eyes. Ren was like me in that way—pained when a human life was lost, unlike some of the other Order members.

But he hadn't even batted an eyelash at this.

~

Once I was out of the warehouse district and standing near Palace Café on Canal, I snapped out of what felt like a bizarre trance. That's how I'd felt since I was at Ren's place. Like I was under some kind of spell and was only capable of walking out of his apartment and getting into a car. My head had been strangely empty, but now as I started walking toward Royal, the numbness vanished. Reality was the chilly wind whipping down the street.

I took deep, even breaths. Okay. What went down back there had seriously happened. Ren had killed Henry and right now he was most likely disposing of Henry's body. My hands opened and closed at my sides. Part of me wanted to vomit a little, but that wasn't going to solve much. I didn't even know what *would* solve this.

Turning onto Royal, I wasn't even sure where I was walking. I just needed to keep my legs moving so I could make this right in my head, because right now everything was the furthest thing from right.

I needed to get the facts straight. Henry was a danger to me. Ren rectified that threat. That was all that had happened. It wasn't like Ren had . . . had murdered someone.

But hadn't he?

I stopped walking and moved until my back was pressed against the cool stone of a building. I squeezed my eyes shut and cursed under my breath. I couldn't make this right in my head. My stomach roiled.

I loved Ren. I was in over my head, under water and drowning in love with him, but what he'd just done didn't sit right with me. I opened my eyes. It didn't match what I knew about him. It would've been one thing if Henry had done something in that moment to prove that he was an immediate danger, but he hadn't.

"Okay," I whispered to myself. "Time to focus."

I might not know how to feel about what Ren had done, but I knew I wasn't okay with it. We needed to talk about it, even though deep down I knew talking wasn't going to magically fix anything or bring Henry back to life. I didn't know what else to do though.

I wish Val were here.

I sucked in a breath as a sharp pang lit up my chest. The truth was, if Val were still alive and she hadn't betrayed us, I would've called her. She'd been the type of friend, or at least I'd believed so, that would hide a body with you and go down in a ball of flames by your side.

But Val wasn't here anymore, and it wasn't like I could call up Jo Ann. That poor girl would have a heart attack. I had to deal with this by myself.

I pushed away from the wall, starting to walk again as I packed away what Ren had just done. If he was right about the other Elite members knowing what I was and using me as bait to lure out the prince, it was no longer safe for me to be here. The ticking clock over my head had sped up.

My phone ringing cut off my thoughts. Digging it out of my purse, I saw that it was Brighton. A flash of guilt caused me to wince. I'd totally forgotten about Merle and everything.

"Hey," I answered, scanning left and right as I stopped at the corner. A police officer was across the street, and a small group of people were huddled in a half-circle. I could see two straight legs on the ground.

"I've found something," Brighton said, her voice pitched with excitement. "Finally, I've found something."

It took me a moment to catch up. Her mom was missing. Community of fun loving faes. Right. "What?"

"One of the old hand-drawn maps of the city shows a totally different city," she said.

I frowned as I crossed the street. "What does that mean?"

"It means exactly that," she said, sounding out breath. "At first I thought I was just looking at a normal map. It has a lot of the landmarks and businesses, but holy crap, you're not going to believe this. They are *everywhere*, and they were right under our noses the entire time."

A horn blew, and I placed my hand over my other ear. "Brighton, you're going to have to give me more detail, because I have no idea where you're going with all of this."

She took an audible breath. "Okay. Sorry. It's just . . . This is big, Ivy. So big."

Laughter spilled out from a restaurant as a door opened, and I sidestepped a slow-moving couple. "Details, Bri."

"It wasn't really the map that caught my attention at first. There are dozens of these hand-drawn things, but one of them had these strange markings in front of certain homes and businesses. They looked like crudely drawn wings, and I remembered seeing the same thing in one of Mom's journals," she explained. "It took me forever to find the journal it was in, but those wings on those buildings symbolize a safe haven for the fae."

I almost stopped in the middle of the street. "Are you sure?"

"That's what it says. Now, we know that the fae obviously have some kind of network in the human world. It's the Order's responsibility to ferret out locations where they're clustered together, but I don't think these locations are the kind my mom wrote about—the good fae."

"Wait," I said. "I don't get it. If your mom knew about these places, then the rest of the Order had to, right?"

"I can't answer that, but that's not all," she added in a rush. "I think I know where my mom is. There's this house—a mansion really—that keeps popping up on all the maps. It has that symbol drawn on it. Mom had circled it on another map, too. I know that's not the best evidence, but I . . . I just have a feeling."

"A feeling?" I repeated.

"Yes. I know it sounds stupid, but I just know that's where she is," Brighton insisted.

I bit down on my lip. The conversation with Brighton was all over the place, much like my life right now, and a "feeling" really didn't mean anything, but she was desperate to find her mom. That meant she would probably go knocking on the door of this house. "Where is this place you're talking about?"

"Okay, so that's the weird part," she said, and I waited. A moment passed. "It can't be where it says it is on the map."

My brows lifted. "Explain."

"I've double-checked and triple-checked the location," she said. "And I keep coming up with the same place. This mansion is located over on South Peters Street."

"Really?" I was trying to think of what was down there, but all I could muster up were images of old warehouses. Definitely no mansions.

Brighton drew in another deep breath. "It's where the Market Street Power Plant is."

My lips parted wordlessly and I paused to think. "That huge, abandoned and creepy-ass building on Peters Street?"

"Yes," she said. "I told you. I've compared the different maps. Some of them show a different city—places that, as far as we know, don't exist. That's what I'm trying to tell you."

That didn't entirely make sense. "Are you going to be home all day?"

"Yes. Where else would I be?"

I stopped beside a delivery truck. "I'm going to swing by. Just promise me you will not go to that plant. Okay? I'll check it out first."

She didn't answer.

My hand tightened around the phone. "Promise me, Bri. There are a lot of crazy things going on right now, and the last thing I need is you getting kidnapped or falling through a rotten floor. I'll be over shortly. Just hang tight, okay?"

Brighton hesitated and then sighed. "Okay."

"Thank you." I started to hang up and then stopped. "I talked to Jerome. He knows something, but he warned me to not poke around about these fae." I kept my voice low as people passed me. "You haven't mentioned this to anyone else, right?"

"Who else would I tell?" She laughed, and it sounded forced. "Everyone already thinks my mom and I are crazy. No reason to give them further ammo."

She had a point. "Okay. I'll be over soon." As soon as I disconnected the call, the phone rang again. This time it was my home number. I answered. "Tink?"

"How'd you know it was me?" he asked.

I rolled my eyes. "Who else would be calling me from inside my apartment?"

"I don't know. People. Ghosts."

"Ghosts?" I turned, walking back toward Canal.

"Maybe they can use phones. You don't know."

"I'm pretty sure ghosts can't use the phone," I replied dryly. "Is there a reason for you calling me?"

He huffed. "I have a reason. I was calling to tell you I set up the answering machine for you."

I'd forgotten all about that. "Thanks."

"And I also might've ordered something else. Okay, I definitely ordered something else. But not from Amazon. You can't get these from Amazon."

"Okay." I picked up my pace, knowing more cabs would be on Canal. "What did you order?"

"It's a surprise."

Oh no. "Tink, I don't like your surprises."

"You'll like this one."

"Doubtful. What is it?"

"You'll see when you come home. Bye!" Tink hung up on me.

I glanced down at my phone, half-tempted to call him back, but figured I didn't have the brain space to deal with whatever he was up to. Catching a cab on Canal, I gave him the South Peters address, which earned me a puzzled look. Whatever. I'm sure the cabbie had driven people to weirder places.

As I stared out the window, I remembered the crack of Henry's neck and winced. What was I going to do about that? I knew I had no intentions of going to David or law enforcement, and I knew that didn't say great things about me. What I needed was more information from Ren about what he knew that led him to believe there was now such a risk.

Traffic was a pain, and it took about twenty-five minutes to get over to the old power plant. The moment I stepped out of the cab, the man tore out of there like an army of bats was chasing him. Guess I was going to have to Uber it back out.

I eyed the sprawling brick building that was several stories high and had many broken windows. I approached one that looked like a basketball had been thrown through the glass, and peered inside.

"Yikes," I murmured, seeing overturned, broken workbenches and chairs. I really couldn't see more than that through the window I was peering into. The place was incredibly dark.

Stepping away, I made my way to the end of the building and down the side. A tall metal fence enclosed the back and obscured most of the rear of the building, but there was no mansion inside. A trailer could fit back here and be hidden. Maybe a single-story home, but definitely no mansion. I walked the length of the fence, looking for a possible opening and not finding one as the scent of the nearby river grew stronger. A narrow alley appeared, and it looked as abandoned as the power plant.

There was nothing here.

Shows a totally different city.

I was going to have to get in front of Brighton and see whatever she was looking at to figure it out. Pivoting around, I hurried back up the side of the building, toward the front as my phone went off again. This time it was Ren. My stomach dropped, a mixture of excitement and unease. "Hey," I answered.

"Where are you?" he asked.

"Um." I glanced inside one of the broken-out windows and saw a flutter of wings. A pigeon. "Nowhere. Where are you?"

"At the apartment. It's been taken care of."

I wrapped my arm around myself, glancing up at the thick clouds as a shudder worked its way through me. That was extraordinarily quick. "Ren . . ."

"What?"

I swallowed hard as I looked around. There was some kind of industrial business across from the old power plant. There were a ton of white utility trucks, but no one was moving about. "We need to talk about what happened."

He didn't respond.

I lowered my chin as I worried the inside of my lip. I needed to go to Brighton's, but I had to take care of this first. "I'll meet you back over at your place, okay?"

There was another gap of silence and then he said, "I'll be waiting."

I hung up the phone and started walking again. I'd taken a handful of steps when I caught a sweet, minty scent that reminded me of Ren's earlier kisses.

I turned and looked over my shoulder. I don't know what I expected to see, but there was no one here, and nothing that could be responsible for the scent. Weird.

It took no time to get to Ren's since the power plant was close to his place. I shifted from one foot to the next the entire ride up the elevator. He opened the door as soon as I knocked, appearing the same as when I'd left, tall and beautiful, and I wasn't sure why I was looking for something different. Like he'd have the words "I killed someone for you" stamped across his forehead.

Ren stepped aside, and I walked in. The scent of coffee was strong in the air. My stomach turned. He'd snapped Henry's neck, got rid of the body, and returned home to make coffee.

So cold.

I stared at him as he closed the door, and the unease in the pit of my stomach doubled. Turning away, I lifted the strap of my bag off my shoulders and placed it on the arm of the couch. I didn't look at the spot on the floor where Henry had fallen.

Ren brushed past me, walking into the kitchen. "Would you like something to drink?"

"No." I followed, keeping my arms at my sides. "What did you do with Henry?"

"You probably don't want to know." He picked up his cup of coffee and took a drink. "No one is going to find him, though."

My gaze flitted to his and then I looked away, shaken by his blasé attitude. "Who are you?" I blurted out.

Ren slowly lowered the cup. "Excuse me?"

"You're freaking me out a little. Okay, a lot," I admitted, placing my hands on the kitchen island. "You straight-up murdered Henry and you're acting like today is just any normal Wednesday."

"I did not straight-up murder someone. He was going to hurt you. So will Kyle. I cannot allow that to happen." He stepped back, crossing his arms. "I am protecting you."

I stared at him. "I get that you were protecting me, but Henry didn't even try anything. I wasn't in immediate danger."

"You would've been. You still are," he reasoned. "And if you're wondering if I will do the same to Kyle, the answer is yes."

My mouth dropped open.

"Why are you so surprised? They *will* kill you, Ivy. Just because they haven't tried anything yet doesn't mean they won't once they realize they can't easily use you to trap the prince."

He had a point, but it was the method in which he had carried it out. And it was more than that, too. This wasn't like Ren. Not at all. Frustrated, I reached across the counter and picked up his coffee mug. "May I?"

"Have at it." He gestured with one arm.

I took a drink and immediately recoiled at the bitter taste. "Whoa." I placed the coffee cup down as I stuck out my tongue. "Holy crap, that is some strong, black coffee."

"It's the way I like it," he stated.

My brows furrowed together. "No, it's not."

Ren cocked his head to the side.

"You like sugar in your coffee, like me. Actually, you usually put, like, six or more packets of sugar in your coffee. You don't drink it black."

His lips parted. "I like it both ways."

"No one likes coffee both ways." Okay, maybe someone out in the world enjoyed coffee both ways, but I'd never met one in real life.

He raised one shoulder. "It's just coffee."

It wasn't just coffee. Something occurred to me then. He'd thrown away the beignets this morning, claiming they tasted bad. I was eating out of the same batch, and mine were fine. Once Ren had been introduced to beignets, he loved them like all people with good taste in fried pastries did. It's like he'd developed a sudden allergy to sugar. And what he'd done to Henry? That wasn't like Ren either. Not the Ren who enjoyed sugar in his coffee and on his pastries, but the Ren who viewed all human life as something precious.

A biting chill slammed into my chest as I took a step back. Deep in my heart of hearts, I already knew. I *knew*, and I was seriously going to be sick. "What was I studying in college?"

Ren blinked those cool green eyes at me. "What?"

My heart started pounding in my chest. "What was I studying at Loyola?"

He laughed quietly under his breath. "Why are you asking that, Ivy? Are you feeling well?"

No. I was not feeling well at all. "Just answer the question, Ren."

The half-smile disappeared, and the iciness spread in my chest. "What did you call me the first time we met?"

A muscle flexed along Ren's jaw as he slowly unfurled his arms. He didn't answer, because I knew he couldn't. There was no way, because this . . . this wasn't Ren.

Chapter Twenty

Heart thundering in my chest, I placed my right hand on my hip, just below where the iron dagger was secured. His gaze flicked to my hand and back up to my eyes. He didn't miss the movement.

Of course not.

Horror rose swiftly as full realization kicked in. This . . . this thing standing in front of me wasn't Ren. It hadn't been him in Jackson Square. It hadn't been Ren kissing and touching me on that couch. My hand shook with revulsion. It looked like him, but it wasn't him, and that meant the real Ren . . .

Oh God.

Pain lanced my chest. "Where is Ren?"

The thing in front of me raised its brows. "What are you talking about? I'm right in front of you."

"You aren't him." I slipped my hand under my shirt and wrapped my fingers around the handle of the dagger.

"Okay." It lifted its hands. "I do not know what's going on in your head, but we can work this out together."

Oh my God, even its speech patterns were different. This thing spoke too formally. How had I not noticed that until now? I unhooked the dagger and braced myself. "Where is the real Ren?"

It stepped out from behind the island, and I tensed.

"Ivy—"

"Don't say my name," I ordered, fingers tightening around the dagger. Oh God, how long had it not been Ren? My stomach twisted like a cold knife had been thrust into it. No. It had to have been him the evening the knight showed up. We made love. I would've known if it was him, and I couldn't focus on that right now. "Tell me where Ren is, or I am seriously going to make this hurt for you before I kill you, whatever you are."

The only creature this thing could be was a changeling, but as far as we knew, none of them had come through the gates since the last time they'd been closed. We'd never caught one before, and according to lore, for a changeling to be in our world, the human they'd taken over was typically in the Otherworld. And that wasn't possible. The gates were closed.

The worst possible scenarios were going through my head as I widened my stance. "You need to start talking *now*."

It lifted its chin and eyed me for a moment. Then a slow, cold grin crept across the mirror image of Ren's face. The thing blinked, and when its eyes reopened, they were icy blue instead of emerald. I sucked in a sharp breath.

"I was hoping you wouldn't catch on so quickly," the thing wearing Ren's face and body said. "Unfortunately, you are more clever than I anticipated."

The thing came forward, and I held up the dagger between us. "Stop," I demanded. "Don't come any closer."

"What are you going to do to stop me?" it queried.

I opened my mouth to tell it that I was going to cut off a very important part of it and shove it down its throat, but the thing leaped at me. I spun out of its way at the last possible moment and jumped back. I swung with my free hand, and it caught my wrist.

"You could've tried to stab me but you didn't." Fake Ren yanked me forward, up against its chest and onto the tips of my toes. "As long as I look like him, you will do nothing to me."

Fake Ren was right. Dammit. Even though I knew this wasn't Ren, I'd swung a fist at it and not the dagger. That folly had cost me. It grabbed my other wrist with its free hand and twisted. Biting pain radiated down my arm and my fingers twitched. The dagger clanged to the floor.

I cursed as Fake Ren let go. Shifting back a step, I brought my knee up, aiming for a sensitive area, but it anticipated the move and twisted. My knee slammed into its solid thigh.

It grunted. "That was not very nice, little bird."

Little bird. My gaze snapped up, and ice shot down my spine. "You," I whispered, and the full horror of what was happening, of what I'd come so close to doing with him earlier, was realized. "Drake."

The prince wearing Ren's face smiled.

Panic blossomed in the pit of my stomach. The prince had the ability to take on another form? I knew he'd appeared as a raven, but a human? I had no idea he was capable of this, and there was no way I could have prepared myself for him masquerading as someone else—as Ren. None of that mattered at the moment, though.

"Where is Ren?" I yelled, yanking myself away.

I twisted as I pulled, putting some space between us. I rocked back, bringing my other fist down, pounding on him and breaking the hold on my arm.

"You are so aggressive," Drake said with a low laugh.

Springing back a step and keeping my eye on the prince, I went to reach for my other dagger. "Where is he?" I asked.

"He's a bit . . . occupied at the moment."

I brandished the dagger and willed my hand to still. "What does that mean?"

Drake continued to smile as he stepped forward.

"Is he alive?" When he said nothing, I almost lost it. "Answer me!"

"The last time I checked." He shrugged one shoulder. "That could change at any moment."

Oh my God. The bubbling panic almost pulled me under. "You better pray he's still alive."

A smirk replaced the cold smile. "And if not?"

I didn't answer. Instinct screamed that I should run, should get as far away from the prince as possible, but he was my only link to Ren—if Ren was truly still alive.

"You have to admit this was impressive," Drake said. "If it wasn't for the stupid cup of coffee, you wouldn't have known."

"I would've figured it out." And I would have. Hopefully before things progressed further than they had already. I should have caught on immediately. There had been warnings that this wasn't Ren from the moment he showed up at the Square. His speech patterns. The fact he hadn't driven. The way he tasted of—oh God—of winter mint. The coolness of his touch.

And the fact that he'd killed Henry without remorse.

"Would you have figured it out with my tongue in your mouth or while I was thrusting between your legs?" he asked. "Because when I fucked you, it would have been me and not this pathetic excuse for a creature."

I didn't think.

Reacting out of pure, unadulterated fury, I launched myself at him, sweeping the dagger in a wide arc. The prince darted to the side, but I'm fast when I'm angry. I caught him over the chest, tearing his Henley and drawing dark, shimmery blood. He might have looked like Ren right then, but he wasn't. I moved to strike again.

Drake made a sound that raised the hairs along the back of my neck. His hand snapped out. One second I was bringing the dagger down, the next I was thrown backward. I hit the wall, but didn't drop the dagger, and before I could move, he was on me.

He caught my right wrist and pushed forward, pinning my arm and body to the wall. "You would have known it was me when you starting coming," he said, his lips glancing over the curve of my cheek. "And you were so close earlier, weren't you?"

Red-hot anger flooded my senses. "I thought it was Ren. *You* disgust me."

"Keep telling yourself that." His teeth caught the fleshy part of my ear, and I shrieked again.

"Let go of me," I growled.

"I do not think so." His head lowered, and I sucked in a shaky breath. A moment passed and he lifted his head, leaving a cold chill racing down the side of my throat. "You want this body and form. I am not sure why, but if this is what it takes—"

The only weapon I had was my head, so I slammed it forward into his jaw. A burst of pain momentarily stunned me. He swore violently, but he backed off. I cocked my arm back and threw the dagger, knowing it wouldn't kill him but would do some damage.

The dagger flew true, embedding itself deep into his chest. A raw curse exploded from the prince as he reached up, grabbing the handle. He tore it out and threw it with enough force that the tip pierced the tile. The handle vibrated.

Oh crap.

Bending down, I reached for the thorn stake. My fingers brushed the smooth length a second before a hand curled around a knot of my hair. The prince yanked me to the side and pushed with enough force that I skidded across the kitchen floor. A burn of pain radiated down my hip.

Drake caught my booted foot and lifted it so high that my back hit the floor. Material ripped as he tore several inches of my pant leg. He gripped the thorn stake and threw it across the room. It hit the wall near the fridge and fell to the floor. He dropped my leg. "You are not stabbing me with that."

Dammit.

I flipped over and leaped to my feet. Standing up, I grabbed the coffee cup off the counter and threw it at him. He dodged it easily. Ceramic and coffee exploded onto the wall.

"Really?" He laughed.

Diving for the stake, I screamed in frustration when his arms encircled my waist. My nails dug into him as he dragged me out of the kitchen. I kicked my legs out, catching the black metal lamp. It fell to the floor, the white shade caving in.

"Why are you even fighting me, Ivy? You know you

cannot win."

Bull. Shit.

I let myself go limp. Drake wasn't expecting that move, and his arms loosened a bit, so I slammed my foot down on his and thrust my elbow back into his stomach.

"By the old gods, you are testing my patience." He dragged me to the right and wrapped his arm around my chest, pinning my arms.

Then I was flying.

I hit the couch and landed face-first in the back cushions. For a moment I was stunned, and then I flipped onto my back. I started to swing my legs, but Drake was there, standing over me and then on me. A heavy hand wrapped around my throat.

Thrashing, I kicked out and beat my fists on his arms. I lifted my hips to throw him, but his weight was too heavy and there was no moving him. The heaviness caused pressure to clamp down on my chest. I went wild, my panicked instinct taking over. I went for his eyes with my nails, but he kept his head back.

Then Drake pressed down, and I felt what I hadn't felt when we'd been on the couch and I thought I'd been making out with Ren, seconds from taking it to the next level. A different kind of terror filled every cell as he lowered his mouth toward mine, stopping just shy of our lips meeting. "I like it when you fight back."

I immediately stopped. "Gross," I spat.

"Shame," he murmured. "But there will be time later."

Forcing myself to go still, I tried to suck in air as I stared up at the prince. He looked like Ren. He sounded like him with the exception of the speech pattern, but this wasn't Ren causing me pain, slowly cutting off my airway. It wasn't Ren turning my insides out, terrifying and infuriating me.

It just looked like him.

It was the cruelest kind of evil wrapped in the most familiar beauty.

His gaze moved over my face as he reached between us with his other hand. He gripped the front of my shirt, and for a heart-stopping moment, I had no idea what he was going to do. Then his fingers wrapped around my chain. He yanked. My body jerked, and then he was holding the necklace—my tiger's eye with the clover enclosed.

My eyes widened.

"I'm going to enjoy this far more than you'll ever know."

Drake lowered his mouth to mine, and I clamped my lips shut. "So difficult," he said, grasping my chin. His fingers dug into my cheeks, forcing my jaw open. The winter mint taste filled my mouth, but he didn't try to kiss me.

He inhaled.

My entire body jerked as an icy burn traveled down my throat and exploded in my gut. He was feeding—oh God, he was *feeding*. With each breath he took, the precious commodity was stolen from me. The feeding was draining, stealing away my energy. A heavy weight settled in my stomach, barb-tipped and razor sharp. It tore through me, and distantly I recalled Val saying it could be pleasant, better than sex. I called bullshit

on that, because it felt like he was sucking out every ounce of my being.

Darkness crept in, crowding out all light and sound, and then it was more than just energy he was stealing. I fought to stay aware in my body. Too much was at stake, but the burn was everywhere, and I was shrinking away from it, pulling myself back. My hands slipped off his arms, and pieces of my will vanished, crumbling away until my body went lax, my arms falling to my sides. I saw the inky blackness filling the veins in my hand, spreading outward.

And then I saw nothing.

Chapter Twenty One

Waking up was like dragging myself out of quicksand. Every time I thought I'd reached the surface, I was sucked back down until I was finally able to pry my heavy eyelids open. Bright light greeted me, an intense warm sunlight.

Was I dead?

I turned my head to the left and saw a large window. Gauzy white curtains were held back by sashes. I quickly deduced that I was, in fact, still alive.

And I was on a bed.

A large bed.

Jerking upright, I gasped as a rush of dizziness nearly dragged me back under. My throat ached, as did several other places. My hip felt like it needed a replacement. I squeezed my eyes shut, counting slowly as everything that had gone down with the prince resurfaced.

He'd been masquerading as Ren.

He'd fed on me.

I opened my eyes and looked at my right hand. The veins there were more prominent and a darker blue, but the black was gone, along with most of the poison. The sluggishness would linger for several hours. That I knew from personal experience.

Ren.

My breath caught as I stared down at the pale blue bedspread. I didn't know if he was alive or dead or . . . worse. All I did know was that he wasn't safe. The prince—Drake—had said that he was alive for now, but I wasn't sure if I could trust those words. Sorrow welled up until a knot formed deep in my chest and tears burned my eyes.

If he was . . .

My fingers dug into the comforter as I exhaled harshly. I couldn't let myself feel grief right now. Too much was at stake, and I was *not* safe. I needed to figure out where I was and how I could get far, far away from this place.

I lifted my gaze, scanning the ornate bedroom. The room was huge, with lavish furnishings. Two oversized chairs that reminded me of thrones sat in front of a large window. Across from the bed was a massive oak dresser. A standing mirror was in the corner next to an open door that led to what appeared to be a sizable bathroom.

The room smelled of rich balsam.

Gathering up my energy, I scooted toward the edge of the bed and peered down at the shiny hardwood floors. A plush white throw rug that looked as soft as a lamb covered half the floor. Carefully, I swung my legs off the bed. It was then that I realized my feet were bare. My boots and socks were gone, as was the iron stake hidden in my left boot.

I was weaponless.

"Shit," I muttered.

With a shaky hand, I reached for the torn collar of my shirt. My necklace was gone, too. Double shit. I was susceptible to manipulation now. Tendrils of fear grew within me, washing over my chilled skin. The only way I could protect myself was to be careful, and to not let the fae make eye contact with me, but that was equivalent to the pull-out method when it came to not getting pregnant.

My hand closed into a fist and fell into my lap. As my feet hit the soft rug, a dozen horrible thoughts assaulted me. How long had Drake been masquerading as Ren? Instinct told me it was after the night I had told Ren about what I was, and he'd subsequently disappeared. I was praying that was the case, because the longer Ren could've been under their control, the worse things were.

Drake had touched me. He had kissed me, and I . . .

"Oh God," I moaned, squeezing my eyes so tight that I saw tiny bursts of light.

Acids churned in my stomach as a mixture of betrayal and shame collided with anger. I was so going to kill the prince. I was going to find a wire brush and scrub down my body first, and then I was going to kill him with it.

I stood and took in my surroundings. Shuffling over to the door, I unsurprisingly found it locked. Another closed door led to an empty closet. There were no windows in the bathroom, but there was a ginormous Jacuzzi tub.

There was a small table between the throne chairs. A fancy, ceramic water pitcher that I doubt was ever used sat in the middle. Stepping around it, I checked out the window. No locks. I peered outside, and my shoulders slumped when I saw that I was several stories off the ground. There was no way I'd survive the jump. I scanned upward. Tall trees surrounded the property. The dull grass down below didn't look like it had been touched in ages. Through the trees, I thought I saw muddy water.

I was definitely out of the city.

Footsteps echoed in the hallway. Turning around, I frantically scanned the room for a weapon of sorts. The pitcher was the only thing I could find. I grasped the cool handle, surprised by the heaviness. I tensed as the door opened.

A tall woman stepped inside. Even though I was without the clover, I still saw through the glamour. She was a fae, all silvery smooth skin and pointy ears. Her pale gaze moved to the bed. She frowned and turned to where I stood.

"She's awake," she said, speaking out into the hall.

My grip tightened on the handle. "Where am I?"

The female didn't answer as she drifted further into the room.

"Where am I?" I repeated.

She raised a single eyebrow. "I don't answer to you, cow."

Cow? I fought the urge to roll my eyes. "You guys really need to come up with better insults."

Her laugh was cold. "You should put that pitcher down before you hurt yourself."

"No, thank you." I glanced over her shoulder. The door was still open. I could make a run for it. I just needed a distraction. Once I was out in the hallway, though, I had no idea what I would face.

She cocked her head to the side. "We are having food brought to you. If you misbehave, you will net the consequences."

"Ooh. Scary."

The female's lip curled. "I think we should starve you. Maybe then, when hunger is gnawing at you, you will gladly open your thighs—"

I threw the pitcher and then took off. Well, tried to take off. My muscles weren't exactly cooperating in a timely fashion. The pitcher smacked into the side of the fae's head, and her outraged shriek hit the air at about the same I got my legs to actually move. I stumbled around the chair, heading for the doorway.

The fae crashed into me from behind, taking me down. I hit the floor, and it knocked the air right out of my lungs. She flipped me over, and I took a swing. My knuckles glanced off her cheek, knocking her head to the side.

"Bitch!" she spat, grabbing my arm, and then it happened so fast.

Her teeth dug into my skin, and fiery pain erupted. Screaming, I pounded the side of her head with my free hand. She was biting me! The bitch was actually biting my arm. I hit her again, along the temple, and she let go. Bright red blood trickled down the side of her mouth.

She licked her lips. "Tastes like wine."

I rolled out from under her, scrambling to my feet as a pair of legs entered the room, blocking my way out. I was fully prepared to bum-rush whoever was standing in the way.

"Do it," the female shouted. "Or I will break her in two."

"The prince will not be pleased to see her injured," a male said.

I tried to lift my head but was stopped. Cool metal hit my throat, and a loud *click* thundered in my head. Panicked, I reached up and my fingers slipped over a metal band—a band connected to something. A chain. Holy shit—a chain.

"Like a dog. A breeding bitch," the female fae said a

second before pain exploded alongside my head, followed by intense, white light and nothing more.

~

Waking up happened differently this time. There was no quicksand or struggling to open my eyes. I was knocked out one second and then I was sitting up in a rush. I swung my legs off the bed, ignoring the ache along my head. A white bandage circled my left forearm. I made it another three steps before I was pulled back.

My hands flew to the band around my neck. It was smooth with the exception of a small keyhole. Wide-eyed, I spun around. The length of the chain rested on the blue bedspread. It was thin and light when I gripped it.

Oh my God.

I pulled on the chain, seeing that it was connected to the upper-right bedpost. I rushed over to it, swallowing down the nausea. No. It wasn't connected to the actual bed. There was a metal hook in the bedpost, like it had been planted there just for an occasion like this, and it was locked in place.

Oh my God.

"Son of a bitch." I yanked on the chain. Metal rattled, shaking the bed, but I got nowhere. He had me chained to a damn bed! "I'm going to kill him. I'm so going to kill him!"

Fury coated the inside of my mouth. I couldn't believe it. Wrapping my hands around the chain, I yanked with everything in me. Wood creaked but didn't give. I guessed I should've been grateful that the chain wasn't heavy. Tears of anger burned the back of my eyes. I pulled on the chain until my palms ached, until the tears hit my cheeks. *This can't be happening.* Over and over, I repeated those four words, but it was happening. This was reality.

Behind me, the door opened without any warning. I dropped the chain and turned, breathing heavy. There he was. The prince. Drake. And it *looked* like him—dark, shoulder-length hair and olive skin. It was a small relief that he no longer looked like Ren.

"I'm going to kill you," I promised.

He arched a brow. "Is that so?"

"Yes."

Drake chuckled as he walked toward the bed, stopping just out of arm's reach. "You haven't touched your dinner." He gestured to the nightstand. A covered plate sat untouched. "You should eat."

I reached for the plate, and Drake seemed to sense that I had no intention of eating. He was wicked fast, snatching the tray away before I could beat him upside the head with it. My hands closed around empty air. "Unchain me," I commanded.

"I don't think so." He placed the tray on the table where the pitcher had been. "You're awake for all of five minutes and you abused one of mine."

"One of yours bit me." I lifted my left arm.

"And she has been dealt with." Drake faced me, crossing his arms over his chest. "I do not want you injured."

"Really?" I laughed harshly. "You have no problem injuring me."

"That was before I knew what you were."

"Oh, so beating the crap out of other females is okay? Feeding on them against their will?" I said when he looked like he was going to speak. "And I'm pretty sure you injured me earlier—"

"You were fighting me," he replied coolly. "Am I supposed to stand there and not defend myself?"

"You have me chained to a fucking bed!" I shrieked like a banshee.

The dry smirk remained fixed on his face. "That is to protect others. Obviously, you cannot be trusted to behave like a civil creature."

"Behave like a civil creature? Are you insane? You fed on me and brought me here against my will, and I'm supposed to *behave*?" I lurched for him out of anger and was immediately snapped back by the chain. A curse of frustration tore out of me. I couldn't believe I was actually having this conversation. "I am going to kill you."

"How? You can't even reach me."

My head was going to explode. "But you're going to get close enough to me eventually."

"True," he said. "And when I do, you'll be willing."

"Not likely."

Drake's smile grew.

My anger matched it. "You can't pretend to be Ren anymore. I know."

"I don't need to pretend to be him."

I started to pace as far as the chain would allow, which was from the nightstand to the halfway point of the bed. "I thought for a child to be conceived, it couldn't be done with any trick or coercion," I said.

"You would be correct."

I eyed him as he moved closer. "But you pretending to be Ren would be trickery."

"Would it? There isn't exactly a handbook on these things. If you said yes, you would've given me consent."

The bitter taste of shame clogged my throat even though I knew what had happened between Drake and me wasn't my fault. I *knew* that, but the mortification was still there. "I would've given Ren consent. Not you."

"Semantics." He sat on the edge of the bed. I could probably have reached him, but only to grab his hair, and that wouldn't have helped. "It was worth trying."

Backing into the nightstand, I put as much space as the chain would allow between us. "You *sicken* me."

He smirked. "And I love seeing you with this." He reached over, running his finger along the taut chain, and I tensed. "It's like having a rabid cat on a leash."

"Fuck—"

Drake yanked on the chain, and I toppled to my knees. "I also love seeing you down there, little bird."

Tears of humiliation stung my eyes as I stared at his boots. "Do you think that I would ever, in a million years, be with you after all of this?"

"I think so." Drake rose, forcing me to stand with him.

"I hate you," I seethed, watching him.

One shoulder rose as he reached into his pocket, withdrawing a key. "I'm not particularly fond of you either."

"You're not even attracted to me." I recalled the moments on the couch when he was pretending to be Ren. "How's that going to work out?"

"Oh, there are times when I find you deliciously attractive." He unhooked the chain from the bed, but before I could do anything, he wrapped it around his fist. He yanked me forward, against his chest. "This is one of those moments. So don't worry about my ability to perform." Lowering his mouth to my ear, he said, "I've had worse."

I strained away, leaning as far back as I could. "Well, I haven't."

"You'll change your tune soon enough." He shortened

the length of the chain and started walking. I had no choice but to follow.

The hallway was wide with several closed doors. At the end, two ancients stood as sentries. Their lips curled in disgust as we passed. I wanted to drag my feet, but his pace made it impossible. I struggled to keep up with him as we went down the wide stairs.

"You're like my pet," he said as we reached what I assumed was the first floor. Bright sunlight streamed in through numerous windows. He tugged on the chain when I stopped.

Fae were everywhere. Lounging on the couches and chairs in the sitting room. Leaning against the walls. My wild gaze roamed over them as Drake tugged me toward the back of the large house. All of them watched with varying degrees of amusement or disgust etched onto their striking, coldly beautiful features. Except one. A female fae with silvery hair braided and tossed over one shoulder. The look on her face was one of horror. I didn't get it. The fear in her pale eyes was palpable as the prince dragged me toward another door that an ancient stood in front of.

But then the ancient opened the door, revealing a narrow hallway, and I was being pulled through it, much like a dog on a leash. "The humans who owned this house said that this once was the servants' quarters," Drake explained. "I think they used the term 'servant' loosely."

I was led into a wider room that used to be a servants' kitchen. The cabinets were still attached to the wall and an old fridge hummed softly. The room still served as a kitchen.

Well, not the kind of kitchen I ever wanted in my

house.

Dozens of cots lined the room, and they were occupied by humans in various states of being fed on. Their complexions were pale and marred by inky, black veins. A male was currently being fed on. His moans were a mixture of pain and something else entirely. And he wasn't pushing away the male fae that was feeding on him. He was clenching the fae's shoulders, holding him close.

"Oh my God," I whispered, horrified, my stomach twisting painfully. "You—"

"We need to feed," Drake replied, tugging on the chain until my gaze found his. "They enjoy it. You would too if you'd stop fighting me."

"They enjoy it?" I whispered, sickened. "What kind of life is this?"

The prince didn't respond. He opened another door, and I thought about what had happened at Flux. I had no idea if all the humans who worked at the club knew about the fae, but some did, and look what had happened to them. They were murdered. "You killed all those people at the club. You—"

He tugged on the chain until I was brought to the tips of my toes. "They crossed me. It would be wise of you to learn from their example."

I wanted to ask how they'd betrayed him, but I was pulled into a room about the size of a walk-in pantry. It was dimly lit by a bare, hanging bulb. I gasped. I was no longer thinking of the club or the humans lying on the cots. A figure was hunched against the wall, his hands secured together. A heavier chain ran from his wrists to the wall. Russet, wavy, limp hair fell over his pale, high cheekbones. A purplish-blue bruise covered the left side of his face. He was shirtless, his pants were undone, and his chest was a mess of scratches and bite marks.

No. No, no, no.

I didn't want it to be him, but it was. It was Ren.

Chapter Twenty Two

"Ren," I cried out, rushing forward.

Drake caught the chain, jerking my head back. The metal dug into my windpipe. I grabbed the chain, fighting for length. "Did I give you permission to go to him?" he said.

A powerful surge of hatred boiled up in me, stronger than I knew was possible. Ren's chest was moving with slow, shallow breaths. He was alive, but the network of veins under his skin was abnormally dark. I didn't have to ask to know what they'd been doing to him.

Not taking my eyes off Ren, I struggled to get oxygen in and words out. "Please. Please let me go to him."

The prince didn't respond for what felt like forever, and then I felt the chain loosen. "Don't make me regret this concession. He will pay for your actions if you displease me."

Hating the prince with every fiber of my being, I went

to Ren's side, kneeling down on the scuffed wooden floor. "Ren," I whispered, placing my hand on his right cheek. Carefully, I lifted his head. Lashes fanned the deep, dark circles under his eyes, but he was still the most beautiful thing I'd ever seen. "Oh God, Ren . . ."

"Don't feel too bad for him," Drake said, approaching us. "He's caught the eye of Breena, and she has been real . . . hands on with him."

I didn't know who this Breena was, but she was officially on my to-kill list. Brushing back the flop of hair from his forehead, I brushed my lips over his brow.

"How romantic," Drake said dryly.

I closed my eyes against the burn of salty tears, but I couldn't un-see the ragged scratches and the surface bites. I didn't know everything that this Breena and the others had been doing to him, but I knew it wasn't pretty. "I'm sorry," I whispered, pressing my cheek to the top of his head. "I'm so sorry."

Ren's shoulders rose with a ragged breath, and as I drew back, his eyes fluttered open. Oh God, those beautiful green eyes were all his. They were slightly dull and a bit unfocused, but they were his. Tears snuck free as his gaze found mine. How had I ever mistaken the prince for him?

I forced a weak smile. "Hey."

"Ivy?" Ren murmured.

"It's me." I smoothed my hand down his cheek, feeling several days' worth of stubble.

Another breath shuddered out of him. "You . . . shouldn't be here."

Pressure clamped down on my chest. "Neither should you."

His eyes drifted shut as he leaned into me. His lips

moved, but there was no sound. I had no idea what kind of mental state he was in, but if it was anything like how he looked, it couldn't be good, and I wanted to tear the room apart. I had no idea if he remembered anything about our conversation the last time we saw each other or if he hated my guts because of what I was and the position it put him in, but I didn't care if he loathed me. I couldn't bear to see him like this.

"I told you he was still alive," Drake said, "but him staying alive depends solely on you."

Pressing a kiss to Ren's temple, I then looked over at the prince. He stood a few feet from us, my chain dangling from his grip.

Once he had my attention, he smiled coldly. "I will let him go in exchange for you."

I stilled, not sure I was hearing him correctly. "What?"

"I will let him go, right now, if you agree to be with me."

My lips parted as I sucked in air. His offer echoed in my head, and I was almost too horrified to consider it. He couldn't be serious.

"If not, I cannot promise that Breena will make things . . . as pleasurable for him as she has in the past," Drake said.

I flinched at the insinuation.

"No," Ren groaned, lifting his chin. My gaze shot to his battered face. "You can't . . ."

"You can," Drake stated. "If you want him to live, you can."

"This . . . this is coercion," I whispered, looking up at him.

"Not if you truly decide to give yourself to me freely."

Bile rose swiftly as I stared at him. He was being a

hundred percent serious. To save Ren, I had to give myself to the prince . . . and possibly end the world by having a baby that blew open all the gates to the Otherworld.

"You have a choice," the prince said. "I let this human male go free and you submit to me. Or I hand him over to Breena completely and he won't survive the night."

That was no choice.

I couldn't let Ren die. Even if he hated me, I couldn't do that. The Order needed Ren. The world needed him to fight the fae and the ancients. I needed him alive.

Ren stirred, trying to shift forward, but he slumped over to the side. I caught him before he toppled over completely. My thoughts were a jumbled mess, but I knew I couldn't allow any more harm to come to him. There had to be another option. I needed time.

Time.

We needed time.

An idea sprung to life, and I latched onto it like it was the only preserver in the ocean. If I could get Ren to safety and somehow negotiate time, I could hopefully figure a way out of this mess.

"How do I know you're not lying? How will I know that you've let him go and he's safe?"

"I give you my word." Victory gleamed in his glacial eyes. "Once given, it is only breakable by death."

That was true. I had no idea why the fae were bound by promises, but they could not go back on them. Not even a prince or a queen. "And you would promise to let him go immediately and harm him no more?"

"Yes."

"Ivy, don't. You can't," Ren groaned.

It pained me to ignore him, but I had to. "I need time."

The prince cocked his head to the side.

"I need time to . . . to be with you." I forced the words out as Ren tensed against me. "I can't just do it. That's not who I am."

Drake's eyes narrowed. "No—"

"All I'm asking for is time. If you don't give it, and you hurt Ren further, I will find a way to end this, and you'll be back to square one, looking for another halfling."

His grip tightened on the chain, and I felt it around my neck. "How much time?"

"A month."

"No. A week," he countered.

That was not enough time for me to hopefully find a way out of this damn place. "Four weeks."

"That's a month." The prince sighed. "Two weeks."

"Three," I shot back. "I need time to grow accustomed to this. To become comfortable."

"You don't need to be comfortable. You just need to let me plant my seed in you."

I winced. "Yeah, okay. That's why I need time, because you say stuff like that while I have a chain around my neck, and I just want to throw up in your face."

The prince's lip curled in disgust. "Revolting."

"Exactly," I spat. "I need time."

"Son of a bitch," Ren grunted, pulling against his chains. His eyes opened to thin slits and his cheeks were flushed with anger. "You're not going to touch her." Muscles popped in his arms and shoulders. "I'm going to fucking kill you. You sick son of a bitch, I will fucking end you."

The prince shot Ren a dismissive glance. "Three weeks and you'll submit to me?"

My stomach soured, but I nodded.

"Say it," he ordered.

"Three weeks and I'll . . . submit to you," I gritted out.

The prince smiled, flashing bright white teeth that were shockingly sharp. "Deal." He turned, calling out in a language I didn't understand. The door opened, and one of the short-haired ancients stepped in the room. "He is to be released."

"Wait. Promise me that you will cause him no further harm and free him, and that you will give me three weeks," I demanded. "Promise that."

A muscle flexed along his jaw.

My heart was pumping. "I need to hear you promise that."

"Ivy . . ." Ren's hands opened and closed fitfully.

"I promise that he will be released without any further harm, and I will give you three weeks, not a day longer, to grow accustomed," Drake stated.

The band seemed to constrict around my neck as I whispered, "Deal."

"No," Ren exclaimed. "Ivy, you can't—"

"It's okay," I told Ren, cupping his cheek. "I got this, okay? Trust me." Before he could respond, I pressed my lips to his. "It'll be okay," I said.

Ren reached for me, but Drake yanked on the chain, and I had no choice but to stand and step back. Ren caught himself with his bound hands, and the pained expression on his face broke my heart into a million little pieces.

"Don't do this," he said, voice gravelly. "I'm not worth it. You can't do . . . this."

"You *are* worth it," I told him. "I couldn't live with myself if . . ." Pressing my lips together, I held his stricken gaze as Drake started out of the room. "I love you," I stated. Walking backward, I kept my gaze trained on Ren's face until he blurred, until all I heard was the rattling of his chains as he struggled to his feet. "No matter what, I love you."

The ancient obscured my vision of Ren, but I heard him shout, "Don't you fucking touch her. I will rip you into fucking pieces. Ivy, no!"

I took a shaky breath as the door was shut, muffling Ren's threats, and a second later, my back was against the wall and the prince was leaning into me. Beside us, a human male whimpered on a cot.

The prince was in my face. "If you think to cheat me or trick me, I will do things to you that will make you beg for death, but I will withhold it from you until your hair turns gray and your skin wrinkles," he said, his voice low and deadly calm. "And that is a promise I will not break. Do you understand me?"

Thinking of the humans I saw hanging from the rafters of Flux, I shuddered. "I understand."

Chapter Twenty Three

I stared at the plate of roasted chicken, inhaling the savory herb scent. It smelled amazing. I should have been hungry. The last thing I'd eaten was a bowl of some kind of soup last night, almost twenty-four hours ago, but my stomach churned unsteadily at the idea of eating anything.

It probably had a lot to do with the chain around my neck. Every swallow was a painful reminder of my captivity. The only time it would be removed was tonight, when I finally got to shower. Bathroom breaks were periodic, and even then, the chain was only unhooked from the bed, and the bathroom door was left open.

Anger burned through me as I stared at the plate of food, half-tempted to throw it across the room. I was going to go crazy in this room, wondering and worrying about what was happening out in the world.

Was Ren truly okay? The prince had promised his

safety, but that didn't mean he was okay. Had Brighton found Merle and this supposed group of warm and fuzzy fae? Was Tink okay, or had he burned down my apartment in a panic? Did he even know what had happened to me? And what about David and the rest of the Order? They had to know that Henry was missing by now, that I'd been taken. I didn't even know if Henry or Kyle had really believed that I was the halfling or if that had been a lie Drake had told.

So many questions and no answers. None.

I stretched out my legs as I pushed a limp, greasy curl out of my face. Drake had only visited me once since he'd taken me to see Ren. Yesterday. It had not gone well. I was trying to be on my . . . best behavior. Earning his trust was the only chance I had at escape, but the man made me crazy insane with anger.

Looking around the room, I saw the same thing I'd seen before. No avenue of escape. The only chance I had was to get this chain off my neck and somehow get outside. I had no idea where we were, but out there, I had a chance. In here, I had nothing.

The bedroom door opened and I tensed, drawing my legs up. Two female fae entered the room. I recognized one. It was the silvery-haired female who'd had that horrified look on her face when she saw me outside the room Ren had been kept in. She'd brought my food earlier and last night, along with the prince and another ancient. I believed her name was, coincidentally, Faye.

I had no idea who the dark-haired fae was, but she was beautiful and lithe like all fae. It wasn't often that I saw a dark-haired fae, but the combination with the silver skin was stunning. Dressed in tight jeans and a slinky, nearly see-through tank top, she was the kind of woman who had perfectly shaped breasts that looked amazing when braless. I knew this, because I could see her nipples.

Faye glanced at my untouched plate. "You haven't eaten."

I didn't answer, because I really didn't see the point.

The other female closed the bedroom door and reached into the pocket of her jeans. "Well, we're here to make sure you shower, so you've lost the opportunity to eat."

"She can eat afterwards, Breena." Faye stood several feet back. "The prince doesn't want her to starve."

I swung my legs off the bed. "You're Breena?"

Breena's lush red lips curved into a smirk as she eyed me. "I am."

Slowly, I stood. "You're on my to-kill list."

"Is that so?" Breena shrugged. "I bet I know why."

Fury dug into my bones. "I bet you do."

"I told you it wasn't wise for you to be here," Faye replied with a weary sigh. "The prince spoke of you. She wasn't going to forget."

"I was hoping she wouldn't." Breena paused, her pale eyes full of malicious intent. "And you know who else is never going to forget my name? My little human pet."

"Stop it, Breena," Faye warned, glancing at the door.

My hands curled into fists. "You're disgusting."

"That's not what Ren thought," she replied, pulling the key out. "Especially not when I had my mouth on his skin, my tongue on his, and his—"

Screeching, I lurched at her. Breena easily evaded me, stepping just out of my reach, causing the chain to painfully jerk my neck back. "You sound proud of forcing yourself on someone," I shouted.

"Who's saying I forced myself?" She laughed darkly. "I can be very, very convincing."

"And you're going to be very, very dead," I promised.

Breena snorted. "My pet had the most amazing tattoo. I traced those vines with my tongue."

"Shut up." Rage filled me, mingling with the bitter sting of jealousy. It was stupid to give her that kind of power, but I couldn't help it. I knew that Ren didn't want whatever had gone down between them. I wouldn't have done what I'd done with the prince if I'd known it wasn't Ren, and the mortification over that still burned brightly, but she was getting under my skin and setting up a home there.

"Give me the key," Faye ordered.

Breena handed it over without taking her eyes off me. "He tasted like man and salt. Not a bad combination. I may have to pay him a visit."

"You won't get the chance," I said as Faye approached me. My gaze snapped to her.

She stopped, wariness etched into her face as she lifted her hands. "I'm going to unchain you so you can shower. That's all."

The moment I was unhooked, I was going to take this chain and wrap it around Breena's neck.

"Please don't." Faye's eyes met mine, and it was like she'd read my mind. "If you go after her or cause any trouble, one of the males will come in. Do you understand?"

My jaw ached from how tight I was clenching my mouth shut.

"They'll be in here while you shower," Faye explained, tone almost pleading, which surprised me. "You don't want that, right?"

"No," I forced out.

"Then please don't go after her," she said, voice low. "She wasn't with him that long. She fed on him, but that is all."

"Keep telling her that if it lets her sleep better at night." Breena's laugh tinkled like wind chimes.

"Ignore her," Faye insisted. "She just wants to get a rise out of you, see you punished. Don't give her that."

The breath I took felt like fire in my lungs. "Why do you even care?"

Faye's gaze flicked away from mine, and she didn't respond. I honestly didn't get why Faye cared if I had to strip down in front of an army of fae, but she was right. I didn't want them in here while I showered, and I really, *really* wanted a shower.

"Okay," I said.

Relief shot across Faye's face, but Breena smiled like she had won some kind of battle. My answering smile was grim, because *after* I took a shower and had clothes back on, I really didn't have anything to lose, and that bitch was going down.

Faye unlocked the chain, but held the end in her hands. "You ready?"

I nodded.

We walked over to the bathroom, and Breena followed. I did my best to ignore her presence, which was probably one of the hardest things I'd ever done in my life, especially when she started talking again.

"You need to leave the door open," she said, smirking.

Faye winced.

"That's not necessary," I told them. "What am I going to do in here?"

"I don't trust you." Breena bumped my shoulder as she walked past me and sat on the ledge surrounding the tub, gracefully crossing one leg over the other.

I tensed as Faye unlocked the band around my neck

and removed it. Immediately, I reached up, touching my bare skin, and swallowed carefully while Faye moved to the shower stall. She turned the water on, adjusting the temperature.

"Strip," Breena ordered.

I lowered my hands, glaring at her.

Her smirk grew. "Either you take off your clothes or I will take them off for you."

Faye sighed. "Breena."

"It's not an empty promise," Breena added.

My skin prickled with anger and irritation. Part of me wanted to let her try to strip me down, but the last thing I wanted was a room full of fae while I showered. Breena had already gotten to me—she'd done things to Ren, with Ren, and now she wanted to intimidate me. No way was I giving her one more thing.

I reached down, wrapping my fingers around the hem of my thermal, and yanked the soiled material off. Then I threw it at her.

Breena's hand snaked out, catching the shirt. The smirk faded from her face as she dropped the material onto the ground. "Cute. Does your bra actually have daisies on it?"

It did. Whatever. Unbuttoning my cargo pants, I shimmied them down my hips and thighs, then stepped out of them. Steam was quickly filling the bathroom.

"Pink panties?" Breena snickered. "How old are you?"

"Go fuck yourself," I said, reaching behind and unclasping the hooks of my bra. My cheeks heated as the straps slipped down my arms.

"How about I go fuck your boyfriend?" Breena responded.

I'm gonna kill her. My hands trembled as I let the bra

slip to the floor. *I'm gonna kill her.* I kept repeating those words as I slipped off my undies.

"I have no idea what he sees in you," Breena observed, arching a dark brow. "Your tits aren't that bad. The rest of you? Probably a good thing you skipped dinner."

"Shut up, Breena." Faye shot her a dark, scolding look. "Just shut up."

Breena ignored her. "Oh, look. Your tattoo is in the same place as your boyfriend's. How cute."

I stiffened. The tattoo—the symbol of freedom that all Order members had—was way too low on Ren's stomach for her to have seen it without his pants coming off. Stomach twisting, I struggled to take my next breath. Our gazes met. Challenge filled her pale eyes.

"Shower, Ivy." Faye lightly touched my arm. "Go ahead and shower."

Skin burning, it took every ounce of self-control to turn and step into the shower. The warm water hit my skin, stinging the bruise along my hip. Faye closed the door behind me, but it was clear glass, so there was absolutely no privacy. Embarrassment made my movements jerky as I picked up the bottle of shampoo.

Breena talked the entire time I showered. She spoke of how alive she felt after feeding on Ren, and how his muscles had flexed under her hands. Then she moved on to how things would be with the prince once I got "knocked up" and delivered his child. I'd be cast aside, and she would take my place. From what I was gathering, she had a lot of experience with Drake.

So cliché.

I ignored her and focused on the simple joy of being clean, even though I wanted to shove the bottle of body wash down her throat. I was biding my time. So I swallowed the humiliation and held the anger close as I finished showering. The door opened once, and a disposable razor was offered to me. I stared at it and then slowly lifted my gaze to Faye's.

Pink flushed her silvery cheeks. "He wants you to shave."

"He wants . . ." I knew why. Sickened, I swallowed a dry heave. "No. No way."

"Gross," muttered Breena. "Humans are so hairy."

Did the fae not get hair in the same places we did? I had no idea, and frankly, I didn't care. I wasn't shaving. "It's not happening," I said.

Something akin to approval flashed in Faye's gaze, but I figured I had to be seeing things. She nodded and stepped away from the shower. I wanted to be clean, but if being hairy and dirty kept the prince away from me, then I'd gladly be as gross as humanly possible. When I was done, Faye handed me a towel.

Goosebumps raced over my skin as I stepped out of the shower. It was then that I realized Faye was holding a bundle of black cloth. Water dripped from the ends of my hair as I clutched the towel close to my body.

"The prince wants you to wear this," Faye explained.

This turned out to be a black gown. It was long-sleeved and low-cut with a high waist. Without even touching it, I knew it was incredibly thin.

"Are you serious?" I asked, and when Faye nodded, I grimaced. "There has to be something else."

"It's either that or you're naked." Breena rose fluidly. "Your choice."

I watched her roam out into the bedroom and then I faced Faye. I didn't get why she was being kind or helpful, but I hoped it extended to finding me something else to wear. "Please. I can't . . . I can't wear that."

"I'm sorry." And she sounded sorry. Again, I was surprised by this.

The chain and metal band lay on the bed, waiting for me. Frustrated, I took the dress from her. There were no undergarments, and I figured that was on purpose. Disgusted, I turned my back to Faye.

She stepped outside the bathroom, giving me the closest thing she could to privacy while I dropped the towel and slipped the silky dress on over my head. The hem fell to the floor, and my toes peeked out from underneath.

With no undergarments on, I felt nude.

I scooped my wet hair out of the dress, refusing to look at myself in the mirror. The top was tight, leaving very little to the imagination, and it gaped slightly if I bent over. Great.

"How long does it take one person to get dressed?" Breena sniped from the bedroom.

Smoothing my hands down the sides, I smiled tightly as I lifted my head. I walked out of the bathroom, stepping around Faye. Calmly, I stalked up to the bed and stopped a few inches from Breena.

"You make the gown look like you're playing dress-up," she said.

My smile widened as I faced Breena. She looked at me expectantly. I cocked my arm back and punched her right in her stupid face with everything I had in me.

Faye gasped as Breena fell backward onto the bed. I didn't give her a chance to recover. Straddling her thin hips, I gripped the sides of her head and thrust my thumbs deep into her eyes.

"I'm going to kill you," I promised, ignoring the bite of pain as she clawed at my arms through the stupid dress.

"Maybe not right now, but one day I will kill you."

Breena screamed, bucking her hips, but I held on to her like an octopus, waiting for Faye to intervene. The bedroom door flew open, and an ancient rushed into the room. I kept digging my fingers in, relishing Breena's shrieks of pain until two hands gripped my shoulders and tore me away. My butt hit the floor.

Metal closed around my neck and the chain was pulled tight, forcing me to stand. Breena jumped to her feet, shimmery blood dripping from the corners of her red eyes. Screaming like a banshee, she rushed me, but didn't get far.

Faye caught her around the waist and started dragging her, arms and legs flailing, around the bed and toward the open door. A hysterical laugh bubbled up in me as the ancient shoved me back toward the bed. I caught myself and whipped around.

His arm shot out, the back of his hand connecting with my jaw. Pain erupted along my mouth. I touched my chin, wincing when red smeared my fingertips.

"The prince will be displeased with your actions," the ancient warned, looking like he wanted to knock me upside the head.

Lip bleeding and aching, I gave him a bloody smile. "Worth it."

Chapter Twenty Four

I ate my lunch on day four, even though mustard was not exactly pleasant with a split lip. Faye brought me a sandwich a little bit after one o'clock. She didn't hang around and chat, which sucked because I was curious about her and what drove her to be so kind to me. Granted, it wasn't like we were going to go out and get matching "best friend" bracelets, but she wasn't like the others. But the only thing she said to me on the way out was that I shouldn't have attacked Breena.

Maybe I shouldn't have, but oh well.

Out of all the things I could regret in life, that wouldn't even make the top thirty.

My thoughts went to a strange place, and I thought of Val. How would she treat me if I was here and she was still alive? Would she be kind or spiteful? Part of me wanted to believe she would step up and help me, but it hurt to realize there was very little I knew about Val.

Thinking of her made every part of me ache.

I'd just finished my sandwich when the bedroom door opened. I tensed when I saw that it was Drake. He was dressed in linen pants that most men wouldn't look right in, and his shirt was half-unbuttoned. His feet were bare.

He was dressed way too casual, and unease stirred in my stomach. Drake had stopped by last night, mostly to yell at me for nearly gouging out Breena's eyes and to tell me that he was glad I was no longer "filthy." I was guessing Faye hadn't told him the razor had gone unused.

"Miss me?" he asked as he stopped in front of the bed.

I snorted. "Not even in the slightest."

"If I had feelings, I still wouldn't care."

Rolling my eyes, I scooted to the edge of the bed and placed my feet on the floor. I didn't have a lot of space to move around, but I didn't like being on the bed with him in the room. I stood like I did whenever he came in.

"Do you like the dress I picked out for you?"

He hadn't asked that question before. "No," I said, shaking my head.

"I'm not surprised." He chuckled, and then moved like lightning, curling his fingers around my chin. He tilted my head back. "You know, Valor could've done worse to your face."

Valor, ironically named, was the ancient who'd backhanded me yesterday. "We've already had this conversation," I said, jerking my chin out of his grasp, hating that he'd *allowed* that and that was the one reason he wasn't doing worse. "And I'll say it again. I'm going to kill her."

"Not likely."

My eyes narrowed and my hands closed into fists. "You don't think I'm capable of it?"

One side of his mouth curled upward as he tilted

his head forward. His dark hair slid over his shoulders. "You'd kill her because she touched your human male?"

"I'd kill her because what she did to him wasn't something he wanted," I shot back. "It wasn't mutual. If it were mutual, then my problem wouldn't be with her."

"How do you know?" he challenged.

I sucked in a sharp breath. "Because I know—because *this* isn't mutual. Because being fed on isn't something Ren would've wanted. Because—"

"And you think he truly wants you, even knowing that you're a halfling?"

My shoulders tensed. Wondering if Ren still cared for me hadn't been a priority since I was brought here.

"Let me ask you a question," he said as he pulled the key from his pocket. "How do you think we captured your male so easily?"

"I doubt it was easy."

His full lips twisted into a smirk. My muscles locked up as he reached around, scooping my hair up with one hand. "It was last Monday," he said.

My chest squeezed. That was when I'd told Ren I was the halfling, which was what I'd expected. Ren had gone missing that night until Tuesday, then Drake had shown up, masquerading as Ren, on Wednesday.

"It wasn't me who snatched your human male." He unlocked the band around my neck and dropped it onto the bed. "It was Breena."

I didn't dare move, even though I now had a small measure of freedom. He still held on to my hair, and he was too close. When he spoke, his cool breath caressed my cheek.

"She caught his attention and lured him in quite easily," he told me.

My hands balled into fists. "He saw past her glamour. It's our job to go after fae when we see them."

"And how do you know he was just doing his duty? Breena is beautiful, and you . . . well, you have this hair." He lifted it up. "Not sure what to make of it."

"Gee. Thanks."

He chuckled, dropping the curly mass, but didn't step back. His hand landed on my shoulder, a heavy, suffocating presence. "She rendered him helpless quite easily," he continued. "I guess he was distracted."

Of course he was, and it wasn't for the reason Drake was suggesting. "I know what you're trying to do, and it isn't going to work."

"It isn't?" His hand moved from my shoulder to the back of my neck, and he forced my head back so I met his gaze. "Do you know when we feed, we can pick up thoughts? See inside someone? Pieces of their personality, their wants and desires?"

I didn't know that.

His eyes were like pools of blue ice. "How do you think I was able to convince you I was Ren for a period of time?"

"Only for a handful of hours," I reminded him.

Drake's fingers tightened around my neck. "If we hadn't been interrupted, I would've gotten what I came for."

Anger and embarrassment flushed my skin. I tried to pull away, but he held me in place.

"I learned certain things about him when I fed, as I am sure Breena did." He paused. "One of the things I picked up from your human male was his concern over those two men—Henry and Kyle."

Great. But right now that wasn't one of my biggest problems.

"You should thank me for removing at least one of those threats," he said, and I clamped my mouth shut. "I did what your human male couldn't do."

"Murdering someone in cold blood isn't exactly a desirable trait," I shot back.

"We'll have to disagree on that." Letting go of my neck, he stepped back. "Do you know what else I learned?"

I all but darted across the room, putting as much space between us as possible. The bedroom door was closed, and I was smart enough to know I wasn't going to get past him. I wasn't sure why he'd let me go, but I wasn't going to look a gift horse in the mouth. I needed to keep my cool, because the only chance I had was to earn his trust.

"What?" I asked.

Drake smiled tightly. "Your human male isn't sure how he feels about you. He's *torn*. He cares for you, but he loathes half of what you are. He cannot reconcile those two halves."

The breath I sucked in burned, and a knot formed in the back of my throat, making my voice hoarse. "Why should I believe what you're saying?"

"Because I've been inside your head and you share those same fears," he replied. "You fear that he feels that way, and you would be right. He does."

I paced in front of the dresser, folding my arms around my waist. The knot expanded in my throat.

"Why would you want to be with someone who does not fully accept who you are?" he asked.

That was a great question, and one that lingered in the back of my thoughts far too often. Frustrated, I started wearing a path in the plush carpet that surrounded the massive bed. Keeping my cool probably wasn't going to happen. "Do you really think telling me these things is going to help?"

"Yes."

My hands curled into fists. "It's not."

"You made a deal, so in the end, it doesn't really matter, does it?" he replied. "You have seventeen days left."

I shuddered. "I'd rather you kill me than remind me of that."

"I thought you didn't want to die." Drake dropped into the chair by the window, and he sat like he always did, thighs spread wide and shoulders pressed back. He turned every chair into a throne, and it annoyed me greatly. "When you were on your back and I'd broken some very important things inside you, didn't you want to live? Has that changed?"

"Yes." I made another pass in front of the bed, the stupid dress whispering around my ankles. "Your mere presence makes me wish for a fifty-story window to jump out of and a cement sidewalk below. Or a moat. A moat with a dozen hungry alligators in it."

He smirked. "You always paint such lovely pictures with your words, little bird."

"I'm going to paint lovely pictures with your intestines," I shot back.

Drake laughed.

I hated him.

Seriously.

"Resist all you want." He dismissively flicked his wrist as he turned his gaze to the window. "We have a deal. In the end, you will be under me and I will plant my seed in your belly."

My lip curled with disgust and I stopped pacing. I told myself to shut up, but my mouth moved without my control. "That has to be the most revolting thing I've ever heard."

He raised one shoulder, managing to make a shrug look elegant.

Anger rose inside me, my nearly constant companion. "Do you really think I want this?" He opened his mouth. "Don't answer that question," I warned. "We made a deal, because you gave me no other option. I don't want you, and I sure as hell don't want to bear your child."

A smirk graced his perfect lips and his pale gaze centered on me. "Oh, we'll see about that."

I laughed bitterly. "Oh no, me wanting this is never going to happen. Like, the never-ever part is Taylor Swift level of never-ever."

A look of confusion appeared on his face.

"I know I'm no longer of any use to you once I pop out the apocalypse baby—"

He sighed. "I wish you would stop calling the baby that."

I ignored him. "Once I pop out the apocalypse baby, you're going to kill me. I don't care how hot you think you are, or how skilled you like to believe your magic cock is, me not wanting this is my life insurance policy."

"I thought you wanted a window to jump out of and a moat full of hungry alligators."

My eyes narrowed. "Maybe I don't plan to honor our deal. Unlike the fae, I'm not bound by my promises."

He tipped his head back, closing his eyes. My back stiffened. I was insulted. *Offended.* I was a badass fighter, and he was so not scared of me that he was about to take a freaking nap!

"You know, little bird," he said slowly, his fingers tapping along the arm of the black chair. "I plan to keep you afterward. Your mouth amuses me. Perhaps I will have a pretty cage fashioned to hold my pretty red-headed bird."

I gaped at him. "You should go update your *Match. com* profile with that information. The ladies will be lining up outside, because nothing screams romance like being held captive in a cage."

Drake chuckled darkly. "Ah, you are amusing."

"I am *not* amusing!" I lifted my chin. "I'm *pissed*."

"Really," he replied dryly. "I never would've guessed that."

Heat swept over me as my anger creeped into cut-a-bitch territory. "I'm going to kill you. I *will* find a way, and I *will* kill you for everything you have done to Ren, and everything you're doing to me."

The prince tipped his head to the side.

"And that's not a warning. It's a promise I won't even consider backing out of."

His fingers stilled, and that should have been warning enough, but I was too pissed to recognize that I'd gone too far.

The prince was out of the chair and in front of me in less than half a second. Not even a heartbeat had passed. How fast he could move would never cease to amaze and terrify me.

He gripped my arm and spun me around. His hand landed in the center of my back, but I didn't fall forward. Oh no, I *flew* forward. Like the length of the room. I threw my hands out, and my palms smacked into the paneled wall a second before my face would have.

The prince was at my back in under a nanosecond, pressing and sealing my body to the wall. "My amusement has its limitations, little bird." His breath was icy against my ear. "There's something you haven't realized, and I am done waiting for it to connect. There are worse things I could do to you than end your life. And it's time you learned that."

Oh. Shit.

Chapter Twenty Five

I wasn't surprised when the metal band was snapped around my neck again, but when he took the chain and dragged me out into the hallway, I had no idea what was about to go down.

The whole earning his trust thing had belly-flopped out the window.

Drake didn't speak as he led me downstairs, and there was no way I was getting away from him at this moment. Not when he was this angry.

I wasn't stupid. Running my mouth may have made it appear that way, but I was smart enough to taste fear on the tip of my tongue.

There was a blur of fae faces as he took me back toward the room full of cots and humans. The ancient guarding the door eyed the chain wrapped around Drake's fist, smirking as he stepped aside. My cheeks burned with humiliation. Being led around, dragged from one room to the next with a chain in this ridiculous dress went beyond public shame.

He moved to the center of the room, and I stopped just inside, my toes curling against the cool wood floor. The cots weren't nearly as full as they had been the last time I was here. Three of them were occupied. One of the humans, a female who looked like she was in her mid-thirties, was awake, staring listlessly at the ceiling. The other two were guys who looked like they were barely in their twenties, and they were asleep or passed out.

There was only one other fae in the room, a male who was leaning against the wall, his attention focused on the cellphone in his hand. I wondered if he was checking his Facebook account, and I squelched a hysterical giggle.

Drake looked over his shoulder, brows furrowed. Our gazes met, and a smile formed on his lips, turning cruel. A second later, he jerked the chain.

I resisted, and pressure clamped down on my neck, making it hard to swallow or breathe. Panic balled in the pit of my stomach, heavy like stones. Reflex took over, and I gripped the chain.

"You fight me even though you know it's pointless." Drake walked toward me, and the tension in the chain eased. Air rushing down my throat pushed back the panic. He stopped in front of me. "It's either incredibly foolish or courageous. Which is it?"

I met his stare but refused to answer his question.

One eyebrow rose as he leaned in. His mouth was next to my cheek. "You're a fighter, even when it's useless. I can respect that, but that doesn't mean I won't break you."

Turning my head from his, I exhaled roughly. "You're not going to break me."

"Is that so? I think I'm already well on my way." He

lifted the chain, rattling it. "You're in my chains, eating my food, sleeping in my bed, and wearing my clothes." His head tilted as he reached up with his other hand and traced a finger along my neck. I leaned back, and he chuckled as if I amused him. "You've already agreed to be with me. How exactly am I not breaking you, little bird?"

Anger flashed through me, causing my heart to pound in my ears. I lifted my gaze to his. "You will not break me."

His grin widened, freezing the fire in my veins. It was also secretive and knowing, like he'd already read the book and knew how it would end. "I've only met a few halflings over the many centuries I've been alive."

Centuries? I knew he was old, but good lord.

The prince turned, leading me over to where the woman lay. She didn't move or look up at us. "We once had many humans in the Otherworld. They didn't last very long. The feeding or the environment always got to them in the end, but we bred them, replenishing our stock before their inevitable deaths."

I shuddered with disgust. The fae truly treated humans like cattle.

He didn't seem to notice my distaste. "Unfortunately, the Otherworld is dying. Everything is turning cold and dead. The environment is no longer suitable to sustain human life, and without humans, we age . . . and we die."

Something occurred to me. "Turning cold? Like the weather?"

Drake nodded.

My eyes widened. "It's happening here. The cold spell." I thought of the withered, dying vines outside of my apartment. "It's because you're here."

"It's adjusting to our needs," he replied.

"But will your presence have the same impact here,

like it did in the Otherworld?"

He shrugged. "It could, but it will take thousands of years. The weather will continue to cool. Winter is in our blood, after all."

Shock rendered me speechless for a moment. "I thought the courts were dismantled. That summer and winter joined together and—"

His deep laugh silenced me. "The two courts did not simply join together. We overtook the summer court centuries ago. Winter rules all."

I was barely able to process this before he started speaking again.

"Every so often, a fae would impregnate a human. Things sometimes got out of . . . control while feeding," he said, grinning, and I remembered what Tink had said he'd seen once in the clearing in the Otherworld. The prince with several women. I imagined that could get kind of complicated. "Before we knew of the prophecy—the loophole surrounding the doorways—halflings were generally seen as an abomination. They were killed."

"God," I muttered.

"As if your kind treats halflings any better?"

I pressed my lips together, because he had a point, but whatever.

"But there were times when one of our kind took a liking to the human, to the child, and the halfling would grow." Drake walked between the cots, tugging me along with him. The woman's gaze drifted toward us. Placing a hand on my shoulder, he pushed me down with enough pressure that I couldn't resist. He forced me to sit beside the woman. "Do you know what we discovered about halflings?"

A prickle of unease quickly grew until it felt like a

thousand tiny needles dragging across my skin. Every muscle in my body grew rigid as he sat beside me. The cot was small, so there was very little room. The side of his body pressed against mine, and my thigh rested against the woman's leg.

Drake leaned in, curling an arm around my waist, tightening the chain. "We learned that halflings could feed just like us."

My wide eyes met his as a new horror gave birth, chilling my skin. "No," I whispered.

"Yes," he replied, his voice low. "It's quite simple. It's like a kiss. You just have to inhale and want it, and it will happen. You just need to know that you can do it. The first couple of times is like . . . taking a hit. It's a lot for your system to handle, but you will get a handle on it."

I shook my head, suddenly understanding his earlier smile. This wasn't going to happen. No way.

"I think you need to explore your other half." His hand left my waist, moving behind me and toward the woman. She stirred and started to sit up. "It's time that you discover who you truly are."

"No way." I tried to stand, but he held the chain, forcing me to stay seated. Panic clawed at my throat, and I couldn't get enough air into my lungs. "There is no way I'm feeding off of anyone. That's not who I am."

"You don't know what you are," he responded. "You have no idea."

"I know who I am." I glanced at the woman. She was staring at us. Waiting. Her expression was blank, devoid of all thought and emotion. Did she know what was happening? "I'm Ivy Morgan. I'm a member of the Order. I'm *human,* and I don't feed on other humans."

"You are a halfling, and you will do as I say."

"Never," I whispered, my hands curling into fists.

The prince leaned over as he curled his hand around my chin. His grip was controlling, and I hated every place his skin touched mine. "You do remember that I can make you."

My heart plummeted as realization set in. Drake *could* make me. He could make me do anything. Strip naked and dance around the room. Get on my knees before him. Jump through a window. I no longer had the protection of the clover. I could be manipulated just like any other human. For some foolish, horrible reason, I'd relied on the fact he couldn't force me into bed to conceive a child, but that barrier didn't extend to anything else.

"No." I tried to yank my head out of his iron-clad grip. Real fear erupted in my gut. "Don't do this. Please. Don't make me do this."

"You will want to do this." He guided my gaze to his, and before I could squeeze my eyes shut or even prepare myself, our gazes locked and there was *something* in his eyes, *something* about him that I couldn't look away from. Time seemed to slow down, and all that existed was the fast, erratic beat of my heart and his gaze. His eyes weren't just one shade of blue, I realized. They were several dizzying shades of pale blue and violet. Like a glacier deep in the ocean, there was so much depth. "You may even like it," he murmured, smoothing his thumb over my jaw. "My will is yours."

My lips parted. I didn't agree with him. I couldn't exactly remember why, but I knew I should, especially when Drake spoke to the woman beside me. I'd forgotten her and jumped a little when she placed her small, frail hand on my shoulder. I twisted toward her even though I knew that wasn't wise.

"Show her," Drake said.

He was talking to this woman, and I didn't understand what he meant, but she seemed to know, because her eyes drifted shut and she leaned into me, the front of her body against mine. I thought she was going to kiss me. Her mouth lined up with mine.

Drake's hand slipped from my chin to the band around my neck. I hated that band. It symbolized everything that I had lost.

"You're hungry, aren't you?" Drake murmured in my ear, derailing my thoughts. "You're so thirsty. A need is burning bright in your stomach, lighting up every cell in your body. You need."

He was right.

My stomach felt hollow. My throat felt parched. I'd eaten earlier, but I was . . . I was starving now. I *needed*.

"It's not food you desire. It's not water that will quench your thirst. You need life. You need a part of her. And she can give you what you need," he explained, his voice as smooth as a lullaby. "Take it."

My heart thundered in my chest. I couldn't . . .

"She wants to give it to you," he said, and I thought for some reason that might not be true. "Show her."

Another hand curled around my shoulder, and I was tugged forward. There was no chain stopping me. The woman spoke and her hands moved, but I didn't understand what she was saying. My eyelids were too heavy, and I couldn't keep them open.

"Inhale," the voice ordered, and that one word was everywhere, outside of me and in me, and I did what felt . . . right.

I inhaled.

The woman jerked, her fingers spasming around my arms. An odd coolness slid over my lips and tongue. It reminded me of iced coffee on the hottest summer day. It was like stripping down and diving into water. But it was more. It was like electricity. A jolt of pure caffeine wrapped in ice. It rushed down my throat, hitting that empty spot.

And then it hit every place in me.

It was too much.

My senses sparked to life. Senses I didn't even know existed. Something surrounded me, and I . . . I was *invincible*. My eyes were still closed, but I saw every shade of color. Red. Blue. Green. Yellow. And more, over and over, a rainbow that was inside me. The hunger dulled and the thirst eased off. I wasn't hollow anymore. Oh no, I was so very full and warm even though the tip of my tongue felt cool.

"That's it," a deep, rough voice said. "Feed."

I inhaled again without thinking.

Nails dug through my thin dress, pulling and tearing at the cloth. There was a sound, a pitiful whimper, but I was alive and my skin was tingling with electricity. I had no idea how much time had passed, but I slowly became aware of the woman no longer clutching my arms. She was on her back, and I was leaning over her. Then I wasn't on the cot. I was on my feet, and the prince was beside me, his mouth on my throat and his hand in my hair, but I didn't understand a single thing he said. Then we were moving—walking.

When I stumbled out of the room, my gaze collided with someone I knew. Someone who had been kind to me. *Faye.* Maybe it wasn't her. I wasn't sure. I couldn't focus on her. Not when the walls were shaking and the floor was rippling.

Then I wasn't walking anymore. I was floating, and I was surrounded by warmth as cool air washed over my tingling, sparking skin. I moved restlessly and I didn't move at all. I wasn't here. No. I was nowhere near here. It was like being blanketed in clouds. Maybe that's where I was. Up in the sky where nothing could ever harm me.

Sensation burned my skin, jolting me out of my daze. I blinked slowly, recognizing the ceiling. The bedroom. I wasn't in the clouds. I was on the bed. The burn on my leg was a hand, and the heaviness settling over part of my body wasn't comforting.

I looked up.

Hair as dark as a raven's wing. Not russet-colored. Not warm. Those eyes weren't green. They were pale blue ice. My heart sped up again, and this godawful feeling in the pit of my stomach spread. This couldn't happen. I didn't want this. I never wanted this.

"No." The word was weak, a whisper. I cleared my throat. "No," I said louder.

He stilled, and I saw pieces of his chest and stomach. His shirt was undone. My stomach churned. *He can make you do anything.* I squeezed my eyes shut.

"You want—"

"No." The word scalded my tongue, and it felt like I was fighting quicksand. It took everything to force the words out. "No. I don't want this. I don't want you. No."

For a moment, I thought he would continue, that he would keep speaking and force my eyes open. That I would fall under that spell again, and even though I had a hard time remembering why it was bad, I knew it was terrible. It was *evil*. It was something I wanted no part of.

The prince grunted in exasperation. "Soon." He lifted himself up, but I could still feel his weight, and I thought I might be sick. I no longer saw rainbows. "Soon you will say yes," he said. "There is no other option."

Chapter Twenty Six

I slept for what felt like forever.

I didn't remember the prince leaving the bedroom or the door closing behind him before I fell asleep, but the sun had set and rose before I woke up. I was a little disoriented upon waking, only because I wasn't sure of how much time had passed, but I sat up and I was full . . . of energy. Like I'd received the deepest, most rejuvenating sleep possible. It wasn't an abnormal level, like I'd done speed or anything, but I felt *good* and I . . .

And I remembered everything.

I fed on a human yesterday.

I jolted forward and winced as the heavy chain dragged over my still-sensitive skin. I realized that I wasn't chained to the bed, but I didn't move. I sat frozen, realizing something else. My dress was torn, the material pooling around my elbows. Scratches marred my upper arms. The woman—she had done that, because of what I had done to her.

"Oh God." I leaped from the bed.

Dragging the chain behind me, I raced into the bathroom and dropped to my knees. Seconds later, everything that I'd eaten in the last day came back up. When I was done, my sides ached. I sat back, holding the top of the gown to my chest and supporting my weight with my other hand. Cold sweat dotted my forehead.

Oh God, I had hurt that woman. I'd taken from her what was not mine to take. I didn't even know if she was okay or if I had taken too much. Feedings could kill humans.

I hadn't known I was capable of feeding like a fae.

My fingers curled around the top of my dress as I stared blankly at the tile floor. I didn't know who I was anymore. My breath caught in my chest. I'd forgotten how easy it was to fall under a fae's control. It had happened to me before, when I was younger, but I'd truly forgotten how easily it could happen.

One look and I'd been under the prince's control.

I'd been in complete control of myself, and a second later I hadn't been, and I'd done something that went against everything I believed in.

That poor woman.

I knew I hadn't willingly fed on her, but that didn't lessen any of the guilt festering deep inside me, and that guilt quickly grew, because it wasn't just a consequence of what I'd done to that woman. My stomach churned again.

I couldn't remember the details of what had happened between the prince and me. After I . . . I'd fed, it was like I'd been detached from my body, gone someplace else. It was like being slipped a roofie, but I was *somewhat* lucky, because he had stopped. I remembered that, but it didn't make me feel any real sense of relief.

An oily feeling settled over me, blanketing my entire body. I felt heavy, weighed down, and my skin, the bones and muscles, didn't feel like my own. And they hadn't been my own yesterday. I had no control. I knew that. My brain told me over and over that what happened yesterday with that poor woman wasn't my fault. I'd been under a manipulation, a compulsion, and I hadn't given Drake permission to touch me, to do *anything* with me. It wasn't my fault, but I still wanted to flay layers of my skin off. I wanted to strip off the dress and burn it, along with the bed and this entire house.

I wanted to cut what little memories I had out of my head with a butter knife.

What he had done wasn't remotely okay. I hadn't been in the right frame of mind. He'd controlled me, forcing me to feed, and then took advantage of me being as high as a kite.

My stomach twisted again and I lurched forward, clutching the toilet. I heaved, and the only thing that came up this time was spittle and air, but it burned my throat and hurt my stomach. Once I thought I wouldn't be sick again, I pushed away from the toilet.

I leaned back against the tub and dropped the end of the chain in my lap, closing my eyes and waiting for my heart to slow down. I focused on taking deep, even breaths and figuring out what my next steps would be. I had to have next steps. Something. I couldn't sit on the bathroom floor.

I needed to shower.

I could do that.

I opened my eyes and forced myself off the floor. I closed the bathroom door, and was dismayed upon realizing the lock had been removed. I had no idea when that had happened. I cranked on the water, turning it up as hot as I could stand, and then I placed the chain on the sink. I stripped off the gown and picked up the chain without looking at my reflection.

I stepping under the hot spray of water, gasping as it hit my arms. The scratches stung as they got wet. I didn't care if showering rusted the stupid band and chain. I stood under the hot water until my skin turned pink. Then I grabbed the bar of soap and lathered up not once but three times, and I still felt like I could do it again. Hot tears burned my eyes.

I can't do this.

Oh God. I wasn't sure I could deal with all of this for a moment longer, let alone until I figured a way out of here. I didn't regret making the deal. I'd had to make sure Ren was safe, but my plan had been so incredibly clueless, foolish even. Gaining time to figure out an escape only put me further under the prince's control, giving him opportunities I had never foreseen. And now what? I had no idea how I could work at gaining Drake's trust when I wanted to gouge out his eyeballs the next time I saw him.

I have to do this.

There was no choice—not really. Giving up wouldn't stop time, and even though I didn't plan on honoring our bargain when our time was up, I had to get out of here. I had to pull it together, because the only other option was that I . . .

I removed myself from the equation.

I stared at the mosaic tile of the shower stall. Could I do it? The chain hung heavily from my neck. It would be easy to use the chain, far too easy, but even in my darkest moments after Shaun's death, I'd never seriously considered ending my own life.

This situation was different though, because it wasn't grief or depression guiding the thought. My very existence was a means to an end, and I couldn't continue living like this, being forced to feed on humans. I also knew that eventually Drake wasn't going to stop.

A sob shook my shoulders and I stepped back, pressing against the tiled wall. Pressing my hands over my face, I struggled to hold it together. My entire body trembled. I wanted out of here. I didn't want to spend another second in this place, but what I wanted wasn't going to happen.

"Pull your shit together, Ivy." I gripped the chain and forced myself to turn off the water and step out of the shower. "You can deal with all this crap later, but you need to get your shit together."

Repeating those words over and over, I slowly stitched myself back together, because I had to—because I wasn't going to wake up and find myself safe. There were gaps in the stitches, gaping holes, but it was the best I could do. The only chance I had to get out of here with my life and my sanity was by following my earlier plan while keeping it together. That was the only thing I could control now.

~

Faye brought me a sandwich that evening, but I wasn't hungry. Anxious energy upset my stomach, and every time I heard footsteps outside the door, I expected Drake to come through. But he hadn't.

Yet.

She avoided eye contact with me as I picked at my food, managing to eat the slices of honey ham only because I knew I needed to eat something. When I couldn't swallow anymore, I set the plate on the nightstand and looked up to find Faye by the window.

I remembered seeing her yesterday when I went into that room and also when I left it. Or at least I think I saw her when I left. "Are you going to hook this chain back to the bed?"

Her shoulders stiffened as she finally focused on me. "I have not been told to. I hope I will not, but I guess it will depend on you."

My blood pressure shot up. "I'm not sure how being chained to a bed really depends on me."

"It shouldn't," she agreed, surprising me. "But it does."

Staring at her for a moment, I shook my head. "I . . . I don't get you."

Her silvery-blonde eyebrows rose.

"You know what I am, right? Not the halfling part or why I'm here. You know I'm an Order member—"

"And it would be your duty to murder me if you saw me on the streets?" she interjected. "Yes. I know."

Holding the end of the chain, I scooted over so my feet were on the floor. "Then why are you nice to me?"

She stepped away from the window. "Do I need a reason?"

I looked around the room. "Uh. Yeah. All things considered."

Faye frowned, and she still looked, well, magical. All fae did. They were stunning in an eerie, unreal way. "Is it so hard to believe that when I see you or anyone like you that my first inclination isn't to feed off you and kill you?"

Again, I looked around the room. "Considering where I am and where you are, uh, yes."

Gliding forward, she stopped a few feet from me. She started to speak, but the bedroom door flew open, and the ancient called Valor stood there.

"The prince wants her brought to him," he announced, pushing the door open further.

"No," I said.

Faye nodded and then stepped back. "If you come willingly, I will not have to lead you."

What seemed like such a small token of freedom was far more powerful than even I could have realized. My throat tight, I nodded and rose, holding the end of the chain. I wouldn't be led to wherever the prince was. I would walk there of my own free will.

"Thank you," I whispered to her as we followed Valor through the door.

Faye didn't acknowledge my words, and we were silent as I followed them down the hallway. We weren't going toward the stairs. I had a sinking suspicion that we were going to Drake's bedroom, and I really didn't like that idea.

We stopped in front of a set of large double pocket doors. Valor knocked once. The prince called out, "Come in."

Valor slid the doors open, then stepped aside. Faye walked in, then me. The first thing I noticed was the giant, four-poster bed in the middle of the room, one even larger than the one I'd been sleeping on, and then I noticed what was *in* the bed, and didn't notice anything else after that.

Drake wasn't alone.

He was on his back, arms folded behind his head, and a woman was on top of him, riding him backwards, cowgirl style or whatever they called it, and that woman was that fucking bitch Breena, and she was completely hairless. Everywhere.

Holy sex show, this was so not what I was expecting.

They were so naked. Like, I was seeing everything. *Everything*. Breena lifted her hips, and I got a good idea of what the prince had going on downstairs. Then she slammed back down, her lips curved into a grin, and her eyes, unfortunately not permanently damaged, focused on us. The prince groaned in a way that told me we'd come in at the tail end of their escapades.

"Jesus," I gasped, stepping back and bumping into Valor. "Do you need us to come back or something?"

"No." Drake's chuckle was deep and husky. "I was expecting you."

"Seriously?" I squeaked.

He grasped Breena's slim hips and lifted her off of him. She landed on the bed beside him with a jiggling bounce, and I quickly looked away, not wanting to see anything else. "Did she eat?" he asked Faye.

"A little," she responded, her voice surprisingly level, as if holding conversations with the prince while he was having sex was something normal. Maybe it was.

"If you don't eat your dinner, you don't get dessert," the prince stated.

My gaze shot to him. I didn't want to look, but I kind of had to, because it was like a train wreck of sex right in front of me. "Yeah, I don't want any dessert."

"You sure about that?" He reached over, curling his hand into Breena's mass of dark hair. He dragged her up onto her knees. "Do *you* want dessert?" he asked her.

Breena's gaze shifted to him and she licked her lips. "Of course I do." Placing a hand on his thigh, she leaned into Drake, pressing her front to his side. Then she licked the side of his face. "Do you know who else liked dessert?"

I tensed, knowing what she was going to say. "Do you want your eyes gouged out for real this time?" I said.

Turning her head to me, she smiled. "I'd like to see you try."

"I think I've already proven that I can." I returned her smile as my hands tightened around the chain I held.

"Enough." Amusement colored Drake's tone. He looked over at Breena. "You know what your mouth is better used on."

"Nice," I muttered.

Drake eyed me as Breena got down to making a better use of her mouth. "As if your human male doesn't feel the same."

"Actually, I'm pretty sure he respects me," I shot back.

"Respect?" Drake laughed as he stroked Breena's head like she was a damn pet. "What does that have to do with it?"

I almost couldn't believe he was asking that question, but then again, I wasn't entirely surprised. "Everything."

"Is that so? You know what I find amusing?"

"No." But I was betting he was going to tell me.

He leaned back, giving Breena more room to do her thing. "You stand before me as if you will still be reunited with your human lover. I find that amusing. I also find it amusing that you think he would have you back even if I hand delivered you to him in a pretty bow."

I sucked in a sharp breath.

"If he felt the same way about you, don't you think he would've found his way back here? That he would be storming the doors of our compound? We are well hidden, but where there is a will, there is a way."

His words were like a well-placed smack in the face. Drake didn't know what he was talking about. He didn't know what Ren and I had shared, but those words still stung. Those words still spoke to the fear and insecurities rooted deep inside of me.

"I don't need him to save me," I said, stating the truth.

He smirked. "You can't even save yourself."

Resisting the urge to pull a Princess Leia and charge over to the bed to wrap the chain around his neck like he was a slimmer version of Jabba the Hut, I asked rather haughtily, "Did you have me brought here just to talk about Ren while you have sex?"

"Is it that obvious?"

Breena laughed. Well, it was a muffled sound, because her mouth was otherwise occupied. Her head was bobbing and her hand was between her legs, and my face was on fire. Holy canola oil, this was . . . wow, there were no words. I looked over at Faye and she was staring at the floor. Maybe that was what I should do.

Totally going to do that.

But I looked over my shoulder at Valor instead. He was avidly watching the show on the bed, and I really just wanted to throw myself out the nearby window. Since I couldn't do that, I stared at the floor and tried to ignore the sounds coming from the bed. I didn't dare look up until I heard Drake groaning again.

Pulling Breena's head out of his lap, he then tossed his legs off the bed and stood. Buck-ass naked, of course.

I thought of Tink. He would freak if he was here right now. A weird giggle started to rise and I squelched it down.

He walked over to a chair and picked up a robe, slipping it over his shoulders. He left it hanging open, of course, because why not? I mean, what was the point since I'd just seen—

"It's time."

Those two words jerked me out of my thoughts. A chill

tiptoed down my spine, quickly turning into dread. "Time for what?"

The prince walked toward us. "It's time to feed."

Chapter Twenty Seven

I could barely keep track of time.

Minutes turned into hours, hours into days. I think ten days had passed since the first time I'd fed on that woman, but I wasn't exactly sure. Every ounce of my being was dedicated to keeping my head above water, but with every passing minute, I drowned a little more.

A sick and disturbing ritual started, one I wanted no part of but couldn't fight. No matter what I did, I was dragged under.

The prince would show every day, sometimes in the afternoon. Those days were better because I didn't spend hours waiting for him to show, knowing that he would and fearing what was to come. Part of me would rather get what was coming over with. Other times he showed in the evening, and I was wired after hours of dread eating away at me.

But he always showed, and I was never taken to his

room again.

I tried to resist the manipulation by keeping a distance between us, since I hadn't been chained to the bed again. But it didn't work. There was nowhere for me to go, and I . . . I didn't remember leaving the room with him after that.

I only remembered bits and pieces. Going down the stairs. Sitting on the woman's cot and wondering why her veins were so dark. Then I *fed*. I remembered feeling good and then not feeling anything at all, then falling asleep. Each time I woke up, I was full of energy—life that I'd been forced to steal from someone else—and then I showered. I *always* showered. Details of the time after the feedings were vague shadows I didn't dare examine too closely.

Every day was like that.

By around day twelve or thirteen, the chain was removed, but the band remained as a reminder—a stupid, pointless reminder, because if the prince wasn't there, I was sleeping or pacing. The door was locked and there was no busting through the heavy wood like a ninja. No one else came near me.

Not Breena.

Not Faye.

Food was always on the nightstand when I woke. I had no idea if it was Faye who brought it to me or one of the other fae, but it was always a sandwich of some sort. That was the only food I saw all day, and sometimes I wasn't hungry, because I . . . I was already full from a different source.

When I had complete control over my mind and body, it took every ounce of willpower that I had in me not to claw his heart out with my bare hands. It would've been hard and messy, but there was a damn good chance I could have done it. The hate building inside me burned brighter than a thousand suns, but even with that rage, I always, *always* felt cold. With each passing day, it was like I was filling up on the inside with ice and shadows. The only time I didn't feel this way was when I slept.

I felt nothing then.

Once he explained to me why I slept after . . . after feeding. The way he described it reminded me of how you want a nap after Thanksgiving dinner, but I also thought it sounded kind of like any time you were high. Eventually you came crashing back down and your body sort of gave out. There was no hangover or recovery for me though. All I needed was sleep, and I was better than before, as sickening as that was.

I didn't think of Ren during these times. I couldn't allow myself to, because when I thought of Ren, I worried about how safe he was. I knew the prince couldn't hurt him. He couldn't break his promise, and that meant he couldn't indirectly cause Ren harm, but that didn't stop any other fae from deciding a way to please their leader was to serve up Ren's head on a platter. And even though I tried not to allow it, Drake and Breena's words haunted me. Those words messed with me, just like they'd intended, and I thought maybe if I wasn't stuck in this room, being forced to do horrible things every damn day, I would have the strength not to give in to those words.

I didn't know anymore.

But in the minutes and hours I was alone, pacing the length of the room, no matter how hard I tried not to, I mourned Ren, because if I made it out of here alive and was reunited with him, I still couldn't see a happily ever after for us.

On the sixteenth day, the prince arrived in the afternoon. I was ready for him, restless and antsy, standing by the dresser in another dress, much like the first one, but in a deep forest green this time. I don't know what the fae around here had against pants, but I really looked like the chick from that Disney movie now.

The prince stopped just inside the room, his gaze moving from the bed to where I stood. Based on previous experience, I knew he would immediately pull me under, and once that happened, I would be lost.

"Can we talk for a little bit?" I blurted out before he could do anything.

His brows rose. "Talk?"

I nodded as I folded my arms across my chest. "Yeah, that's what people typically do."

"But we're not people."

Irritation spiked, and I took a deep, even breath. *Keep your cool, Ivy.* "I know, but I think talking wouldn't hurt. I only have a couple more days—"

"Six days if you're counting today," he interrupted.

"Thanks for keeping track," I replied, and he smirked. "But I'm still not . . . comfortable with you."

He stalked forward, and I tensed as I dropped my gaze, focusing on his booted feet. That would only work for so long. When a fae used manipulation, something changed in their voice. It was like a lullaby, and you had to listen and look. And once you looked, you were a goner.

"I would think by now you'd be comfortable," he said as he stopped a few feet in front of me.

Loathing of the deepest kind flared in my chest. He hadn't . . . God, I couldn't even bring myself to think it let alone say it, and I hated that, because it made me feel *shamed*, and I had done nothing wrong. Nothing.

He repeatedly took advantage of me, proving he was the worst kind of creature, and the only reason I think why he hadn't gone there was because he really didn't want me.

The prince was aroused only when I fought him, as disturbing and twisted as that was.

It took a couple of seconds before I trusted myself to speak. "You manipulate me into feeding, and then after that I'm not really me. None of that counts and doesn't help me get comfortable with you."

He leaned against the dresser, loosely crossing his arms. "I'm not sure it's actually necessary to get more comfortable."

"I disagree."

"I'm sure you do," he replied. "I've been incredibly lenient with you."

I blinked, and almost looked up at him. "Seriously?"

"Yes. I have removed the chain. I have not pushed, and if you think I have, then you haven't learned anything." Straightening, he curled his hand around my arm. "I could've gotten you to say yes several times over the last couple of days. I haven't. Should I have?"

"I would've said yes only because I'm not in control of myself," I said, shifting my gaze to the floor. "And I assume the reason why you haven't done that is because you know it won't work. Sure, you can get me to agree, but I cannot be under your control, and I am the entire time."

Drake didn't respond for several moments and then he dropped my arm. "What do you want to talk about?"

Surprise flickered through me. He was actually relenting? "I . . . I have questions."

"Then ask them."

His bored tone irked me, but I let it go. "Do we have to stay in here?"

He was silent for a moment. "I guess not. Where would you like to go?"

Hope sparked alive. "Outside."

"Not going to happen."

Out of instinct, I lifted my gaze, but stopped at his chest. "I have been locked in this room and in this house for over two weeks. I would like to breathe open air. Is that really too much to ask for?"

"Yes."

I unfolded my arms. "Being cooped up in here is going to drive me insane."

"I thought you already were."

I was seriously going to throat punch this guy. "All I'm asking for is a couple of minutes outside, in the sun and in the open air. That's it."

Drake muttered something in a different language and then pushed away from the dresser. He started for the door and I lifted my gaze. "If you try anything, you will not like what happens."

Triumph flashed within me. "Also, just a heads up, but threats don't exactly make me feel comfortable either."

He held the door open. "And just a heads up, I really don't care."

I pressed my lips together as I walked past him, knowing if I ticked him off now, I wouldn't just be starting all over. He'd have me down in that horrible room and I would be doing terrible things to innocent people.

That horrible cloudy feeling swept over me, and I was cold down to the marrow. Just standing beside him and having to breathe the same air made me feel like there was an iceberg taking up residence in my chest.

I hated it.

But I had to deal with it.

Pushing those thoughts aside to dwell and stress over later, I followed him down the winding staircase. There was an ancient by the front door. He said nothing as he opened it and stepped aside.

Cool air rushed over me, spreading goosebumps up and down my arms. The thin dress was no protection against the chilly temperature, but I wasn't going to complain. I was outside, and even though I knew I wouldn't make it far at all if I ran for it, there could be other opportunities. I just needed to . . . *behave* myself. Ugh.

Drake walked out onto a sprawling, vacant porch. I imagined at one time it had bushy ferns hanging above the railings and comfy chairs perfect for a lazy day of reading. There was nothing human about it now. Just cold. Empty.

A driveway that hadn't been repaved in ages cut into the dead grass and disappeared into the woods several yards from the front porch. I walked down the old stone steps, stopping in the sunlight. I inhaled, closing my eyes for a few seconds, centering my thoughts. There was a deep, rich earthy scent that reminded me of a pile of grass clippings. I recognized it. I opened my eyes, looking around. I didn't see it, but I knew we had to be close to the bayou.

"Ask your questions."

I hated a lot about the prince of the Otherworld, but I really hated his demanding tone. "Can we walk?"

Sighing, he practically stomped down the steps. "Ask."

I shot a nasty glare at his back, but I started walking. I did have a lot of questions and decided to start with the most important one. "What do you plan to do once you have your apocalypse baby?"

Drake looked over his shoulder at me. "Would you please stop calling it that?"

"What's your game plan? The baby is born and the gates open. What next?" I folded my arms again as I scanned the landscape. There were no other roads except the driveway we were walking down. I knew there were none at the back of the house, because the bedroom I was staying in faced that portion of land. It was just tall weeds and trees back there. "There are a lot of humans. Like seven billion or something. I know that sounds like an all-you-can-eat buffet, but that's a lot of humans who aren't going to want to be on a menu."

He chuckled as he glanced over at me. "Humans are stupid."

I shook my head. "Wow."

"They ignore the obvious. They have a tendency to stick their heads in the sand and fabricate logical explanations that assuage their fears rather than face what's right in front of them," he said, and I kind of had to agree with some of that. "They won't know we have taken control until it's too late."

"And how will you take control?" I asked.

He stood in the middle of the cracked driveway and faced me. I immediately lowered my gaze out of instinct. "There may not be seven billion fae in this realm, but there are hundreds of thousands of us now."

The Order always knew there were a lot of fae, but hundreds of thousands? Holy crapola, that was a lot.

"One fae equals a thousand humans," he said, and I figured his math was a bit biased. "And once we open the gates, all will come through, and there are millions of us."

Wind tossed my curls across my face as I stared at his chest. There was no way, for obvious reasons, we could allow that to happen. "There are still more of us."

"You mean more of *them*," he corrected. "Do you think

we haven't been planning for decades? Centuries?" He stepped forward, and my muscles locked up. "We are not barbarians who can only conquer by war. Not that we'd completely rule out that option if it came to that."

Good to know. I started walking past him, toward the end of the driveway. "But?"

"But we have planned," he repeated, easily catching up to me with his long legs. "We are everywhere. Some are just ordinary citizens. Others have willed their ways into positions of power."

I thought of Marlon. He was known as a huge developer in the city, and he had a lot of power locally, but I knew Drake wasn't just talking about land development. "You've infiltrated the government, haven't you?"

Without even looking at his face, I knew he was smiling when he spoke. "Local. Federal. Global. We are everywhere, and it's only a matter of time before we have complete control."

He made it sound so simple, and in a way, it was. If they got into enough positions of power, they could take over, slowly changing the world into what they wanted.

"It still won't be easy," I said. "Once we figure out what's happening, we'll fight back. And yes, the fae have abilities we don't, but we have a reason to fight no matter what."

"And what reason is that?"

We'd reached the wooden area, and strangely, but not exactly surprising, there were no sounds of life. No birds. Insects. Nothing. "We value freedom above anything else."

"Except most humans will already be bent to our will and they will fight *for* us," he said. "Human cannon fodder."

Disgusting. Terrifying.

"I'm done with this," he said abruptly, startling me. "It's time."

Heart lurching in my chest, I took a step back. "Wait. We haven't been out here long enough. I still have questions."

"You can ask them later."

Taking another step back, I struggled to keep the panic down. "Can we walk for a little bit longer? I don't—"

"You're delaying the inevitable." Impatience rang throughout his tone.

Sweat dotted my palms. "I don't have to . . . have to feed. You've made your point now. I get it. You can make me do whatever you want. I don't need to do that. I don't want to."

"You obviously haven't gotten the point since you keep referring to yourself as a human. It's time for you to remember what you are," he said. I knew there was no winning this argument with him.

I spun around quickly, prepared to run back to the house.

"Ivy. Stop."

I stopped.

Just like that, my body was compelled to answer even though my brain was desperately yelling at me to get away, to move—to do anything to stop what was coming.

"Look at me."

His voice slipped over my skin like silk. My ears buzzed as I felt my body slowly turning to face him. Against my will, my gaze lifted to his. I waited.

Drake's eyes deepened. "You will do as I say."

And I did.

It was strange. One minute I was outside, skin chilled

from the cold air, and the next I was in that room. There were different people in here now. The woman was gone, and I wondered what had happened to her. Then I was sitting next to an older man I didn't know. He had silver hair at his temples, and then after a few whispered words, I was . . . feeding, and then I was upstairs, slipping into a deep sleep.

I was shaken awake, a demanding hand biting into my shoulder. I woke to a dark room and a pale, silvery face.

Faye.

I leaned away from her, rolling onto my side. My thoughts were full of cobwebs, and I couldn't quite recall the last several hours. All I knew was that I wasn't supposed to be awake yet. I needed more time. My eyelids started to drift shut.

"You need to wake up," she said, grabbing my arm and squeezing hard.

Confused, I resisted when she tugged on me. "I . . ."

"There's no time to explain. You must get up now," Faye said. "It's your only chance if you want to escape."

Chapter Twenty Eight

"W-what?" I whispered.

Faye leaned over and turned on the bedside lamp. Soft light flooded the room. "You must get up, Ivy. The prince is not here and this will be your only chance."

Her words tumbled through my brain like tumbleweeds rolling down a vacant street. I was slow to make sense of them, but I didn't close my eyes again. I pushed myself up into a sitting position. Nausea hit me, clearing enough of the cobwebs for me to realize that was different from when I woke normally after . . . after feeding.

Feeding.

My gaze lifted to Faye's. "I fed again."

Frustration pinched her features as she reached toward me, unlocking the band around my neck. She tossed it onto the bed. "I know. And if you keep feeding, you're going to get addicted. You probably already are."

"Addicted?" I repeated dumbly. That was the first I'd

ever heard of that. "What do you—?"

"Ivy." She clutched my shoulders and shook me until my head snapped back. "You need to focus. We have to go now. Do you understand me? This will be your only chance before your time is up and the prince will be in this bed, creating a child that will open all the gates to the Otherworld."

Creating a baby . . .

Holy shit. I tossed my hair back from my face as the remaining tendrils of sleep cleared and the fogginess left my thoughts. "The prince isn't here?"

"No." She pushed off the bed and stood. "He left about thirty minutes ago, taking three of the ancients with him. It was a planned trip, but we don't have a lot of time. There's only a small window of opportunity."

Pushing off the bed, I moaned as a wave of dizziness hit me. I fought through it, straightening. "Sorry," I gasped out. "I'm not feeling too well."

"Of course not. You have to sleep off the more unpleasant effects until you get used to them." She walked over to the door, pressing the side of her face against the wood. "Fae don't necessarily experience the adverse reactions, and only the younglings, when they first start feeding, experience the euphoria and following sleepiness, but for halflings . . . it can be different. But that's not important right now."

I raised a brow as I tucked the bushy mass of hair behind my ears. I had a feeling what she was saying was going to be important later, but right now, it wasn't a priority. Later, I was going to have so many questions for her. "So you're going to help me escape?"

She nodded. "And before you ask why, all you need to know right now is that the Order is not the only ones who want to prevent the gates from opening."

I stared at her carefully. Trusting her was risky, but then again, why would this be a trap? And if it was, could the consequences be any worse than what I was already facing?

"Okay," I said. "Let's do this."

"I couldn't get a thorn stake." She reached around to the back of her jeans and pulled out an iron dagger. She pressed the handle into my hand. "But this will do."

My fingers curled around the handle of the weapon I was oh so familiar with. It felt like ages since I had held one, and I welcomed the weight in my hand. "It will do," I said as she reached for the door. I thought about something. "Wait."

She looked at me.

Grabbing a handful of the dress, I lifted the skirt part and used the dagger to cut a slit halfway up my leg to allow for more movement. "Ready," I said.

Faye grabbed the doorknob but paused. "I won't kill any of them," she warned me. "I will incapacitate, but I will not kill."

I thought about that for a second. "Okay. I'm probably going to kill them, though."

She made an exasperated sound, but opened the door and peered out. "It's clear."

Knowing this could somehow blow up in my face, but willing to risk it for a chance to get out of this place, I took a deep breath and pushed everything aside. Now was not the time to think about what I'd been forced to do while being imprisoned here, or about Ren, or anything other than escaping.

I followed her out into the hall, and we made our way to the stairs. At the top, she said in a low voice, "There are three fae downstairs in the main room. There are more in the house, but I hope we can get out before they know what's happening. Valor is . . . he is occupied at the moment in the back room."

Knowing what the back room was used for, I couldn't suppress a shudder. "Can you incapacitate quietly? Because I can kill quietly."

"Yes."

I looked down the stairs, not seeing anyone yet. "Let's go."

We crept down the stairs, and of course the steps creaked every couple of steps, sounding like cracks of thunder. The truth was, I wasn't sure how quietly I could kill. I had never really attempted to do it without making noise.

Faye reached the landing first. We were about twenty feet from the front door, and we were so close, but the foyer opened into two rooms. There was a good chance we'd be seen. My pulse pounding, I stepped down into the foyer, pressing the dagger against my leg. I took two steps before a voice rang out from the adjoining room.

"Where are you two going?"

Cursing under my breath, I looked over to see a male fae walking toward us with another fae behind him. Faye didn't answer, so I decided to go the "whole kill me some fae" route.

I stepped toward the male. A flicker of surprise scuttled across his features a second before I slammed the dagger into his chest. He did the poof-begone thing.

"What the hell?" The second fae charged toward me, but Faye intercepted him. Spinning gracefully, she dipped behind him and caught his arm, easily flipping him onto his back. She twisted as she went down, snapping bone.

The fae screamed. There went being quiet.

"Sorry," Faye said a second before snapping the fae's neck. Damn, she was a beast.

Snapping a fae's neck wouldn't kill them, but it would definitely take them out of the equation for a bit. I darted past her and threw open the front door. She was right behind me.

The cold night air greeted us. So did the third fae, who was outside smoking.

She spotted us, and as she turned, she flicked her cigarette off the porch and rushed us. I easily side-stepped her and jerked my arm back, preparing to deliver the killing blow.

"You don't need to kill her," Faye cried out. "They don't know any better."

"Not kill her?" I ducked as the female swung at me. "Oh, we're really going to have to talk about the whole 'they don't know any better' part later."

Shifting onto my back leg, I spun and delivered a kick that sent the female flying into the porch railing. Wood splintered and gave way. Arms pinwheeling, she fell backward, off the porch.

Not so graceful then.

Charging forward, I hopped off the porch and picked up a long piece of splintered railing. I could have taken her out right then, and I wasn't even sure why I felt I should try to follow Faye's wishes, but she was helping me. Hopefully.

The female fae started to sit up, but I swung down, using the railing to impale her to the ground. Blood spurted, and as she opened her mouth to scream bloody murder, I knocked her out with an elbow jab to the temple.

I stood up, tossing my hair back.

Faye gaped at me.

"What?" I demanded. "It won't kill her."

She slowly shook her head. "We need to go down the driveway. Leads to a road about a mile out. We're going to cross it and keep going. Okay?"

A mile out? God, I hated running. But I also hated being forced to do things against my will, so I'd run five miles if I had to. It might kill me, but I would do it.

The cracked pavement was cold under my bare feet as we ran with only the moonlight and stars to guide us. Faye was faster, staying several feet in front of me. Hope was welling up in my chest. We were almost to the woods, and then we'd be out of sight of the house and close to the road. We'd be closer to—

"Stop!" a deep male voice shouted.

Faye looked over her shoulder. "Dammit, two fae. We need to keep going."

I was going to take her word for it, and I was also going to ignore the fact that she wasn't even out of breath. "They will catch up," I gasped out as we entered the wooded area. "We have to take them out."

Faye stopped suddenly, eyeing my location and how far behind her I was. "You're right."

Looking around, I slowed down and then stopped. There wasn't even time to hide for an ambush. We had to face them. "I'm killing this time," I warned, glancing over at her. "It's too risky not to."

Her jaw was set in a hard line, but she nodded.

One of the fae reached us ahead of the other. It was the male who'd been in the room the first time I'd fed, the one who had been on his phone. I sprung forward, thrusting the dagger out. He spun to the side, narrowly avoiding my stab. Anger twisted his features into something animalistic. He swung on me and I dipped as Faye caught the other fae, a female, by the waist and drove her to the ground like a linebacker. Damn.

I knelt, avoiding the next blow. On the ground, I kicked out, taking the male's legs out from under him. Leaping up, I came down on him, bringing the iron dagger home. I lifted up as he sucked into himself, earning a one-way—hopefully—ticket back to the Otherworld. When I looked up, I saw that Faye had broken another neck.

I heard rustling and spun around, praying to God an alligator didn't try to eat me. Scanning the area, I didn't see anything. Thank God for small—

"Ivy, watch out!"

I spun around and gasped. Valor was less than a foot from me. I jumped back, but that didn't help. He caught my arm and I went flying across the driveway. Barely able to brace myself for the impact, I hit the soggy ground on my side and rolled into a bush. Pain arced across my back, but I pushed through it as I sat up.

Faye was tossed aside. She smacked into a tree and hit the ground face-first. She didn't get right back up, and I hoped she was okay.

"Shit," I muttered, pushing myself up. I still had that dagger and I was sort of proud of my mad skills there.

"What were you two thinking?" Valor demanded as he stalked toward me, crossing the driveway. "Did you really think you could escape?"

"Uh. Yes."

"Stupid," he growled. "And because of your actions, she will die and you will wish you had been smart enough to know better."

I didn't feel necessary to point out that my actions hadn't driven Faye to do this. I waited until he was a foot in front of me and then feinted to my left. Valor fell for it and darted in that direction. I spun out, delivering a kick to his right side. He stumbled and threw a punch. It connected with my jaw, stunning me for a second as tiny bright lights burst across my line of vision. I knew I had to fight hard. I had to get him down and not give him a chance to use any of his special ancient abilities or to get the best of me, because I knew taking down an ancient wasn't going to be easy.

Kicking out again, I hit his right leg and then straightened, jabbing the dagger deep into his side. He grunted and swung, but I anticipated the move and dipped under his arm. Now in front of him, I caught him in the chest again with the dagger, and immediately brought my leg up, kneeing him in the nuts.

Valor doubled over, and I caught his shoulders, shoving him down with my weight. He went, clutching his poor boys. He rolled onto his back, and I saw the opportunity. I had to do some major damage to keep him down.

I dropped to the ground next to him, the damp soil soaking through my dress. He rolled onto his side, grabbing my left arm and yanking hard enough that I worried he'd pull it out of its socket. He shouted, and I didn't think about what I was doing, because it was *so* gross. I just did it. Slamming the blade down, I went for the eye, and I hit my target. His roar was cut off and his arms dropped limply. Dark blood and other liquid I didn't want to think too closely about, because it might make me puke, spurted into the air, hitting my face and chest.

The hit wasn't going to kill the dumb son of a bitch, but I figured it would keep him down for a while.

"Ivy!" Faye shouted, up and apparently alive. "Let's go!"

Yanking the iron dagger out of Valor's eye socket, I stood up and took off, darting across the street, following Faye's moonlit form. We ran for several more yards, twigs and fallen branches tearing at my feet. Small rocks dug into my skin, but I kept going. My heart felt like it was going to pound right out of my chest, but this was my only chance. If I didn't get away now, I was never getting away.

Feet pounded behind me. Sparing a look over my shoulder, I saw the ancient I'd just stabbed in the damn face tearing through the woods, dark liquid pouring down his face. Jesus, he was like the Terminator Ancient. I dug in, giving it everything I had.

But it wasn't enough.

Air exploded out of my lungs as he crashed into me from behind, taking me down. The impact knocked the dagger out of my hand, and his weight drove me several inches into the mush where I got a mouthful of soil and grass. Dirt clogged my nostrils, and for a moment I couldn't breathe.

Spitting the mess out, I dragged in gulps of air as Valor grabbed a handful of my hair and jerked my head back. "You fucking bitch," he spat. "I could snap your neck in a second."

My fingers dug into the soil as I reached for my dagger. "I don't think your prince would be happy about that."

Valor flipped me onto my back and loomed over me, one hand still tangled in my hair. His face was a mess—really not a pretty sight. "Do you think that will stop me? He'll find another halfling. You're not the only one."

"I'm the closest," I spat out, lifting my hips to throw him, but he wouldn't budge.

His grip in my hair tightened, and fire spread across my skull. I was going to be bald if he kept it up. "He's going to think you escaped, but in truth, you're going to be dead."

I started to point out that my escaping on his watch was probably not going to over well, but I didn't get the chance. His other hand came down, landing on my throat, squeezing and cutting off my air before I realized I'd taken my last breath.

That was it.

My eyes widened as I grabbed his wrist, scratching and tearing at his skin, but it did nothing to alleviate the pressure. Where in the hell did Faye go? He was choking the life out of me! A deep, unholy burn bloomed in my chest and rapidly crawled up my throat. I went for his gouged-out eye, but he leaned away, keeping just out of reach. Panic exploded, raw and all-consuming as the corners of my vision darkened.

Valor was really going to kill me.

This was it.

I was going to die in the bayou like I was some poor victim in an episode of an investigative Discovery Channel show.

My strength was waning and I could no longer keep swinging at him. My hand slipped down his arm, and all I could think—

Valor suddenly jerked and his grip on my throat loosened. Air rushed into my lungs as he looked down at his chest where a stake had burst through. And not an iron one, either.

His body trembled but no sound came out of his gaping mouth as I scrambled out from underneath him. The ancient was a goner. Dead. Oxygen burned my raw throat and my eyes watered as I rolled sideways. My brain kept telling me to get up and start running again, but all my limbs were tingling and they felt sort of detached.

A gentle, warm hand touched my shoulder. "Ivy."

I stilled. Slowly, I lifted my head, and with a shaky hand, pushed my hair back from my face. My voice was hoarse and weak as I said, "Ren."

Chapter Twenty Nine

Shocked and utterly speechless, I stared up at Ren, and a part of me wondered if I was hallucinating, because I couldn't understand why he was here.

Ren slowly knelt beside me. Moonlight highlighted his cheekbones and full mouth. "Ivy, are you okay?"

I had no voice as I stared at him. His hair fell in waves over his forehead. In the darkness, his green eyes were nearly black. He looked a little pale, almost shaken. It looked like Ren and he'd killed Valor, but I . . . I wasn't sure of anything anymore.

My heart, which never really slowed down, kicked into high gear, pounding so fast I felt like it would give out any second.

I'd been fooled before. I'd let my own wants and desires to be reunited with Ren clog all my sense of judgment. If I had been paying attention, had been less emotional, I would've noticed right off the bat that something was wrong with Ren, that it wasn't him.

He reached out, as if to touch me.

Unable to trust my own judgment, I scuttled back across the ground. He froze and I threw out my hand, warding him off. He didn't move toward me. That was a good sign, I thought, as I unsteadily got to my feet. He did the same, and I noticed then that he held the thorn stake in his hand. It had to be him, right? Drake wouldn't have one of those. He'd thrown aside the one I had while we'd been in Ren's apartment, but he could've went back and got it. He could've had anyone go back. This could be a trap. I had no idea where my dagger was, not that it would do much good if this was Drake. Slowly, I stood.

Feeling sick, I took a small step back as I glanced at the mushy ground. It was too dark to see my weapon.

"Ivy," Ren spoke, causing my gaze to snap to his. "It's okay. Everything is okay."

I wet my lips. Everything might not be okay. When I spoke, my voice cracked. "Is . . . is it really you?"

His brows knitted together as stark pain flickered across his face. "Yes, it's me." His voice was hoarse. "It's really me, sweetness."

Sweetness. Ren called me that. Drake as Ren never had.

My hands started to tremble. Could it really be him? He came back after . . . after everything? The tremble traveled down my legs. No. There was no reason.

"Ivy." A voice intruded on my thoughts. Faye. She was still alive and standing behind Ren. And she wasn't alone. Two more fae were with her. I tensed. "We have to go. We're out of time," she said.

"You . . ." I swallowed, feeling out of it. My gaze shot back to Ren. I was frozen in place, my mind and body snagged. "I don't know if it's you," I said. "I don't know why there are more fae here."

"It's me." Ren's voice was gruff. "I'll explain everything later, but we have to go, and I know it's a lot to ask, babe, but I need you to trust me right now. To trust us. If we don't go, we will lose this window. We—" He cut himself off, then reached into his pocket, pulling out his cellphone. "We have a couple more seconds," he said, hitting a button on his phone.

He was calling someone, and I couldn't think of who he would be calling right now.

Faye shook her head and came forward. The other two male fae stayed back, scanning the area. "We don't have time. More will be coming."

"Hey," Ren said, ignoring her. "I need you here. Yeah, I know I told you to stay in the car, but you need to get here. Right now. We're about a mile from where you are." There was a pause as Ren stared at me. "She's here, but I need you to be—" He paused abruptly, and frustration deepened his tone. "Dammit. Just get here. *Now*."

I had no idea what was happening, but I was shaking, and I didn't even know why. Confusion clouded my thoughts as Ren disconnected the call and put the phone in his pocket. His gaze never left me, not once, and it made me uncomfortable, because of, well, everything. *Everything*.

I suddenly didn't feel like myself. I wasn't Ivy Morgan. I wasn't a fighter relying on instinct, because Ivy would be running since this could be a trap. Ivy would risk it all then go down fighting. Ivy wouldn't be locked in place, full of indecision and fear. I was this . . . thing who had fed on people because a monster made me do it just to survive. I didn't . . .

I didn't even know who I was anymore.

God, I didn't need to think about that right now. I needed to pull it together. I was losing my damn mind at the most inopportune moment ever possible, in the history of—

"Ivy!"

I twisted to the right and my eyes widened. A tall form was cutting through the trees, moving as fast as a sprinting deer. I knew that voice, and if he was here, then this was Ren and it *was* okay.

Tink burst into the clearing. He was man-sized and wearing jeans. And a shirt. He actually had a shirt on.

"Ivy!" he yelled.

"Lower your voice," Faye said.

Tink didn't listen, because he was Tink, but I had never been happier in my life to see him. He shouted my name again, and then he was crashing into me, nearly taking me to the ground. All the aches and bruises screamed in protest, but I wrapped my arms around him.

"Oh my Queen Mab, I thought you were dead! Or at least knocked up! And I thought I'd be dead, because no one but Jerk-Face over there knew about me, and I thought I would starve. Starve to death!"

"Tink," Ren warned, voice low.

"And I was just sitting at home, all by myself. Well, not by myself, but I don't think you want to hear about that right now, but I was worried. You didn't come home for days and days, and I was down to ordering cereal off of Amazon and"—he took a quick breath—"I never thought I'd see you again. Even when Renny showed up. I thought all was lost," he wailed, squeezing me so tight as he swayed back and forth. "And I was going to have to live with him now, and . . . Wait, why are you wearing a dress?"

I clung to Tink, my arms wrapped tightly around him. Tears burned my eyes and hit my cheeks, because I . . . I never thought I'd see him again.

~

We had to run again.

Once Tink got himself under control, I was able to get myself moving. His presence was more than just comforting. With him here, I knew this wasn't a trap. Ren was real. Faye and her mystery fae friends weren't going to try to drag me back to Drake or lock Ren in the pantry again.

With Tink here, and his hand clenching mine, I was Ivy again. Sort of. I was enough of my old self that I knew what I needed to do to have the highest chance of survival. Indecision took a back seat.

Faye and the two mystery fae flanked the three of us— Tink, Ren, and me. And I wasn't doing much running at this point. Tink was mostly half-dragging me. We ran another mile and then came upon a dark stretch of narrow road. The scent of earth and dank water was strong as we slowed down. An oversized black SUV was parked on the shoulder of the road.

The two fae opened the tailgate and climbed in, getting in the very back. Then Tink slid in. He didn't sit. His long body was folded, cramped as he bent over, waiting. A hand touched my shoulder, and I jolted.

"It's just me." Ren removed his hand, his face shadowed. "I'm just helping you get in."

I flushed as I nodded jerkily, then placed my hand in his. I climbed up into the back of the SUV and sat in the seat.

"Dammit," Ren exploded, and I looked up at him. He

was staring down.

"What?" I asked.

"Your feet. Jesus." Concern flashed over his face as he held open the back door. "We need to look at them as soon as we get back."

I didn't even feel my feet anymore, but I looked down and saw that they were covered in dirt and blood.

Ren hesitated for a second and then closed the door. I watched him jog around the hood of the SUV while Faye climbed into the front passenger seat, and then he was behind the wheel. I sat, tensed and ready for Drake or an ancient to appear out of nowhere.

Then we were moving, hitting the road and quickly speeding up. I looked over at Tink. He was quiet, which was really odd. Tink was *never* quiet.

I drew in a deep breath and glanced up at the front. Ren's hand was clenching the steering wheel so tightly that his knuckles were bleached white. His gaze flicked up to the rearview mirror for a second, finding mine.

What was going through his head? I had no idea, but I shouldn't have been surprised that he was here, taking part in this rescue mission. He was a member of the Elite, and obviously I couldn't be left with the prince.

I pressed my lips together and turned to the window, staring out at the dark scenery racing by. Faye was speaking to Ren in a low voice, and I wanted to know how they had met. How their two worlds had crossed. Was it when he was held captive at the mansion, or after? And who were these fae sitting behind us? There were so many questions, but I didn't ask them. I just stared out the window, watching the woods blur and give way to the grasslands and swamps.

Part of me wondered if this was a dream. Was I really

out of there, sitting in the car with Tink and Ren? I rested my forehead against the cool glass. Yes, this was real. The ache in my hip and the soreness in my throat told me it was. When I dreamed, I didn't feel this . . . cold inside. When I dreamed, I didn't feel like I was full of shadows.

I was happy—thrilled that I was out, and with each passing second, I was further and further away from that place, but I couldn't . . . I just couldn't relax. It was like I was too tired to, and that didn't even make any sense. My hands shook, so I shoved them between my knees.

Eventually, we hit the city and I started to recognize where we were. It had taken a while to get back to the land of normalcy, which gave me an idea of how far out I'd been the last couple of weeks. Once we got close to the Mississippi River, I realized where we were heading as Ren turned onto Market Street.

I slid my hands out from between my knees and turned toward the front. "Are we"—I cleared my throat—"are we going to the old power plant?"

"Yes," answered a fae in the back. When I looked over my shoulder, I saw it had been the one sitting on the right. He had fair hair, lighter than the other male. He didn't look at me when he spoke. "My name is Kalen," he said. "And this is Dane."

They were some . . . fae-like names. "Ivy," I murmured.

"I'm Tink," Tink announced. "But you guys know that."

"Yes," Dane said, sighing. "We know that."

Tink grinned.

I turned back to the front. "I don't understand. I checked out this place. It was on a . . ." I trailed off, not wanting to explain how I knew about it.

"It was on a map that Merle drew?" Kalen answered, and I twisted back around. His smile was faint. "We know.

Merle is with us. So is her daughter. They are safe."

Then it struck me, and I felt a little stupid that it had taken me so long to figure it out. "You . . . you guys are the *good* fae?"

"I told you that not everything is as it seems," Faye replied from the front, drawing my attention. "Good and evil are subjective," she continued, peering back over the seat at me. "But we do not kill humans. We do not use our abilities to manipulate humans beyond protecting what we are and where we live. And most of us don't feed on humans."

"They age," Tink said. "And die like humans. I'm a brownie. Therefore, I do not need to feed. I just age very, very, very slowly."

"I'm guessing you're probably still in your toddler years then," Ren muttered from up front.

Tink snorted. "I'll have you know that I'm two hundred years old."

My eyes widened as I looked over at him. "What?"

Faye laughed softly. "Brownies can live to be over a thousand years old. In human years, he's barely twenty."

Ren snickered.

Tink's eyes narrowed.

I jumped in before those two got into it, and while that was a welcome thing to hear and see again, I had so many questions. "Okay. I checked the power plant out. It's rundown and abandoned."

"We know you checked the place out." Dane leaned between the seats. "We saw you, but we only let you see what we wanted you to see. It keeps the humans away. Allows us to live in peace away from the . . ."

I got it. "Away from the Order."

"Exactly." He sat back. "The kind of glamour we're

using on the building can't be seen through. No wards will break it."

"And this isn't the only building like this?" I asked.

"No," Ren answered as the vehicle slowed. "It's not."

I exhaled slowly and sat back against the seat. There was a lot I didn't know. Big surprise there. Outside the window, the old power plant came into view. It still looked like a place where a serial killer would leave their victims' body parts. Ren turned down the road, heading towards the back of the building. We passed the old metal fencing and then we entered a narrow alley where the vehicle stopped.

Ren killed the engine, and as I stared at his profile, my heart started kicking around in my chest. His hands slipped off the steering wheel, and I saw his shoulders rise. He turned, his gaze finding and holding mine in the dimly lit interior for what felt like forever. Neither of us spoke in those precious seconds that felt like forever and yet not nearly long enough.

Faye spoke, breaking the spell. "We're trusting you, Ivy. We brought in Ren. We trust him, and I swore to my people that bringing you here would be safe," she said. "We can protect you from the prince, but we cannot put our people at risk."

"Aren't your people going to be at risk once the prince finds out I'm missing?" I asked.

Kalen spoke up from behind us. "The prince is not our only concern. The Order cannot know where we are either."

My gaze flew to Ren. Obviously if he was here, then he had agreed to keep this all from the Elite and the Order, and that was a big deal. I had no idea how he had come about finding this place and why he had decided to trust them, because that was a huge leap for any Order member to be working with the fae, no matter how good they claimed to be. It was still hard to believe what Merle had wrote in her journals.

But Faye had gotten me out of that place, away from Drake, and Tink was here, along with Ren. "Okay," I said, agreeing to the one thing that was sure to get me kicked out of the Order. Then again, being a halfling also revoked my card-carrying membership. But I still felt uneasy, even though it was the right thing to do. "I won't betray you."

Chapter Thirty

Faye studied me a moment.

"She won't." Tink opened the door on his side. "She kept me all this time and never told anyone. Renny-Tin-Tin didn't even know about me until he walked out into the kitchen naked with his junk all hanging out, swinging—"

"I'm going to punch you," Ren cut in. "And it will hurt."

Tink was already out of the car when I spoke to Faye. "I won't say anything. Tink's telling the truth. I never told anyone about him until Ren . . . um, accidentally discovered him."

Another second passed and then she nodded. "Okay."

Tink opened my door from the outside as I heard Dane whisper to Kalen, "Naked?" I was glad Ren was out of the SUV.

I climbed out, wincing as my feet hit the ground. The pain registered now, and it sucked. Each step I took felt like I was walking on fire.

Dane walked over to the gate while Kalen got into the driver's seat of the SUV. He took off, going somewhere, as Dane placed his hand on the building. The metal shook and began to slide to the side.

"The glamour will fade in a few seconds," Ren said, coming to stand beside me. "Once you're inside, you'll see what's really here."

Having no idea what to expect, I waited until Dane had created an opening large enough for us to walk through. He went in first, followed by Tink, who stopped just inside, waiting for me.

"Can you walk?" Ren asked.

I really didn't want to, but I nodded. I got my legs moving, feeling Ren right behind me. Faye was the last to come in, closing the metal wall behind us. At first, I just saw murky darkness—possibly a scrap yard, but then the air shimmered like a thousand fireflies had taken flight. A veil of dizzying sparks suddenly dropped, revealing what truly existed.

"Oh my God," I whispered.

We were in a beautiful courtyard—a garden straight out of a fairytale. Tall trees rose up to the night sky. Paper lanterns hung from the limbs, illuminating the way. There were vines and plants everywhere, virtually untouched by the cold. It did seem warmer here, at least by ten or so degrees. The place carried a magical, almost surreal feeling.

"Crazy, isn't it?" Ren said, his voice low. "When I first saw it, I couldn't believe my eyes. That this has been here the whole time." He looked down at me. "What Merle wrote in her books was true, Ivy. They've been here a long time, and this place—places hidden like this—are everywhere."

"You make it sound so creepy," Faye said. "We aren't really *everywhere*. I mean, we're hidden in a lot of places, but we do it because of safety."

"That's just Ren, being all ominous." Tink walked ahead, his arms swinging at his sides. "He's not really what you'd call a people person. I think he's socially awkward. Or maybe just intellectually stunted."

Ren sighed and appeared to be counting numbers under his breath.

Wrapping my arms around my waist, I followed them down the grassy pathway toward a pavilion that butted up to the back of a building that was—wow—no longer an abandoned factory.

Nothing was dilapidated. There were no missing bricks or busted windows. One whole section was nothing but a glass wall. A set of large French doors were open, and I could see that the insides were brightly lit.

Tink was inside by the time I crossed the pavilion, walking past numerous thick-cushioned, comfy-looking chairs. Warm air heavy with the scent of coffee and vanilla tickled my nose as I stepped into what only could be described as something similar to a hotel lobby.

Golden chandeliers hung from the high ceiling, and the building had to be bigger than it appeared outside, because the ceiling alone was two stories high. Chairs were everywhere, some spaced around fireplaces, others in front of large TVs that were currently turned off.

Further in, I saw that there was an honest to goodness coffee shop. My mouth was probably hanging open.

"You hanging in there?" Ren asked quietly. He was by my side. Had been the whole way in here. The sleeves of his shirt were pushed up now, and I saw the tattoo on his arm.

Drake had the same tattoo when he was pretending to be Ren, but for some reason it looked different now. More real. More Ren.

"Ivy?"

Realizing he'd been waiting for me to answer, I forced a nod even though I really wasn't okay. This was a lot to process. Everything was a lot to process. I felt like I had fallen down a rabbit hole, and a cat was going to appear out of nowhere and start talking to me like I was on some kind of acid trip.

"What is . . . what is this place?" I asked, hearing how shaky my voice was.

Faye faced me, not a strand of her long silvery hair out of place. "It's a safe haven of sorts, but on any given day, there are about a hundred fae who live here."

My lips parted on a sharp inhale as my arms fell to my sides. "A hundred fae . . . ?"

"We can house more. We have a store down at the end of that hall." She gestured to my left, pointing to somewhere beyond the coffee shop. "And we have a cafeteria."

I started to ask if it served humans or food, but luckily and wisely stopped the dumb, needlessly smartass comment. I wanted to ask, though.

"Ivy needs to shower and rest." Tink grabbed my hand suddenly. "What room can she stay in? I think she would like the one that overlooks the garden. And it's not super far up, only on the eighth floor."

There were how many floors? Then again, this place could house over a hundred fae. Holy fae overload, this place was under some powerful-ass glamour.

Faye's brow furrowed while she thought about it. "The garden room is fine."

"Okay." Tink started dragging me to my right. "We'll

head up. See you guys later."

I looked over my shoulder at Ren. He was standing next to Faye, his arms crossed and jaw hard, but the look etched onto his face, in his bright green eyes, was a wealth of sadness that was hard to look upon. With a knot in my throat, I turned away and let Tink lead me to the elevators.

He didn't say anything as he hit the button for the eighth floor, but he held my hand. It was kind of weird, but also good. There was something comforting about it.

"This place . . . it's like a hotel," I said as the doors opened.

"That's what your boy toy said too." We stepped inside, and as the doors quietly slid shut, he looked down at me. "You don't need to shower if you don't want to, but you *are* kind of filthy. Your eyes are a bit messed up, and you have dirt all over you."

"I can shower," I said dryly.

"But I also thought you'd like some time alone, because it's about two in the morning, and the fae around these parts get up at the butt crack of dawn. And there are a lot of them, Ivy. A lot. Like I couldn't spit and not hit one."

"That's . . . reassuring."

"But they are good. I promise you. Some are a little nervous right now, because of Ren. Not me." The elevator stopped, and he led me out into a wide hall. He hung a left, leading me toward a room that had "GARDEN" written on the door. "They love me. You see, brownies are, like, the shit in the Otherworld. So I am the supreme shit here."

I frowned, wondering if he knew how that sounded.

Tink opened the door to a large room that reminded me of a studio apartment. On one side there was a decent-sized bed, a nightstand, and a dresser, and on the other was a small couch in front of a TV. There was a fridge, and no stove but a microwave. A door led to a bathroom.

Overwhelmed, hurting physically, and more than just a little mentally and emotionally bruised from everything, I turned in a slow circle. "How . . . how did all of this happen?"

Tink seemed to know what I meant. "It's a long story, Ivy-Divy."

"I need to know—need to understand what happened while I was at . . . at that place," I explained. "How did you guys end up here? How did they get Ren to trust them? Are Brighton and Merle—"

"I'll tell you everything, but maybe you should shower first? And then you should maybe get off your feet," he offered. "Okay? Glad you agree."

I stared at him, having the distinct feeling there was something he was avoiding. Probably a lot of things.

"I'll get you some clothes. I brought some here, because I knew we'd find you. I just have to get them. There's a robe on the door. It's not yours, but it's nicer. Doesn't have holes in it." He stopped at the door. "Oh, and I'll grab you a key."

I halted, my breath catching. "Does the door lock?"

Tink cocked his head to the side. "You can lock it. When you're in here or when you leave, but you don't have to."

Swallowing hard, I said, "Oh, okay."

He stared at me a moment, and with a rare show of seriousness, he said, "You're not being kept captive here, Ivy."

I closed my eyes, breathing through my nose. Then I nodded and made myself go into the bathroom. Closing the door behind me, I walked over to the small shower stall and turned the water on. My thoughts raced a million miles a minute as I stripped off the ruined gown and stepped under the hot water. I focused on the stings and aches as I showered, getting all the dirt and blood off me. Then I turned off the water, dried off, and found the robe. Tink was right. This fluffy gray robe was much nicer than mine.

I didn't look at myself in the large mirror as I left the bathroom.

Tink wasn't back yet. I went to the bed and sat down. There was a mountain of pillows at the head of the bed. I looked around as I slid my hands along the robe. This room was nothing like the one at Drake's, but my stomach churned.

"I'm not there," I whispered.

I kept repeating that over and over as I scooted back against the pillows. Yes, I was in another house full of fae, and in another bedroom, but this wasn't the same. It was nothing at all like that, and I—

There was a knock on the door and then it cracked open. Tink came in, carrying one of the weekender bags I rarely used. He walked it over to the dresser and placed it on top. He also had what looked like iron daggers and stakes in his hands, but I wasn't paying attention to either of those things.

Tink had on some kind of sling, like the kind mothers carry their newborn babies around in. What in the world . . .

"I brought you some weapons, but don't let the other fae see them." He arranged them on the dresser like I had them at home, and I thought I saw the sling *wiggle*. "Iron kind of wigs them out."

"Understandable," I murmured, squinting. "Tink—"

"I grabbed some of your jeans and sweaters, and yeah, I kind of had to grab the unmentionables, so I sort of rifled through your underwear"—something made a sound from the sling, a tiny, tinny sound—"and honey child booboo, you should buy some thongs, because really, the boy shorts are so yesteryear."

My lips pursed. "Um, Tink, what's up with the sling?"

"Oh, this?" He smiled nervously as he ran his hand through his hair. White-blond strands stood straight up. "Well, do you remember before you got all kidnapped by the prince of the Otherworld? I left a message about it, but you probably don't remember."

Left a message?

"I'm not even sure you got the message." He crept toward the bed, and I heard the sound again. Something small in the sling squirmed, and Tink stopped beside me. "I didn't get it from Amazon. Well, I got this sling from Amazon, but not Dixon." He reached inside the sling and took out this tiny little ball of gray fur. Holding it up, he said, "Dixon, meet Ivy."

It meowed pitifully.

My mouth dropped open.

Tink held a kitten—an extraordinarily adorable kitten. A kitten that I had told him not to get, but he had it and he was carrying it around in a sling. Tink sat down and placed the little fur ball on the bed.

It meowed again, prancing up the bed, then clawed its way up my robe-covered leg, continuing until it was in my lap. The kitten was all gray except for the tip of its tail, which looked like it had been dipped in white paint.

"I needed a pet," he reasoned. "And I haven't accidentally killed it yet, so win."

"Yeah," I whispered, picking it up and lifting it so it was eye-level with me. It gave another admittedly cute meow, and I was lost in the kitten's brilliant blue eyes.

"Are you mad, Ivy? I know you said no, but well, I don't have a real excuse. I kind of just did what I wanted."

I brought the kitten close to my face, smiling when it stretched out a tiny leg and planted its paw on my nose. "I'm not mad. Honestly." I sat the kitten down on the bed and it waddled off to investigate Tink's fingers. "Dixon? Named after a certain *Walking Dead* character?"

"Of course." Tink jerked his thumbs at his shirt. "Proud Daryl lover over here." I laughed, and it sounded strange and hoarse to my own ears. I couldn't remember the last time I genuinely laughed. I took a shaky breath. "What happened?"

Tink wiggled his fingers for the kitten. "Maybe you should tell Tink what happened to you."

Biting my lip, I shook my head. "I . . . I . . . Can you just tell me first?"

For a moment, I thought he was going to protest. "You left Wednesday morning and that was it. Then, about a week later, Ren showed up. He told me that you'd been taken by the prince. He didn't know how to get back to you. He said he barely remembered his time at the house where you two were kept, and he had no idea how to find it."

God, I hoped that was the case. I really did. It would be a blessing, a true gift, to have no memories.

"Then a fae showed up at your place. Not a good one. We took care of that. Together." He paused, grinning proudly. "The fae was totally gunning for Ren. Said he was going to take Ren's body back to the prince, and he would be awarded something creepy like humans for dinner for life, but that obviously didn't happen."

My hands curled into fists. Son of a bitch. I knew it. The prince couldn't touch Ren, but I knew the other fae would be going after him to gain some kind of favor from their leader.

"We talked about going to the Order, but he knew that wouldn't be smart, because of what you are. You told him."

I opened my mouth.

"Can't get pissed at you for that, because it's kind of a moot point considering he got captured and would've found out anyway. But you lied to me. When you were upset and said you two had a fight, it was because you told him the truth. Actually, that doesn't even matter now." As he talked, the kitten grew tired of trying to jump on his fingers and moseyed on up my legs, plopping down in my lap. "Anyway, it was only like a day after the fae attack when Kalen showed up. Or maybe Dane? I don't know. They all look alike."

My brows inched up my forehead as I scratched Dixon behind the ear.

"Dane or possibly Kalen said that he could help us get you back. Of course, Ren tried to kill him. It was kind of dramatic, but finally Dane slash possibly Kalen mentioned this Merle person, who by the way, is pretty cool but a bit of an odd bird. And Ren started listening to him. Dane slash possibly Kalen said that they had someone on the inside who would get in contact when they thought they could help you get out," he continued. "We tried to look for you first. I left the house with him. It was loud. I forgot how loud the world is, but we didn't know where to look."

"You worked with Ren?" I asked. At least now I knew

how they came to be with these fae. Not all my questions were answered, but things were starting to fall into place. "I'm surprised."

He raised a shoulder. "I had to find my Ivy-Divy."

I smiled as the kitten stretched out his tiny legs. Tink leaving the house and pairing up with Ren was a big deal even if he didn't say it. "Thank you," I told him, drawing a shaky breath. My skin felt too raw as he lifted his gaze to mine. "Thank you for looking for me and—"

"You don't have to thank me," Tink said. "It's what friends do. And we're the very best friends."

My smile returned.

"And it's what boyfriends do, right? I wouldn't know. Don't currently have a boyfriend or a girlfriend," he added, and then rolled his eyes. "Ren wasn't going to stop until he got you back."

Air caught in my throat. Boyfriend? Girlfriend? Oh God, pressure clamped down on my chest and my throat burned. It had nothing to do with Valor's earlier death grip. "I don't know if Ren is my . . . I think he was just doing his duty, Tink. He knew I couldn't be left there."

Tink frowned. "I don't think it's just his duty. He wanted to storm that house from the moment Dane slash possibly Kalen told him he had someone on the inside. The Order hasn't been involved in any of this."

I continued petting Dixon, liking how his little body rumbled like a tiny engine. There was no way that things were the same as before. No way.

"As much as it hurts my soul to say this, and yes, I believe I have a soul full of glitter and rainbows, I don't think you're giving him enough credit," he said, and if I wasn't already sitting down, I would've fallen down. "I don't know exactly what happened between you two or what came afterward for both of you, but he . . . he barely slept or ate during this time. He . . . he *missed* you, Ivy. He worried."

I watched Dixon's paw twitch as he slept, thinking about what Tink was saying. I could think of a lot of reasons why Ren would have had problems eating or sleeping even if he didn't remember exactly what had happened to him. And of course he would have worried. My womb was a ticking time bomb.

"What happened to you?" Tink asked quietly.

I met his gaze, words rising to the tip of my tongue. I could tell him, but I didn't want to dump this on him. And I wasn't sure what I could even say. My head was a mess of thoughts, and that darkness in me was everywhere, infiltrating my every cell. I felt *cold*. "A lot," I said.

"You aren't . . ." He lowered his chin, and I knew what he was going to say. I wasn't the same. I wasn't. "I know . . . how the fae can be. I know they can be cruel." His eyes closed, and I tensed. "I know what they are capable of, but I know . . . I know you are strong. You will be okay."

The breath I took got stuck in my throat, and I suddenly wanted to climb out of my skin and become someone else. But that wasn't possible. Even if I could have, I never got the chance. A knock on the door woke Dixon, and Tink rose, walking to answer it.

I held my breath, hoping that it was who I thought it was but praying that it wasn't at the same time. But it was. It was Ren. He looked like he'd showered and changed. The gray Henley he wore hugged the lean lines of his body, and the sweats hung low on his hips. He was barefoot.

Ren's gaze swung right to the bed. He stopped just

inside the door, not moving, and he didn't look away.

"I'm sleepy," Tink announced suddenly. He rose before I could say a word, then scooped up the sleeping kitten. He leaned over, kissing my cheek. "See you in the morning."

Tink was surprisingly quiet as he exited the room, not saying anything to Ren as he closed the door behind him. There was no doubt in my mind that he was a bit worried about my mental state, not that I could blame him.

I was a bit worried myself.

Sitting up against the stack of pillows, I clenched the comforter as Ren approached the bed, his steps slowing.

He sat down on the edge, and those eyes, so green and so warm, so *human*, met mine. I had to ask myself once again how I could have ever mistaken the prince for him. The eyes had been the same color, but that was it. When I'd seen him in that horrible place, his face had been battered. Now, there was no sign of those bruises or cuts, but he was haunted. I saw it in his eyes.

It struck me then that this was the first time Ren and I were together, both of us in a stable and safe environment, no one tied up or chained, since I'd told him I loved him and that I was the halfling.

So many things had happened since then.

Too many things.

And neither of us was the same.

Chapter Thirty One

Ren exhaled slowly as his gaze roamed over my face. I had no idea what I looked like, and it was only then that I realized I was still in the robe that was now covered with tiny, gray cat hairs. My jaw ached, and I knew it was probably bruised, and my hair was a wet, curly mess.

"Your eye," he said quietly. I didn't get what he was saying at first. "It looks like a vessel burst in your left eye."

"Oh." I blinked, having no idea that had happened. "It doesn't hurt."

He tilted his head to the side and then his gaze flicked to my neck. "I should've gotten there sooner. There was a damn accident on US 11, and it slowed us down."

"It's not your fault." I crossed my arms, staring at the paisley design on the bedspread. "And you *did* get there in time. You stopped him."

"It's my fault."

My gaze lifted, and I found him staring at me. "What?"

I said.

"All of this." He gestured with his arm. "It's my fault. I handled things wrong. I got caught up in my head and wasn't paying attention. Walked right into a damn trap. And because of me, that bastard was able to get his hands on you."

The tightening around my chest increased. I couldn't believe he was blaming himself. "Ren, you can't hold yourself responsible for any of this."

"Yeah, I can. I left you that night when you told me what you were. My head was fucked up. I should've known better than to go after the fae when I did. I wasn't in the right frame of mind, and I got myself captured."

I looked away, drawing in a shallow breath. "Then isn't it really *my* fault? I blindsided you, and I didn't even tell you about the prince. I . . . I kept that from you. If I had warned you about him being around, you would have been better prepared."

"I didn't give you a chance to tell me about him," he said, and paused. "I wish you hadn't waited to tell me. I get why you did—why you felt you couldn't. I'm a member of the Elite—*was* a member, anyway."

"Was?" I whispered.

"Not officially an ex member, but I've been MIA for weeks. That's not going to go over well with those in charge."

"No," I agreed. He was right. "Doubt it's going to go over well for either of us."

Ren turned his body toward me. Our gazes met for a moment, and then I focused my eyes on the bedspread again. Deep inside, my chest ached as if it had been cracked wide open. A moment passed. "I really don't care about any of that right now," he said. "Maybe that's the wrong thing to be thinking, but I don't give two fucks about the Order. I don't want to talk about them. I want to talk about us."

My heart turned over. I wasn't sure I was ready for this conversation, because I knew what was coming. I bent my knees, tugging the edges of the robe over them. "I'm kind of sleepy. I mean, it's been a really long night and I just want—"

"Don't," he said, his voice so soft that I had to look at him, and I lost the ability to look away. "Don't shut me out, Ivy. I know I deserve it if you do, but please don't."

"You deserve it?" My voice cracked. What in the world was he talking about? I didn't get it. How could he really think all of this was his fault? Words tumbled out in a rush. "He pretended to be you."

Ren drew back, his shoulders stiffening.

"Did you know that?" I asked, but went on before he could answer. "After you left Monday night, no one knew where you were Tuesday. Then you—or I thought it was you—showed up on Wednesday, and you said it didn't matter what I was. That you still wanted to be with me, and I was . . . I was just so desperate to believe that, that I didn't see what was right in front of me. He pretended to be you—looked like you, sort of sounded like you, but he wasn't you. I should've realized immediately that it wasn't you, but I didn't until later that day. I should've known immediately."

"I know he pretended to be me," Ren stated. "Or at least that was what I was told the first day at that damn house. He told me what he was going to do. I remember him feeding on me, and then he fucking turned into me. I tried to get out of there, but fuck, I was chained to the goddamn wall."

My stomach clenched. "How much of your time there do you remember?"

His chest rose with a deep breath. "Not a whole lot after the first day, but enough to have a to-kill list a mile long."

"Do you . . . do you remember a Breena?" I asked, and then winced, because maybe I shouldn't have asked about her.

His eyes narrowed. "She's number two on my to-kill list. The prince is number one. She was a fucking parasite who had serious boundary issues."

I flinched, knowing what he meant. I wanted to ask him if what Breena claimed was true, if they did things—if she did things to him—but the words died on my tongue. I could be honest with myself. I wasn't mentally or emotionally ready to hear all of that. So all I said was, "I gouged her eyes out. Well, I tried."

One side of his mouth curled up. "You did?"

I nodded. "I really did not like her."

His grin faded as he studied me. Maybe he knew why I'd done it. "What did you—?" He stopped himself with a shake of his head. "You're being too hard on yourself. That bastard didn't even make it a day pretending to be me."

"I should have known."

Grief settled into the striking lines of his face. "Ivy—"

"He didn't like beignets. I should've known right then that he wasn't you. And it was the way he talked. It was so formal. He killed Henry. Snapped his neck. Right there, in front of me, for no reason, and I still didn't realize it wasn't you. He claimed that Henry knew what I was, and I believed him, even though deep down I knew if Henry or Kyle knew I was the . . . the halfling, they wouldn't have let me live for any reason. But I . . . I wanted it so badly to be you, for you to be magically okay with what I was," I explained, wrapping my arms around my knees. "And if Henry hadn't showed up, I . . ."

"I heard from Brighton that Henry was missing. I figured he was dead. I don't know the details," he said after a moment. "What about if Henry hadn't showed up?"

I closed my eyes, resting my cheek on my knees. Acid churned in my stomach. "I thought he was you," I whispered.

"I know that. When I saw him, *I* thought he was me. Total mind fuck. So I get it." A heartbeat passed. "Did he . . . did he touch you?"

Turning my head so my face was between my knees, I made fists with my hands. "It didn't get very far." My voice was muffled and my face burned. "We were at your place. Henry showed up, looking for you. He . . . he interrupted it."

Silence.

Then Ren growled. "*Fuck.*"

The bed shook as he rose, and I squeezed my eyes shut until I saw tiny bursts of light. The wanting to crawl out of my skin sensation returned with a vengeance.

"When they let me go, they dumped me down in Little Woods," he said, and I opened my eyes, thinking holy crap. "I was fucking out of it, but I made it back to my place. It took me hours. The place was a wreck. I found your bag and phone. Found your necklace. Knew you'd been there. Knew he'd gone for you, because he'd told me what he planned to do. It's all he fucking talked about." He cursed again, and a knot formed in the back of my throat. "I'm going to fucking kill him. Fucking cut off his dick and fucking feed it to him."

I raised my head, watching him pace back and forth. He stopped at the foot of the bed, placing his hands on his waist. His head bowed and his jaw was clenched.

"It never . . ." I tried, voice reedy. "He never got to that point. Ever. I got out before . . ."

Ren looked up, and a muscle twitched in his jaw. "That doesn't change that he did things to you. That he tried. That doesn't change how fucked up any of that is or that so many goddamn lines have been crossed, or that you didn't deserve this shit. No one deserves this shit!" he exploded. Turning away, he thrust his hand through his hair. His waves fell in every direction as he twisted back to face me. "He kept you chained. I remember seeing you. I remember you being brought to me with a fucking chain around your neck."

Oh God.

My hands shook, and I straightened out my legs. I couldn't do this. Tucking my hair behind my ears, I started to scoot toward the edge of the bed.

"You made a deal with that bastard to set me free," Ren said, stopping me. I froze as I heard the anger in his voice. "You sacrificed yourself for me, and I couldn't do anything to stop you from doing it, to stop him from hurting you."

I opened my mouth, saying nothing as I shook my head. I wasn't ready for this. I felt like I couldn't breathe, and I had to get moving. I stood on weak knees, my thoughts swirling. I walked toward the door, but veered away from it at the last second. Stopping in the center of the room, I stared at the window above the TV and willed my lungs to expand. Then I slowly turned to him.

His eyes shone like glittering emeralds. "You're the bravest person I know," he said.

My hands closed into fists. He had no idea and was

absolutely crazy. "I'm not brave. I just . . . I couldn't let him hurt you anymore. I . . ."

"You love me," he said, voice low. "That's why."

Part of me wanted to deny it and save face, but what was the point? *I love Ren* was practically tattooed across my forehead at this point. "I do, but—"

"I love you, Ivy."

I blinked once and then twice, thinking I was having auditory hallucinations. "What?"

"I love you. I'm fucking in love with you." Ren took a step forward. "I don't know how long I've been in love with you, but it was probably that night you flipped me onto my back, straddled me, and held a dagger to my throat. If it wasn't that night, it was the first time you let me get close to you, let me see the real you under everything."

"You're crazy," I whispered.

"Crazy in love with you."

I started to laugh, but stopped myself because it wasn't going to be a good, jolly belly kind of laugh. "I'm a halfling, Ren."

"I know," he said, taking another slow step toward me. "I know what you are."

"Apparently not," I croaked out. "I'm not completely human. I'm part fae. I'm—"

"You're Ivy Morgan." He was breathing rapidly. "You're this beautiful, wild, and brave woman. You're incredibly loyal, and I don't deserve your love, but I'll take it. I'll keep it close to me and I'll never regret a damn second of doing so. You just also happen to be a halfling. That doesn't change who I fell in love with."

Tiny pinpricks of light illuminated my insides, whipping over the cold darkness. I wanted to believe what he was saying. I wanted to so badly, but it made no sense.

"When I told you, you walked away from me. I told you I was the halfling and that I loved you, and you walked away from me."

"And that is something I regret with every breath I take."

"No. No." I closed my eyes and scrubbed my hand down my face. "You shouldn't regret that. I caught you off-guard. I get why you needed time."

Ren was inching closer. "I knew I cared deeply about you the moment I had you under me and I was in you," he said, and my body flushed hot at the reminder. I was kind of pleased to realize all that seemed to be functioning normally. He took a shallow breath. "I didn't know it was love then. I'd never felt for anyone the way I did about you, but I also had never been in love before. But when I was sitting in that damn room, before my head got all foggy, all I could think about was you. Getting out of that place and getting back to you. Being with you, keeping you safe. I didn't give two shits that you were the halfling."

"You were sent here to find and kill me," I reminded him.

His jaw hardened. "Fuck that. Fuck why I came here. I would never lay a damn finger on you that you didn't want there."

"You can't feel this way," I protested, backing up. "Remember what happened to Noah? He was your best friend and you had—"

"I remember what I had to do, and now I know I did the wrong damn thing," he said. "But this has nothing to do with Noah."

"You can't go through that again," I told him.

"I don't plan to. And I don't care what you are. Trust me, when I was taken—when you were taken—I got real one on one with the way I felt about you. Those weeks you were there and I couldn't get to you? Yeah, I figured out real fucking fast what I cared about and what I didn't," he told me, his eyes flashing a deep forest green. "I love you, Ivy. You aren't going to talk me out of that."

"But you . . ." He didn't know all the things I'd done. He had no idea. I dragged my hand down my face again. "He—the prince—he made me do things, Ren. I don't think you would feel the same way if you knew."

He closed his eyes for a moment and then reopened them. "I can't imagine what he made you do, but I want to know everything—everything you're comfortable sharing with me, whenever you want. But I'm telling you right now, it's not going to change the way I feel about you. It's only going to make me want to kill him even more."

My stomach dipped. It wasn't unpleasant, but my thoughts were. "You don't know that, Ren. You don't."

"I do." His voice was hard. "I love you. That's not going to change. I love—"

"He made me feed on people!" I shouted.

Ren drew up short, his face paling.

"You see? You can't love someone who did that. You can't be with me, knowing what I am, knowing what I've done!" Tears burned my throat and eyes. "I hurt a woman. I know I did. I might've—oh God, I might've even killed her. I don't know. I didn't even know I could do that, but I did. I did it, and I hurt her and she tried to make me stop, and I couldn't. And I could do it to you."

Something flickered over his face, an emotion that was damn near feral. "You would never do that to me."

I fisted the side of my robe. "You don't know that."

"Did you feed of your own free will or did he manipulate you into doing it?"

"Does it matter?"

"Yes!" he shouted. "That fucking matters, Ivy."

Looking away, I bit down on my lip. "He forced me."

"Son of a bitch!" he exploded again, and I turned to him. His hands were in fists at his sides. "He forced you to feed. He fucked your head up. That's totally understandable, but he forced you, Ivy. You didn't have a choice, and the Ivy I know, the Ivy I first found sexy as hell every time she told me off, and the Ivy I grew to respect and fucking admire—the Ivy I fell head over fucking ass in love with would never do that without being forced. So don't put that on you. Don't wear that kind of guilt."

I opened my mouth, but he . . . he was right. God, Ren was right. I knew who I was. That Ivy was still inside me—under the coldness and the darkness, she was still there. I would've never fed on anyone if I had a choice, but I hadn't had one. This was different now, though. Before, I hadn't known I could feed, but I could, and it was horrifically simple. All I had to do was want it and inhale.

Fear formed in my stomach, settling like a heavy knot, and I let go of my robe. "But what if I hurt you?" I whispered. Tears blurred my vision. "I could never live with myself. That would be it. That's my breaking point."

Ren was wicked fast.

Clasping my cheeks, he lowered his mouth to mine and kissed me with not a moment of hesitation or doubt. He wasn't careful, and there was no fear in his kiss. His mouth parted mine, and it was hungry and desperate, raw and tortured, and full of a thousand other emotions, but most importantly, it was full of love. Then I was kissing him back, my fingers grabbing the front of his shirt. One of his hands left my cheek and fisted my hair. And I knew this wasn't going to turn into something twisted. I didn't want that from him. I didn't want that from anyone.

I just wanted *him*.

Ren loved me.

He was *in* love with me.

Oh God, the kiss tasted like him—like toothpaste and Ren—and he was warm, every part of him. His hands, his lips, his tongue. This was him *kissing* me. This was him *loving* me. This wasn't lust and this wasn't a trick. I knew that in my core, in my very bones, and in my soul.

He pulled back, breathing heavily. "You would never hurt me. Never. It's not because I love you. It's because you love me."

I stared up at him and then . . . then the worst possible thing happened. Or the best possible thing. I started to speak, but a sob came out, the messy kind, and the tears I'd been holding back for what felt like forever burst free.

Somehow we made it to the floor in front of the bed. I don't even know how, but I was half in his lap, half sitting on the floor, and our arms were around each other. He held me like he had never expected to do it again.

I had never expected him to.

"It's okay," he said, arms tight around me. "It's okay."

Ren kept saying that, over and over. And I wanted it to be okay. I wanted to explore the ray of light his words had created. I wanted to focus on the fact that against all odds, despite everything, Ren loved me, and I loved him, and we were together. We were in each other's arms, and there was something so powerful about that, but there was a lot of darkness in me, a lot of coldness, and a lot that Ren didn't know.

But he knew enough and he still . . . he was still here, and he was still holding me. Ren still loved me.

Hands clenching his shirt, I pressed my face against

his chest, inhaling the fresh outdoorsy scent that always clung to him. I cried and my entire body shook with the force of my tears. My cheeks were soaked. The front of his shirt was damp, but I couldn't stop crying. The tears were for him and everything he'd gone through, what he'd suffered. The tears were for Val, and there was still a well of grief for her that I realized in that moment I hadn't even fully tapped into. I cried for the woman I'd fed on.

And I cried for me.

I sobbed for everything I'd seen and the things I'd been told. For what I had to sacrifice to get Ren out of there and just keep my head above water. I cried for everything I'd been forced to do, and I knew it would be a long time before the ghost of those actions stopped haunting me.

And those tears came from the dark, cold place inside me that his words, those three beautiful words, had begun to thaw and shine light upon.

Chapter Thirty Two

My body gave out at some point, and I passed out on the floor, curled up between Ren's legs and against his chest. I vaguely remember him putting me to bed, and he stayed next to me for a long time. I knew this because I woke in the middle of the night and didn't recognize the room.

Panic exploded through me like buckshot, and I shot straight up in bed. For a horrible series of seconds, I thought I was back in the other bedroom, locked away and waiting for the prince to show. I'd reached for my neck, feeling for the metal collar.

Ren had woken to find me sitting up and feeling my neck like a freak, and he seemed to know what was going on inside my head. He'd wrapped his arm around my waist and eased me back down beside him.

"You're here," he'd whispered into the dark room. "You're here with me."

I'd eventually fallen back to sleep, and I slept like the

dead. There was a good chance I didn't move once. I might have even snored. I don't know. I just remember listening to Ren's calming voice, and then when I opened my eyes again, daylight was streaming into the room, and I was alone.

Rolling over onto my side, I winced as my muscles ached and protested at the movement. I noted how that was different from all the other times I'd woken up after such a deep sleep. The difference was, I had fed those times. But I didn't want to look too closely at that. Not right now.

I scanned the room, my gaze landing on the sofa in front of the TV. My heartbeat sped up as I saw Ren rising and turning to me.

Relief was etched into every line of his face. "Hey there," he said, approaching the bed. "I was beginning to wonder if you were going to wake up."

Feeling a little dizzy, I sat up and pushed the matted strands of my hair back from my face. "How long have I've been sleeping?" My voice was hoarse.

Ren sat on the bed next to me. "You woke up on and off the first night, but once you fell into a deep sleep, you slept straight through yesterday and last night."

"Geez." I dropped my hand, clearing my throat. "I didn't mean to sleep that long."

"It's okay. You needed the rest." Reaching over, he gathered my robe together. The material had fallen open, giving him an eyeful. I hadn't even noticed. A slight flush traveled down my throat as he found the tie and redid it. His voice was thicker when he spoke. "Everyone understands that."

"Sorry . . . for crying all over you."

"Never apologize for that. Ever. You want to cry all

over me again, I'm right here. I don't want to be any place else."

My gaze traveled over the black thermal he wore and how it stretched over his broad shoulders, and then I moved my gaze up to his full lips that had said such amazing words to me. My eyes met his. There were shadows of worry under them. "You love me," I blurted out, and then immediately wanted to staple my mouth shut, because that sounded so dumb.

His smile traveled up to his eyes. "That sounds about right."

Those words wrapped around me like a warm, soft blanket. Ren loved me. That hadn't been a dream. None of this was a dream.

"You have something you want to say to me?" he asked, tone teasing. "I think there is definitely something you want to say to me."

A grin tugged at my lips. "I don't have anything to say."

His brows rose.

The grin was slow to turn into a smile, but it did. "I love you," I said.

"That's what I wanted to hear." Leaning in, he brushed his lips over mine. I tensed just a little, still half-afraid I'd inadvertently start sucking his life force out of him, but he wasn't worried. He stayed right there, his mouth hovering over mine. "I do wish you were awake yesterday just to bear witness to what I saw."

"What was that?" I asked, resting my forehead against his.

He placed his hand next to my leg, supporting his weight. "Tink fashioned some kind of leash for that cat of his."

"Dixon."

"Yeah, Dixon. I saw him outside in the garden yesterday. Your window looks down on it. He was walking the little thing, but that's not the random part," he explained. "Tink was back to his other size. You know, bite-size height. He was flying and walking the kitten. I'm pretty sure he was also naked. Too far up to make out any details, thank God."

A giggle parted my lips. "Dear lord, when that cat gets bigger, it's going to eat him if he stays that size."

"One can only hope." He laughed as I drew back. "Just kidding. He's kind of growing on me. Like a fungus."

"Nice," I murmured, relaxing.

Ren kissed my cheek and then leaned back. "You feel up to talking to anyone today?"

"Of course," I answered at once.

His eyes searched mine. "You sure? You can take another day. I can grab you some food. They got cable in these rooms. We can find some movie and just chill."

While that sounded amazing and I honestly would have loved nothing more, the world was still churning outside. The prince was still out there. Nothing was going to wait around. "I'm fine. I just need to shower. I feel like I need to wash a layer of sleep off me."

"You look beautiful," he said.

I rolled my eyes. "I think you need your head examined."

"Nope." He paused. "After you shower, we'll grab something to eat and then we'll meet up with everyone. Okay?"

His steady gaze snagged and held mine. We still had a lot to cover. There were a lot of details he didn't know. Details I needed time to come to terms with myself and time to share.

"Okay," I said.

I closed my eyes as Ren kissed the tip of my nose. He pushed off the bed, and I got up after him. My legs felt a little wobbly as I grabbed the bag Tink had brought me and walked into the bathroom, closing the door behind me.

I wondered if Tink was out walking the kitten naked again.

Taking a quick shower, I stepped out and dried off. I rooted through the bag, finding a pair of worn jeans and a long-sleeved green shirt. I got dressed and then gathered up my wet hair, twisting it into a knot.

Steam had evaporated from the mirror, and I caught sight of my reflection. I stopped right in my tracks. It was the first time I'd seen myself in days. I barely recognized the girl staring back at me.

There was a streak of red still in my left eye, which reminded me of someone infected with the zombie virus. My face was paler than normal, and a bluish bruise stretched along the side of my jaw. I looked . . .

Haunted.

Definitely not beautiful. That was kind of Ren to say, but there was a bone-deep exhaustion in the unforgiving shadows under my eyes, and a wariness in my blue eyes that hadn't been there before, not even after what had happened to Shaun, Holly, and Adrian. It mirrored the coldness inside me that had dug its claws in.

Now was not the time to think about the cause of all that. I grabbed the bag and pried it open, realizing Tink hadn't brought any of my makeup. There was no camouflaging this hot-mess express. Maybe I could sneak a trip back to my apartment. I had to. There were not enough clothes to get me through a week.

Ren was waiting out in the room, sitting in the chair, flipping through a magazine when I stepped out. Something occurred to me then. "Did you stay here the entire time I slept?"

"Mostly." He closed the magazine and tossed it onto the coffee table. "Tink stayed while I left to get a change of clothing, but I showered here. Didn't want you to wake up alone."

Oh.

Oh man, that was sweet.

"Hell, I almost forgot." He stood up and reached inside his pocket as he walked over to me. "I think you'll want this back."

My breath caught. Ren held out my necklace, the four-leaf clover dangling from his fingertips.

"The chain was broken, so I got you a new one." He unhooked the clasp and draped it around my neck, securing the clasp.

The moment the tiger's eye hit my chest, I had to press my lips together to stop from crying like a baby all over him again. I placed my palm over the stone, feeling a relief that couldn't be described. Four leaf-clovers were not easy to find, and the process the Order took to preserve them was unbeknownst to me. Having this necklace back was a godsend.

"Thank you," I told Ren.

He said nothing as he curled his hand around the nape of my neck and drew me to his chest. We stood there for several moments and then he kissed my forehead before drawing back.

"You ready?" Ren extended his hand, and I took it without hesitation.

I was as ready as I would ever be.

~

"This is so weird," I whispered to Ren as we walked down a long hall on the first floor. We'd just gotten done eating breakfast in the cafeteria, eating with fae who apparently didn't feed off humans.

"Tell me about it." Ren's hand squeezed mine. "It's only been me these last couple of weeks. It takes a lot to get used to." He paused as we passed a fae woman and a young child who was staring up at us with wide eyes. The woman, I assumed the child's mother, smiled faintly in our direction. "Going from hunting them down to eating dinner with them and sleeping in the same building with them is a trip."

It most definitely was, especially when I'd been with the kind of fae that were more likely to punch you in the face than smile timidly at you.

Ren stopped in front of a pair of double doors and knocked. A second later, the right side swung open, and there was Brighton.

"Ivy!" She folded her arms around me, squeezing tightly. I was a little stunned. I don't think we'd ever hugged before. "I'm so glad to see that you're okay," she said.

I patted her back awkwardly, swearing I heard Ren chuckle. "It's good to see you."

She drew back, her blonde hair swept away from her face. "Come in. Everyone is here."

Glancing back at Ren, he winked at me. Alrighty then. I walked into what reminded me of a corporate boardroom. There was a conference table at one end of the room, next to a credenza stocked with liquor. A huge desk sat at the other end, in front of a window overlooking the street.

I saw Merle and Faye, happy to see that the former

was alive and well, but my attention was snagged by the male fae rising from the desk. Everything about him was a shock to the system.

He was older, his dark hair salt and peppered. Fine lines creased the silvery skin around his ears and mouth. In human years, I would've pegged him to be in his sixties, and I had never seen a fae that old before. Never.

Holy crap, he was aging just like a human.

Ren placed his hand on my lower back. "Ivy, this is Tanner. He runs this place."

The male fae smiled as he walked around the desk and extended his hand. "It's nice to finally meet you, Ivy, and that the mission to retrieve you was a success."

In a daze, I reached out and shook his hand. "Nice to meet you, too."

"My real name is a bit unpronounceable, but Tanner is a good abbreviation of it." He laughed as he squeezed my hand. "You look a little shocked."

I checked out his ears just to make sure they were pointy. "I . . . I'm sorry. I'm a little out of it."

"Understandable," he replied smoothly. "And I also understand that it must be a shock to be here, around my people."

I nodded slowly.

"You'll find that a lot of things about us will come as a shock," he added, dropping my hand.

I nodded again.

"As Faye explained to you, this is a safe haven for fae who have the same principles and moral compass as we do," he explained. "We do not believe in feeding on humans, and as such accept our much shortened lifespan. Once upon a time, we used to work side by side with the Order. Unfortunately, our joining did not last very long."

Merle muttered something under her breath, but I couldn't make it out.

"Our ancestors left the Otherworld, because they didn't agree with what the ruling court was doing. They were killing our world and turning all of us into monsters. We did not come here to do the same to your world," he explained. "And we will do everything to ensure the prince and those who follow him do not succeed."

"Most of the fae here are descendants of the summer court," Brighton explained. "They started escaping before the gateways were closed because they were being hunted."

"Hunted much like your friend Tink and his kind were—hunted to near extinction," Tanner said. A wistful look crossed his face. "He is the first brownie I've ever seen, but my parents spoke of his kind. What you've done to save him is awe-inspiring."

I glanced over at Ren.

He rolled his eyes.

I grinned.

"The fact that you took care of him, healing him when he was injured, and kept him hidden told me that we could trust you." Tanner inclined his chin. "It is also how we knew we could trust Ren."

It's a good thing Tanner didn't realize the antagonistic nature of their relationship. Something completely random occurred to me. "Did you guys try to seek me out before this?" I asked.

"No," Tanner replied. "Why do you ask?"

I glanced at Ren. "Before . . . before the whole thing with the prince, a fae followed me into a parking garage in the city. Where you parked that Monday night? I was looking for your truck," I explained. "Anyway, he didn't do anything. Before he got the chance, a female fae showed up, killed him, and then literally impaled herself on my dagger."

Tanner blinked. "That was not us."

"Any idea what could be behind that?" Ren asked.

He shook his head. "I will put some feelers out. See what I can find out."

I turned as Merle approached me from the side. She looked calmer than the last time I'd seen her. Her blonde hair was smooth, and her eyes were alight with curiosity and intelligence.

Merle clasped my cheeks. "Did he plant his seed?"

I cringed. "Can you never phrase it like that again, ever?"

"Did he?" she demanded.

"No," Ren answered, standing beside me. His hand was still on my back. "We got her out in time."

Merle's eyes held mine. "I need to hear her say it."

"Merle," Tanner said quietly.

She ignored him too. "We need to know for sure."

"He didn't," I said, feeling my cheeks heat. "I swear."

"Good." Merle smiled, and then hugged me before stepping back. "I would've hated to have to kill you."

My eyes widened.

"Mom," exclaimed Brighton from where she stood by the table.

"What?" Merle shrugged as she walked over to one of the chairs and sat. "If she was carrying the prince's child, we would have had to kill her. It's a fact."

Faye cleared her throat as she walked to stand beside Tanner. "We wouldn't have had to kill her. There are other options."

"Why *didn't* you just kill me, though?" I asked Faye.

"That would've taken care of the problem. You had plenty of opportunity."

Ren stiffened beside me.

Her expression tightened. "We do not believe in killing humans, no matter the situation."

I arched a brow. "You might want to tell Merle that."

Merle chuckled as if I had suggested Faye tell her about a new pot roast recipe.

"She is human," Faye replied. "Humans tend not to value life."

Deciding it was time to change the subject, I focused on Merle again. "Why did you tell Brighton that Ren would know what to do with the info in the journals?"

She smiled faintly and nodded in his direction. "The young man has trust in his eyes."

I opened my mouth, but I wasn't sure how to respond to that. When I peeked at Ren, he was grinning at his booted feet.

Tanner gestured for us to sit in the chairs. Ren and I did so. "I know you have a lot of questions and there is a lot we need to tell you, but we don't want to overwhelm you. Faye has explained that the last few weeks have been . . . stressful for you."

I tensed. "Stressful" isn't exactly the word I would have used. It was also something that I didn't really want to go into right now.

Ren leaned forward, resting his elbow on his leg and his chin in his hand. "Let's focus on the most important part," he suggested, tone firm. His gaze slid to me. "They know how to send the prince back to the Otherworld."

"What?" I sat up straighter. "How?"

Tanner leaned against the desk and crossed his ankles. "You want to take over?"

Faye didn't look like she wanted to, but she started talking anyway. "When my family left the Otherworld many decades ago, they took a very special, very powerful crystal from the head of the king's throne and brought it into this realm. The crystal was then taken by the Order for safekeeping. Or at least, that's what they said. Their decision to move the crystal without our permission created . . . a rift between our two kinds."

I wondered if that was why the Order and these fae stopped working together, but a rift didn't seem like a big enough reason to have everything about their union now stripped from our history.

I thought of the crystal Val had taken from the Order the night the prince had come through the gate. Since I had spoken to Miles about it, I really hadn't thought about it. Granted, a lot of things had been going on, but I knew where that crystal was. "The prince has it."

"Did you see the crystal?" Tanner asked, pale eyes sharpening.

"No." I shook my head. "But my . . . but one of the Order members who'd been working with the prince took it."

"Hussy," Merle muttered under her breath, and Brighton sighed once more. "The crystal should've never been in the hands of the Order. They do not understand the power or its importance, not truly."

"I haven't seen it," I said, looking around the room. "The Order hasn't explained its importance. One of the guys there even went as far as saying it's basically nothing. I'm guessing that's not the case?"

Faye folded her arms over her chest. "The crystal can send the prince back to the Otherworld, but it is not an easy task."

"And we don't know exactly where the crystal is," Tanner added. "Faye looked for it while she was at the prince's compound."

"Never saw it," she said. "But there were many places I simply had no access to."

I wanted to know how she came about working for the prince, but that wasn't exactly important right now. "So, we have to get the crystal and then what?"

Faye took a deep breath. "Then we need the blood of a royal and the blood of a halfling—"

"Only a small amount," Ren clarified, sitting up. "Like a drop of a halfling's blood."

Tanner smiled. "He's still not happy about that."

His eyes narrowed. "Finding the crystal and getting the blood of the prince and a drop of yours isn't the hard part."

"It's not?" Doubt lifted my brows. "That sounds pretty hard when we don't know where the crystal is. And getting blood from the prince is not going to be easy."

"The ritual of the blood and the stone," Faye said, drawing my attention, "has to be completed in the Otherworld."

~

There was a little conversation going back and forth after that. Getting the crystal was the first step, but we'd have to figure out where the hell it was. I couldn't really even think about getting the prince's blood, because I really didn't want to be in the same time zone as him. And then there was the whole issue of getting to the Otherworld.

The whole point of me not getting knocked up with the

prince's baby was to keep the gates closed, but we had to open them. Temporarily.

And we'd need the Order for that.

I had a suspicion baby Jesus was more likely to attend dinner tonight wearing suspenders than getting them on board with opening a gate.

Faye spoke of how they were fully aware of the prince's plan to go all super-villain on the world. It was about an hour or so later when Ren and I left the room. There was still a lot to discuss, but my head was already bursting with the limited knowledge I'd gained, and it was just good to get out.

Out in the hall, I stopped and looked up at Ren. "Can we go outside?"

"Whatever you want."

So that's what we did. We headed out to the courtyard. It was surprisingly free of fae, but then again, it wasn't particularly warm out here. Drawn to a large swing, we sat side by side.

I had no idea how we were going to deal with the prince and his minions, find the crystal, and get his blood without him kidnapping me, and then somehow magically do all of this *inside* the Otherworld.

We were only outside for a few minutes when Tink rounded the corner, carrying little Dixon in his arms.

"At least he's clothed," he muttered.

"There is that."

"There's really not room for three," Ren grumbled as Tink walked up to the swing.

I smiled faintly as Tink plopped down on the other side of me. "There's totes room for three," Tink said, shooting Ren a look. "If you have a problem with our closeness, you're more than welcome to leave."

Ren sighed. "I should've let you starve."

"Whatever." Tink put Dixon in his lap. "You wouldn't know what to do with me."

Dixon promptly climbed out of Tink's lap and into mine. I stared down at the little guy, and he stared back up at me and started making bread on my stomach with his little paws.

"Heard you met with Tanner," Tink said. "He thinks I'm amazing."

"Let's ask him what he thinks of you in a few days," Ren replied. "I bet it changes."

"Hate the game," Tink said, leaning forward. "Not the player."

"What?" Ren frowned. "That doesn't even make sense."

"I'm just going to ignore you now," Tink commented, and then jabbed me in the side with his elbow. "I was worried about you, Ivy-Divy. You slept like you were a Disney princess who ate a rotten apple."

I arched a brow as I scratched the kitten above its tail. "I think you mean a poisoned apple."

"Whatever. Same difference. Prince Charming over there couldn't wake you with a kiss," he said. "That's all I know."

"You're going to need more than a Prince Charming to wake you when I knock your ass unconscious," Ren said with little heat behind the threat, watching Dixon as he curled into a little ball and promptly went to sleep.

Tink huffed and then laid his head on my shoulder. I was used to him doing that when he was much, much smaller.

The three of us sat there in silence, and I don't know why, but I felt like crying again. I was such a mess. Such a mess. Maybe I just needed to sleep another two days. The knot in my throat was expanding, but there was something I needed to say.

"I . . . I just want to thank you two for not giving up on me," I said, focusing on Dixon. I cleared my throat. "For looking for me and for caring."

"You don't need to thank us," Ren said. "You never need to do that, sweetness."

"For once, I agree with the loser," Tink replied. "I already told you. That's what we do."

Tears burned my eyes. "Yeah," I croaked out, pressing my lips together.

"You're going to be okay," Ren said, seeming to sense I needed to hear that, because I really did. He stretched his arm out along the back of the swing, curling his fingers around my shoulder.

Tink nudged my arm, careful not to wake Dixon. "Of course she will be. She has us."

Us.

That was the first time I think Tink had ever referenced himself and Ren in the same sentence and had it not end in insults. Wow. Progress. Or he was *that* worried about me.

Tink was probably just that worried about me.

And that was okay. He worried because he cared and loved me. And even as hard as it was for me to believe and understand, Ren cared too.

Ren loved me.

Sitting in between Ren and Tink, I turned my face up to the sky and closed my eyes. I let the sun soak my skin and start to warm places inside me that were cold and dark.

I was a little torn, frayed around the edges, and it was going to be a long, bumpy road to being a hundred percent okay. And nothing was going to stop and wait for me to get there. Drake would be coming for me, or he would be going after another halfling. We had to find the crystal, and we had to stop him. None of that could really wait.

But I was going to be okay.

I was a halfling. I wasn't the same Ivy from a few months ago. Everything was different now. *I* was different. There were places in me that were still cold, that were still full of insidious shadows, but I wouldn't be cold forever.

Careful not to disturb Dixon, I reached over and placed my hand on Ren's leg, palm up. I felt the sharp breath he took. A second later, he folded his hand over mine, and he squeezed.

I lifted my gaze to his, but I didn't need to say anything. I leaned into his side, resting my head against his shoulder. I felt his body relax almost instantaneously. My gaze slid over to Tink. He was watching us with those pale, blue eyes. He winked.

I was not alone in any of this.

I was only a little torn, but not broken.

"Yeah," I said. "I'll be okay."

And I *was* brave.

The *Wicked* Saga continues with the final book
BRAVE
Coming summer of 2017

Acknowledgements

Thank you to my team who helped bring this book to life—Kevan Lyon, Patricia Nelson, Kara Malinczak, R.S., Sarah Hansen, Taryn Fagerness, Christine Borgford at Perfectly Publishable, Stacey Morgan, and all my friends and family. Special super thanks to the readers, who were incredibly patient while I wrote the sequel.

About Jennifer L. Armentrout

Jennifer L. Armentrout is the # 1 New York Times and International best selling author who lives in Martinsburg, West Virginia. Not all the rumors you've heard about her state are true. When she's not busy writing, she likes to garden, work out, watch really bad zombie movies, pretend to write, and hang out with her husband and her hyper Jack Russell named Loki.

She writes young adult contemporary, science fiction, and paranormal romance for Spencer Hill Press, Entangled Teen, Disney Hyperion, and Harlequin Teen. Don't Look Back was nominated as Best in Young Adult Fiction by the Young Adult Library Association. Her book Obsidian has been optioned for a major motion picture and her Covenant Series has been optioned for TV.

Under the name J. Lynn, Jennifer has written New Adult and Adult contemporary and paranormal romance, including the # 1 New York Times best seller Wait for You. She writes for HarperCollins and Entangled Brazen.

Made in the USA
Middletown, DE
29 January 2021

32714997R00205